LIBERTY'S WRATH

LIBERTY'S WRATH

CHARLES BRITTON

LIBERTY'S WRATH

iUniverse books may be ordered through booksellers or by contacting:

iUniverse
1663 Liberty Drive
Bloomington, IN 47403
www.iuniverse.com
1-800-Authors (1-800-288-4677)

ISBN: 978-1-4917-8987-2 (sc)
ISBN: 978-1-4917-8988-9 (e)

Library of Congress Control Number: 2016903021

Print information available on the last page.

iUniverse rev. date: 03/11/2016

AUTHOR'S NOTE

The natural progress of things is for liberty to yield and government to gain ground.

—Thomas Jefferson

Any society that would give up a little liberty to gain a little security will deserve neither and lose both.

—Benjamin Franklin

Liberty is the foundation of the American identity, and the source of American exceptionalism. No people in the history of nations have enjoyed the blessings of liberty more acutely than citizens of the United States of America. Yet, throughout the course of human events, Americans have willingly ceded liberty to promote the common good. The push and pull between absolute liberty, and a willingness to cede liberty to a social contract that promotes the common good, has been the front line of America's ideological battlefield since 1776.

I wrote *Liberty's Wrath* because the pendulum of America's liberal-conservative politics has always fascinated me. With each swing of the pendulum, it seems we cede a little more of our liberty in an effort to create a more perfect union. The essential question that continues to frame America's destiny is simple: How much freedom is too much freedom? *Liberty's Wrath* follows America down a rabbit hole to what I believe is the logical conclusion for those who posit that absolute freedom will form a more perfect union.

I welcome the opportunity to discuss *Liberty's Wrath* with anyone willing to invest the time to read this text. I may be reached by email at Charles. Britton2000@gmail.com.

PART 1

ROSEWOOD

November, 2012

WILLIAM stepped into the cool November air. Not even the excitement of learning where he would spend the spring semester of his senior year student teaching could dull his ill-tempered mood. The maestro conducting his executive function directed a mental orchestra to alight a cascade of tears in one moment, and a torrent of abuse the next. William inhaled deeply, hoping the crisp autumn air would settle his angrily churning thoughts. He hawked a mouthful of phlegm and spat violently as he crossed the gravel driveway in front of the three-family home where he rented an apartment on the top floor. He kicked at the stones. His toe struck one of the larger stones at a right angle, and sent it careening across the driveway as though skipping along the surface of a glassy lake. He gritted his teeth and held his breath as he watched the stone skip twice and take flight in the direction of his car. The stone missed the passenger-side window by a few inches and sailed over the roof. William exhaled with a deep sense of relief; a cracked window would be the cherry on top of an already miserable morning.

He unlocked the front door, dropped into the driver's seat, and slapped a key into the ignition. The Volvo's engine grumbled to life. The car's electrical system chimed once, and the radio captured AM waves from the morning broadcast. A DJ's tinny voice carried over the AM static, "Even with Florida still undecided, the results are official - Barack Obama and Joe Biden have been re-elected."

William punched the radio in an effort to silence the report. "Ouch, fuck," William whimpered, caressing a bruised knuckle. The broadcast continued by cutting to Obama's re-election acceptance speech. "Stupid fucking Americans," William hissed. He pushed the power button on the radio to silence the report.

William had stayed up into the wee hours of the morning watching the results roll in. State after state on the map behind the Fox News announcers turned blue. When Ohio was called for the Obama ticket, not even the Fox News crew could deny the landslide. Sometime around 3:30 a.m., William turned off the TV, popped two Tylenol PMs, and fell into a heavy, medicated slumber.

William steered the Volvo into the Quinnipiac University student parking lot. He parked the car, and crossed the campus towards Dalton Hall. The commons was slowly filling with fleece-clad undergrads making their way to the 10:30 a.m. classes.

William was the first student to arrive on the third floor of Dalton Hall for the Instructional Methods course. He sat in the back row by the window, and stared blankly out over the commons. His iPhone buzzed. He retrieved the phone from his jacket pocket and read a text message from Mary, *Sad day for America.* William typed a reply, *Can't fucking believe it. Country going to hell now.* His thumb hovered over the send button for a moment while he re-read the text. He touched the space on the screen in front of the word *fucking,* and pressed the backspace arrow seven times. Mary despised profanity. The iPhone chimed as the message was sent.

William leaned back in his chair and stared out the window. He watched a pair of students high five one another, and another pair exchange an excited hug. He couldn't hear the conversation, but he knew they were celebrating Obama's reelection. He imagined zeroing in the crosshairs of the scope on a high-powered rifle and pulling the trigger. He wondered if the bullet would pass through pure air as it pierced the skulls of the dimwitted campus liberals. The iPhone chimed with a reply from Mary - *I know. Stop by after class.* William tapped a two-letter response, *OK.* He closed his text messages and opened his university email account. He found one message distributed over the student listserv from the Quinnipiac University President. William opened the email and read, *The Quinnipiac University Poll was one of the most accurate in the nation, beating out the NY Times and NBC/Washington Post Polls. The Quinnipiac Poll accurately predicted the presidential race and all down ticket races within the margin of error. On behalf of the University, we extend our congratulations to the faculty, staff, and students who conducted this year's polling.*

"What-the-fuck-ever," William grumbled.

Students began filtering into the classroom. By 10:40 a.m., the class had assembled, and the professor began the instruction. Halfway through a lecture on the alignment of curriculum, instruction, and assessment to the Common Core State Standards, William raised his hand and interrupted the professor.

"Yes, William," the professor said.

"Why is the Quinnipiac University Teacher Preparation Program supporting a federal takeover of public education?" William asked.

A low groan from the other students filled the classroom. The professor's shoulders slumped forward as he removed his glasses, pinched the bridge of his nose, and then set the glasses back in place.

"I'm not sure I understand the question," the professor said.

"The Common Core is nothing more than another Obama administration attempt to take over state and local control. Just like he did with health care, the Common Core is a bald-faced attempt to destroy states' rights and usurp local control of education," William said.

"The Common Core was not developed in Washington, DC. The National Governors Association commissioned the development of a common set of national standards. It had nothing to do with the federal government. The Common Core is a state-based initiative," the professor said.

"That's a bunch of crap and we all know it. Obama used his Race to the Top grants and No Child Left Behind waivers to bribe the states into adopting the Common Core so that the federal government can direct education policy. This is another example of Obama's tyranny."

A pretty, blonde student in the front row turned and faced William. "Why don't you just be quiet," she said. "Nobody cares about your political nonsense. It might be helpful if you stop getting your news from Glenn Beck."

"It's not nonsense," William said. "The Common Core is a blatant attempt to limit state rights and expand the authority of the federal government."

A boy sitting next to the blonde co-ed turned and faced William. "You heard the lady, right? So, shut up. No one gives a damn about your Tea Party nonsense."

The boy and girl exchanged a tender glance, and turned back to face the professor.

"All right, all right," the professor said, regaining control over the conversation. "William, this is an instructional methods course. If you want to debate the merits or political baggage that come with the Common Core, I suggest you do so in a political science class."

William lowered his eyes and stared submissively at his desk. He hated himself for not having the balls to continue the fight. He daydreamed about catching up with the boy who told him to "shut up" after class, and kicking his ass in front of the pretty, blond co-ed. William knew he would do nothing more than avoid eye contact, and scamper out of the classroom like a frightened field mouse when the professor dismissed the class.

At the end of the lecture, the professor reviewed expectations for upcoming assignments, and then updated the class on the status of their student teaching placements.

"So, the moment you've all been waiting for," the professor said. "Dean Handler just released your student teaching placements. Your faculty advisors have them. If you haven't heard from your advisor yet, I suggest you email him or her, or stop in during office hours."

The students began accessing email accounts on cell phones, iPads and laptops. One student reported that she had received her placement, and announced she would be heading off to an elementary school in Hamden. The other students began emailing their advisors, anxious to learn their placements. William packed his books and notebook, and made his way out of the classroom. He knew where to find Professor Wisan.

Professor Wisan served as William's faculty advisor since William's sophomore year. In his first year at Quinnipiac University, William took US History 101 with Dr. Wisan, and subsequently enrolled in every course that Dr. Wisan taught. As the sole conservative on the liberal-dominated faculty, Dr. Wisan was the only professor in the Quinnipiac University Humanities Department that William trusted and admired. Over the years together as advisor-advisee, their relationship quickly transcended that of professor and student; they considered one another friends.

Dr. Wisan held office hours every afternoon from 12:30-1:30. He sat perched in front of a bookshelf lined with dusty volumes. Instead of a laptop or desktop computer, a Royal Scrittore Portable Manual Typewriter sat on a small desk in front of Dr. Wisan. William smiled when he heard the familiar clickity-clack of the typewriter as he made his way down the hallway. He could already picture Dr. Wisan, clad in his familiar tweed coat, with disheveled white hair, and thick sideburns that framed a ruddy complexion and enormous red nose. Dr. Wisan reminded William of a character from a Herman Melville novel – some salty New England seadog with a penchant for dirty sea shanties and hard alcohol. William knocked on the door and waited for Dr. Wisan's jocular entre.

"William, my boy, is that you? Come in, come in," Dr. Wisan bellowed. William opened the door and stepped into the office. "How do you fare?" Dr. Wisan boomed, leaning back from the typewriter to allow his enormous potbelly enough room to fold out over his lap.

Dr. Wisan's jocular greeting instantly lifted the melancholy in William's mood. "As well as I can be," William said.

"Bah, let not your heart be troubled. Live hale and hearty, hearty and hale."

"You're always in a good mood, even on days like this. It's amazing."
"And what is it about this day that should leave me glum?" Dr.
Wisan asked.
"What? Really?" William asked. "You have seen the news today,
right? Obama... The election... Four more years of socialism..."
"Things are as they are meant to be. Have faith my young friend."
William watched a knowing twinkle flicker in Dr. Wisan's eye. "You
can't tell me you're happy about this," William said.
"Happy, no, of course not. But are you assuming I voted for our
president's opponent?"
William was dumbfounded. During the hundreds of hours they
spent together talking about politics and the Constitution in the lead-up
to the election, William never once asked Dr. Wisan who he was voting
for. He simply assumed that Dr. Wisan's conservative principles would
compel him to vote for Romney.
"What? Come on, you voted for Obama? No way!"
"Of course not. But that's not what I asked. I asked why you're
assuming I voted for the president's opponent."
"If you didn't vote for Romney, and you didn't vote for Obama,
then who - Bob Carr, Ralph Nadar? Or what, didn't you vote at all?"
"I consider the right to vote a sacred duty. I haven't missed a vote
since I was first eligible in 1954."
"I don't understand. Who did you vote for?"
"I voted *present*."
William sat down heavily in a leather chair across from Dr. Wisan.
"Come, come, William, don't look so angst-ridden. What's on your
mind?" Dr. Wisan asked.
"How could you not vote for Romney? I don't get it."
"Why would I trade one overbearing imperial president for another?
Republicans are just as serious about stripping us of our freedoms as
Democrats; they just have a slightly different agenda, full of different
types of freedoms they want to take from us. I will only vote for a
politician who aims to restore our freedom. Until then, I will continue
to vote *present*."
"I don't understand. Romney promised to return us to small
government, just like Ronald Reagan. He sees government as part of
the problem, not the solution."
"Some may see it that way, but unfortunately Mr. Romney, like
President Reagan, would be all-too-willing to use the force of the federal

7

government to limit individual rights without consent of the governed. He just happens to have a different set of rights that he would be willing to curtail. Thomas Jefferson, like Romney and Reagan, may have felt that government that governs least governs best, but I happen to agree with Thoreau on this principle: government that does not govern at all governs best. I refuse to be forced into a choice between big government liberals, and slightly less big government, so-called conservatives. I will save my vote for the individual who promises to restore a true state of nature that empowers the individual."

A flash of anger surged through William. "I killed myself on the Romney campaign. We needed every vote; a non-vote was just as good as a vote for Obama."

"I know. I watched you and your Young Republican classmates work very hard. You must be disappointed. I'm very sorry."

"We have to listen to four more years of liberal propaganda. I don't think I can take it."

"I believe we'll be better off for this moment in time. Through Obama, Americans will see the affront to liberty that the federal government is exercising. With time, just like the Anti-Federalists who handed us the Bill of Rights, a new breed of liberty-loving Americans will rise up against the scourge of progressivism."

"I hope you're right," William said.

"Have faith my young friend. The forces of liberty are already gathering. Now, let me see if I can lighten the mood a little. I have your student teaching placement," Dr. Wisan said.

"Where?" William asked excitedly.

"Cheshire High School."

"Oh, that's perfect, right down the road," William said.

"And I have another even more compelling offer for you to consider."

"What?"

"Rosewood."

WILLIAM crossed the commons, keeping an eye out for an errant Frisbee launched by a group of undergrads who decided it would be more fun to toss a disc in the commons rather than attend morning classes. By the looks of them, William could tell the boys were just starting to spike a marijuana buzz from a wake and bake session in their dorm room. The perennial smell of marijuana and sounds of

Phish and the Grateful Dead emanating from the dorm rooms of boys like the Frisbee-players prompted William to get out of the dorm and into his own apartment as quickly as possible. William watched the boys take turns launching the disc and chasing it down, unbuttoned flannel shirts trailed out behind sandal-clad feet that scampered after the Frisbee as it sailed through a cool, cloudless, perfectly blue sky. The Frisbee silhouetted against a spectrum of reds, oranges and yellows that burst forth from the head and body of a Sleeping Giant who rested on his back next to the campus. William paused for a moment to regard the autumnal pyrotechnics on display the full length of the Sleeping Giant State Park. The colors were peaking; soon, the world would collapse into the dull, grey hue of another bitter winter, a winter that William speculated would grasp America for at least four more years.

William made his way slowly across campus to Chelsea Hall. He entered the building and climbed five flights of stairs to the top floor of the dormitory. Several years earlier, the Quinnipiac chapter of the Christian Coalition convinced the university administration to reserve the fifth floor of the residence hall for values-driven, female students. There had been some minor uproar among the residents on campus when the university administration announced the decision. The fifth floor of Chelsea Hall was the most coveted residency on campus, boasting up-to-date amenities, including a spacious student lounge, and large, comfortable suites. Chelsea Hall sat on a precipice at the highest elevation on campus. The million-dollar view from the top floor was nothing short of magnificent, offering residents a view of the full stretch of campus, and full expanse of the Sleeping Giant State Park. The student lounge on the fifth floor was a showcase location for the university, and a regular stop on campus tours conducted for prospective students. Potential students and their parents would breeze through the lounge, oohing and aahing over the panoramic view of the entire campus offered up from floor-to-ceiling windows. Professional photographers regularly captured the view and featured it in many university publications. The Christian residents kept the floor meticulously neat and orderly; the parents of prospective students were always impressed with the polite young women on the floor. The administration allowed the Christian Coalition to govern the floor independently. The rules and expectations for students living on the floor were far stricter than the rules in other dormitories. A Christian-values themed social contract featured a code of resident conduct that banned the use of alcohol, established a rigid 10:00 p.m. curfew, and limited all male visitors to daylight hours only. William stepped onto the floor. He paused at a bulletin board to read Christian-themed literature, and dates for upcoming Christian Coalition meetings and events. He turned and walked down a hallway lined with whitewashed doors to a single room at the end of the hall. He knocked softly. While he waited, he read from a whiteboard on the door. The whiteboard was headed *Resident Assistant, Mary Malfronte - Floor Rules*. At the bottom of the list of rules, Mary had written in neat block lettering - *It is up to St. Peter to determine if failure to obey God's commandments will deny you entrance to heaven when you stand at the pearly gates. It's up to me to determine if your failure to follow residency rules will get you expelled from this floor.*

Mary managed the floor with crisp efficiently that earned her the nickname Mildred, after the nurse in *One Flew Over the Cuckoo's Nest*. None of the residents dared to refer to Mary directly as Mildred, only throwing the nickname about among the guffaw of snickers and sneers that followed in the wake of the dorm mistress when she patrolled the floor, liberally doling out reprimands for behavior she perceived as slovenly, slothful, or otherwise full of sin.

On a whiteboard next to the dorm rules, Mary posted a two-column list. The first column was headed *warning,* and the second column titled *probation.* Since William's visit the day earlier, two names appeared under the warning heading, and one name was scrawled in the probation column. William immediately recognized the names. Tension in the dorm was growing between residents who Mary disdainfully referred to as freewheeling, hippie Christians, who believe that God is love, full of forgiveness and hope, and Mary, who fiercely believed that the true God was a jealous God, ready to smite the indolent and rain fire on sin.

The door creaked open. "Good morning," Mary said.

"Is it?" William asked, nodding towards the names on the warning and probation list.

Mary interlaced her fingers in front of her belly, stiffened her back, lifted her chin, and declared, "Not for them."

"What happened?" William asked.

"That one is a harlot. The other two are her co-conspirators," Mary said.

"A slut, huh, not surprised. Stupid and morally bankrupt tend to go together," William said. William had despised the girl on the probation list ever since she had the gall to pin a *Christians for Obama* campaign button to her backpack. "What're you going to do with them? Are you taking them in front of the residency board?"

"Not yet. But time isn't on their side," Mary said. "They'll get what they deserve soon enough."

William smiled, reminded in that moment why he loved Mary, or at minimum deeply regarded her. William and Mary met as freshmen at a Christian Coalition meeting. William had been attending the meeting as a representative from the campus Young Republicans. The Young Republicans planned the visit as part of an outreach effort to drum up support for a voter-registration drive. William was smitten, not by the spark that follows a love-at-first-sight dynamic, more by the dull glow that evolves through begrudging respect for shared values.

Common beliefs and shared values framed William and Mary's relationship; the Evangelical fire that burned white-hot in Mary, and William's uninhibited passion for conservative politics were perfect bedfellows. Together, they evolved and adopted one another's worldviews; William allowed his Protestant faith to be co-opted by Mary's Evangelical Christian fervor, and Mary, who would otherwise prefer a Christian theocracy, melded her worldview to favor limited government, so long as the limited government used the force of law to compel Christian-tinged social values. As one of a handful of conservatives on the liberal-dominated campus, William and Mary wore their beliefs on their sleeve, and found solace in one another's faith.

Mary made it clear at the outset of their relationship that intercourse was off the table until they were married. She guarded and cherished her virginity. William was chaste for another reason – personality and physical appearance. In high school, a particularly verbose and colorful schoolyard bully regularly reminded William that he 'couldn't get laid in a whorehouse with a fistful of twenties.' Pent-up sexual frustration mounted as William transitioned from his teen years into his early twenties, a time when most over-sexed undergrads on the Quinnipiac campus could not get enough. He channeled the frustration into a conservative fervor that manifested in deep-seeded despise and hatred for all things that framed the sexually uninhibited, politically correct, liberal culture on campus.

William followed Mary into her room. Per dorm rules, Mary left the door open to accommodate her male guest. William sat down in a chair in front of a metal desk in the crisp, Spartan room. Mary glanced over her shoulder, making sure William was in full view of anyone peering into the dorm room from the hallway. She crossed the room and sat cross-legged on the mattress of her small, single bed. William stared up at a wooden crucifix above Mary's bed, and then lowered his eyes to meet Mary's gaze. She was dressed in a long prairie dress, her stout frame completely filling the folds of the paisley-pattern dress. Her hair was tied back in a firm bun, emphasizing a large, bulbous forehead and sunken eyes the color of sliced grapes. William imagined that somewhere not so deep in her genetic line was a slew of individuals with Down Syndrome. Mary's countenance matched the stern Christian values manifested in every aspect of her core being.

"Bad night," William said.

"Yup," Mary said. "Another win for the abortionists and homosexuals."

"We did all that we could."

"Did we?" Mary asked.

"Too many takers in America."

"Guess so."

William felt the weight of Mary's accusatory glare. He wanted to remind her that she had never particularly liked the idea of voting for a Mormon, but he decided it wasn't worth the argument, so he changed the subject. "I found out where I'll be student teaching."

"Where?"

"Cheshire High School."

"Nice and close."

"Yup, right up Route 10."

"I'm happy for you."

"I was invited to something else, too."

"What?"

"Something called Rosewood."

"What's that?"

"I'm not entirely sure. Dr. Wisan told me about it just a few minutes ago; he went out of his way to recommend me. He had to run off to teach class, so I didn't get too much detail. It's somewhere in Virginia. I think it comes with a teaching job offer, something about new charter schools being started by some group he's affiliated with. It sounds interesting."

William knew that Mary would recoil when she heard the invitation came from Dr. Wisan. Dr. Wisan's reputation as a radical preceded him. His political views were the stuff of legend on campus. As a hard-right libertarian in the 1960's, he had been actively involved with a group of radicals branded as anarchists by the federal government. In the era of free love and anti-war protest, Dr. Wisan aligned himself with a virulent strain of anti-government forces. His writings framed much of the intellectual fervor spurned by the likes of Ayn Rand and the John Birch Society. William understood the discrete difference between the vision advocated by Dr. Wisan, and the worldview of the counter-culture, left wing, 1960's anti-war activists. Though their anti-government aims were similar in many respects, the nuanced yet profound philosophical differences were lost on Mary, who held the same disdain for anyone who didn't share her Christian-tinged conservative principles.

"You know how I feel about that man," Mary said. "Be careful, he's not like us. I don't want to see you get roped into anything."

"You've got him all wrong, Mary. He believes in the same things we believe in, he just takes a different philosophical road to get there."

"Oh, I understand his principles perfectly well, thank-you-very-much. He's all for letting the homosexuals, abortionists, and do-whatever-you-want liberals have their Sodom, just so long as we're allowed to have our Eden. That's not what we stand for. It's our responsibility to make sure everyone is provided a path to Jesus, even if that path comes with a crop and a cane in the hand of government."

William didn't take the bait. He admired Mary for her unwavering commitment to conservative principles, even if they came with a heavy dose of fire and brimstone. "There's no harm in checking it out," William said.

"Why don't you just stick to the plan? Finish up your Masters in Education, and then we'll find you a nice job in the parochial or public school system."

"I already told him I'd go; it can't hurt to see what they have to offer."

"When?" Mary asked.

"Winter break."

"I thought you were planning on coming home with me for the holidays."

"I can do both. The conference is only one weekend. I can drive down to Virginia for the conference and then head back to upstate New York. It's a bit of a haul, but not unmanageable."

"Sounds like you've already made up your mind," Mary said.

"I have. I want you to get behind me on this one, Mary. I want to know more about these schools. From the little Dr. Wisan told me, it sounds like they're putting together something very special."

* * *

December, 2012

GPS GUIDED William through the Virginia countryside. An endless expanse of fallow tobacco fields stretched to the limits of his vision along a secondary, two-lane Virginia State Highway.

"Prepare to turn right," the female voice of the GPS navigator advised.

"Turn right? What are you talking about?" William asked, taking his foot off the gas and scanning the edge of the highway.

"Now, turn right," the navigator said.

"Where in the Sam hell…" William said, peering through the windshield. A narrow, one-lane dirt road materialized along the shoulder of the highway. William pressed the brake and turned the car onto the hard-pack dirt road. The car skidded when the tires left the firm embrace of the asphalt highway. William took his foot of the brake, and straightened the Volvo. "Geez, talk about the boonies," William said to himself.

The Volvo bounded over the dirt and gravel road, deep into the agrarian expanse of a tobacco plantation.

"Unable to find GPS signal. Please point GPS unit skyward to regain signal," the navigator announced.

"Really…" William said, staring out the windshield, up into an enormous expanse of clear blue Virginia sky. "Not sure how much more skyward I could point you." William reached over and pulled the GPS charger out of the cigarette lighter on the dashboard. The GPS unit went dark. "No turning back now," William whispered.

William stared out the windshield, gazing over mile after endless mile of lifeless fields. The landscape was equal parts beautiful and barren; William felt like he was leaving civilization behind, drawn backwards into a more primitive American epoch, a time when men and women were dependent on whatever bounty their hard labor could eek from the landscape. A subconscious inkling radiated a low-pitched fight or flight instinct deep in William's psyche; his heart beat fiercely, adrenaline pumped through his veins, senses heightened, vision narrowed, hearing peaked; awareness of the surroundings intensified with a sense of pending danger that hung thick in the Volvo's cabin. He took his foot off the gas and moved it over the brake. If he stopped now, he could throw the car in reverse and head back to the highway, back to upstate New York, where Mary was waiting for him, back to life as a parochial school history teacher, back to a life of quiet desperation. He moved his foot off the brake and stepped on the gas; the Volvo responded with a leap, jumping forward over the dirt and gravel one-lane road. Exhilaration replaced the fear; something pulled him forward, like the soft blue glow of an electric bug zapper hung on the covered front porch of a farmhouse.

The Volvo bounded over the dirt road for several more miles, crawling ever deeper into the Virginia countryside. The monotony of the fallow tobacco fields created a strange sense of vertigo, like travelling through a desert landscape - a sense of stillness even when travelling at sixty miles per hour. The road took a slight bend and climbed a gently sloping rise. William slowed and navigated the Volvo through an open gate. A wrought-iron sign set atop the gate announced his arrival at Rosewood. There was another bend in the road. The dirt and gravel transitioned into a cobblestone driveway that snaked around the front of a pristine, whitewashed, three-story residence framed by four enormous, Doric columns.

"Wow," William said to himself.

William drove the car around a circular driveway in front of the residence. Two valets dressed in crisp white coats held up their hands and signaled him to stop. William stepped on the brake and rolled down his window.

"Good morning, sir," a valet said. "How can I help you?"

"Hello. Is this the Rosewood Plantation?"

"Yes, sir."

"I'm here for a seminar."

"Name?"

"William Blake."

The valet spoke William's name into a radio. The response over the radio was garbled. The valet opened the front door of the Volvo. "Welcome to Rosewood, Mr. Blake," the valet said.

"Thank you. Where should I park?"

"I'll be happy to park the car for you, sir. Head through the front door, you'll find a reception desk in the foyer."

William put the car in park and stepped outside. The cool, mid-December air was laden with a heavy waft of foliage from the season's tobacco harvest. The scent mixed with subtle overtones of a chimney fire. Fallow tobacco fields surrounded the house for hundreds of yards in every direction. Small, windowless brick houses that William recognized as the slave quarters of a bygone era were clustered in a neat row along one edge of the house. Whoever owned the estate had clearly invested the TLC and resources necessary to maintain the nineteenth century plantation. Unlike the estates at Monticello and Mt. Vernon, Rosewood radiated the hard edge of a working plantation. Rosewood's beauty was balanced with a purpose that belied beauty for the sake of beauty. Rosewood was not an estate designed to lure tourists and look pretty in wedding photographs, this was an estate designed for manual labor - the whisper of an 1840s' lash trickled across the tobacco fields on a soft, cool breeze.

William climbed up the front steps and entered the Rosewood residence. He approached a small table in the foyer staffed by a middle-aged woman.

"Good morning, you must be William," the woman said with a pleasant, southern drawl.

"Yes, ma'am."

"I trust you had a nice trip."

"Yes, ma'am. You guys sure are out here in the boonies," William said.

"Did you have any trouble finding us?"

"No, not particularly. Lost the signal on my GPS a few miles back, but I just assumed I was headed in the right direction."

"You assumed correctly. Welcome to Rosewood. I'm sure you will enjoy your afternoon. The orientation session will begin shortly; everyone is assembling in the great room as we speak. Before I show you the way, we have one rule at Rosewood - no electronic devices of any kind are allowed inside the residence. You'll have to leave your cell phone here."

William removed his iPhone from his pocket. "No problem. Mind if I check my messages first?"

"Won't do you any good, there's no cell service here, and the Wi-Fi is restricted."

"Okay," William said, placing the phone on the table.

"Thank you," the woman said. She picked up the iPhone, affixed a sticker with William's name to the back of the phone, and placed it in a basket. "We'll make sure you get this back before you leave. Now, please raise your arms while we wand you."

"Wand me?" William asked.

A man dressed in a business suit stepped from behind the reception desk. In his right hand, he held a metal-detecting wand. "Place your arms out straight, sir," the man said.

"Geez, what is this, the TSA or something?" William asked.

"This will only take a second, sir," the man said. William held his arms out straight while the man ran the wand down his sides, back, and front. The wand beeped once as it traversed the buckle on William's belt. The man stepped back and nodded to the receptionist.

"Very good," the woman said. "Here's your nametag. Please follow me."

William peeled off the sticker on the nametag and stuck it on his shirt. He followed the woman down a hallway.

"You guys take security pretty seriously, huh?"

"Yes, sir. We have to. Too many noisy, liberal media types out there sniffing around. We wanna make sure you're not snooping around for Rachel Maddow or Chris Hayes."

"You don't have to worry about that with me. I'm definitely not part of the MS-LSD crowd."

The woman smiled at William. "Well, here we are, go on in and introduce yourself to the other young people. Feel free to have some refreshments. Mr. Birch will make his remarks shortly."

William stood in the doorway of a large, dimly lit ballroom. The entire room was gilded with innate and festive Christmas trimmings. A crystal and bronze chandelier hung from a vaulted ceiling. Crystal droplets on the chandelier dangled over the crowd, capturing the orange glow of a fire that blazed in wide, stone hearth centered on a wall at the far end of the room. The fire and crystals on the chandelier encased the room in a soft orange and red flicker, creating a macabre aura, as the combination of shadow and flames danced across the room.

"Thank you," William said.

"You're more than welcome, sweetie," the woman said.

The ballroom was organized for a presentation. Twenty rows of fifteen chairs faced a podium centered in the middle of the room. A table loaded with refreshments was the center of activity. The crowded room was alive with conversation. William guessed that there were a hundred or so men and women in their early-to-mid-twenties socializing throughout the room. He walked casually to the refreshment table and helped himself to a bottle of water and a few miniature carrots. He began carefully dipping the carrots in Ranch dressing and popping them into his mouth. He scanned the nearly full room. The majority of the men and women in the room looked like a normal group of young people, though very few minorities. The Polo shirts, designer dresses, and well-coiffed assemblage smacked of a Young Republican convention crowd; it certainly wasn't the group of anarchists William had been expecting, unless the sons and daughters of anarchy were raised in a suburban, country club set. William scanned the crowd further, searching the faces and eavesdropping on the conversation. He felt awkward, standing alone, dipping an endless parade of miniature carrots in Ranch dressing and popping them into his mouth.

A single word stole William from his self-absorbed people watching - "Hello." William turned. A pair of intense, deep-set hazel eyes stole the breath from William's lungs. William reflexively pulled his head back and blinked twice, physically shaken by the force as every paradigm of physical beauty was instantly shattered. He gently closed his eyes and pinched the bridge of his nose in an effort to calm his manically churning thoughts. When his gaze resettled on the woman, vertigo scrambled his senses; an intense cognitive dissonance flooded his stream of conscience. He shook his head slightly, trying desperately to conjure words through the jumble of thoughts. The entire stretch of the English language seemed foreign. His executive function raced on overdrive, trying in vain to re-conceptualize the mental model for physical perfection.

"So, you're William Blake," the woman said. She reached out and brushed her fingers across the nametag affixed crookedly over William's heart.

William felt the ever-so-soft caress of her fingers across his nametag. A thud the equivalent of the deep, concussive boom of fireworks unleashed during the grand finale of a July 4th cascade pounded in his chest. William's knees turned to Jell-O. He stumbled backwards into the table, and managed to steady himself without upending the entire array of refreshments. A piece of half-eaten miniature carrot caught in his throat. William coughed in a reflexive fit, but the burst of air failed to dislodge the meddlesome vegetable from his throat. Terror gripped William as the once easy breaths refused to traverse the carrot. The panic intensified when the specter of someone giving him the Heimlich maneuver in front of the exotic woman materialized in his mind. William punched his chest with his right fist, buckled over, and coughed violently. The carrot dislodged and launched from his mouth, landing with a wet thwack on the floor next the woman's high-heeled foot.

"Geez, are you all right?" The woman asked.

William struggled to steady his breath. His eyes burned with tears. "Oh, uh, yeah, I'm fine. Wrong tube," William stammered.

"Here, take a sip of water," the woman said, extending her half-empty bottle of Evian.

William took the bottle and raised it to his lips. The threaded top of the Evian bottle glistened with peach-flavored lip gloss. William slurped from the bottle; the sweet nectar of peaches flowed with the refreshingly cool water across his tongue and down his throat. He drank as though he had just marched across Death Valley without a canteen, his tongue working violently on the bottle, desperately chasing the sweet nectar that once adorned the woman's lips. The water disappeared from the bottle in three gigantic swigs. William lowered the bottle and exhaled.

"You sure you're all right?" The woman asked.

"Yes," William answered, forcing the words from his mouth.

"Come on. Let's sit down."

William followed the woman to the back row of chairs facing the podium. "Are you sure you're okay?" The woman asked. William cleared his throat and tried to answer. A dry rasp was the only sound he could muster. "Stay here. I'll run over and get you another bottle of water."

With the fear of choking to death forestalled, William refocused his internal deliberations, and tried to rationalize the existence of the divine creature who had caused his brush with mortality. He watched her stand and walk towards the refreshment table; his mind churned, turning over every superlative and adjective used to conceptualize his understanding of beauty. The woman stood 5' 9" tall, with long, raven-black hair, and creamy-white skin that hugged toned muscles that flexed in perfect proportions under the wool fabric of a knee-length skirt and a skin-tight black turtleneck. William watched her delicate, avian movements as she plucked a bottle of Evian from a basin loaded with ice, and wiped the water from the bottle with a napkin. She turned and faced William. The view from the front was even more tantalizing than the back. Perky breasts popped seductively under the cotton fabric of the black turtleneck. Everything about the woman was perfectly symmetrical - sleek and sultry. She crossed the room and settled into the seat next to William.

"I'm Tabitha Couture," she said, handing William the bottle of water.

"Hi, uh, I'm William," William sputtered awkwardly. "William Blake."

"It's nice to meet you, William. I'm glad you didn't choke to death back there."

"Thanks. Me, too."

"Is this your first time at Rosewood?" Tabitha asked.

William had a sneaking suspicion that she already knew the answer, but he responded "yes" so as not to appear rude.

"Oh, so you're a virgin," Tabitha said teasingly. "I still remember my first time. You're in for a real treat today."

A man stepped to the podium. Speakers in front of the podium crackled to life. A peal of feedback echoed across the room. The man stepped back from the podium and covered the microphone with his hand to silence the feedback. He adjusted the volume and spoke into the microphone, "Good afternoon. How do you fare?"

Half the audience boomed, "Hale and hearty, hearty and hale."

"Hale and hearty indeed. Welcome to Rosewood. Please take your seats." The speaker waited while the rows filled. "My name's Aldous Manner, I'm a special assistant to Edward Birch." An exhale of adulation and a few schoolgirl giggles filled the room at the utterance of the name Edward Birch. The man continued, "As a reminder, the use of any recording devices is strictly prohibited. We have staff throughout the room. Anyone observed with a cell phone, iPod, iPad, or any other electronic device will be removed. It is now my pleasure to introduce, Mr. Edward Birch."

The lights in the room dimmed, and the audience erupted with applause. A man in khaki pants, a white dress shirt with the collar unbuttoned, and a blue blazer stepped to the microphone. For the second time that morning, William's mental models were shattered; the paradigm of masculinity and leadership was immediately unpacked and reformed around the image of the man behind the podium.

"Good morning, good morning, one and all, good morning," the man said. "How do you fare?"

The audience boomed with a response in perfect rhythm, "Hale and hearty, hearty and hale."

"It warms my soul to hear those words resound through my beloved Rosewood. Let not your heart be troubled, America; here are the footmen and women in your army of liberty."

Edward Birch towered over the crowd. He stood well over six feet tall, with the build of a triathlete. Perfectly trimmed, dark hair framed a strong, square jaw, and piercing blue eyes.

"You are here today because you have been identified as the next generation of great American patriots. I am convinced that when future historians chronicle the contributions of your generation, you Millennials will be remembered as revolutionaries, those who united to stand up against the soft tyranny of our age, the same way the great men and women present at America's birth stood up to the tyranny of their age. It will take your hard work, courage, and spirit to put America back on a path to liberty. I have every confidence you will live up to the challenge that awaits."

William felt himself and the entire crowd swoon. Edward Birch captured the crowd with the same ecclesiastical fervor that enraptures the congregations of snake-handling churches in Appalachia. The audience fell prey to the pull of Edward Birch's charisma; the force was irresistible, Edward's voice hypnotized the crowd of acolytes and soon-to-be acolytes.

"The forces of oppression are equal parts brilliant and cunning," Edward said. "They have played on the sympathies and good nature of Americans, convincing a majority that refusal to sacrifice at the altar of big government is at minimum selfish, and at worst, treason. For three generations, these forces of oppression have duped Americans into believing that their devotion to America is devotion to the system of bureaucracy that now controls every aspect of our lives. But we are equally as brilliant and cunning as they are. We see through the deception, and we have a plan that will lead America out of the wilderness - a great awakening is at hand. You will help ignite the tinder and fan the flames of independence, a fire that will soon burn brightly across this nation." Edward paused dramatically. As if on cue, the fire popped and crackled; flames leapt in the hearth and flickered brilliantly, the crystal droplets on the chandelier shimmered over the crowd in a brilliant orange and red hue.

William turned and looked at Tabitha. She stared up at Edward with a mesmerized expression, completely transfixed by his speech. "Who is he?" William asked.

"Shhh," Tabitha said. "Just listen."

"Those of you assembled here today are the kindling, and with your devotion to The Movement, I will be the spark. I hear you ask, 'how?' What is my role in the revolution? This revolution does not require you to shoulder a rifle, or lob a grenade. Our founding fathers blessed us with the instruments we need to sustain our revolution. Our revolution requires nothing more than the will and consent of a majority. Your role is to sow the seeds of liberty in the conscience of the majority by capturing the hearts and minds of America's youth. You are here today because your professors, advisors, and mentors, those few remaining freethinkers in the halls of liberal academia, have identified you. Your zeal and determination earned their respect, and merited the opportunity that now awaits - the opportunity to transform America, and restore her to our founders' original intent."

The audience leapt to their feet and erupted with applause. William stood and stared into the faces of the young people around him. A mixture of adulation and orgasmic delight twisted across the countenance of about half of those in attendance. The other half applauded politely and tried to play along. William looked to his left and stared at Tabitha. She was on her feet, bouncing lightly on her toes, like a two-year-old about to receive a balloon at the circus. Her hands clasped in front of her face as if praying.

"Thank you, great Americans, thank you. Let the revolution begin!" Edward raised his fist in the air and stepped back from the podium. Two handlers escorted Edward out of the room. The crowd slowly settled down. A euphoric murmur filled the ballroom.

"Wasn't that wonderful?" Tabitha asked, tugging gently at William's arm. "Every time I hear him speak, oh, it just makes me want to burst."

"Who is he?" William asked.

"Edward Birch," Tabitha said. "He's the reason we're here."

The sparse lights in the room were turned off and the shades drawn. For a moment, the only light was cast in gently lapping orange and red waves from the fire. Two screens set up on each side of the podium illuminated under the glow of LCD projectors. The scene opened with a dramatic helicopter flyover of a lighthouse somewhere along the rocky, wave-swept Maine coast. Gigantic words introduced the segment - *Beacon Academy – Restoring America's Promise*. Images of decrepit schools and rundown neighborhoods illustrated the points made by a female commentator who narrated the video.

"Today, there are over fifty-six million children enrolled in America's pre-kindergarten through grade twelve system of public education. The taxpayers of this great nation spend approximately eleven thousand dollars each year to educate each one of these children, over six hundred billion dollars annually. That's more money spent on education than all other industrialized nations spend on education combined. Yet, the vast majority of America's children is wholly unprepared for a self-sufficient life." The images on the screen showed graffiti-covered walls and urban blight. "What's worse than the dearth of skills and content knowledge America's students develop is the fact that America's children are being purposefully inculcated to believe that an expansive social contract will provide for them, and even more appalling is the purposeful cultivation of an attitude and belief that all Americans are entitled to these provisions. This is happening because the men and women overseeing the education of our children - America's public educators and the politicians their unions support - know that their livelihood and power depend on the development of a generation of voters who will continue to commit America's treasure to the vast wasteland of public institutions. Our children are being indoctrinated to support a regime of tyrannical Statists, men and women who sit atop a mountain of spendthrift local, state, and national systems of governance, each with the power to tax and spend the wealth of Americans through sales, income and property levies and fees."

"It's outrageous, isn't it?" Tabitha whispered.

"Sure is," William whispered back.

"Then let's do something about it."

The video ended and the lights rose in the ballroom. A woman dressed in a sharp, navy blue business suit stepped to the podium. "Welcome… Welcome… One and all…Welcome," the woman said, waiting for the trickle of conversation in the room to hush. "My name is Jeanette Evans. I am the Executive Director of Beacon Academy. As Beacon's Executive Director, I serve as the superintendent of schools, overseeing the operation of the Beacon Academy enterprise. Let me start by illustrating what we're up against."

PowerPoint slides filled the screens. The slides advanced, displaying data and information to support Jeanette's points.

"The literacy rates and math skills of America's children are the lowest in the industrialized world, and the lowest among any generation of Americans previously assessed. So, we're left to ask, why; why is this happening to our children? What does our system of public education stand to gain from the cultivation of a generation of citizens who can't read, write, or think critically and creatively? The answer is as simple as it is despicable – servitude."

The crowd oohed and aahed as Jeanette illustrated the underpinning of the conspiracy.

"A century and a half ago, it was illegal for the slaves who resided on this very plantation to be taught how to read and write. The government strictly forbade any effort to educate blacks in the South. The reasoning was simple – education was power. Education was the power to organize, the power to communicate, and the power to rebel. Education today has the same power as it did in the 1860s. And for the same reason, our government-funded institutions are purposefully calibrating the quality of public education to ensure that Americans are kept just ignorant enough; just ignorant enough so that they remain indentured servants to the state."

"Holy shit," William said.

"That's right," Tabitha said. "Crazy, isn't it?"

"It's un-fucking-believable."

"Just keep listening."

"This conspiracy is managed by the teachers' unions, and political lemmings they have elected to sit on the local and state boards of education that oversee a monopoly on public education," Jeanette said. "The evidence of this conspiracy is found in the standards and curriculum our schools follow, the menial instruction they provide, and the halfhearted efforts they make to assess student learning. Our students learn nothing that offers them any real insight or depth of knowledge, and absolutely no skills individuals can use to fend for themselves. When confronted about the mediocrity they are sustaining, the refrain is always the same - we need more money, more money, more money; more money to line their pockets, more money to feed the beast of government monopoly."

Jeanette raised her hands in an effort to quell the growing unrest in the audience. The room was about to ignite.

"But let not your hearts be troubled. It's great Americans like you who will help right our ship of state. Beacon Academy offers a new direction, a way out of this mire. Next fall, we will open ten Beacon Academy charter schools in states across America. We have plans to expand rapidly after our inaugural year. And you great Americans stand to become the pioneers; a new breed of American teacher, a teacher committed to the principles that made this nation great.'

'The mission of Beacon Academy is simple. We aim to restore America's greatness by tapping into that which made it great – Americans. Students today are taught that America is great because of the institutions that enslave us; they are purposefully conditioned to believe that it is the collective, not the individual, which is the wellspring of our greatness. Our approach is different; we aim to maximize the value of self; we aim to restore the sense of rugged individualism that built this nation into a shining city on a hill. Beacon Academy offers a new attitude and a new approach - an approach grounded in the principles of freedom, personal responsibility, rugged individualism, and the self-reliance that once defined America and American values.'

'Beacon Academies are charter schools; we are accountable only to the state granting the charter, and a national board of directors. As charter schools, we are schools of choice - we derive our students from a variety of public school districts. If accepted, students who choose Beacon Academy sign a contract that commits them to the principles and operating conditions of the Beacon Academy enterprise. Our long-term goal is nothing short of a complete revolution of America's system of compulsory public education. I'm sure by now you have many questions. If you're still interested, we'd like to invite you to Richmond for the weekend. A binder is being distributed with an agenda and overview of the next forty-eight hours."

Two women began distributing blue binders emblazoned in gold with a lighthouse and the words *Beacon Academy - Restoring America's Promise*. William took one of the binders, and turned back the cover. He found a single sheet of paper inside.

"Could have just handed this out," William said.

"What?" Tabitha asked.

"Why do we need an enormous three-ring binder for a single sheet of paper?"

"If you come to Richmond, that binder will fill up pretty quickly. We don't want to give you everything until you commit."

"Oh," William said. "That makes sense."

Jeanette reviewed the agenda, and then said, "We have rooms reserved for each of you at the Richmond Marriott. We hope you will join us; if not, you are free to return to your homes, go with our best wishes. For those who want to learn more, I promise your time will not be wasted."

"So, what do you think?" Tabitha asked.

"It's very interesting," William said. "Basically, this is all a big teacher recruitment fair, right?"

"That's a fair description, but we're not looking for just any teacher, we're looking for the right teachers."

"That's the second time you've used the word *we*. I'm guessing that means you've already signed up."

"Yes. I will be teaching and serving as the assistant director next year at a Beacon Academy in New Haven, Connecticut. I've been assigned to be your sponsor."

"My sponsor?"

"Yup. All new recruits are assigned a sponsor to help with the orientation."

"How did you get stuck with me?"

"That's a longer story than we have time for right now. Come to Richmond and I'll tell you."

"You certainly have my attention."

"Good," Tabitha said. "Does that mean you're going to spend the weekend with us?"

"Definitely."

"Great. You won't be disappointed, I promise."

"How long a drive is it to Richmond?"

"A solid two hours depending on traffic."

"Are we driving ourselves?"

"Yes. I'm going to get going. I have a few phone calls to make back at the hotel."

"I guess I'll see you tomorrow morning at the orientation meeting," William said, looking over the agenda.

"I have a better idea," Tabitha said. "Do you work out?"

"Work out? Oh, sure, of course I work out, I work out all the time," William stammered.

"Cool. Grab a bite to eat and get yourself settled at the hotel. There's a fitness center on the first floor. Meet me there at Six O'clock tonight. We'll get in a good work out and then take a dip. They have an indoor pool and a hot tub on the patio outside."

26

"I'd love to, but I didn't bring a swimsuit or shorts. I didn't think I'd need them," William said.

"That's fine, it's only Two O'clock. There are a bunch of strip malls between here and Richmond. Stop off and grab yourself something to wear."

GPS GUIDED William to a Target outlet in a strip mall on the outskirts of Richmond. He parked the Volvo and made his way into the store. After a few trips up and down the aisles, he grew frustrated and asked a sales associate where they kept the bathing suits.

"We don't have any bathing suits out now. It's the middle of December. We won't have our spring and summer lines out for another couple of months," a sales associate informed William.

"Is there anywhere around here where I could find one?"

"I don't know. You could always just grab a pair of shorts in the menswear section. We have a full line of workout clothing."

William walked to the men's section and picked out a pair of black, Umbro running shorts. He held the shorts up to his waist, guesstimating his size. It was the first pair of shorts he ever purchased for himself. He avoided wearing shorts like the plague; his large waist, long trunk, and stumpy legs always made shorts sag awkwardly, like a full diaper on a toddler. Even in the dog days of summer, William was more comfortable in a pair of jeans or khaki pants.

A growing anxiety was beginning to snarl William's stomach and chest. The last thing in the world he wanted was for Tabitha to see him in shorts with his shirt off. The panic intensified when he realized he might have to perform physical exercise prior to their promised swim. A potential train wreck of embarrassment was beginning to stream through his mind's eye. William considered putting the shorts back on the shelf; he could always tell Tabitha that he had stopped at a store, but couldn't find a swimsuit. The sales associate said that spring and summer clothes wouldn't be available for another couple of months, she had handed him a plausible excuse.

"Don't be such a coward," William whispered to himself. A surge of courage washed over William as he carried the shorts to a cashier at the front of the store.

The trip to downtown Richmond through rush hour traffic was grueling. A three-car accident snarled traffic in both directions. The digital clock on the Volvo dashboard flashed 5:45 p.m. when William pulled into the Marriott parking garage. William carried his overnight bag and the Target shopping bag into the Marriott. He walked to the reception desk and found a line of guests waiting to check-in. A sense of relief washed over him; it would be at least another thirty minutes before he was checked-in, there was no way he'd make it to the fitness center by Six O'clock. He could take his time checking in, drop off his bag, and make his way to meet Tabitha around Seven O'clock, just as she was finishing her workout and swim. He would apologize, explain that traffic delayed his arrival, and then suggest they share a late dinner together. The snarl of anxiety loosened in his chest as the plan materialized in his mind.

"Hey, there you are. Did you just get here?" A voice asked from behind William.

William turned, Tabitha was standing behind him in a pair of sweatpants and matching jacket. "Oh, hey, yeah, I just got here. Traffic was a mess," William said.

"Well, I'm glad you made it in one piece, were you able to stop and get a swimsuit?"

William held up the Target shopping bag. "Yup," he said.

"Perfect, I was just heading to the gym. Get yourself checked-in and then change and meet me there."

"No, it's okay, really. You don't have to wait for me. I don't want to hold you up," William said.

"Don't worry about it, it's no problem. I'll just take my time stretching before I start with some cardio. See you in ten," Tabitha said with a perky cadence, skipping off in the direction of the indoor pool and fitness center.

The snarl of anxiety tightened William's chest. "Shit," he said under his breath.

William used a key card to access his room on the second floor. He placed his overnight bag on a dresser and unzipped the main compartment. He found a Quinnipiac Bobcats t-shirt that he planned to sleep in, and changed into the Umbro shorts and t-shirt.

On the first floor, William crossed through the lobby and followed signs directing guests to the fitness center and indoor pool. William pushed the crash bar on a set of double doors and stepped into the pool area. Two kids splashed in the small, kidney-shaped pool. A morbidly obese woman, who William assumed was the kids' mother, sat on the edge of the pool, watching the children play in the water. Above the woman, an enormous sign warned guests that there was no lifeguard on duty – swim at your own risk. William stepped into the pool area and spotted the fitness room. Floor to ceiling windows separated the fitness center from the pool. Stairmasters and treadmills ran the length of the windows.

William walked across the pool deck, staring into the fitness center. He spotted Tabitha on the last Stairmaster. She had stripped down to a pair of tiny, skin-tight yoga shorts and a sports bra. The wire from a pair of ear buds ran down her arm to an iPod in an armband wrapped around her bicep. William walked slowly in front of the floor-to-ceiling windows, hoping to catch Tabitha's eye. She was absorbed in her workout. William walked up a small flight of stairs and entered the fitness center.

Tabitha was the only guest in the fitness center. The electric whine of the Stairmaster echoed through the room. William paused at the entrance and watched Tabitha's arms and legs piston up and down on the Stairmaster at breakneck speed. Her black hair was tied back in a tight ponytail that bounced playfully back and forth across her shoulders. Beads of sweat poured down her long, slender neck, across her shoulders, and down the length of her perfectly toned back. The sweat caught in the fabric of the obscenely scant, black yoga shorts that covered two perky ass cheeks. Her legs were impossibly long and slender, with ripped muscles flexing in powerful thrusts up and down on the Stairmaster. William stood in the entrance, mesmerized. Tabitha turned her head and made eye contact with him in the floor-to-ceiling mirror that covered an entire wall of the fitness center. She waved. William returned the wave and walked across the room, holding Tabitha's gaze in the mirror.

He caught a glimpse of himself in the full-length mirror, and wondered what Tabitha must think of him. He stood a shade over six feet tall. The height added to the all-around awkward appearance of his pear-shaped body. Since childhood, William had been hyper-aware of his disproportionate physique, caused by narrow shoulders, wide hips, and slightly bowed knees. When he walked, he led with his hips, making it look as though he might topple backwards. All through middle school, he was subject to the scorn of belittling classmates who would mercilessly tease him with a schoolyard chant, 'weebles wobble, but they don't fall down.' His odd body shape was complemented by a long, narrow head, and a face framed by bushy dark eyebrows, hair that hung flat and thick like the Beatles circa 1964, and an angular, Roman nose.

"Hey, there you are, I was wondering if you were going to show up," Tabitha said.

"Hi," William said. "Sorry I'm late."

Tabitha pressed a button on the Stairmaster to slow the rapid pace, and pulled one of the ear buds out of her ear. "Are you gonna work out?"

"I was planning on it," William said, deeply unsure of where or how to begin exercising.

"Cool. I've got another half-hour on this, then I'm gonna do some abs to finish up. After that, let's jump in the pool and then soak in the hot tub."

"Where's the hot tub?" William asked.

"Outside on the patio. It's nice and cold out there tonight, perfect for a good soak."

Tabitha increased the speed on the Stairmaster and placed the ear bud back into place. William began surveying the array of machines. The treadmills, elliptical machines, Stairmasters, and variety of exercise equipment looked to William like they had been plucked from one of the Marquis de Sade's dungeons. William considered his body nothing more than a means of transportation for his brain. He despised all athletics, and considered the process of perspiring a filthy necessity to be avoided at all costs. A small bout of scoliosis as a child earned him an exemption from elementary, middle, and high school gym classes, and empowered him to skip out on all athletic competition growing up. Prolonged inactivity covered William's underdeveloped muscles with a layer of fat. He wasn't fat in a classical sense; his twenty-two-year-old metabolism still speedy enough to burn the bulk of excess calories. William never developed the habits of a foodie; he had no tongue for sweets, or taste for alcohol, which otherwise would have put him on the fast track to obesity.

Beyond food, William denied his physical needs and cravings with a chaste, Puritan spirit. His hardline Christian beliefs became the curtain behind which he hid all physical desire. He associated bodily needs and desires with sin - gluttony and lust at the top of the list. Yet, standing in the fitness center, staring at Tabitha's perfect body, William felt an irrepressible surge of lust. The desire vanquished all pretense of fidelity to his faith. He tried to repress the sexual urge, but it was overwhelmingly powerful. He needed to impress her. She expected him to work out, and he was determined not to disappoint.

Panic captured William's chest in a vice grip when he realized that he didn't have the slightest clue how to use any of the machines. He began stretching his legs and arms, pulling awkwardly and leaning this way and that, recalling from memory the positions of athletes he observed the few times he'd passed various Quinnipiac teams warming up for practices and games. He used the feigned stretching to buy himself a few minutes to devise a game plan. He figured the safest bet was one of the manual, stationary bikes. The free weights and Nautilus machines were out of the question. The last thing William needed was Tabitha watching him struggle to lift a fifteen pound dumbbell, or elevate the lightest weight plate on a Nautilus machine. Even if he could fake the proper form, he knew he would appear both awkward and weak. The electric treadmills, elliptical machines, and Stairmasters were also out of the question; even if he could figure out how to turn the machines on, he was likely to wipe out. The specter of flying ass-over-teakettle off a machine would be humiliating, and could well earn him a trip to the emergency room. The manual, stationary bike was the safest bet.

William walked to a water fountain near the entrance and took a long, slow drink of water, doing his best to kill time. He felt Tabitha's eyes on him. He inhaled a deep breath to steady his nerves. The stagnant smell of sweat mixed with the scent of industrial air freshener and chlorine from the indoor pool. William wiped his mouth and walked slowly down the line of cardio equipment. He passed Tabitha. She smiled at him. William smiled back and gave a slight wave. The manual exercise bike was at the far end of the line of cardio equipment. The bike looked ancient and awkward in the line of shiny, high tech, electric cardio equipment. It would be the last choice for anyone accustomed to modern fitness machines, but it was William's best chance. All he had to do was sit on the bike and pedal at his own pace. There were no buttons to push or speeds to adjust - just a seat, handle bars, two pedals, and a chain connecting the pedals to a free-spinning wheel.

"Hey, William," Tabitha called from the Stairmaster, pulling out one ear bud.

"Yes," William said, looking up.

"I'm sorry to bother you. I forgot to grab a towel. I've got my heart rate in the zone, and I don't want to stop now. Can you get me one?"

"Absolutely, no problem," William said, feeling like a condemned man who had just received a temporary stay of execution.

William walked back towards the water fountain where a pile of towels was set on a table. He plucked a towel off the top of the pile and carried it to Tabitha.

"Thanks," Tabitha said, slowing the speed slightly on the Stairmaster and wiping sweat from her face, neck, chest, and stomach, then running the towel up and down her arms. "All right, back to work."

William walked back to the stationary bike and climbed onto the seat. He put his feet on the pedals and pressed forward. The pedals stubbornly refused to budge. William pushed downward, standing slightly and directing all his weight against the pedal. The pedal slowly turned one hundred and eighty degrees under William's weight. For a horrifying second, William realized he would have to stand and allow his weight to revolve the pedals, his leg muscles lacked the strength to revolve the pedals the full three hundred and sixty degrees necessary to get the wheel spinning from a sitting position. He examined the bike and spotted a knob next to the handlebars. He twisted the knob and felt the pedals loosen. He thanked God, and adjusted the tension to the lightest setting. Within seconds, he was freely pedaling.

For the first ten minutes, the exercise was bearable. William enjoyed the slight breeze that the whoosh of the wheel sent up his t-shirt. He leaned back and watched Tabitha in the mirror. She was in amazing physical condition: Her legs and arms pumping powerfully up and down, head and back straight, core engaged, toned abs locked in a tight ripple, and eyes staring forward with a steely determination. William's eyes lingered over her perky breasts. The sports bra revealed a lot of skin while holding her breasts firmly in place. William would have preferred a little bounce to the breasts, but was satisfied to let his imagination wander. He pulled his imagination back to reality when he felt an erection grow in his shorts. He lowered his eyes and refocused his thoughts on something less prurient. The bike seat was chaffing and uncomfortable, even a semi hard-on would make biking difficult, if not impossible.

Fifteen minutes into the workout, William's heart pounded angrily in his chest, and even on the lightest setting, the muscles in his thighs and calves began to tremble with each revolution of the pedals. The worst part was breathing. He sucked at the air, wheezing as though trying to breathe through a straw. The air stubbornly refused to traverse his windpipe and fill the capillaries in his lungs. He glanced into the mirror; the contrast between his laughable attempts to pedal, and the ease with which Tabitha pumped up and down on the Stairmaster, each step more powerful than the last, was striking. As he closed in on twenty minutes, William began pleading with God, begging the Lord to hurry Tabitha through her workout.

"Oh, thank you, Jesus," William said quietly under his breath when he heard the electric whine of the Stairmaster slow. The machine beeped as Tabitha's manic climbing eased when she entered the cool down cycle of the hour-long workout. Five minutes later, the machine stopped. William stopped pedaling and hunched over the handlebars, desperately trying to fill his lungs.

"You all done?" Tabitha asked, removing the ear buds and stepping casually off the Stairmaster.

"Yes," William sputtered.

"Quick one, huh," Tabitha said. William nodded, unable to expend the breath necessary to form any words. "Want to do some abs?" Tabitha asked. "Come on over, I've got a killer ab ripper workout for you."

Tabitha walked to an open area and spread two towels on the floor. She sat with her knees in front of her and wrapped her arms around her shins. William climbed off the exercise bike. He took a step forward and stumbled, his leg muscles devolving into a gelatinous mass. He reached out and steadied himself on an elliptical machine, managing to regain a precarious balance over his wobbly knees. He tried another deep breath, his lungs constricted in an asthmatic vice, allowing only a harrowing wheeze of oxygen through his windpipe.

"You okay?" Tabitha asked.

William held out a hand and nodded. With a Herculean effort, he managed to fill his lungs. His heart rate slowed. "I'm okay," William said, the words starting to flow. "I worked out really hard yesterday, and I'm just getting over a cold." William impressed himself with how quickly he pulled the lie from thin air. The ruse worked.

"Then don't push yourself," Tabitha said. "Sit down and relax. I'm gonna finish up and then we'll hit the pool and hot tub. A soak will do you good."

William sat on a weight bench next to Tabitha. He watched her progress through an ab routine of sit-ups, bicycle kicks, side crunches, and single and double leg lifts. Her perfectly formed stomach and leg muscles popped and flexed with each exercise. There wasn't a single roll of fat on her entire body. The urge to possess her was overwhelming. The heat of a primeval and simian anger surged through William in a hormonal rush. He wanted to dominate her, own her, and, for some dark reason, hurt her. The word shocked William when it materialized in his mind – rape. When Tabitha rolled onto her belly and finished the routine with some light yoga and stretching, it was more than William could bear. The view of her ass and groin in the obscenely scant yoga shorts as she moved back and forth from plank position, into downward facing dog, and then into spider pose created a lustful rage that seared through William's belly.

William's words tumbled out of his mouth before he could bite his tongue, "fucking bitch."

"What was that?" Tabitha asked.

"Oh, no, ah, nothing," William said, feigning a grimace and rubbing his thigh. "I have a little cramp."

"The hot tub will feel good. Come on, let's hit it," Tabitha said, gathering the towels off the floor and tossing them in a basket.

"Ready when you are," William said.

"Grab a couple clean towels," Tabitha said, nodding towards the stack by the water fountain.

William lifted a towel and wiped his face. He followed Tabitha out of the fitness center and into the pool area. "Did you bring a bathing suit?" William asked.

"No. I'm gonna jump in just like this," Tabitha said.

Tabitha leaned over, untied and removed her sneakers, and pulled off her socks. She placed the socks and shoes on a lounge chair and walked to the edge of the pool. The kidney-shaped pool was too small and shallow for a dive, so Tabitha walked casually down cement steps built into the side of the pool and dipped into the water. She leaned backwards and dunked her head. "Ahhh, that feels great," Tabitha said, breaking the surface and rubbing her hands over her face. "Come on in."

William sat in a lounge chair and removed his sneakers and socks. He reached over his back and grabbed the cotton fabric of his t-shirt around the collar, preparing to pull the shirt over his head. He froze for a moment, feeling Tabitha's eyes on him. The image of underwear models with perfect six-packs and chiseled chests formed in William's mind. He contrasted this image with what he was about to reveal for Tabitha – flabby, pasty white rolls of fat, narrow shoulders, and a flat chest peppered with a patchwork of clumpy black hair. He pulled off the t-shirt and dropped it on the lounge chair. William crossed his arms over his chest, hiding as much of his body as possible, and walked to the edge of the pool.

"Is it cold?" William asked.

"Luke warm. Rinse off real quick, and then we'll hop in the hot tub outside."

William walked slowly down the steps. The water reached up over his thighs and soaked his testicles. William sucked his teeth as his scrotum and penis shriveled into folds of skin.

"I've heard that's the worst part for men," Tabitha said playfully.

"Oh yeah, not fun," William said. He stepped gingerly off the last step, and then hopped up and down a few times before lunging forward and fully submersing himself in the pool.

Tabitha ducked under the water and swam a few laps. "All right," she said, popping up at the far end of the pool and pulling herself out of the water. "I'm ready for the hot tub."

"Lead the way," William said.

William climbed out of the pool and followed Tabitha across the pool deck to a set of doors that led to a veranda. "Are you ready for this?" Tabitha asked.

"Ready as I'll ever be."

"The hot tub is right over there. I'm gonna move quick, try to keep up."

Tabitha pushed the crash bar and stepped through the door. The warm indoor air breathed a few wispy tendrils into the near freezing night. The plate glass door immediately steamed over. The cold air slammed into William's half-naked, soaking wet body. He instinctively wrapped his arms around his chest and hunched over, leaning sideways into the icy blast. Tabitha walked quickly across the flagstone patio in the direction of incandescent blue, underwater lights that glowed at the edge of the patio. William hot-stepped across the patio behind Tabitha. Tabitha stepped gingerly into the eight-person hot tub. William tried to step lightly into the in-ground hot tub. He stumbled and splashed into the water sideways.

"That was graceful," Tabitha said, laughing.

William rose to the surface, ensconced in the soothing embrace of the one hundred and four degree water. "Oh, man, that's good," William moaned, sitting back in one of the seats.

"Let's get some of the jets going," Tabitha said, turning a few knobs on the side of the tub.

The water erupted. William and Tabitha leaned back against the jets, letting the burst of water massage their lower backs. After a few minutes adjusting to the tub, Tabitha turned to William. "So, what do you think so far?"

"Think?" William asked, his thoughts still awash in a hormonal buzz after staring at Tabitha's ass in the downward facing dog position.

"About Beacon Academy, silly. You must have some questions."

"Oh, yeah, well, I mean, I like everything I've heard so far. This is some kind of Tea Party thing, right?"

"Absolutely not. We're not some group of crackpots parading around waving Gadsden Flags with assault rifles slung over our shoulders. Please be careful about that. When we go mainstream, there are a lot of people in the liberal media who will try to write us off by lumping us together with those folks, so don't give them any more ammunition - this is not a Tea Party thing."

"But you're conservatives, right? School choice, vouchers, charters, that's all straight out of the Republican playbook. That's what this is all about, isn't it?"

"Okay, look, I understand your need to attach this to something you know and understand. We're all innately pattern-seeking creatures, so go ahead and call us conservatives - that's close enough. But open your mind a little wider than that; don't box us in too much."

"Fine. But before we get too far ahead of ourselves, let's start with some simple questions. What is Rosewood? Why did we have to meet way out there in the boonies before coming here? Why not just hold the conference here?"

"Rosewood is Edward Birch's plantation. It has been in his family since Virginia was a colony. Someday, Rosewood will be considered in the same breath that we mention Independence Hall, or maybe Bunker Hill. It's the seat of a new revolution. Edward wants all the new recruits to experience it."

"Who is Edward Birch?"

"Great question. I suppose that's like asking 'who is John Galt?'"

"What's his story?"

"Amazing, isn't he?" Tabitha asked, a dreamy expression radiating across her face in the iridescent blue underwater lights.

"No argument, the man can capture an audience. He's got a little Barack Obama in him when it comes to public speaking. I'm glad he's on our side."

"Obama! Puh-leeese, banish the thought. Edward Birch is nothing like Obama. Although, in a strange sense, we may look back on all of this and realize that Barack Obama was the greatest thing to ever happen to The Movement."

"The Movement?"

"Yup, short and sweet, isn't it? That's what this is all about – The Movement. Edward Birch is one of the intellectual and spiritual giants behind The Movement. Someday he is going to be the face of everything we accomplish."

"What's his background? Why haven't I heard of him before?"

"Edward and the other Movement engineers have been working quietly in the background, building the infrastructure for several decades now. We don't want to spring ourselves on America, yet; that would be like blowing your load too soon - we're patient lovers, we need to get America's juices flowing, make sure she's good and ready for it."

William shifted uncomfortably in the hot tub, the temperature rising with Tabitha's X-rated analogy. "Oh," William said, clearing his throat. "So, when are they going to make their move, the next election cycle - 2016?"

"No, I doubt it will be that soon. I'm sure they're moving forward in a few key locations, but nothing big, yet. First, we have to rack up some successes on the ground level, prove to America that there is a practical aspect to our principles. We need to give America a taste of our formula for success."

"Is Beacon Academy part of that formula?"

"Exactly. That's why it's so critical that we invest the time and energy to find the right people, people like you."

"I get it. You've been scouring teacher prep programs, looking for teachers who are conservative. Very clever. I suppose that Dr. Wisan is one of your scouts."

"Dr. Wisan has been an important member of The Movement for a great many years. He personally recommended me as your sponsor."

"Why?"

"He cares about you, William. He thinks I'll be good for you – help stiffen your spine a little."

"Stiffen my spine?"

"Or other things," Tabitha said teasingly. "I read the dossier Dr. Wisan assembled on you. You have the right stuff, but you're a little too, how should a say, uptight."

"Dossier? What are you guys like the CIA or something? That's a little creepy. What does it say?"

"It's not the slightest bit creepy. It's called due diligence, the foundation of any successful movement. As for what it says, well, let's just say your principles are well-grounded, but we're gonna need to do a little work to bring you all the way around."

"What kind of work?"

"A few tweaks around the edges, just give you a little nudge in the right direction, bring some of your principles into focus a bit."

"Well, good luck with that; I'm not going to compromise my principles, not ever."

"No one is going to ask you to compromise your principles, we're not some cult that's out to brainwash you," Tabitha said. "Boy it sure is hot in here. I need to cool off for a minute."

Tabitha climbed out of the hot tub. She stood at the edge of the tub, pulled her ponytail over her shoulder, and began wringing water from her ponytail; a small stream of water trickled down over her chest and stomach. Tabitha's body steamed in the frigid air, the night's icy fingers tickled her flesh and firmed her nipples. She walked around the side of the hot tub, sat down on the edge next to William, and dipped her feet into the water. Her thigh rubbed against William's shoulder.

"We just need to make sure we're all on the same page, that's all," Tabitha said, laying her hand lightly on William's neck and caressing softly.

William leaned into the caress. "Okay," William said. "What do you need from me?"

"Well, let's start with one thing – you're a Republican, right?" Tabitha asked.

"Yes. I consider myself a conservative first and foremost, but I am a member of the Republican Party."

Tabitha slipped back into the hot tub and slid into the seat facing William. "For the moment, that's all well and good, but in the long run you're going to have to let that go. The Republican Party is playing a key role in helping us establish the framework for what we have in place so far, and for what we're building. We consider the Republican Party our syringe, but it's not the vaccine - The Movement is the vaccine. Once we get going, we're eventually going to scuttle the Republican Party just as thoroughly as we scuttle the Democrat Party. We need to make sure your allegiance is to your conservative principles, not to any party."

"What's wrong with the Republican Party? There are plenty of RINO's, but there are plenty of true conservatives in the mix," William said.

"Republicans are just as willing to trample our freedoms as the Democrats; they just have a slightly different set of liberties they aim to take."

"I'm not following you?"

"The Movement is about one thing - complete liberty. We aim to fully empower each and every individual across this nation to live his or her life the way nature intended it to be lived – free."

"There's no such thing as absolute freedom. People can't just run around doing whatever they want, that's absurd, there would be anarchy."

"I disagree. So long as I'm not hurting you, your family, or the communities you choose to freely associate with, what gives you the right to tax me, take what's mine, or force me to live by your rules and values?"

"Now you're sounding like some commune-living, do-whatever-you-like, liberal. There's nothing conservative at all about that worldview."

"Nonsense. I'm for limiting government, completely. Republicans pay lip service to this conservative principle, but when they end up in power, they write just as many laws and regulations as Democrats. The Movement aims to roll back all centralized authority, not impose more. We're going to cultivate a nation of rugged individuals, individuals who are self-reliant and free to choose his or her path through life, even when it means facing the unpleasant consequences of whatever decisions he or she makes."

"So, you're all about states' rights. Sort of like the old Anti-Federalists," William said.

"In a sense, yes. The Anti-Federalists gave us the Bill of Rights; thank God for that, it's the only thing that prevented the federal government from creating utter tyranny in this nation. But even the state level is too centralized and far-reaching. The Movement is about liberating the individual, restoring God-given natural rights to every man, woman and child in America."

"The big idea sounds good, but I'm not ready to buy it. If Republicans throw in the towel and surrender, the Democrats will ride herd over this nation, just look at what Obama and his Dummycrat cronies have done for the past four years. If you're talking about a third party that will split the Republicans by peeling off conservatives, well, no way, that's another train wreck in the making. No thank you, I'll stick with the Republican ticket any day."

"The Movement is not a third party; we have absolutely no party affiliation at all. Let me ask you something: How many people do you think are Democrats simply because there is a Republican party; and vice versa, how many people are Republican simply because there's a Democrat party?"

"I don't understand the question."

"Think about it," Tabitha said. "How many people do you suppose choose one party or the other simply because there are only two viable options? Most people choose one or the other party because they desire to protect the freedoms that one party wants to limit more than they mind giving up the freedoms that the other party wants to limit. Let me put it another way: How many people are Democrat or Republican simply because they're forced to choose between two liberty-inhibiting evils?"

"I never thought about it that way. I suppose that would be a good question for me to take back to the pollsters at Quinnipiac."

"I'll tell you the answer - everyone. And that's the problem, that's what is going to cause the downfall of this nation. The Movement is America's only real chance at survival. Otherwise, the pendulum is just going to keep swinging back and forth, from one brand of progressive liberalism to a slightly less virulent brand of progressive conservatism. And with each swing of the pendulum, a new crop of know-it-all leaders proclaiming a mandate to reshape America will be handed the centralized power to tax and spend, legislate and regulate, increase the size of government, and grow the police state necessary to enforce the will of government. Where does it all end? Just look at history for your answer to that question, it ends where every previous empire ended, in complete and utter collapse under the weight of its own bureaucracy."

"That's not a very pretty picture."

"That's what makes the opportunity you're about to be handed ripe for the taking. The opportunity to get in on the ground floor of real change."

"All right," William said. "I'm interested. So, tell me, what got you involved in all this. What are you, twenty-three years old? How did you get in so deep at your age, you're barely out of college, aren't you?"

"I'm twenty-four. I finished college two years ago – SUNY Oneonta. The Movement provided me a full scholarship. I've been involved with it since I was a kid. I guess you could say I was born into it."

"So, what, were your parents involved, is that how you got hooked?"

"Look, it's getting late and I'm starting to prune up. We have to get an early start tomorrow, and I have an inbox full of email that I have to return before I turn in. Why don't we call it a night? After the seminar tomorrow, we'll go out and have a couple of drinks, and I'll tell you all about me."

"Okay," William said.

"You ready for a mad dash back inside? Try and keep up if you can."

Tabitha hopped out of the hot tub and sprinted across the patio towards the indoor pool. William climbed out of the hot tub, stooped over against the cold and speed-walked back inside. William and Tabitha dried off by the pool and slipped back into their socks and sneakers.

"That was fun, thanks," Tabitha said.

"Yeah, I thought so, too," William said. "So, what's the plan for tomorrow morning?"

"We're going to start the morning with breakout meetings by branch location. You're going to meet with me and the Long Wharf prospects."

"What's Long Wharf?"

"With a little luck, it may soon be your second home," Tabitha said.

"Where are we supposed to meet?" William asked.

"I don't know off the top of my head. One of the seminar rooms, it's on your agenda."

Tabitha and William walked through the lobby to the elevator. "What floor are you on?" William asked.

"I'm here on the first. You?"

"Second," William said. "So, I guess this is where we'll say goodnight."

"Guess so," Tabitha said. "Well, William Blake, it is very nice to meet you. Let's hope this is the beginning of a long and fruitful relationship," Tabitha said, extending her hand stiffly and formally.

William shook her hand. "Nice to meet you, too." The elevator doors opened and William stepped in. He watched Tabitha wave as the doors slid shut.

THE next morning, William showered and dressed. He double-checked the agenda to make sure he knew where he was supposed to go, and headed down to a free continental breakfast. He helped himself to a bagel with cream cheese, orange juice, and a cup of coffee. He was anxious to see Tabitha, so he ate the bagel quickly, gulped down the OJ, and carried the coffee through the reception area to the Marriott conference center, where Beacon Academy reserved an array of seminar rooms for the breakout sessions. William found the seminar room reserved the Long Wharf teachers. He was the first to arrive. To kill the time, William sat in one of the chairs arranged in neat rows and began surfing the internet on his iPhone.

"Uh-oh, someone didn't read their orientation packet, did they?" Tabitha asked, stepping into the room.

"Good morning," William said, standing bolt upright. His eyes ran up and down Tabitha. She was dressed in a crisp, navy blue business suit with a red scarf tied around her neck. "What orientation packet?"

"The one you got when you checked in?"

"I didn't get anything. All they gave me is the key card to my room," William said. "Have I done something wrong?"

"Likely excuse, but we'll let you slide this time. You're not allowed to have any electronic devices with you during the seminars - no cell phones, laptops, iPads – nothing."

"I didn't know. I'll run up to my room and put it away."

"Don't worry about it, just turn it off and put it in your pocket. You can drop it off later. I trust you won't record any of this."

"Cross my heart," William said.

"Great. Help me get these chairs into a circle. This morning's session is more conversational than anything else. There should be twelve of us, unless anyone dropped out since last night."

William helped Tabitha rearrange the chairs into a circle. The group ambled into the seminar room in pairs. Tabitha busied herself shaking hands and introducing herself. In each pair, she already knew the sponsor, and was animated and excited to meet the recruits.

"Good morning, everyone," Tabitha said. "Please find a seat." The sponsors and recruits took seats around the circle. "It's nice to see you all. Let's get started with some introductions. My name is Tabitha Couture. Next year, I will be serving as the assistant director at the Long Wharf Beacon Academy in New Haven, Connecticut. Our director, Jason Brigham, is back in Connecticut, he has a meeting in Hartford to work out some of the details of our charter; otherwise, he'd be here. So, I see you folks who are new to us have already met your sponsors, I trust you all spent some time getting to know each other last night, and debriefing from our time together at Rosewood." Heads nodded around the circle. "Excellent. Then why don't I let those of you who have already signed a contract to teach at Long Wharf Beacon Academy introduce yourself and your recruit."

One by one, the Beacon Academy teachers who had already signed-on to teach at Long Wharf took turns introducing himself or herself, and then introduced his or her recruit. The recruits said hello, provided a brief biography, and an overview of what they were planning to teach.

"It's nice to meet you all," Tabitha said after the penultimate Beacon teacher introduced himself and his recruit. "Like I said earlier, I'm Tabitha Couture. I will be serving as the assistant director at Beacon Academy. I will also be teaching a full load of classes as an English teacher. I finished my teacher prep program two years ago at the State University of New York in Oneonta. Since then, I've been working with the central committee planning and recruiting students and teachers in Southern Connecticut. It's a pleasure to introduce my recruit, this is William Blake."

"Good morning." William said. "I'm just finishing up my Masters in Teaching at Quinnipiac University. I student teach this semester, and if this is as good as it sounds so far, I'm hoping to join you all in New Haven as a social studies teacher."

The sponsors and recruits around the circle nodded and said hello to William.

"So, let me start with a little background about the Long Wharf Beacon Academy. As the name suggests, the school is located in Long Wharf. Is anyone familiar with this section of New Haven?" Tabitha asked. The recruits shook their heads. "All right, no problem, Long Wharf is in eastern New Haven, it's on the Long Island Sound directly across from a town called East Haven. It's an industrial area, and a little rough around the edges, but we have a beautiful piece of property picked out, we're directly on the Long Island Sound. We're in the process of converting a facility that used to be a YMCA. We expect to open next year with two hundred and fifty new students and twenty-five teachers. After our inaugural year, we have plans to double in size, and then triple in size by the start of our third year. The current facility can serve up to eight hundred students. Any questions so far?"

A handsome boy with blond hair and chiseled features raised his hand.

"Christopher, what's on your mind?" Tabitha asked.

"How much do we make? What's the contract like?" Christopher asked.

"I like a man who gets right to the point," Tabitha said. "This afternoon, you will hear a presentation from the Beacon Academy CFO. If you're still interested after the presentation, you will speak individually with our program director and me to negotiate your contract. We'll set up a time for that to happen before you all head home tomorrow afternoon. That will give you a chance to see the specifics of your base salary and potential bonuses. As a first-year teacher, you will have the opportunity to earn well over one hundred thousand dollars."

"How is it possible to pay that kind of salary?" Christopher asked.

"First, let me be clear about one thing, this is not your normal teaching assignment. We're asking for your complete commitment to the school, and more broadly to The Movement. We're doing more than just teaching our content areas; we're cultivating a generation of young adults ready to stand on their own two feet. We're able to pay a healthy salary because working conditions that foster self-reliance and salary go hand-in-hand," Tabitha said.

"What are the working conditions? I mean, this is a public school, right? Where does that kind of money come from?" Christopher asked.

"Yes, we're publicly funded. But we will not operate like any public school you've ever known. In traditional public schools, nearly half of the operating budget goes to fund the salaries and benefit packages for administrators, custodians, maintenance people, food service personnel, special education teachers and programming, extracurricular and co-curricular stipends and programming, school counselors, psychologists, social workers, security guards, transportation, and on and on. At Beacon Academy, we have none of those positions. We only have teachers and students. We count on teachers and students to work together to address all of the school's needs. Because we don't have to account for all of those non-educational allocations, we have the funds to invest in what matters most – our teachers and the school community."

A woman with straight, shoulder-length brown hair and a stern countenance raised her hand.

"Yes, Tiffany," Tabitha said.

"Then who does all the non-teaching work? Who cleans and repairs the building, makes the schedules, helps kids when they have problems, disciplines students when they misbehave? Who's there to support what's happening in the classroom?"

"You do. We do. If there is a need in the community, the community addresses the need. Our mission is based on the concept of self-reliance and personal responsibility. The mission applies to teachers and students alike, and we're serious about practicing what we preach. We will live our mission."

"I don't get it," Tiffany said. "How do you live a school's mission with dirty bathrooms and no janitors to clean up if someone vomits in the hallway?"

Tabitha took a sip of water and leaned forward in her chair. "Let's take a step back. How many of you attended public school?" Tabitha asked. Every hand in the room went up. "Then you're stuck in what you know; the ineffective and inefficient paradigm of traditional public education. You have to tear that mental model apart in order to understand what Beacon Academy is all about. Let's compare the two models: Today, in the traditional model of public education, students are not trained to be independent or self-reliant. One symptom of that mindset is manifest in the fact that students in traditional public schools simply expect someone to clean up after them. Traditional public schools condition students to take zero responsibility for their schools. Public school teachers are just as guilty. They, too, simply expect that someone else will address the school's needs when they skirt out of work every afternoon. Students and teachers take no responsibility for their classrooms or any part of the school facility. Everyone is completely dependent on the overreach of the existing public education social contract, a social contract that encourages laziness and dependence. At Beacon Academy, we have a different approach. Everyone is responsible for every aspect of the school. If the academy needs to be cleaned, we clean it; if it needs to be repaired, we repair it; if it needs to be fed, we feed it - we rely on ourselves."

"So, then you're expecting us to teach all day, and then spend the afternoon cleaning toilets?" Tiffany asked.

"You are expected to take care of yourself and take care of the community, a community which is formed based on the concept of free association – no one is forcing you to teach at Beacon Academy. If you enjoy using a clean toilet, then it may mean cleaning it, as opposed to expecting someone else to clean it for you. It strikes me as ridiculous that taxpayers across this nation spend enormous sums of money to pay the salaries for custodians to clean up after their children. We prefer to invest that money in a process designed to make education work. In order to do that, we will expect students and teachers to clean up after themselves. The money that would have been spent to pay a custodian is then available for us to compensate teachers for that labor – that's essentially how we're able to offer such generous contracts to our teachers," Tabitha said.

"I don't know," Tiffany said. "I'm not really interested in signing up for a job that will have me teaching science all day and cleaning public bathrooms all night. Even if it does pay a hundred thousand dollars."

"That's fine," Tabitha said. "Then Beacon Academy may not be the right fit for you. However, you may be assuming that if you join our faculty you will be assigned a job you dislike. You may have other talents to bring forward, a talent or skill we can rely on, something aside from the ability to scrub a toilet. If so, then you can rely on someone else to clean the bathrooms, and they will rely on you to satisfy other needs. Everybody gives something back. What you give back and how you give back will be a function of the school's needs, and how those needs match your skills and talent."

"Tabitha," William said. "What are the hours and work year at Beacon Academy?"

"Beacon Academy will be open twenty-four hours a day, seven days a week, and three hundred and sixty-five days a year. We have no attendance policy for students or teachers. You are free to come and go as you please. You will make your own schedule, and share that schedule with your students. There may be some coordinating with the other teachers, but essentially, you make your own hours. The learning expectations and outcomes for students and teachers will be set by the school, you work as long and hard as you feel necessary to meet or exceed those expectations," Tabitha said.

"Really?" A recruit named Mark asked. "You're open all the time, all night?"

"That's right. Students and faculty are welcome at the school any time they feel the need or desire to be there," Tabitha said.

"Aren't you worried about vandalism or theft?" Mark asked.

"How many of you are planning to go home tomorrow and spray paint the walls of your home, or throw rocks through your windows?" Tabitha asked. "And how many of you are going to stick gum under your living room table, or stuff a roll of toilet paper down the toilet?"

Everyone around the circle shrugged and shifted in their seats.

"Of course you're not going to do those things," Tabitha said. "No right-minded person would destroy his or her home. But I'd be willing to bet that if I stuck any of you in a prison cell and told you there was no way out, you might be inclined to trash it. Public schools do that exact same thing to their students. Schools tell kids they have to be in school during school hours. If they come late, or leave early, they're punished. If they don't come at all, they're told truancy police will come arrest them and their parents. In the same breath, they're told at the end of the day they have to get lost; buildings are locked up tighter than a drum, and students are threatened with arrest for trespassing or loitering if they show up after school or on weekends and vacations. It's no wonder some kids lash out, they're facing threats of punishment for both being in school and not being in school. That's antithetical to our mission at Beacon Academy. If you want to be a part of our community, you are welcome; if you don't want to be there, don't come. The mission of the school, and one of the primary tenants of The Movement, is grounded in the concept of free association. Of course, there are strings attached. If you choose to be a part of the community, you are committing to serve the community. It's the same for our teachers. Teachers are at-will employees, just as students are at-will students. Students may be expelled at any time if they violate the trust of the community or fail to live up to the school's core values, beliefs and expectations. A teacher may be dismissed at any time, with or without cause. There are no expulsion hearings or just cause provisions in teacher contracts. If the community decides you are not positively contributing to the school - you're out. So, if a kid vandalizes the school, he will be cast out, it's that simple."

"It sounds good in theory," William said.

"It's more than a theory," Tabitha said. "It's a belief. We are looking for teachers with missionary zeal who are willing to live that belief." The recruits nodded in agreement.

A recruit with a perplexed expression raised his hand. "Yes, Adam," Tabitha said.

"You said there's no principal or assistant principals. Who runs the school? As the assistant director, are you our supervisor? How are we evaluated?"

"We are responsible to ourselves and to the community. You will be supervised and evaluated based on the quality of your contributions to the success of the school. Ultimately, the community will hold you accountable; if the school is succeeding, we will all experience that success, and you will be rewarded; if the school fails, we will objectively reflect on the causes of that failure, and if it is determined that you are a source of weakness in the community, you're out."

"I love the philosophy, but I still don't get it on a practical level," Adam said.

"I'm not surprised; this is an entirely different paradigm. What exactly are you struggling with?"

"Well, for one, student behavior," Adam said. "I finished my student teaching two years ago. For the past two years, I've been teaching at an inner city public school that has been labeled by the city and state as a failing school. I, personally, haven't had much trouble with classroom management. The kids seem to like me, and I like them. But the majority of teachers in my school complains constantly about student behavior and motivation. They divorce themselves from the school's awful student performance by blaming the students for not wanting to learn. They blame the school's administration for not enforcing rules or disciplining students effectively, or they just throw the blame on the parents."

"That's pathetic," Tabitha said. "At Beacon Academy you won't have to worry about any of that. There will be no principals to help you with classroom management, and no counselors to refer students to who lack motivation."

"How is that going to help me? What happens when students cut class or behave poorly?"

"The system in public schools enables teachers to abdicate responsibility for student learning and behavior. At Beacon Academy, those problems are your responsibility, you will need to figure out what's not working and fix it. At the same time, you are fully empowered to manage student behavior. If a student's behavior is disruptive to your class, you may expel him or her from your class. However, if you do so, that doesn't remove your responsibility for that student's learning. You'll just have to figure out a different way to teach that student apart from a full class of students. You will have to confront, manage, and solve the problem; you will not be able to give the problem to anyone else, or blame the problem on anyone else. Once again, we're talking about self-reliance and personal responsibility. What's the matter? You look perplexed?"

"I'm struggling with it," Adam said. "I had a student who slept through my entire first period class every day. Nothing I did could motivate him. How are we supposed to motivate students who are completely unmotivated?"

"You know, it amazes me, in our teacher prep programs we all took a class called learning theory, right?" Heads around the circle nodded. "And in that class we all read the research on motivation. You all probably journaled your reactions, wrote an essay, or made a class presentation, remember?" Heads nodded again. "Good. Then you all remember reading and discussing the research about intrinsic versus extrinsic motivation. I guarantee that there was one brief moment when you all learned that intrinsic motivation is the greatest motivator of all. Then, you stepped out of those classes, and observed a system of public education that relies exclusively on extrinsic motivation to engage students. So, Adam, if you have problems with student motivation, I would encourage you to go back and re-familiarize yourself with those concepts of learning theory. I think you'll find that Beacon Academy is perfectly designed to capitalize on students' intrinsic motivation. The concept of self-reliance is the core of our mission. Self-reliance is also the heartbeat of intrinsic motivation."

"You're losing me," Adam said. "How are you going to foster intrinsic motivation?"

"Two things intrinsically motivate anyone – choice and relevancy. In traditional public schools, students are provided absolutely no choice in determining what they learn or how they learn it. And the material they are exposed to is completely irrelevant, wholly disconnected from their lives, void of any transferability to what actually matters. The only motivation students experience is extrinsic - grounded in threats and fear. They're told, do this or you'll be punished in the short term, and, in the long-term, if you don't do this, you won't amount to anything in life – you'll be doomed to failure. At Long Wharf, we're going to turn this paradigm upside down. Students and teachers will be fully empowered to choose, and motivated by a program that makes the application of learning the cornerstone of everything we do. We will ground our students' education in a process that promotes independence and self-reliance, the cornerstones of liberty. Think about it: What is it that all teenagers truly crave? Freedom. If we do our jobs well, students will be given a full range of skills that will empower them to stand on their own two feet. They'll have a powerful and empowering education."

"It sounds too good to be true," Adam said.

"It's a relatively simple formula based on the concepts of liberty and independence. Well, look, I'm conscious of the time. You're all scheduled to meet in your content areas to review the curriculum. Let's take a quick break to re-caffeinate and then you can head off to your content locations. I'll see you all after dinner for the presentation by our CFO."

The group broke and began mingling around the room. William stood next to Tabitha.

"So, what did you think?" Tabitha asked.

"I agree with Adam – sounds too good to be true."

"It's not. This is the real deal. If we do this right, we'll show America the new face of education. I have to run. Don't forget to bring your cell phone back to your room. I'll catch up with you later. I'm looking forward to going out for a few cocktails with you tonight. You're still interested, right?"

"Absolutely."

WILLIAM refreshed his coffee and brought his iPhone back to his room before walking to the seminar room where the social studies and history curriculum was scheduled to be presented. William and the social studies teacher recruits spent the rest of the morning reviewing curriculum maps and resources. Marriott staff brought in a platter of cold cuts for a working lunch. By early afternoon, the group finished reviewing the curriculum, and began designing lesson plans. They worked straight through dinner. At 6:30 p.m., the seminar coordinator announced that they had to break for the evening presentation by the Beacon Academy Chief Financial Officer. William organized his binder and walked with his newfound colleagues to the largest presentation room. They sat together at a table near the back of the room.

A hand landed on William's shoulder. "I told you we'd fill that up," Tabitha said, pointing at the three-ring binder.

"Oh, hey there," William said.

"I was looking for you at dinner," Tabitha said.

"We forget all about dinner."

"Too engrossed, huh?"

"Absolutely. It's amazing. I can honestly say that I got more out of the last eight hours than I got out of three semesters of teacher preparation courses at Quinnipiac. I can't wait to start using some of this stuff when I student teach this fall."

"I'd hold off on that if I were you," Tabitha said.

"Why?"

"You get a grade for student teaching, don't you?"

"Yeah, so?"

"Your cooperating teacher is going to have a say in that grade, right?"

"I guess so, why does it matter?" William asked.

"Just trust me, stick with what they tell you to teach, and how they tell you to teach it. You're going to be behind enemy lines when you step into a traditional public school classroom. Don't make waves."

"Maybe your right."

"Trust me, I'm right. You'll have plenty of time to teach the Beacon curriculum next fall. If you try teaching kids in public school with that material, they'll run you out of there. For the time being, just go along and get along."

"That's good advice, thanks."

"No problem. I'm heading up to my room to get some work done. I don't need to sit through this presentation, I've heard it before. Are we still on for a drink tonight?"

"Yes."

"Okay, good. There's a restaurant bar in the lobby. Let's meet there at Nine O'clock."

"Sounds good."

"Order me a glass of white wine if you beat me there."

"Sure."

For the next two hours, William and the recruits sat through a presentation by the Beacon Academy Chief Financial Officer. The CFO provided an overview of the contracts offered Beacon Academy teachers. William sat quietly at his table, wishing the time away. The CFO finished his presentation at Eight O'clock. William hustled back to his room to shower and get ready for his date with Tabitha.

WILLIAM walked into the Marriott restaurant bar. Fewer than a half-dozen patrons sipped cocktails at the bar. Three stocky men in flannel shirts and NASCAR baseball hats watched an NFL game on a flat screen television. William climbed onto a stool at a two-person pub table. A waitress sidled up to the table and asked William if he wanted a drink.

"Yes, please. I'll have a glass of white wine and a beer," William said.

"Any particular kind of beer and wine, sweetie?"

"Oh, ah, sure," William said, feeling a little foolish for not knowing how to order wine and beer. "Just a normal white wine and beer, what do you suggest?"

"How about the house white?"

"That sounds fine."

"And what kind beer would you like? We have Budweiser, Bud Light, Harpoon, and Guinness on tap, and just about anything you'd like in bottle."

"Budweiser, I guess," William said.

"You got it."

William watched the waitress walk back to the bar and enter the order on a touch screen set up in the bar's service area. A few minutes later, the waitress returned and set the drinks on napkins.

"Are you going to want anything from the kitchen?" The waitress asked.

"Not right now, thanks."

The foam on the head of the beer flowed over the side of the frosted pint glass and soaked the napkin. William picked up the beer and gingerly sipped. He wrinkled his nose as the cold beer slipped across his tongue and shocked his taste buds. For the past four years, his Friday and Saturday nights were spent sipping Coke with Mary and other Christian Coalition students; he never had occasion to grow accustomed to the taste of alcohol. William placed the pint glass on the napkin and wiped foam from his lips. He sat back on the stool and looked at the holiday decorations that adorned the bar. For a corporate outfit, the garlands, ribbons, and wreaths were tasteful.

William's attention was stripped from the festive décor when Tabitha stepped into the bar. She was dressed in tight jeans with a slight bell at the bottom, and a skin-tight, black turtleneck sweater. Her hair was tied back in a ponytail. She looked like she should be stepping into a smoke-filled café on the West Bank of Paris in the early 1950s, about to sip wine, smoke clove cigarettes, and discuss some existential dilemma with Jean-Paul Sartre.

"Hey there," Tabitha said, climbing onto the pub stool across from William.

"Hi. Is that what you wanted?" William asked, nodding to the wine.

"Perfect, thanks. I'll get the next round," Tabitha said, lifting the wine glass and taking a healthy swig. "Ah, just what I need after a long day, comfy clothes and a glass of wine, is there anything better?"

William lifted his beer and pretended to enjoy a gulp.

"Cheers," Tabitha said, offering her wine glass.

"Cheers," William said, clinking her glass and taking another drag off the pint.

"So, you've experienced the whole Beacon Academy sales pitch. What do you think? Are you ready to commit?" Tabitha asked.

"It's great, but I still have a lot of questions."

"I'm all ears. Ask away," Tabitha said.

"Okay, so, I think I've got this figured out. The Movement, it's some kind of libertarian thing, right?"

Tabitha took another long sip of wine. "So, we're back to labels. Why can't you let go of that?"

"I'm just trying to get myself grounded in this whole thing, that's all."

"Many of our principles are guided by libertarian ideology. But it would be too easy for mainstream America to write us off as radicals if we call ourselves libertarians. Language is important, so before we start calling ourselves anything, we need victories to illustrate what we're trying to accomplish."

William rubbed his forehead and stared around the room. The bartender turned up the music. Christmas songs added warmth to the room. The waitress dimmed the lights and began moving around the bar lighting a red candle on each pub table.

"What kind of victories?" William asked.

"The leaders of The Movement need to be able to point to what we stand for. It's too easy to talk ideology. We need to match the ideology with reality by providing examples. That's what Beacon Academy is all about; we're going to practice what The Movement preaches. Our success will be an example of what we can accomplish if we empower the individual. We're going to become an inspiration - the way things ought to be," Tabitha said.

"Is it reasonable to think that a handful of schools is going to collectively change the mind of America? We'd have to be pretty darn successful for that to happen. I mean, come on, that's a little ambitious, don't you think?"

"This is bigger than that. We're only one small sliver of what Edward Birch and The Movement Executive Committee is planning. They're laying the groundwork for something amazing. It's not just about education; it's policy and practice in economics, medicine, and foreign policy - every corner of society. When we go mainstream, we're going to have hundreds of examples to point to, examples of how individual freedom succeeds where the collective fails. Right now, we need to focus on creating the structures that match the ideology with the practice. In our case, the practice will be in public education, which is why we need teachers committed to the cause."

Tabitha finished her wine with a long swig. "Ah," she said. "You want another? I'm gonna have one."

William still had half a pint to finish. He picked up the pint glass and swallowed the beer in three long gulps. "Sure," William said, turning in his chair, and scanning the bar for the waitress.

"She's over there," Tabitha said. "She looks busy. I'll get us a drink at the bar."

Tabitha climbed down from the pub stool and walked across the room. She spotted an empty chair at the end of the bar. The empty chair offered her an opening to sidle up to the bar and get the attention of the bartender. William watched a broad-shouldered man in a flannel shirt watching a football game at the far end of the room notice Tabitha. Her sleek, avian movements and perfect body was sure to garner the attention of any predatory male, especially a testosterone and alcohol-fueled man watching football with his buddies. The man elbowed his buddy and leaned back in his chair to get a good look at Tabitha's ass. William couldn't hear what the men were saying, but he could only imagine the sexually charged remark. The bartender placed a glass of wine and fresh draft beer on the bar. Tabitha lifted the drinks and carried them back to the pub table. The men unabashedly leered at her. The broad-shouldered man made eye contact with William as Tabitha placed the drinks on the pub table. They exchanged unspoken hostility, holding eye contact longer than the polite, fleeting moment.

"You okay?" Tabitha asked.

"Oh, yeah, fine," William said, removing his gaze from the man.

"I forgot to ask what kind of beer you're drinking, so I got you an IPA. Is that okay?"

"Sure," William said, completely oblivious to what an IPA is.

Tabitha climbed back on the pub stool. "Oh, that's nice," Tabitha said, noting the burning candle on the table. "Very romantic."

William dropped his eyes bashfully and reached for the beer. "So, how did you get wrapped up in all this?" William asked.

"All what?"

"The Movement, the school, everything?"

"I've been involved for a long time."

"What got you started? Family?"

"Yes. My family and I know what our out-of-control federal government is capable of. My father owned a printing business in upstate New York. We weren't rich, but we were definitely well off. When I was in middle school, the IRS started investigating my father's business for tax evasion. He served eight months in a federal prison during my freshman year in high school. They took everything - our house, cars, savings accounts, retirement, they essentially cleaned us out. We were completely destitute by the time they were done with us. When my father got out, he tried to put things back together, but could never bounce back. He died of a heart attack a couple of years after getting out of prison. The stress killed him," Tabitha said. She picked up her wine and swallowed half the glass.

"That's awful," William said. "Do you have any other family?"

"My mother fell into a major depression and killed herself after my father died. My brother is living somewhere in California. Last I heard from him he's in San Diego. He's addicted to heroin. Every once in a while he reaches out to me for money, but I haven't seen him for a few years."

"Wow, that's terrible."

"After my father died, I did a little research; you'd be surprised how many families out there have been crushed by the federal government. The media never says a damned word about it; they just let the feds use their police state to run roughshod over us. That's when I stumbled onto The Movement, and the worlds just kind of aligned."

"So you're in this for payback."

"That's where it started. But I've evolved a little; let's just say I want to make sure nothing like that ever happens to another family,"

Tabitha said. "So, how about you? Where do your conservative roots spring from?"

William picked up his beer and took a long swig. He nearly gagged on the bitter hops that framed the overtones of the IPA. "Wow, that's good," William said, coughing a little into his sleeve. "I don't know exactly. I guess I'm more of a cultural conservative than anything else. I was raised in a conservative family. I'm sickened by the perversion that's being shoved down our throats. What used to be way out there is now freakin' mainstream, and it's getting worse by the day. It pisses me off when the moral majority raises objections and we're called bigots and homophobes by the politically correct liberal media."

"You'll have to temper that a little," Tabitha said, sipping her wine.

"What do you mean?"

"Our principles are simple – freedom is the purest disinfectant. Nobody has the right to assert his or her will over you without your consent, and you have no right to assert your will over others. We believe freedom is an absolute value."

"I agree. That's why I'm a conservative."

"Are you sure? Freedom is a sword that cuts both ways. Some of your conservative beliefs are going to have to be curtailed if you truly embrace The Movement's values."

William stared into his beer, fighting the slow creep of the alcohol. The waitress walked to the table.

"Can I get you another drink?" The waitress asked.

"Sure. I'll have another glass of wine," Tabitha said. "You want one?"

William wanted to say no, but he nodded.

"Are you still working on the Budweiser?" The waitress asked.

"That was the Harpoon IPA," Tabitha said, pointing to the half-empty pint.

"I'll have another one of those," William said.

"One Harpoon and a Chardonnay. You got it," the waitress said, heading off towards the service bar.

"So, where were we?" Tabitha asked.

"You were about to tell me to let go of some of my conservative principles."

"No. Not let go. You are welcome to whatever beliefs you hold dear. You'll just need to let go of the notion that you can impose them on anyone else."

"Impose them? What do you mean?"

56

"Just what I said - freedom is an absolute value. Liberty is never something that should be limited by any governing authority that is not established through a principle of free association."

"Let me see if I've got this right," William said. "You don't object to same sex marriage or abortion? You're completely okay with those perversions of our moral fabric?"

"No, of course not. I object to those things just as deeply as you do. But I more strongly object to the notion that a centralized government can use its authority to force me, or anyone else, to embrace or reject those things."

"So, you would be okay with a law allowing gay marriage?"

"No. That's the exact opposite of what I just said. I reject any law that limits my freedom, one way or another. I would reject a law that allowed gay marriage just as vehemently as I reject any law that bans gay marriage. There is no role for a federal government in any of those matters. Those are matters of faith, of personal responsibility; they need to be decided in the home, church, and local community, not some centralized power structure with a police force to assert its will over mine."

"Then you'd leave it up to the states?"

"No, not really. An expansive state government is just as bad as an expansive federal government. I would leave it up to the individual, the family, and whatever community individuals choose to embrace."

"Then by default you believe that gay marriage is okay as long as the individual thinks it's okay?"

"I, personally, don't believe in gay marriage, abortion, drug abuse, gambling, prostitution, or any other immoral behavior. I would never engage in those things, nor would I associate with people who engage in those things. Any community I choose to be involved with will not allow those things. If it did, I would leave immediately. But at the same time, I do not believe I have the right to use government to assert my beliefs. I have the freedom to choose not to do those things; you have the freedom to choose to do those things, so long as your choice doesn't interfere with my free will," Tabitha said.

"Here you go, guys," the waitress said, placing two fresh drinks on the table and picking up the empty glasses. "You guys want anything else, an appetizer or something to eat?"

"You hungry?"

"I'm good," William said.

"You sure? You missed dinner," Tabitha said, taking a sip of her wine.

William picked up the pint glass and forced himself to pull a long swig off the top. The beer was going down a little easier, and quicker.

"No, I'm fine. Maybe later. Thanks."

The waitress walked away. Tabitha lifted the wine glass to her lips and stared seductively over the edge of the glass. The candlelight swirled in the white wine and radiated across Tabitha's mouth. "So, is this turning you off?" Tabitha asked.

William's voice caught in his throat. "No, ah, not at all," he fumbled.

"I can see the wheels turning," Tabitha said.

"All right, I am having a problem," William stammered, the alcohol slightly slurring his voice. "I believe in God, and I believe that he expects us to live by his rules. I can't let go of that."

"No one's saying you should," Tabitha said. "But you have to admit the realities of America in the twenty-first century. There's no way you're going to convert the entire nation to your point of view, right?"

"Does that mean I shouldn't try?"

"If your approach is to use the power of government to force your beliefs on others, then, yes, in the name of pure liberty, I think you should give up. You have to learn to trust in the power of the individual, trust in freedom. If your way of life is the best, then people will naturally be drawn to it. You can't force people to think gay marriage, or abortion, or any other social issue is right or wrong. Think about it, if you try to use government to force your views on someone, that person is likely to fight just as hard to use government to force his views on you. And in a democracy, well, that's how we end up with people like Obama, Harry Reid, and Nancy Pelosi running our country."

"I guess you're right."

"I am right. If you really want to live in a moral society, then create the conditions where freedom is the only law. If a moral life is the proper life, which I believe it is, then absolute freedom will create the conditions for morality to thrive."

"I see where you're coming from."

"Excellent. Let's drink to it," Tabitha said, lifting her glass.

William lifted his pint and clinked Tabitha's wine glass. Beer sloshed over the side of the pint glass. William took a long swig of beer and thumped the empty pint glass back on the pub table.

The waitress walked across the bar and placed two shots on the table. "Here you go," the waitress said.

"What's this?" Tabitha asked.

"Alabama Slammers," the waitress said.

"We didn't order these."

"You didn't? My bartender said to bring them over. Hang on I'll check."

"We must have a secret admirer," Tabitha said. "Well, let's not look a gift horse in the mouth."

Tabitha lifted her shot glass and held it up to William. William picked up his shot, clinked glasses with Tabitha, and together they threw the shots back. The shot burned down the back of William's throat.

"I have to use the bathroom," William said, sliding down from the pub stool. As soon as his feet hit the floor, the alcohol rushed to William's head. He grabbed onto the side of the pub table to steady himself. The pub table tipped upwards slightly.

"Whoa, easy," Tabitha said, grabbing the stem of her wine glass. "You okay?"

"I'm fine," William said, forcing the words, his tongue refusing to form the correct syllables.

William took a step forward, and stumbled slightly before finding his balance. He felt Tabitha's eyes on him as he searched the bar and charted his route to the bathroom. After a few steps, he managed to find his footing and picked up the pace.

After what felt like an interminably long piss, William flushed the urinal, buckled his pants, and wiped a few dribbles of urine from his slacks. He walked to the sink and washed his hands, his blurry reflection stared back at him in the mirror. "Keep it together, you idiot," William hissed. He turned off the hot water and waited for the stream to run cold. He cupped his hands under the stream, and splashed water on his face. He dried himself with a paper towel and slapped his cheeks, trying desperately to chase the buzz of alcohol from his head.

When he walked back into the bar, William saw the broad-shouldered man who had been staring at Tabitha's ass standing at the pub table talking to Tabitha. Tabitha leaned forward with her elbow planted on the table and chin in her palm, listening intently to the man. William charted an unsteady course across the bar, passing the broad-shouldered man's friends, who were watching their friend go in for the kill.

"Oh, shit. Game on," one of the men hissed at William as he passed the table.

William turned to look at the man. He held his gaze for a brief moment, and then turned his head and continued walking towards Tabitha and the broad-shouldered man.

"Hey, there you are. I was about to send out a search party," Tabitha said.

"Geez sport, were you taking a shit or something? What're you thinking leaving a lady as beautiful as this sitting all alone in a hotel bar?" The man asked.

"Oh, stop," Tabitha said, slapping playfully at the man's arm.

"Excuse me," William said, brushing past the man and climbing back onto the stool.

"I got you another beer," Tabitha said, pointing to a fresh draft on the table.

"Let me buy you guys another shot," the man said.

William's heart sank when Tabitha answered with a perky, "Sure."

"You got it, sweetheart," the man said. "How does a chilled So Co and lime sound?"

"Delicious," Tabitha said.

"I like a girl who can handle her whisky. Be right back," the man said, turning and walking towards the bar.

"What's So Co?" William asked.

"Southern Comfort."

"Never tried it."

"Really? You'll like it, stings a little, but it's pretty tasty with the lime," Tabitha said. "You don't mind that he's hanging out with us, do you?"

"Did he buy us the other shot?"

"Yeah, he seems like a pretty cool guy."

"I kinda wanted to talk a little more about The Movement," William said.

"All right, we'll do a shot with him, and then you can tell him to get lost."

William could feel Tabitha's eyes on him. William turned and stared at the man as he ordered shots at the bar. Courage fueled by the alcohol surged through William; there was no way he was going to allow the broad-shouldered brute to emasculate him. He'd never been in a fight before, but if there was ever a good time to take a stand, this was it.

"Here you go, sweetie," the man said, placing a shot in front of Tabitha. "Here's yours big guy."

"Thanks," William said. "After the shot, you're going to have to excuse us."

The man reached up and adjusted the brim of his NASCAR baseball hat. "Now that's not a very neighborly thing to say, is it? I mean, after all, I just bought you guys two shots, didn't I?"

"Cheers," Tabitha said, holding up her shot glass.

"Salud," the man said, throwing back the shot.

William tipped his shot glass and swallowed the whiskey. A burn unlike anything he had experienced before erupted in his throat. William wondered if the man had filled his shot glass with battery acid. His gag reflex kicked in and for a brief, terrifying moment William was convinced he was going to projectile vomit across the pub table. The burn continued down William's throat and settled with a white-hot thud in his stomach. He instinctively searched for something to douse the flames. The frosty pint glass was the only relief in sight. He lifted the glass and greedily gulped the beer, emptying the pint is three long swigs.

"Now, where were we? Oh, yeah, you were just about to tell me to fuck off," the man said, staring at William. "Well, darling," the man said, turning to face Tabitha. "I'll leave it up to you, would you like me to fuck off, too?"

"I'll leave it up to him," Tabitha said, nodding towards William.

William slid off the pub stool and landed on his feet in one motion. The effort was guided by luck and gravity, rather than will. The first thing to go was depth perception, then balance. William stumbled forward and reached out toward the man in one final effort to grab hold of something, anything, that might keep him from crashing to the floor. The man stepped back and to the right, giving William all the space he needed to fall face-first to the ground. William rolled over and looked up at Tabitha and the man. The last thing William remembered was staring up at Tabitha as an amused expression fanned across her face.

WILLIAM woke up sometime around Two O'clock Sunday morning. He was face down on the mattress, fully dressed, except for his shoes. The room was dark. He lifted his head and fought to assemble a coherent thought. A white-hot migraine pierced his head with the intensity of two ice picks thrust into his temples. William dropped his head back onto the mattress; his cheek landed in something sticky and moist.

At Five O'clock that morning, William peeled himself off the comforter and stumbled headlong into the bathroom. He dry heaved over the toilet, and then crashed onto the tiles. The cool ceramic tiles and porcelain toilet bowl was refreshing. He slipped in and out of consciousness, only once managing to claw himself from the floor to retrieve a towel to use as a pillow.

A rapping sound echoed through the bathroom and tore William from his slumber sometime around Eight O'clock. Each rap pierced his head with the intensity of a jackhammer. William implored God to make the sound go away.

"William.... William…," Tabitha called as she knocked on the door.

William reached up and grabbed hold of the toilet seat. He pulled himself upward and managed to get to his knees. A dry heave erupted in his abdomen. He leaned over the toilet and retched. William took three deep breaths and stood up. He was dizzy and badly disoriented, still partially drunk from the night before. William stumbled forward and steadied himself on the counter around the basin. He closed his eyes and focused all his mental energy on finding his balance.

In between the raps on the door, William heard Tabitha's voice, "William… William… Are you there? Wake up."

"Just a minute," William called.

The sound of his own voice reverberated painfully through William's head. He turned on the water, and washed vomit from his face and hair. He lifted a clean towel from a rack, dried himself, and stumbled out of the bathroom. He opened the door and found Tabitha standing in the hallway. She was dressed in the same clothes as the night before, her turtleneck sweater stretched and badly wrinkled. She looked tired and used; her hair matted to the side of her face, mascara and eyeliner smeared around her eyes, and lipstick smudged across her lips and cheek. William had seen the same look on the face of countless Quinnipiac co-eds making the Sunday morning walk of shame across campus.

"Hey. You all right?" Tabitha asked.

"What happened?" William stammered.

"Come on, you gotta get up. You're scheduled to have a contract negotiation in my room in forty-five minutes. Get yourself together."

WILLIAM showered and cleaned himself up as best he could. He downed three Advil tablets, dressed, and took the elevator to the first floor of the hotel. He knocked on Tabitha's door.

"Come in," Tabitha called.

William opened the door and stepped into the suite. Tabitha stood up from a small table next to the window and walked towards William with her hand outstretched. She was dressed in a business suit with her hair tied back in a bun. There was no trace of a hangover. Tabitha shook William's hand with a crisp, professional efficiency.

"Good morning, Mr. Blake," Tabitha said.

"Geez. I guess it's time to get serious," William said, noting the business suit and formality of her greeting. "If I'd known, I would have put on a shirt and tie."

"You look fine. Come over and sit down. I'm going to get Jason on my cell."

"Who's Jason?" William asked.

"Jason Brigham, he's the director of the Long Wharf Beacon Academy. He's going to negotiate your contract."

"Ready when you are," William said, taking a seat at the table.

Tabitha sat down and dialed the number on her iPhone. She activated the phone's speaker and set the iPhone on the table between them. The phone rang. A male voice answered on the third ring.

"Good morning, Jason Brigham."

"Hi Jason, it's Tabitha. I'm here with William Blake."

"Hello William. It's nice to speak with you. Tabitha has told me a lot about you."

"It's nice to speak with you, too, sir," William said.

"So what did you think of the seminar?"

"It's all very interesting, Mr. Brigham."

"Please, call me Jason. So, are you ready to jump on board?"

"Let's just say you've got my attention."

"Excellent, then let's see if we can come up with something that will hold that attention. William, I'm prepared to offer you a contract with a base salary of twenty-eight thousand five hundred dollars. The salary will be paid out from September through August over twenty-four bi-weekly pay periods," Jason said.

As Jason spoke, Tabitha leaned over and removed a folder from a briefcase on the floor. She opened the folder, clicked a ballpoint pen, and began taking notes.

"Beyond the base salary," Jason said. "I'm prepared to offer you some bonuses. The first bonus is based on student performance. Next year, you will have a caseload of one hundred and twenty-five students. In March of next year, those students will take a standardized assessment called Smarter Balanced or S-Bac. Are you familiar with the Common Core and the S-Bac test?"

"Yes."

"If all your students score at the advanced level, you will receive a fifty thousand dollar bonus. Tabitha will show you a sliding scale that outlines the bonus if less than one hundred percent of your students score at the advanced level."

Tabitha removed a chart from the binder and slid it across the table to William. William studied the chart.

"According to this, the amount decreases pretty rapidly below one hundred percent. If less than ninety-five percent of my students score at the highest level, I will receive no bonus at all. Is that accurate?" William asked.

"Yes. That's correct."

"That's a pretty high bar. Isn't there any wiggle room? I've seen some of the S-Bac sample tests, they aren't easy."

"There's no wiggle room. As part of the Beacon Academy agreement with sending districts, the tuition we receive is determined by student performance on the S-Bac. Has our funding structure been explained to you?"

"No," William said.

"I'll give you a thumbnail sketch. We are going to charge local districts tuition for students from their towns. If our students perform at the highest level on the S-Bac, we charge them one rate. If students do not perform well on the S-Bac, the districts are charged a lower rate. If Beacon students perform poorly on the S-Bac, then districts are charged nothing, and they retain the right to reclaim their students and return them to the local public school. This is a pay-for-performance agreement; if our students don't do well on the S-Bac, we will be starved of resources. That is the only way we can offer the bonuses. The bonus system is based on free market competition; if our students do well, we'll be rewarded; if not, our goose is cooked."

"Interesting," William said.

"Does it makes sense to you?"

"Yes. I get it. I think the approach is reasonable and fair. So, I'll have the opportunity to earn a maximum of seventy five thousand dollars next year, assuming my students are well prepared for S-Bac, right?"

"Hang on; we're not finished, yet. In addition, we offer three more incentives. First, each teacher is assigned an additional community responsibility. You've been assigned building security. You are going to work with a group of teachers assigned responsibility for student and faculty safety, and general facility security. Tabitha will share the job description with you."

Tabitha removed a three-page document from a binder and slid it across the table.

"Do you have the description?" Jason asked.

"Yes. Tabitha just handed it to me."

"Okay. Take a minute to look it over."

William reviewed the job description. "Does the school have security guards or a school resource officer?" William asked.

"No, just you and the security team you assemble."

"The school's located in New Haven, right?" William asked.

"Yes."

"This job description says that I'm responsible for any vandalism or burglary that happens at the school. What's the neighborhood like?"

"I'm not going to lie to you," Jason said. "It's not the best area. You're going to have to be on your toes."

"This says that I'm responsible twenty-four hours a day, seven days a week. That's a big commitment. Isn't there any way to hire a security contractor to keep an eye on things, at least when school is not in session."

"No. We are going to take care of the school; everything will be managed in-house. We're not hiring any external or support personnel; everything is going to be handled by teachers and students. At the end of the year, your performance will be rated against that job description and the indicators of success in the description. If you successfully meet those demands, you will receive a bonus of twenty-five thousand dollars."

"That sounds like a generous bonus. Is it all or nothing?"

"Yes. The full bonus is awarded, or nothing."

"Who makes the ultimate evaluation of my performance? You?"

"No, it will be based on a survey we administer at the end of the year."

"Who takes the survey?" William asked.

"All Beacon students and faculty."

"Okay. Sounds reasonable."

"Good, then let's go through the final two bonuses that we're going to offer you. The next bonus is linked to student creativity and ingenuity, and how that creativity improves the academy. You are going to be assigned twenty students next year. You will work with these students to identify a product or service that the students will develop and contribute to the community. Tabitha will share an outline and the rubric that we've developed for this aspect of the program. If the students you advise excel in this area, you will receive a fifteen thousand dollar bonus."

Tabitha slid several papers across the table. William picked up the rubric and reviewed the categories.

"Oh, I get it. So, if I wanted to, I could use these twenty students as my security team."

"Right, you could. Alternatively, you may find that they have a different set of skills that you could capitalize on. Everyone has to give back something to the community. If we tap into the skills, talents, and interests of our students and faculty, we believe the community will thrive."

"Very interesting. And who determines if I earn the bonus in this area?"

"Once again, surveys and direct observations. The metrics will work themselves out. For example, if a group develops a product, we might assess success based on how much revenue is raised from the sale of that product. Or if a group decides to, oh, I don't know, build a greenhouse, we might assess them based on the quality of the produce raised in the greenhouse."

"That's cool," William said.

"We think so," Jason said. "There's one more bonus to discuss. After we receive the S-Bac results and administer our end-of-year surveys, you will receive a composite rating based on student performance, community responsibility, student-based contributions to the academy, and director input. This rating will be used to rank you against your colleagues in the school and teachers in Beacon Academies nationally. This ranking will be publicly posted in the school. The top ten percent of teachers receive a ten thousand dollar bonus. The top twenty percent receives a five thousand dollar bonus. Any teacher outside of the top twenty percent will receive no bonus."

"And the bottom ten percent is subject to dismissal, right?" William asked.

"That's correct. So, let's review. You will receive a twenty-eight thousand five hundred dollar base salary, a potential fifty thousand dollar bonus for student performance, a potential twenty-five thousand dollar bonus for building security, a potential fifteen thousand dollar bonus for your advisory group, and a potential ten thousand dollar bonus if your composite ranking places you in the top ten percent. That puts your salary somewhere between twenty-eight thousand five hundred dollars and one hundred and twenty-five thousand and five hundred dollars."

Tabitha wrote a note on a scrap of paper and slid it across the table to William - *Don't let him low ball you.* William read the note and looked up at Tabitha. Tabitha offered a sly wink and nodded towards the phone.

"I don't know," William said, holding Tabitha's gaze. "It sounds like a big commitment."

Tabitha mouthed the words - *Tell him you want seventy-five thousand.*

"It is a big commitment. We have very high expectations for you. I am working within some fiscal parameters; the only area I can move is on the student performance on S-Bac," Jason said.

"Can you come up to seventy-five thousand?"

"Okay. But that's the only area where I have any flexibility."

"That sounds reasonable," William said, wondering if he caved too soon.

"Good, then we have an agreement. That will bring your top end package to a potential of one hundred and fifty thousand and five hundred dollars."

Tabitha retrieved a three-page carbon copy contract from her briefcase. She used a ballpoint pen to write in the dollar amounts for each of the bonuses. "I think those numbers are accurate," Tabitha said, sliding the document across the table to William.

"How does it look?" Jason asked.

"Pretty much everything we agreed to," William said.

"Good. Initial next to the dollar amounts Tabitha wrote in, and then sign the last page."

William initialed the document, signed the last page, and slid the contract across the table to Tabitha. Tabitha ripped the back page off the contract and handed it to William.

"Did he sign it?" Jason asked.

"He did," Tabitha said. "And we didn't even make him sign it in blood."

"I'm sure that we'll be getting our share of blood, sweat, and tears out of him," Jason said flatly. "Welcome to Beacon Academy, William."

PART II

BEACON ACADEMY

March, 2021

WILLIAM stood in front of the classroom, reflecting on how quickly eight years had flown by. He stared proudly at his students seated at their desks in six perfectly straight rows; it was another bumper crop.

"Well," William said. "This is the moment of truth."

"I still don't understand why those people are here," a blond girl in the second row said.

"They're from the State Department of Education. They're looking for improprieties in the testing," William explained.

"What kind of improprieties, Mr. Blake?" A boy in the back row asked.

"Cheating. They want to make sure we're not cheating," William said.

"Why do they think we're cheating?" The blond girl asked.

"For the past eight years, we've been giving the SAT to every student in grade eleven. As you know, all juniors in Connecticut are required to take the SAT. In each of those years, Beacon students dramatically outperformed other students in the state. It's actually bigger than Connecticut alone; students across America take the SAT. Beacon Academy students have scored number one in the entire nation for eight years in a row. Frankly, it hasn't even been close - we've creamed 'em. And it's not just the SAT, it's the ACT, NAEP, AP, TIMMS, PISA; Beacon students ace everything they throw at us," William said.

"They think we're cheating because we do well?" A girl with short-cropped hair asked.

"Yup, you got it. But you have to understand, the real reason those people are here is a reflection of everything we've been talking about in this class all year. The expansive social contract that progressives use to grow government has one purpose. Would anybody like to explain that purpose to me?" William asked. Every hand in the room rose excitedly. "Jamal," William said.

"To rob us of our independence and liberty by creating a system that we're over-reliant on," Jamal said.

"Okay, good, now connect that to why the observers from the State Department of Education are here today - what are those observers really here for?" William asked.

The students stared at William. Pensive wrinkles formed across each of their foreheads.

"Come on guys," William said, reading the stumped expressions. "Think. Why are those people here? Although they'd never admit it, heck, I bet they probably don't even realize it themselves; as individuals, they're probably low-information bureaucrats who are just doing what they're told to do, and in the process skimming a few bucks from hard-working taxpayers for their measly paychecks. But in the grand scheme of things, what is their real purpose within the fabric of the smothering progressive agenda? Dashawn," William said.

"To create a level playing field," Dashawn said. "They're trying to force us back into a condition of subsistence by flattening our performance."

"That's exactly right. They use the power of government as a great equalizer. Their goal is to smother the top performers and create a regulated distribution of resources. In our case today, they view your intelligence as a resource that needs to be flattened in order to promote their vision of social order. If you listen to them carefully, that's what they're talking about when they call attention to things like the *achievement gap*. Beacon Academy's performance baffles them because they refuse to believe that any singular system can outperform the system as a whole. Instead of celebrating and replicating our success, they aim to trample it. You're a threat to them. They refuse to accept your performance as an objective fact. So, their first move will be to 'find us out,'" William said, using his pointer and middle fingers to put air quotes around the words. "They would love nothing more than to catch us cheating. They expect it; it's the only excuse they can possibly conceptualize."

"But why, Mr. Blake?" A girl named Amanda asked. "Why don't they just look at the school and talk to us. Then they'd see what an amazing place Beacon Academy is, and they'd understand that we don't need to cheat. We have every incentive in the world to do well on those tests, that's why we study hard for them, that's why you and the other teachers here kill yourselves to make sure we're ready for them. What's so hard to understand? It's not cheating, it's hard work."

"Don't be naïve," William said. "Would anybody like to explain this to Amanda?"

"I will," Dashawn said. "It has everything to do with race, class, and expectations for students in public school. In their narrow-minded little world, only white kids in their pretty little suburban schools are supposed to do well on these tests. Here at Beacon, we've got just as many black kids as white kids. When black kids start doing as well as white kids, and a school from the city starts creaming schools from the suburbs, well, that's just not acceptable to them."

"Well done, Dashawn," William said. "He's right. It disrupts the social homeostasis. The black-white and suburban-urban balance is one component, but you also have to remember that your experience here is entirely different from the experience in any other public school. Long Wharf Beacon Academy has been allowed to operate outside the smothering state and federal bureaucracy, and independent of heavily unionized public school working conditions. Essentially, we were set free to develop our own vision, and that vision has proven successful beyond our wildest imagination. We're viewed as a threat because we're the exact opposite of every dysfunction they've created."

"I still disagree with you, Mr. Blake," Dashawn said.

"Good. Tell me why."

"I think this is more of a race-thing than anything else. They can't allow a system to exist in which black kids succeed. If we start succeeding, they won't need their welfare programs, prisons, and every other nanny state social program that has smothered the black population since the days of the New Deal and Great Society. The power structure in this nation is scared to death of any system that might actually empower black America, and equip black people with the skills necessary to live self-sufficient lives."

"I don't disagree, Dashawn. This is about race, class, social mobility - all of those things. It boils down to the powerful versus powerless. Beacon Academy poses a threat to the systems and institutions that powerful men and women have used for generations to keep the powerless in a state of dependence."

"Motherfuckers," Dashawn said under his breath. A round of grousing and anger bubbled through the classroom.

"Good. I want you to channel that anger by going into that computer lab this morning and showing them what you're made of. Prove the power of our principles."

The students cheered and fist pumped in a show of resolve. William led the students out of the classroom and down a hallway to a computer lab. The students filtered into the computer lab and began logging on to desktop stations set up around the perimeter of the room. A man dressed in a cheap business suit, and an obese woman in a floral patterned dress the size of a bedsheet stepped into the room. The man used his pointer finger to count the students. He tapped the headcount onto the screen of an iPad and opened the online testing session.

"Are you Mr. Blake?" The man asked.

"Yes," William said.

"We'll take over proctoring from here. You need to leave now."

William watched the bureaucrat tap the iPad screen. The overweight woman wrote the time and the session number on a whiteboard.

"Good luck, guys," William called to the students.

"Thank you, Mr. Blake," the students replied in unison.

William stepped out of the computer lab and walked down a hallway towards the Beacon Café at the front of the school. He paused at a door leading to a stairwell that descended to an indoor firing range and Dojo in the basement. He pushed the crash bar to make sure the door was locked. The last thing he wanted was some pencil pusher from the State Department of Education stumbling into the facility that housed the school's physical education program.

The Beacon Café was located next to the front entrance. William peered into the main cafeteria adjacent the Beacon Café. A few students sat quietly at tables reading. Two students in the back of the cafeteria played chess. William walked into the smaller room that housed the Beacon Café, and took a seat at one of the tables along the interior wall. A student walked up to him.

"Good morning, Mr. Blake. How do you fare?" The student asked.

"Hale and hearty, hearty and hale, Anna," William said. "Did you finish your essay last night?"

"Yes, sir. I emailed it to you this morning. I think I nailed it; third time is always a charm," Anna said.

"Excellent. I'll read it tonight and post my notes," William said.

"Can I get you something to eat?"

"Coffee and a toasted bagel. Did you guys make any more of that salmon spread you had yesterday?"

"Yes. They made a fresh batch this morning."

"Smear a wad of it on the bagel."

The student headed off with William's order. William was the only person in the café. The dark, wood-paneled walls and crisp white tablecloths gave the room a clean and professional appearance. William wondered if there was a restaurant in the Greater New Haven area that would earn a stronger review from Zagat's. Anna returned with a tray holding a cup of coffee, a small pewter cup with cream, another pewter cup with sugar and a tiny spoon, and a bagel smothered with salmon and caper spread.

"Here you go. Can I get you anything else?"

"No, thank you, Anna."

"Would you mind if I read a little? I'll be right over there if you need anything," Anna asked.

William looked at her incredulously. As a server in the Beacon Café, she was supposed to be working, not studying.

"Never mind," Anna said, dropping her head.

"Look, I won't say anything. Just grab your book and stand at the hostess station. That way, if anyone comes in you can make it look like you're reviewing the menu or something."

"Thank you, Mr. Blake."

William poured cream into his coffee and stirred in a spoonful of sugar. He sipped the freshly roasted and ground coffee, enjoying the rich overtones. He took a bite of the bagel, savoring the smooth texture of the salmon that mixed with perfect hints of onion, garlic, and capers. As usual, the food was five-star quality. William placed the bagel on the dish and used a linen napkin to wipe his mouth. He looked up and saw Jason Brigham crossing the café in his direction.

"Hey, there you are," Jason said.

"Uh-oh," William said. "You're not supposed to be in here. You didn't make this week's list."

Jason looked over both shoulders. "I know, I know. I just saw you sitting in here, I'm leaving. Can you meet with me and Tabitha in the conference room in an hour? One of the inspectors from Hartford wants to talk to us."

"Sure."

Jason turned and hustled out of the café. William finished his bagel and two cups of coffee while perusing the national news on his iPhone. Shortly before Ten O'clock, he said goodbye to Anna and made his way towards the conference room.

"Hey, wait up," a voice called from down the hall.

William turned and saw Tabitha walking towards him. Even after seeing her almost every day for the past eight years, she still managed to steal his breath. She was dressed in a knee-length, plaid skirt, and white blouse with a black sweater to hold at bay the cool, early spring nip in the air. Tabitha walked up to William and gave him a European kiss on the cheek. William inhaled deeply, swimming in Tabitha's scent.

"Good morning," William said.

"You on your way to meet up with Jason?" Tabitha asked.

"Yup. He's anxious about meeting with some jackass from the state."

"I'm heading there, too."

"I know, he told me you were coming."

"He's a nervous nelly. I don't know why he gets all worked up."

"I guess we'll find out," William said.

Tabitha and William walked side-by-side into the main office. A team of students and teachers had converted the main office into a lounge outfitted with leather sofas, a pool table, flat screen televisions, and pub tables. A teacher sat at one of the pub tables, absorbed in her laptop computer. A man stood off to one side of the room watching Fox News on one of the flat screen televisions.

"That must be him," Tabitha whispered, pointing at the man in khaki pants and a camel hair sports coat watching the news report.

"Good morning," William said to the man. "I'm William Blake and this is Tabitha Couture. You must be the gentleman from the state department."

"Steven Hill," the man said, adjusting the glasses over his nose.

"It's nice to meet you," William said.

"Likewise. This is the main office, right? I was worried that I was in the wrong place."

"You're in the right spot," Tabitha said.

"This isn't like any high school front office I've ever been in," Steven said. "Where are the secretaries?"

"We don't have secretaries," Tabitha said.

"No secretaries? How do you run a school without secretaries? I was a high school principal for twenty-five years; I couldn't have survived without my secretary."

"We don't have a principal, either." Tabitha said. "Just students and teachers. We're pretty self-sufficient around here."

"No principal, huh. I'm supposed to meet with Jason Brigham. He's your program director, right? Isn't that essentially the same thing as a principal?"

"Not even close," Tabitha said. "Well, speak of the devil."

Jason walked into the office. "Hello everyone. I'm sorry I'm late. You must be Mr. Hill," Jason said.

"Yes," Steven said, shaking Jason's hand.

"Did you guys introduce yourselves?" Jason asked.

"Yes," Tabitha said.

"Great. Well, let's get down to business. We'll use the conference room over here."

Jason led the group into a conference room attached to the main office. William and Tabitha waited politely for Steven to step into the room. They followed him in and took seats in red leather chairs set up around a long, Mahogany conference table.

"Wow, you have quite the set up here," Steven said, removing a laptop computer and placing it on the conference table.

"Thanks," Jason said. "Can I offer you a coffee?"

"Sure, that would be nice," Steven said.

"How about you guys, want one?" Jason asked William and Tabitha.

William and Tabitha shook their heads. Jason stepped out of the conference room and asked the teacher in the office if she would mind running to the Beacon Cafe and grabbing a cup of coffee.

"It'll just be a minute," Jason said, stepping back into the conference room.

"Do you guys mind if I use your Wi-Fi?" Steven asked.

"Help yourself," Tabitha said. "The password is 'liberty.'"

Steven logged on to the network. Tabitha, William and Jason exchanged a furtive glance; they knew that student technicians in the building would immediately hack into Steven's computer as soon as he connected to the school's wireless network. The students would download and copy any information about the inspection, and email it to William within the hour.

"Did it work?" William asked.

"Yup, all set."

"So, how did the testing look to your team?" William asked.

"There are still a few groups to finish up. So far, test security has not been an issue. My proctors certified a clean session for all of your students. We can say that things looked good this year."

"I can assure you that every testing session for the past eight years has been clean," Jason said. "We're a little offended by the supposition."

"No need to be offended. If you guys haven't done anything wrong, you have nothing to worry about."

"Well, how'd they do?" Tabitha asked.

"I don't have access to the whole test. The open-ended responses and essays still need to be scored."

"But you have instant access to the multiple choice questions. How'd our kids do on those?" Tabitha asked.

Steven tapped the laptop keyboard and stared at the preliminary reports. "They did well," he said.

"I'm sure they did better than well," William said. "I'm sure they scored off the charts. Frankly, I'd be surprised if you found more than one or two wrong answers among the entire student body. Let me ask you something, in your twenty-five years as a high school principal, did your students ever produce standardized test results anywhere close to that level of excellence?"

"I'll have you know that my students did quite well considering the circumstances I had to manage; I was principal at some very difficult schools," Steven said.

"All right, well, look, I don't want to put you on the spot. So, let's just take the best and brightest students in whatever school where you served as a principal, say all of your National Honor Society kids. If you compared your best and brightest to all of Beacon's students, did they even come close to that level of performance?" William asked smugly, nodding towards Steven's laptop.

Jason shot William a glare across the table. "Come on, William," Jason said. "I don't see this line of conversation heading anywhere productive."

"I'm just trying to shed a little light on what's going on here," William said. "He doesn't have any hard evidence of our students cheating. He just refuses to believe the objective fact that our students are receiving a superior education when compared with anything he's ever experienced before. Isn't that right, Mr. Hill."

"I have plenty of evidence," Steven said.

"What evidence? Show it to us. Why are you so convinced that we're cheating?"

"I'm a data guy. I've been studying student performance for many years. Your students' performance is statistically impossible from a purely psychometric perspective."

"How come?" Tabitha asked.

"When your students arrive at this school in ninth grade they have many years' worth of benchmark data behind them. We know how well they performed on standardized tests they took in grades three through eight. Based on that six years' worth of performance data, we can statistically predict student performance using hierarchical linear models. Statistically speaking, your students are scoring at impossibly high levels."

"Can you give us an example?" Jason asked.

"Sure. Let's look at one of your subgroups – free and reduced lunch..."

"What's that?" Tabitha asked.

"What's what?"

"Subgroup... free and reduced lunch... what's that?"

"These are your students who have the cost of their lunches subsidized by the federal government. They are one of the subgroups, like special education, English language learners, Black, Hispanic, etcetera."

"There must be some mistake. We don't have any students like that here at Beacon Academy," Tabitha said.

"Yes you do," Steven said, staring at his computer screen. "According to these student records, over sixty-five percent of your students are eligible for free and reduced lunch."

"And where did you get that data?" Tabitha asked.

"The state tracking system. We assign all public school students an ID number when they enter kindergarten, it's how we follow them through their twelve years in public school," Steven said.

"That's freakin' creepy," William said. "Sounds very *1984*ish to me. Why don't you just implant a microchip?"

"I still don't get it," Tabitha said. "There is no free or reduced lunch at Beacon Academy."

"You're wrong, I have it right here," Steven said, tapping the keyboard on his laptop. "The majority of your students are eligible for free and reduced lunch based on their parents' recent income tax filings and health care subsidies. These families live at or below the national poverty line; therefore, they are eligible for free and reduced lunch."

"They may be eligible for it, but we don't have free and reduced lunches here," Tabitha said.

"Well, then that's another concern. You'd be violating federal law if that's the case."

"You don't understand," Jason said. "Our kids don't need free and reduced lunch. Our students prepare all the meals in-house. We don't charge anyone for the food we consume. The expectation is that students and teachers work hard and earn those meals. In fact, we have an incentive system: Students and faculty who perform above expectations are entitled to take their meals in our Beacon Café, which is essentially a gourmet restaurant we run. Everyone else eats high quality, homemade meals in our cafeteria. Students and teachers who don't meet expectations are not entitled to eat at all, unless they pack their own lunch. No one gets a free lunch at Beacon Academy."

"Punishing students by not feeding them is equal parts illegal and unethical. I don't understand how you're getting away with that," Steven said.

"Anyway, we're getting off the topic, let's get refocused. Why do these free and reduced lunch students make you think we're cheating?" Tabitha asked.

"Based on how well those students did on the S-Bac tests as recently as eighth grade, there is simply no way they could increase their performance as much as they have when they take the SAT here at Beacon Academy," Steven said.

"That's probably because back in their old schools they were indentured to government subsidies; there was no expectation that they perform well - no accountability. I'm willing to bet it's precisely because they were receiving free and reduced lunches that they were performing so piss poor. Why should we expect anyone to work hard if we're not going to incentivize that performance? At Beacon Academy, we encourage our students to stand on their own two feet, rather than rely on anyone else. Once they do that, well, the results are right there in front of you. Does anyone else see the irony here?" William asked.

"We'll just have to see about that," Steven said. "The test data anomalies combined with the tremendous shroud of secrecy that surrounds your school has produced some suspicion that demands a full accounting."

"Secrecy? We're an open book," Jason said.

"Please, Mr. Brigham, let's not play games. You know as well as I do that this school is far from an open book. I'd go so far as to say you've created something akin to a cult. I'll also have you know that we intend to vet this school and get to the bottom of the matter. This cannot continue without greater accountability and oversight," Steven said.

"More government oversight," William said, spitting the words out of his mouth. "That's exactly what you're after, isn't it?"

"William, please," Jason said, holding out his hand. "What can we do for you, Mr. Hill? We have nothing to hide."

"I have some questions."

"Ask away," Jason said.

A knock on the door interrupted the meeting. William opened the door and let in a teacher carrying a cup of coffee.

"It's for him," William said, nodding towards Steven.

The teacher placed the coffee on the table.

"Thank you," Steven said, lifting the coffee and taking a sip. "Wow, that's really good coffee."

"Are you a coffee connoisseur?" Jason asked.

"I love coffee," Steven said, taking another sip. He closed his eyes and took a long, slow whiff of the coffee. "That is a delicious brew."

"We only buy the best quality beans. We get 'em directly off the boat from the Blue Mountains of Jamaica," Jason said. "We roast the beans in our café. Our acquisition team purchased a terrific brass drum roaster at a coffee shop downtown that was going out of business. We roast the beans while they're still fresh, and grind them in-house."

"Is that part of a culinary arts class or something?" Steven asked.

"No, it's just part of the culture of the school," Jason said. "Our faculty and students expect nothing short of the best in everything we do. Keurig machines have no place at Beacon Academy - we don't cut corners. I'll make sure you get a bag of fresh ground beans on your way out. So, you were saying, you have some questions for us."

"Yes. I've reviewed your charter. It's a strange public-private hybrid. You're publicly funded, but you operate like a private school. Somehow, you got the Connecticut Legislature and State Department of Education to waive virtually every state law governing the operation of public schools. I'm not sure how you managed that; I'm not even sure it's legal. The charter includes a waiver for all labor laws, special education law, civil rights law - essentially everything that frames the structures we value as a nation. My first question then is rather broad: Why would any school need such leeway?"

"Ha," William scoffed.

"Is something funny?" Steven asked.

"What you call leeway, we call freedom," William said. "We've created a school based on simple principles of liberty. Our students and faculty enjoy a condition that is not constrained by the laws you referenced. As a result, we've been able to flourish."

"At a price?" Steven said.

"What price?" Tabitha asked.

"Sure, no arguing, your test results are strong, and to-date I haven't found anything to suggest you're cheating, but there's other data from your school that I wouldn't be so proud of. Over the past five years, nearly forty percent of your faculty has turned over, and thirty percent of your students have returned to public schools in their sending districts. Explain that."

"Freedom comes with a price," Jason said. "Everyone knows the expectations from the day we sign our contracts. Teachers and students are given every opportunity to thrive. If they fail to thrive, they know the consequences. Education and employment is not a right at Beacon Academy - it's an opportunity."

"I guess it's easy to have high test scores when you can just kick out those students and teachers who aren't flourishing."

"It's true that we take great liberty removing ineffective teachers," Jason said. "Teachers who do not excel are removed from the school. But isn't that best for kids? Would you want anyone but this best in front of your son or daughter? Our teachers have no unions to hide behind, no tenure, no just cause provisions in their contracts. Our equation is simple: Beacon teachers either succeed in the classroom, or they are removed; it's a simple and objective process."

"Sounds pretty cutthroat to me," Steven said.

"There is a Darwinian component to it," Tabitha said. "But that's what makes us the best."

"And I suppose that's how you treat your students, too? Do well or you're kicked out."

"Students who leave us do so as a function of their own free will. Enrollment at Beacon Academy is based on free association. Unfortunately, some students are simply unable to reverse years of social conditioning experienced in kindergarten through eighth grade. Some students prefer to remain reliant on your system of laws - laws that sustain mediocrity. Other students learn to value accountability to a school they freely associate with, and, ultimately, they learn the value of self-reliance. Our program taps into the innate desire for freedom that all teenagers possess. Once we tap into that natural instinct, the strength of the individual arises, and our students quickly embrace self-reliance. They become intrinsically motivated to succeed. Once a student is intrinsically motivated, he or she begins learning at the deepest levels," Jason said.

"Yeah, yeah, yeah," Steven said dismissively. "I'm not interested your twisted view of learning theory. It all sounds very Spartan to me. I'm more interested in some of the unusual accounting practices you have around here. How are you able to afford all this; beans from Jamaica, a gourmet restaurant, a conference room that looks like it should be used by Fortune Five Hundred executives, where do the funds come from? And I've heard that you pay your teachers an outrageous salary. On average, your teachers are earning in excess of one hundred and fifty thousand dollars a year. How much did you make last year?" Steven asked William and Tabitha.

"We both earned our contractual max," Tabitha said.

"How much was that?"

"Around two hundred thousand," William said.

"Two hundred thousand dollars! Are you kidding me?"

"And for that amount, last year, one hundred percent of my students reached the highest level on every standardized test you threw at them," William said. "I also exceeded every expectation established by our community outside of the classroom. Look around this building - it's pristine. Have you ever seen a school in a condition like this?"

"That's my point. It must cost a mint to have a school like this and still be able pay your teachers an outrageous salary."

"That's because you're thinking like a traditional public school principal," William said. "In schools you ran, I bet you had a small army of non-teaching staff, and the school was still a shithole. How much did you pay all those secretaries, custodians, maintenance people, security guards, administrators, counselors, psychologists, social workers, special education teachers, paraprofessionals? And what did they give you? A shithole. So, yes, we're very well compensated, but that's because we use our funds wisely. We don't pay for all those useless positions. We are rewarded for our efforts in the classroom, and contributions to the community. In the end, our operating budget is significantly lower than any public high school in the state. In short, we cost taxpayers less, and produce superior results. We do it because we take ownership of our school, and we rely on no one but ourselves."

"I've heard enough of this nonsense. I'm not buying it. You're hiding something, and I intend to get to get to the bottom of it," Steven said, snapping his laptop shut and standing from the table.

"You're welcome back anytime," Jason said. "I can assure you we have nothing to hide. Come on; let's go get you that bag of fresh ground coffee."

Jason walked Steven out of the conference room. William and Tabitha sat quietly until they were sure Steven and Jason were out of earshot.

"What an idiot," Tabitha said.

"I have it in mind to follow him into the parking lot and kick his ass. Liberal scum," William hissed. "Worthless bureaucrats like him are the reason this country is so fucking upside-down. I don't understand why more people can't see through the bullshit."

"Come on, let's get in a workout," Tabitha said. "You need to blow off some steam."

THE basement of the former YMCA building was enormous. The basement once housed eight racquetball courts, two locker rooms, and a boiler room. Over the decades, as racquetball slowly lost its cache, the YMCA knocked down the walls between four of the racquetball courts and retrofitted the space to create room for spinning and yoga classes. When Beacon Academy purchased the building, one of the first orders of business was to renovate the space. A crew of students and faculty spent the first year gutting the basement. The walls between the racquetball courts were torn out and the hardwood floors patched together to construct an enormous Dojo. The crew gutted the locker rooms and transformed the space into a three-lane, indoor firing range. The faculty and students reinforced the foundation and foam-sealed the range to create a soundproof barrier. After soundproofing, the pop of .22 caliber weapons was silent outside the range. The larger caliber weapons barely whispered through the Dojo. Outside the building, complete silence - no one would have guessed that students and teachers were firing assault rifles and handguns in the school.

William stepped into the basement and flipped a light switch. A flood of fluorescent light illuminated the Dojo.

"It's weird to see it empty down here during the day," Tabitha said.

"I know," William said. "We're keeping everyone out until the inspectors are gone. Liberal scum would freak out if they knew we were training our students how to defend themselves."

William walked across the Dojo towards a changing room. "Where are you going?" Tabitha asked.

"To get changed," William said, turning to face Tabitha.

"There's no one here," Tabitha said, dropping her gym bag and peeling off her sweater. "I don't know about you, but there's nothing I haven't seen before."

Tabitha unbutton her blouse. She pulled the blouse over her shoulders to reveal a lacy, white bra. She leaned over, unzipped her gym bag, and retrieved a scrunchie. She stood, slipped the scrunchie over her wrist, reached behind her back, and unsnapped the clasp on her bra. The bra landed with a soft thud on top of the gym bag. Tabitha leaned her head back, pulled her long, black hair off her shoulders, and tied it back in a ponytail with the scrunchie. She lowered her gaze and stared at William. A wry smile curled at the corners of her lips. "Why don't you take a picture, it lasts longer," Tabitha said.

"Oh, uh…." William stammered.

"It's a good thing I'm not shy," Tabitha said.

In one fluid motion, Tabitha kicked off her shoes, and lowered the zipper on the side of her skirt. The skirt fell the length of her legs and bundled around her ankles. She stepped out of the skirt and pushed it to one side with her foot. Under the skirt, she wore a pair of impossibly petite, white, Victoria's Secret hip hugger panties. Mirrors that ran the length of the Dojo walls offered William a three hundred and sixty degree view of Tabitha in nothing but her panties. He watched her casually lean over and lift a black sports bra from her gym bag. She slipped the Under Armor sports bra over her head and slid her arms through the straps. She retrieved a pair of skin-tight yoga pants from the bag and stepped gingerly into them. She sat down and began digging through her bag in search of socks.

"Come on, show's over. Get dressed," Tabitha said.

Frustration burned in William's belly. He dropped his gym bag to the floor and began unbuttoning his shirt. His hands shook. He struggled to get the buttons on his dress shirt open. In a fit of frustration, he ripped the shirt open, and yanked it over his shoulders. Buttons scattered across the hardwood floor.

"Oooo," Tabitha crooned, observing the impact of her striptease on William. "Looks like someone's ready for a fight."

William inhaled a deep, cleansing breath in a vain effort to calm the sexual energy that burned in his gut. He pulled off his t-shirt and caught a glimpse of himself in the mirror. Eight years of working out with the students and faculty at Beacon Academy had shredded his arms, shoulders and pecs, and transformed his abs from mush into a neatly stacked six-pack. William unbuttoned his trousers and stripped down to his boxer briefs.

Tabitha stood and walked over to William. She stared him directly in the eye. "No weapons today," she said.

"Huh…" William said, dumfounded.

Tabitha reach out and slapped playfully at the erection that bulged in William's underwear. "Put that away before you hurt someone."

"Fuck you," William said, turning away from Tabitha.

"You better do something about that before you head over to poor little Mary's tonight," Tabitha said with a devilish laugh. "You might tear that poor girl up."

Tabitha rolled out mats while William finished getting dressed. He joined Tabitha on the mat and began stretching. William was slowly regaining control over his hormones, but the sight of Tabitha in her sports bra and yoga pants kept him on edge.

"You ready to go?" William asked.

"Yup. I've got to warn you, Marc showed me a few new moves this week," Tabitha said.

She threw the name Marc at William like a brick. Marc was a former Marine with extensive Special Forces training. Beacon Academy hired him to run the school's physical education program. Marc trained students and teachers at Beacon Academy in martial arts, with a focus in Krav Maga, a form of self-defense perfected by Mossad and the Israeli Special Forces.

Marc stood over six feet, three inches tall. Short-cropped blond hair, a perfectly square jaw, high cheekbones, and piercing blue eyes commanded the attention of anyone in his presence. He was the picture of physical strength and mental toughness - a modern day Viking. The faculty and students revered Marc for his prowess in the Dojo. His contract awarded a series of bonuses when students and teachers attained increasing levels of proficiency measured by the procession of belts ranging from white to black, and marksmanship demonstrated on the range. Marc pursued his bonuses with relentless determination. He reaped a financial windfall year-after-year. In his wake, he developed a lethal faculty and student body.

For a series of tortuous sessions in the Dojo, William watched Marc take a special interest in developing Tabitha's martial arts skills. Worse still, he watched Tabitha melt in Marc's hands. It was widely known amongst the faculty that Marc had conquered a succession of the most attractive female teachers at Beacon Academy. He dominated them on the Dojo mat and bedroom mattress. He never made a big deal of his conquests; he simply accepted his place as the alpha male in the community - entitled to his pick of the pride. And while William was never entirely sure, he was convinced that Tabitha was one in a long line of notches on Marc's bedpost. William begrudgingly accepted it; supplicating himself to Marc like a dog on its back lifting his legs in submission.

"Let's go," Tabitha said, sliding on a pair of sparring gloves and headgear. "No kicks, I didn't bring my sparring boots - punches and holds only."

"Okay," William said.

William and Tabitha raised their fists and angled their hips towards one another in guard stances. They bounced lightly on the balls of their feet as they faced off. William was still recovering from the sexual charge of Tabitha's strip tease and the allusion to her sexual liaisons with Marc when he threw the first punch. The punch was strong and quick, but as Marc had trained him not to do, driven from a place of anger; sexually charged frustration fueled the thrust. Tabitha slipped to one side and stepped away from the lunge. William found his center and attacked again. Tabitha matched his strength with her agility. She parried and landed a blow to his midsection. They sparred for the better part of an hour, matching each other jab for jab.

"You're clumsy today," Tabitha teased. "Where's your mind at?"

William called forth the last remnants of focus and strength, and dove for Tabitha's legs. He tackled her to the mat and managed to flip her onto her stomach and pin her arms. He held her face down on the mat, and began grinding against her, calling forth the weapon she had slapped. Tabitha slithered to one side, freed an arm, and reached between her legs. She grabbed William's testicles and squeezed with all her might. William groaned and fell limp at her side. She loosened her grip, rolled onto her side, and lightly tugged his scrotum.

"Easy big boy," Tabitha whispered. "Save it for Mary." Tabitha released her grip and got to her feet.

"Ouch, damn it, Tabitha, what the fuck," William hissed, pain radiating upward from his testicles into his stomach.

"You should wear a cup if you're going to try that on me," Tabitha said. "Get up, don't be such a pussy - you'll live."

TWO students finished their assignments and passed their work in to William. William looked up at the clock on his classroom wall. It was past Nine O'clock, still relatively early by Beacon standards, but the students had put in a good night, and William was feeling magnanimous.

"All right, good work tonight. I'll let you guys pack it up and get out of here early," William said to the group of juniors.

"Really?" One of the students asked.

"Yeah, it's okay, go enjoy your weekend. Consider this a gift for your efforts on the SAT today."

"Wow. Thank you, Mr. Blake," the students said as they packed their backpacks and headed for the door.

"Be careful out there," William said. "I read in the New Haven Register that there have been a few muggings in the area."

"Yeah, right," one of the students said playfully.

"I'm not worried about you guys, I'm thinking of the muggers," William said.

The students smiled and made their way out of the room. William's iPhone buzzed with a new text message. The name *Mary* appeared on the iPhone screen. William touched the screen and read a text message - *Can you stop over tonight? Need to talk.* William replied - *Sure, leaving in 15.*

William packed his laptop and a few file folders of student work in a backpack, and made one loop around the building to check on security. Three students and a teacher had the overnight shift. As usual, he expected a few dozen students in and out of the building for the rest of the night and into the morning. The students would shoot pool in the lounge or generally hang out. Marc would leave the Dojo and firing range open for anyone who wanted to get in a workout or squeeze off a few rounds. Before leaving, William checked the school's electronic bulletin board on his iPhone, and accessed the weekend schedule. He found nothing out of the ordinary; the only things scheduled were general custodial work, a crew tending the greenhouse, wait staff and culinary teams running the Beacon Café and cafeteria, and two acquisition teams running errands to supply the school - nothing that merited an added security detail. Comfortable that his team had the school covered, William decided it was okay to leave early.

William parked his truck a block-and-a-half away from the school. He enjoyed the walk to and from Beacon Academy; the salty, brackish breeze that filtered off Long Island Sound helped clear his mind. The first couple of years was a transition, a time when William would have never dared wander through the Long Wharf neighborhood enjoying the sea breeze and lost in his thoughts. The neighborhood thugs and gangbangers quickly learned to leave the school alone. A few bouts of vandalism, car break-ins, and stickups brought the wrath of Beacon Academy's security detail led by Marc. Marc took a perverse pleasure in cracking skulls. Now, the neighborhood was quiet and secure in a three-block radius surrounding Beacon Academy.

With Beacon Academy as a neighbor, the area was experiencing an urban renaissance: Kids played in the streets and parks, small businesses moved in, and formerly boarded up multifamily homes were fixed-up and rented to Yalies. Property values shot through the roof in the wake of the gentrification, and ushered in a new class of homeowners who tended to their investments by upgrading and maintaining the properties. The revitalized charm of a historic waterfront community replaced the urban blight. The New York Times Magazine featured Long Wharf as one of New England's top-ten turnaround communities. In the feature, the Mayor of New Haven and Police Chief claimed success by pointing to community policing and urban revitalization programs. The Long Wharf residents knew the reality behind the community's renaissance lay in the steely resolve of Beacon Academy faculty and students.

William navigated his Toyota pick-up through Long Wharf and onto Interstate 95. He purchased the jet-black pickup with cash from his previous year's bonus. Mary didn't approve of such an extravagance, but Tabitha thought it was sexy. It was a short drive across the Pearl Harbor Memorial Bridge. William drove another five miles down I-95 and pulled off the exit to a small coastal community called Stony Creek.

The drive through Stony Creek took him the long way to Mary's apartment, but the shoreline cruise was worth the extra fifteen minutes. William rolled down the driver-side window and slowed the truck well below the speed limit as he cruised along the shoreline. Just off the

Stony Creek shoreline was a series of tiny islands called the Thimble Islands. Lights from multi-million dollar homes and mansions on the islands flickered across the water. William daydreamed about owning one of the islands as the heavy, salt air filtered through the cabin of his truck.

Mary rented a small apartment in Branford, where she worked as a first grade teacher in the Branford Public Schools. William parked the pickup in the apartment complex parking lot, and walked to Mary's unit. He knocked twice. Mary opened the door.

"Hey, what's up?" William asked.

"You're early, it's not even Ten O'clock, yet," Mary said.

"I know. I let the kids out early tonight. They were wiped out from testing. Are the kids at your school taking the S-Bac this week?"

"Third, fourth, fifth, and sixth graders are taking it. My kids won't take it for another couple of years. Come in," Mary said, stepping into the apartment. William followed her into the apartment. Mary gave him a peck on the cheek. "Well, that's nice to see," Mary said.

"What?" William asked.

"It's Friday night and there's no alcohol on your breath."

William's drinking was a growing source of tension in the relationship. William wasn't prone to benders, but a few beers a night, and one or two long happy hours with Tabitha and other teachers from Beacon Academy had become the norm.

"You mind if I take a quick shower? I'm a little sticky from a workout this afternoon," William asked.

"Sure. Do you want to stay over tonight? I'll pull out the sofa bed."

"Why not? I'm beat. Leave the sofa bed in for now. Let's watch a movie. I'll pull the bed out later."

"Okay. Go shower and I'll make some popcorn."

William walked outside to the parking lot and lifted an overnight bag from the bed of his truck. He returned to the apartment and climbed the steps to a small bedroom on the second floor. He flipped on the lights and dropped the overnight bag on Mary's bed.

The bedroom was meticulously neat. William sat on the mattress and looked at two pictures in silver frames on a dresser. The first picture was of Mary's parents. Mary bore an uncanny resemblance to her mother; add another dozen years, and Mary would evolve into a spitting image of the woman staring blanking out of the picture frame: Flat brown hair, a sallow countenance, eyes seated a little too closely together, and ears that hung too low framed the woman's autistic-looking face. A baggy prairie dress concealed wide birthing hips and a sturdy frame. A bout of Scarlett Fever after Mary's birth rendered Mary's mother's womb barren. Otherwise, William was sure that Mary would be the oldest in a litter of siblings.

Mary's father was as plain and unremarkable as his wife: He was tall and slim, with eyes that barely concealed a deep disdain for his fellow man. He stared out of the picture with fists clenched at his sides - hinting at the fire and brimstone approach to Christianity that burned in his heart, and served as the foundation for his daughter's upbringing. When Mary was in seventh grade, her parents died in an accident when the family pick-up truck rolled over in a snowstorm. A life insurance policy and proceeds from the sale of the family's one hundred acre dairy farm in upstate New York left Mary moderately well off.

William heard popcorn popping in the microwave. He stared at the second picture on Mary's dresser while undressing. It was a picture of him and Mary from their Quinnipiac University days. In the picture, they were standing at the top of Sleeping Giant State Park. As undergraduates, they occasionally hiked a trail leading to a stone castle built by the Works Progress Administration during the Great Depression. The vista from the top of the castle offered a panoramic view of Greater New Haven. Mary had held up her iPhone and captured a selfie. The selfie was the only picture ever captured of the couple that was even close to flattering. William remembered the day fondly; it was a time when the prospect of a happy life with Mary seemed like a real possibility.

"You all right up there?" Mary called from the first floor.

"All set," William said.

"There are clean towels in the closet. Help yourself."

William stripped down to his underwear, retrieved a towel from the closet, and peeked down the staircase to make sure Mary wasn't staring up at him. He heard Mary in the kitchen, and walked across the hall into the bathroom. He turned the faucet and waited for the water to run hot. When he peeled off his underwear, an erection burst forth from the cotton fabric of the boxer briefs. He stepped into the shower. The warm stream of water did nothing to soothe the ache that had been building since Tabitha's strip tease in the Dojo. William reached down to turn the hot water to cold, and then paused. The warm water was intensely pleasing. He leaned his head back, adjusted the showerhead to the strongest stream, and aimed the water at his erection. In his entire life, he only masturbated once; afterwards, he felt so intensely dirty and forlorn that he promised God he would never lay hands on himself again. For thirty years of self-denial and celibacy, he kept his promise. William lathered himself repeatedly, hoping that the release would come of its own volition, so he could keep his promise to God while relieving the pent up sexual frustration. He continued to throb and ache, stubbornly denied the longed-for release. He climbed out of the shower, and dried himself off. He cursed himself for not letting the water run cold to soothe the heat in his groin.

William returned to the bedroom and opened his gym bag. He pulled out a clean t-shirt and pair of sweatpants, and continued digging through the gym bag. "Oh shit," William whispered when he realized that he forgot to pack an extra pair of underwear. Putting on the day's boxer briefs after a sweaty workout would be disgusting. He slid into the sweatpants without underwear. His erection popped obscenely under the sweatpants; there was no way he could stand in front of Mary with the conspicuous bulge. He sat on the edge of the bed and willed himself flaccid. After an uncomfortable and partially successful mental effort, he regained enough composure to present himself to Mary without embarrassment, and walked downstairs.

"Geez, took you long enough," Mary said.

"Sorry, hot water felt good. I worked out extra hard today. My muscles are sore," William said, sitting quickly on a barstool in the kitchen. "Do you still want to rent a movie?"

"There's something I need to show you first," Mary said, handing William a piece of paper.

William took the paper. "What's this?"

"It's from my superintendent. She sent out next year's salary agreements."

William read the paper. "Wow, a whopping forty-five thousand for your fifth year."

"Am I gonna sign it?" Mary asked.

"Why wouldn't you?" William asked.

"Please don't avoid the subject. I need to hear it from you - am I moving back to upstate New York, or am I staying here with you?"

"What are you asking me?"

"You're a bastard," Mary said, dropping her head into her hands and starting to cry. "You know darn well what I'm asking. Get out of here; just go away," she screamed.

William stood up from the barstool and went to Mary. "Come on, Mary," William said.

William put his arms around Mary. She sunk into his embrace. William pulled her tightly against his body, pressing forward with his hips. To his surprise, Mary didn't recoil; she accepted the stiffness under his sweatpants against her belly, and continued to sob.

"I'm not getting any younger," Mary said through her sobs. "I can't wait forever. You know she'll never love you. When are you going to let her go?"

The blunt allusion to Tabitha took William by surprise. He always suspected that Mary understood Tabitha's control over him, but he never expected her to come right out and say it.

"I won't hold on for much longer," Mary said through sniffles.

"I know," William whispered in her ear. "I know. Sign the contract."

"Really," Mary said, looking up at him.

"Sign the contract, Mary."

"You know what comes with this commitment."

"I do," William said.

They kissed. In the past, William and Mary's kisses were always Puritan and awkward - like pimply-faced middle school students petrified that their braces would snarl together leaving their mouths locked in a snag of wires. This time, the kiss was deep and intimate. Mary pulled back and stared at the floor, her face reddened by the flash of passion. William felt Mary pull away from the hard press against her midsection. He grabbed her and pulled her tight, grinding his erection against Mary's fleshy stomach.

"Sign the contract," William said, releasing Mary from his grasp.

Mary placed the contract on the kitchen table and retrieved a pen from her purse. She lowered the pen to the paper, paused, and stared at William.

"Sign the contract, Mary," William said sternly.

The pen flew across the paper. William enjoyed the control he exercised over Mary. He knew it wouldn't last much longer without a show of commitment that came with a ring, but for the time being she was at his beck and call. Mary folded the paper, stuffed it in an envelope, and placed the envelope next to her purse. She smiled and let William hug her.

"Come on, let's watch that movie," Mary said.

William and Mary sat on the couch and ordered a movie. They ate popcorn and watched the first half of the movie, sitting a respectful distance from one another. Ever since their college days, William knew that Mary liked to leave a little room for the Holy Ghost when they were sitting together. Halfway through the movie, William made a bold move. He laced his left arm around Mary's shoulders and pulled her in. She succumbed, leaning into William's chest. He laced his right arm around her midsection, reached down, and pulled her legs across his lap. William expected her to recoil. He was pleasantly surprised when she went limp in his grasp. He pushed her forward towards the edge of the couch.

"What are you doing?" Mary asked, her voice trembling.

"Lay down."

"Why?"

"Just do it."

Mary lay on her side facing the television. William lay down behind her. He wrapped his arms around her. Mary's body went ridged as William spooned her. William waited a few minutes for Mary to relax. He was careful to keep his hips as far back into the cushions of the couch as possible, so that his inflamed erection was a safe distance from Mary's fleshy rear end. He knew that if he moved too quickly she would bolt from the couch. He slid his right hand down across her belly, feeling the prodigious rolls of flesh under his hand. He slowly slid his hand downward.

"No," Mary whispered.

William ignored the plea and slid his hand down over Mary's groin. Mary's legs tightened and squeezed together, but she didn't move.

"No," she whispered again.

"Relax," William said. "I won't hurt you."

William worked his fingers in small, rhythmic circles over the flannel pajamas, kneading the doughy flesh underneath. Warmth radiated through the flannel. Mary buried her head in a pillow, loosened her legs, and let William's fingers probe. An animal instinct surged through William when he felt Mary succumb. Mary reached down and made a half-hearted effort to push his hand away. William grabbed both of Mary's wrists in his left hand and pinned her arms to her chest. He yanked her crotch upwards with his right hand, and used his chest to push Mary face-first into the couch. He rolled on top of her, and started to grind his erection into her fleshly rear end. She tried to push away, but William held her tightly, and began pulling and probing with his fingers against the flannel over her crotch. He found the softest, deepest spot, and inserted his fingers as far as the flannel pajama bottoms would allow. William pushed down and forward, getting harder with each thrust. He summoned the image of Tabitha in her panties, and hissed the word 'bitch' under his breath.

William dry humped Mary in an awkward up and down, side-to-side motion. Mary tried to protest, but William forced her face into a pillow to silence the combination of moans and pleas - nothing would stop him. He was grateful for the Judo holds Marc taught him in the Dojo. Mary was defenseless in William's grasp. All she could do was wait for him to finish.

"Take it," William hissed as his hips twitched.

"Stop, please, William, you're hurting me," Mary begged.

William thrust his hips forward. His entire body started to shake with the pending release. The pleasure was unlike anything he had ever experienced - the entire room began to spin. He gave one final yank at Mary's crotch, and simultaneously pushed his erection against Mary's fleshy ass. Mary gasped. William's body went limp as he collapsed on top of Mary. His sweatpants and the backside of Mary's pajamas were soaked. The smell of chlorine filled the room. Mary wriggled out from under William and slid off the couch. She walked quickly to the stairs, wiping at the dampness on her flannel pajama bottoms. She stopped at the bottom of the stairs and turned to face William.

"Do you want me to leave?" William asked.

"No. You can stay on the couch. Get yourself cleaned up down here. I don't want to see you until morning," Mary said.

*   *   *

May, 2021

THE warmth of summer wafted through the open classroom windows on the late-spring air. William checked his email every two minutes. While he waited, he calculated the bonuses he expected to receive on a legal size pad of yellow paper. Shortly before Noon, an email from Jason landed in William's inbox. The email had a time in the subject line - 1:30 pm. "All right," William said to the empty classroom. "The moment of truth."

William walked into the main office for his appointment. He found Jason sitting on one of the leather sofas reading something on his iPad.

"Hey," William said.

"Ah, there you are, right on time," Jason said. "You ready?"

"Ready as I'll ever be."

"All right, let's get Jack and Jeanette on the speaker phone."

William followed Jason into the conference room. He watched Jason punch a number into a speakerphone set in the center of the table. The Chief Financial Officer and Beacon Academy Executive Director answered on the second ring.

"Good morning, Jack and Jeanette. I have William Blake here with me," Jason said.

"Good morning, William. How do you fare?" Jeanette asked.

"Hale and hearty, hearty and hale," William said. "It's nice to speak with you guys - amazing how fast a year flies by."

"It's nice to speak with you, too. I hope you had a successful year," Jeanette said.

"I guess we'll find out," William said.

"Okay, so, let's get to it then," Jeanette said. "We're here to review Mr. Blake's performance. I assume everyone has a copy of William's contract."

"We've got one here," Jason said, looking at his iPad.

"Yes, I have a copy, too," Jack said.

"Good," Jeanette said. "Jason, please review William's performance."

Jason reviewed the performance results for each of William's students. Over the speaker, William could hear Jack tapping numbers into a calculator; in William's ears, it was the sweet sound of money. After reviewing the test scores, Jason reviewed student survey data and comments harvested from end-of-course evaluations. The scores and comments were overwhelmingly positive.

"Congratulations. Another very successful year," Jeanette said.

"Thank you. We worked them hard this year. It takes a little while to break them in and weed a few out here and there. But, overall, it was another good crop of kids," William said.

"Well, Jack, what's the damage?" Jeanette asked.

"Thanks to Mr. Blake's students' performance, we will be able to charge local boards of education the full tuition rate for all of this year's Long Wharf Beacon Academy students. That means we'll have the resources to pay William his full bonus for student performance – ninety-five thousand dollars," Jack said.

"Congratulations, William. Nice work," Jeanette said.

"Thank you."

"What about the other performance bonuses?" Jeanette asked.

"William is the lead teacher for a team of faculty and students responsible for school security and facilities," Jason said. "The physical plant is in tiptop condition. Mr. Blake and his team of advisory students installed two new chillers this spring. The upgrade to the HVAC system will be a welcome relief when we get into the dog days of summer."

"Excellent," Jeanette said. "That's the type of community service that separates us from the pack. Jack, you used to be a business manager for a public school system, what would something like that have cost us if we hired a private contractor?"

"Geez, it's hard to say for sure. The project would have had to go out to bid. Conservatively speaking, we can say that it would run close to one hundred thousand dollars," Jack said.

"How much did the system cost the Long Wharf Beacon Academy?" Jeanette asked.

"We purchased two top-of-the-line chillers and materials for about fifteen thousand dollars. William and his team installed the air conditioning units; all we paid for were the materials."

"Well done," Jeanette said.

"Thank you," William said. "It was a fun project. The students involved got a lot out of it. The project developed a real sense of ownership and pride; it's the type of self-reliance and commitment we aim for."

"Very good, keep up the good work. Now, let's talk about security."

William slumped forward in his chair.

"We experienced no security concerns related to the school's physical safety. In this respect, those responsible for school security and facilities enjoyed a successful year. Student and faculty survey data reflect positively on a safe school environment. There were zero incidences of vandalism, physical altercations, or violence against individuals or property; all internal and external threats were effectively identified and neutralized," Jason said.

"You folks have done yeoman's work," Jeanette said. "You really turned that neighborhood around. I remember visiting Long Wharf when we were scouting locations - it was a hellhole. Now, well, you can hardly touch a house in Long Wharf for under four hundred thousand dollars."

"Long Wharf is one of the safest neighborhoods in New Haven. William's vision with respect to perimeter security really paid off. We've created a pocket of tranquility for at least a three block perimeter around the school," Jason said.

"That's outstanding. I know it didn't come easy," Jeanette said. "It's an approach that we're duplicating in other Beacon Academies across the nation, William. Kudos. It sounds like you would have had another outstanding year; that is, if it weren't for the cyber-attack. Tell me where we are with the breach."

"As you know, we experienced a major attack on the school's network," Jason said

"Summarize what happened and bring us up to date on the investigation."

"The network was hacked by an outside group. The school's IT system was compromised; the hackers gained full access to all data housed on our servers, and accessed all internal and external email messages sent over the school's network," Jason said.

"Have you completed a damage assessment?" Jack asked.

"Yes, sir," William said. "It's not good. I want you to know that I take full responsibility for this failure. I'm sorry to say, but we have to assume that a large amount of data was compromised. Specifically, six months' worth of email was downloaded from our servers."

"I assume the breach has been fixed," Jack said.

"Yes. We installed added layers of physical and digital security. All of our internal email is now routed through internal servers over a peer-to-peer network. Nothing sent teacher-to-teacher, student-to-teacher, or student-to-student is going out over the web. External email still goes out over the web. We've added some layers of security to those emails, but once they leave our network, there's no guarantee. We're advising faculty and students not to email anything potentially embarrassing to the school," William said.

"I suppose it's like closing the barn door after the horse ran off," Jeanette said.

"Yes," William said.

"What were in the compromised emails?" Jeanette asked.

"Thousands of emails were compromised. It would be impossible to read them all. Most were trivial, everyday notes and messages. However, we have run some keyword searches on the database. It is safe to say that all aspects of the school's programming and curriculum was discussed at some point. We can assume that the individuals who hacked the email have a complete record and detailed understanding of what's been happening inside the school for the past six months. They have full insight into our organizational systems, structure, and mission," William said.

"Do we know who hacked the system?" Jack asked.

"No. That's the most troubling thing. Our students and faculty are good, very good. I'd put our best against the best the digital world has to offer. Still, we haven't been able to figure out who got in. We know how they did it, but the IP addresses and other digital footprints were swept clean. All I can tell you is that this wasn't amateur hour, or some dimwitted liberal media outlet. If it was, we'd be able to trace them. And if we knew who did it, you better believe we'd be getting some payback. Based on the sophistication of the hack, we have to assume this was the work of some high level programmers," William said.

"That's very disappointing," Jack said.

"I'm sorry," William said.

"This is a major part of your responsibility for school security. The school's physical structure must be protected with the same voracity as the school's digital structure. In my mind, there is no difference between the two," Jeanette said.

"I agree," William said.

"We've decided to prorate your bonus in this area by ninety percent," Jeanette said. William listened as Jack tapped on his calculator. "Well, Jack, what's the bonus?"

"All total, Mr. Blake's bonus this year is one hundred and sixty-five thousand dollars," Jack said.

"There's more bad news, William," Jason said. "As a result of the security lapse, for the first time ever, your overall ranking has plummeted into the bottom ten percent of teachers at Long Wharf Beacon Academy. You will receive no bonus for being a top-performer. I think this is the first time ever that you didn't score in the top ten percent. Heck, last year you were number one, weren't you?"

"Yes," William said.

"You must be very disappointed," Jeanette said.

"I am."

"Well, so are we."

"I understand. When will you post the rankings?" William asked.

"This afternoon," Jason said.

"Okay. Jeanette, can I ask you one question?" William asked.

"Go ahead."

"I heard that other branch academies were hacked. Is there any sense that this is a coordinated attack of some kind?"

"We believe so," Jeanette said. "The Beacon Academy structure has been an overwhelming success. We've become a real threat to the status quo. Beacon Academy, combined with other Movement initiatives, is starting to have an impact on the liberal establishment. Plans are underway to begin taking The Movement mainstream. We've had a few leaks along the way; the liberal establishment is aware of some of our planning. We believe these hacks are part of a coordinated effort to gather information, information they'll ultimately use to defend the status quo and discredit The Movement," Jeanette said.

"I understand. That makes the breach particularly harmful, doesn't it?" William asked.

"Exactly. That's why we can't have any more security failures," Jack said.

"It won't happen again, you have my word."

"Would it be okay if I share the exciting news with William? It might take a little of the sting out of this meeting."

"Go ahead," Jeanette said.

"Edward Birch is coming to our graduation," Jason said.

"Really? You mean next month?" William asked.

"Yes, he's going to deliver the commencement address."

THE clip on the 9 mm Glock slipped into the grip and locked into place. William pulled the well-oiled slide to rack a round in the chamber. He lined the front and rear sights over the target, and pulled the trigger once. A round popped. He lowered the Glock a fraction of a millimeter, realigned the front and rear sights, leaned forward, and pulled the trigger in twelve quick bursts. The slide locked open when the last 9 mm round left the weapon. He placed the gun on a table and pressed a button on the wall. A belt whined as the target retracted toward him along a trolley.

"Not bad," Marc said.

"How could it be any better?" William asked, noting that each of the thirteen rounds was placed in the dead center of the NRA police silhouette.

"You fired a tracer round before emptying the clip. In a real situation, that hesitation could cost you. You need to get all your lead downrange in one burst. Otherwise, your target will duck for cover after the first round report. It's always harder to hit a moving target. Be confident in your initial alignment, then empty the clip as quickly as you can. Watch."

Marc changed the paper target and pressed the button. The target slid twenty yards downrange. He picked up the Glock and snapped a full clip into the grip. The slide clapped forward and locked a 9 mm round in the chamber. He placed the Glock in a holster strapped to his thigh. Marc turned his back to the target and faced William. "Time me," Marc said.

William looked at the second hand on his watch. "Ready... go."

March spun one hundred and eighty degrees. In a fluid, rhythmic motion, he yanked the Glock from his thigh holster and raised it to eye level. In a split second, he aligned the sights and unleashed a wave of 9 mm rounds. The semi-automatic Glock barked like a fully automatic weapon until the slide locked open when the final round left the chamber. Marc pressed the magazine release and the empty clip dropped to the floor. He simultaneously reached down to his belt, retrieved a full clip, and slapped it into the grip. The slide snapped shut and the Glock began barking angrily. Thirteen rounds erupted in a single, sustained crack.

"Time," Marc yelled.

William stared at the second hand on his watch in disbelief. "Four seconds," William said.

Marc pressed the button on the wall. The belt whined as the target retracted. The center of the NRA police silhouette was shredded. Twenty-six rounds vaporized an X over the center mass of the target.

"Un-fucking believable," William said.

"Yeah, it's pretty damned good if I do say so myself. I just wish I had the motherfuckers who hacked our network in my sights instead of this stupid piece of paper."

William and Marc shared responsibility for school security. The hack cost Marc a good share of his annual bonus.

"I know. Bastards. Don't worry, we'll figure out who it was soon enough," William said. "I'm actually heading up now to see if they found anything. You wanna come?"

"No. You deal with the eggheads. Just let me know when they find out who did it. I'm itching for a little payback," Marc said.

William walked through the Dojo, climbed the flight of stairs leading out of the basement, and walked to the IT office on the first floor next to the main office. On his way past the main office, William paused to review the list posted in the floor-to-ceiling windows. He stared at the names of all forty-nine Beacon Academy teachers rank-ordered from highest performing to lowest performing; he wasn't dead last, but it was gut wrenching to see his name in the bottom ten percent.

"Mr. Blake, how do you fare?" One of the students in the IT office asked when William entered the room.

"Hale and hearty, hearty and hale," William said. The air was thick with electrical ozone from the servers and desktop computers. Several students and two teachers staffed desktop stations, and monitored the school's IT system. "So, what's the latest?" William asked.

"We've had some luck, I better let Brooke tell you, she found 'em," a student said.

"Where is she?"

"Over there," the student said, pointing to the back of a girl's head.

William walked behind the seventeen-year-old student and glanced over her shoulder. Endless lines of code filled two computer screens.

"Got anything?" William asked.

"Geez, you startled me, Mr. Blake," Brooke said, removing two white ear buds from each ear.

Brooke was the strongest programmer and all-around tech whiz in the school. She was a genius behind the keyboard. As a senior, she was on the cusp of graduating. She didn't know it yet, but at graduation The Movement was going to award her a full scholarship to pay her tuition at MIT. The Movement needed programmers and hackers, and Brooke was a perfect recruit. She was brilliant, and completely devoted to the cause.

"Well," Brooke said. "I've discovered a few things. I still haven't been able to pinpoint the initial attack, but I'm hot on their trail, and let me tell you - they're good. They went the extra mile to cover their tracks. I only found one IP address that I was able to trace to a network in Langley, Virginia."

"NSA?" William asked.

"You might think so, but I wouldn't bet the farm on it. It makes sense that a Langley IP address would pop up if it was the NSA, but those guys would never be so sloppy. I suspect the IP address was placed there as a decoy by the real hackers. The real hackers are probably hoping we'll stop our countermeasures there; you know, chalk it up to the work of the NSA or CIA, and give up. Everyone in the hacker community knows that unless you've got the Red Army behind you, you don't go after those outfits. I'm not buying it; I don't think this was the government or military," Brooke said.

"Then what's the good news?"

"Two things: One, I figured out how they got in. They used a tricky little Trojan horse hidden inside the SAT student files. I copied some of the code; I might use it myself someday – it's an elegant piece of programming. I wrote a script with some countermeasures, so the good news is there's no way they're hacking in again without getting caught red-handed. Second, we had two follow-up hacks; I stopped both of them butt cold. The first was a half-assed probe of our system by some college kids. I traced 'em back the source; you'll love this - Young Democrat Club at a liberal arts college in Maine called Bates. They won't be trying that again anytime soon; I fried their network with my counterattack."

"Young Democrat Club? What the hell..."

"I poked around their network before I fried it. They're just stupid college kids looking for political bogeymen. They had some data on their servers that referenced The Movement and Edward Birch. I guess even the dimwitted liberals on college campuses are starting to make some connections. But, honestly, nothing that interesting; the real interesting stuff came when I counterattacked the second hacker."

"Who'd you catch?"

"The hack came from Manhattan - 30 Rock."

"NBC?" William asked.

"Very good, Mr. Blake. Nice to know you're tuned into pop culture. The NBC hackers were good, but not good enough. I left a trapdoor open in the network, and they stepped right into it. I traced them back to their source servers and snuck in under their noses. I spent a little while snooping around. It turns out they're investigative journalists from the show Dateline. I hacked my way into their files and looked at some of the script they've created. I even managed to snag copies of a few rough cuts. They're doing a story on The Movement. The bastards are trying to discredit everything we stand for, and they're profiling Beacon Academy as an example of what we're up to."

"Show me," William said.

Brooke opened a new window and clicked on a JPEG file. The file opened in Quicktime Player. "This first one is the intro. Here, use these," Brooke said, handing William her ear buds.

William placed the ear buds in each ear and stared at the screen. The scene opened with stock footage of a helicopter flyover of Washington, DC landmarks. A voice-over track played a teaser promo for the Dateline piece.

"Tonight, Dateline investigates the rise of the New Libertarian Movement. For the past decade, a group of radicals who call themselves The Movement has been organizing in the shadows of the American political sphere. At first, The Movement was regarded as a spinoff of the Tea Party, another full-throated conservative backlash against the populist and progressive inroads forged during the Obama administration. But even traditional Republicans and conservatives are backing off from affiliation with this movement - the roots of which can be traced back to the radical ideology of twentieth century libertarians and card-carrying members of the John Birch Society. Unlike their predecessors, these new libertarians have not relegated themselves to the fringes of American political discourse. Over the past decade, The Movement has created a series of alternative structures and institutions - organizations that embody the radical notions of all-encompassing independence and absolute freedom. Many of these structures are showing early signs of success, which is spawning legions of passionate followers; followers whose ultimate aim is to rewrite the terms of America's social contract. Tonight, Dateline profiles The Movement." The footage ended with an image of Capitol Hill shrouded in a bleak, ominous fog.

"Wow," William said.

"That's something, isn't it?" Brooke said.

"This is excellent work, Brooke. You said you snagged this off the NBC Dateline server?"

"Yup. There's more, take a look," Brook said, clicking a second file.

The scene opened with a Dateline reporter on a 30 Rock soundstage speaking directly into the camera. Over his right shoulder was a black graphic with the words Libertarianism 2.0 written in dark red, block lettering. The edges of the words dripped slightly as though bleeding off the screen. The reporter spoke with a deep, grave inflection in his voice. "Extremists have never been far from American political ideology. Perhaps a byproduct of a nation that embraces freedom of speech and association, the American experience has produced wave after wave of radicals; each generation seeming to spawn its own cohort of fringe thinkers and anarchists. The newest generation of American radicals traces its roots to the libertarian epistemology of Ayn Rand and the Austrian School of Economic Thought. These new libertarians aim for complete redistribution of power from any form of organized government, to the individual. Tonight, Dateline investigates the rise and growing influence of a group that refers to itself as 'The Movement.'"

"Unbelievable. Liberal hacks," William hissed.

"Those were the only video clips on the server. But I also found this," Brooke said, double-clicking a Word document.

"You got the script. Outstanding, Brooke. Did you read it?"

"Yes. They're profiling a whole bunch of new institutions - various political action committees, a think tank at some place called Rosewood, and they're coming after Beacon Academy. They're making it look like we're some kind of cult."

"Can you save this on a thumb drive for me?"

"Sure." Brooke snapped an external drive into the desktop and loaded the files. She pulled the external drive from the desktop and handed it to William. "If you want, I can hack my way back into the Dateline server; I left a breadcrumb trail to follow. Once I'm back in, I'll zap everything they have stored and fry the server with some malware. They probably have copies backed up somewhere, but at least I can put a scare into them."

"Not right now. Let me share this with some people and see what they want us to do. Do you have any idea when NBC plans to air this segment?"

"I think so. There was a program lineup and taping schedule in one of the documents I stole. I loaded it on your thumb drive. It looks like their production schedule runs about six weeks in advance of airdates. Dateline airs Sunday nights; so, sometime this summer would be my best guess, late August, maybe."

"Truly outstanding work, Brooke. I'm going to make sure Jason hears about this. At minimum, you can expect to be eating in the Beacon Café for the rest of the month."

"Thank you, Mr. Blake."

"You're welcome. Please keep this quiet for now; I don't want to start an uproar. And keep looking for the original hackers."

"Mr. Blake, can I ask you something?"

"Sure."

"That episode, why? Why are they coming after us?"

"Come on, Brooke, you took my class last year. This is another example of the liberal, mainstream media doing the bidding of the progressive power base."

"I know. I understand that part of the why; I guess what I'm really asking is why now? Why are they coming after us now?"

"I don't know. Something has them spooked."

JASON dialed the number on the speakerphone, and sat back in his chair sipping coffee.

"You sent her all the stuff, right?" Jason asked.

"Yup. I sent her everything last night. I included a full report. She should be briefed on everything by now," William said.

"Hello," Jeanette said over the speakerphone.

"Good morning, Jeanette," Jason said.

"Good morning," William said. "How do you fare?"

"Hale and hearty, hearty and hale. It's nice to hear your voices again so soon," Jeanette said.

"It's nice to speak with you, too," William said.

"I have someone on the line with us. Sage, are you there?" Jeanette asked.

"Yes, I'm here," a man's voice answered.

"Great, that's everyone. Sage is an attorney who works for The Movement. I shared the information that you provided us. He asked to sit in on this call."

"Good afternoon, gentlemen," Sage said.

"Hello," Jason said.

"Hello, Mr. Sage," William said.

"It's just Sage, please," the man said. "I'm very impressed with your work, gentlemen. Jeanette tells me that this information was found by one of your students."

"Yes," Jason said. "Her name is Brooke Rohr. She was working with William and a team of faculty and students investigating the data breach and upgrading our network security profile. Brooke caught the Dateline investigators red handed. She hacked her way into the NBC servers and found the video clips and script that we sent you."

"Very impressive. Please extend our appreciation to this young lady. I understand she's receiving one of the scholarships The Movement awards this spring," Sage said.

"Yes. She's been accepted to MIT. She's going to study computer forensics. She's a very talented young woman," Jason said.

"Excellent. The Movement needs more individuals like her. Do you believe she's committed to the cause?" Sage asked.

"Completely," William said. "I had her in class last year when she was a junior. I have no doubt that she has learned to embrace our principles. She is a freethinker who has complete faith in natural rights and freedom. Frankly, by the time all of our students finish their studies with us, they are equipped with the habits of mind and skills to live self-sufficient lives."

"That's exactly what we had in mind when Beacon Academy was conceptualized," Sage said. "It proves the power of our principles. You're creating a generation of right-minded Americans, and also providing us a wealth of talent to develop as we gather steam."

"It sounds like we might be victims of our own success. At least if Dateline has anything to say about it," Jason said.

"Yes. That's exactly what's happening. Edward Birch is about to take The Movement mainstream. The liberal establishment is aware of what we've been building, and is aware of the groundswell of support that we're cultivating. They're going to come after us with everything they've got. They'll want to control the narrative by painting us as radicals and extremists. The Dateline episode Brooke found is just the tip of the iceberg," Sage said.

"Is there anything we can do to help? Brooke said she can hack her way back into the Dateline server and wipe out the files," William said.

"No, not yet. The time will come, but not now - just be patient," Sage said.

"Have you made any progress determining the source of the original hack?" Jeanette asked.

"No," William said. "We're still working on it."

"Okay, keep us posted," Jeanette said.

"Edward is looking forward to your graduation," Sage said.

"We're all very excited," William said.

"As you plan his schedule, make sure you work in a few minutes for him to meet with you privately," Sage said.

"With who, me?" William asked.

"Yes," Sage said. "He'd like to thank you personally for your contributions to The Movement, and talk about your future."

"It would be an honor," William said.

"Very good. Oh, by the bye," Sage said. "You might want to watch Fox News tonight. Edward is being interviewed on the Hannity Show. The interview might help answer some of your questions about why The Movement is about to come under attack from the left."

ON his way home that night, William texted Mary - *Wanna come over for dinner?* Mary replied - *Yes.* William ordered a pizza from Sally's on Wooster Street. He picked up the pizza, and drove to his home on Orange Street.

William purchased a monstrous, three-family house in the upscale Orange Street section of New Haven. He rented the second and third floor apartments, and kept the spacious, first-floor apartment for himself. The steady stream of bonuses and rental income helped him furnish the apartment with top-of-the-line appliances, furniture, and an enormous home entertainment system, complete with a sixty-inch flat screen television and Bose sound system.

Mary was reading a book in the living room when William arrived. William gave Mary a spare key after she signed her contract with the Branford Public Schools. It wasn't a ring, but it was a strong enough show of commitment to satisfy her appetite, at least in the short-term.

"Hey," Mary said, looking up from her book.

"What's up?" William asked, walking over and giving Mary a quick kiss on the cheek.

"Same old, same old," Mary said. "How about you? Anything new and exciting?"

"Maybe," William said.

They ate pizza and talked casually. William enjoyed a glass of red wine; Mary drank iced tea. At Nine O'clock, William turned on the Hannity Show on Fox News, and waited anxiously for the interview with Edward Birch.

"Good evening, welcome to another edition of Hannity," Sean Hannity said into the camera. "Tonight, I have an exclusive interview with former US Navy pilot and businessman, Edward Birch. Over much of the past decade, Edward Birch has been building a movement based on true American values of self-reliance and liberty. Some call him a radical; others see him as a patriot, an advocate for twenty-first century individual responsibility and independence. The Hannity Show was given the opportunity to profile this reclusive American patriot. With no strings attached, no holds barred, I was offered full and exclusive access into the mind of a truly great thinker and conservative activist. Here, tonight, a fair and balanced look at Edward Birch and The Movement."

The camera cut away from Sean Hannity. B-roll footage captured a panoramic shot of Rosewood. Hannity's voice described the scene. "Here at the Rosewood Plantation in Northern Virginia, some say the second great American Revolution is underway."

"You've been there, right?" Mary asked.

"Yes. Shhhh. I want to hear this," William said.

"Geez. Well excuse me," Mary said with a huff, crossing her arms and sitting back on the couch.

"Edward Birch was raised in Virginia tobacco country. As a boy growing up in the 1980s and 90s, he watched the federal government demonize the industry that his family spent generations developing. By the close of the twentieth century, his family estate and business were on the brink of bankruptcy. After graduating from Annapolis, and serving his nation proudly as a fighter pilot in Operation Enduring Freedom in Iraq and Afghanistan, Edward Birch returned to his family estate here at Rosewood, and guided the family business through the Obama recession. With frugal investment and a spirit of self-reliance, he amassed a business enterprise now valued in the hundreds of millions of dollars," Hannity said.

The camera cut to a live, over-the-shoulder shot of Edward Birch. "Mr. Birch, thank you for speaking with me tonight," Hannity said.

"The pleasure is all mine, Sean," Edward Birch said.

"That's him?" Mary asked.

"Yup," William said.

"He's handsome," Mary gushed.

William turned and looked at Mary.

"Just saying," Mary said, lowering her eyes.

"It's all right," William said, pouring himself another glass of wine. "He is handsome."

"You have a beautiful home here," Sean said.

"Most beautiful place in the world," Edward said. "I've learned the greatest lessons of my life right here at Rosewood."

"So, you're a former lieutenant colonel in the United States Navy, and a decorated fighter pilot. You served in Operation Enduring Freedom," Hannity said.

"That's right. I flew F-14 Tomcats."

"Thank you for your service. As a veteran, you must have strong opinions about America's role in the world," Hannity said.

"I do," Edward said.

"So, what do you make of the left's attempts, even after Iraqis have now enjoyed nearly a decade of freedom as a result of our sacrifice, to continue to slander the successes of the Bush administration, an administration you proudly served?"

"I consider America's role in Iraq and Afghanistan to be one of the biggest blunders in our nation's history," Edward said. "As for anyone's attempt to write or rewrite the narrative of that conflict, I have no meaningful comment to offer. Historians and members of the media are free to say and think what they want."

Sean Hannity shifted uncomfortably in his chair. "That surprises me," Sean said. "I would expect a decorated veteran such as yourself to take the longer view on the value of that war."

"Value of war, huh. I wonder if that's an oxymoron," Edward said, staring Hannity directly in the eye, daring him to continue.

Sean Hannity changed subjects. "So, in addition to your military service and success as a businessman, tell us, who is Edward Birch?" Sean asked.

"The son of a tobacco farmer. An American who has grown up to see this nation, and the great state of Virginia, become something I don't even recognize anymore; something our founders' warned us against. I'd like to think of myself as a catalyst for change," Edward said.

"I've read both of your bestselling books. They're nothing short of brilliant. Your ideas have become the blueprint for something your supporters call The Movement. What is The Movement?" Sean asked.

"The Movement is made up of individuals who ascribe to a simple principle; the belief that the individual is the source from which the greatness of a nation rises - not the collective."

"Your critics say that your libertarian ideas have no place in twenty-first century America. You've been called quaint, and out-of-touch - lost in the nostalgia for an age that has come and gone. Your critics argue that without strong central government, something as complicated as American would crumble and fall. What do you say to those who criticize your principles?" Hannity asked.

"I have no lack of critics, Sean. I've been attacked from all sides, every political stripe – Right, Left, Center, Democrat, Republican, Conservative, Progressive, you name it; everyone with an agenda has taken their shots at The Movement. My principles are grounded in something that can only be fairly called the anti-agenda. The Movement believes that the best government is not the government that governs most, or least; the best government is a government that allows individuals to govern themselves."

"It doesn't sound like much of a platform," Hannity said.

"It's not about a platform. For the past decade, we haven't limited ourselves to thinking and writing about our ideas. The Movement has been creating the structures and organizations that embody our values. We have built an elaborate system of examples of how this philosophy works in contemporary America. In every instance, these examples are flourishing beyond every measure," Edward said.

"Can you give us an example?"

"I will do more than that, Sean. I came on your show tonight to make an announcement. Tonight, I'm announcing my candidacy for Governor of the great state of Virginia," Edward said. He put his hand up with dramatic effect to silence Sean Hannity before he could ask any follow-up questions. "I will not be campaigning; at least not in the traditional sense. Over the next six months, I am going on tour."

"Tour? What kind of a tour?" Hannity asked.

"I'm inviting you and every mainstream and alternative media outlet out there to join me on this tour. My aim is to bring along the entire nation. I will be visiting all the institutions that The Movement has created. We're going to throw back the curtains, and let America take a good look at what we've created. Leave no stone unturned, Sean; we want you and your colleagues in the national media to see it all. Next November, I will ask the people of Virginia to register their opinion. Vote for me, and I will work tirelessly day and night to implement this vision for all Virginians. Vote against me, and you will be voting to continue a system of reliance on the state; you will vote to continue to abdicate your freedom to a system of bureaucracy that has grown unchecked for far too long. I don't want Virginians simply voting for me; I want Virginians voting for a principled belief - a new direction for the entire state."

"So, what's the first stop on this tour of yours?"

"New Haven, Connecticut. I want you to come to a school called Beacon Academy. Meet a group of students and faculty who have been freed from the tyranny of traditional public education. Come see what they've accomplished; then ask yourself, is this what public education in America could become?" Edward said.

"Holy shit," William said, draining his glass of red wine in a single gulp.

*   *   *

June, 2021

IN the weeks leading up to graduation, members of the national press overran Beacon Academy. The Movement lifted all restrictions; faculty and students were encouraged to discuss every aspect of the school's program and curriculum. By graduation day, the Long Wharf Beacon Academy, and branch Beacon Academies across the country, had been lead stories in every major print, online, and broadcast media outlet.

The right-wing media heralded the quasi-private nature of the schools, trumpeting the savings to taxpayers, school choice, and accountability foisted on teachers and students. The left-wing media attacked the schools, slamming them as union-busting institutions attempting to brainwash students with conservative ideology. Good Morning America featured the firing ranges and martial arts program. The NBC hosts made no effort to hide their contempt when the cameras captured images of Beacon Academy students and teachers firing AR-15's and 9 mm Glocks, and practicing Krav Maga techniques designed to disarm knife-wielding foes. One particularly histrionic liberal hostess on The View screamed into the camera, and demanded to know why Beacon Academy was allowed to violate the Gun Free Schools Act.

None of the liberal media outlets could deny the success of Beacon Academy students. The earliest graduates were in their twenties, and already leaders in their fields. Most striking was the fact that not a single Beacon Academy graduate had taken a job with any local, state, or federal government agency. All the graduates were achieving on their own two feet in the private sector, divorcing themselves entirely from government bureaucracies.

The image of Beacon Academy graduates contrasted with the image of graduates from traditional public schools. The right-wing media successfully depicted a majority of traditional public school graduates as individuals floundering through university studies or employment, wholly unprepared for the demands of college and career. The stereotype of the traditional public school graduate was of a twenty-something-year-old living in his or her parents' basement. Right-wing pundits successfully etched this slacker-image into the conscience of America, and contrasted it with the stereotype of Beacon Academy graduates, depicted as rugged individuals confidently charting their own path through life. By graduation day, The Movement had been able to control the narrative. The liberal media couldn't put a dent in the Beacon Academy reputation.

Edward Birch's entourage arrived at the back entrance to avoid the media circus amassed in front of the school. An electric current ran through William when three black, Cadillac Escalades pulled up to the curb.

"This is surreal," Tabitha said. "I can't believe he's really here."

Tabitha wore a distant, star-struck expression. Her eyes were glazed and mouth slightly agape, like a groupie staring up from the front row at some boy band rock concert. Tabitha wore high heels, a scandalously short, black skirt, and a white blouse. The top two buttons of the blouse were unbuttoned. A black choke collar necklace with a silver amulet completed the look. On most women, the outfit would be over-the-top slutty; on Tabitha, it was a strange mix of professional and seductive. William's heart beat in his throat; not even the excitement of meeting Edward Birch could mute his desire for Tabitha.

A security detail exited the front and rear SUVs. Four men in business suits surveyed the scene, and set up a perimeter around the middle SUV. A fifth man opened the back door of the middle SUV. A middle-aged woman carrying an iPad and talking on a cell phone stepped out. Edward Birch stepped out behind her. The men in business suits flanked Edward as he sauntered casually up to the welcoming party.

Jason stepped forward and extended his hand. "Good morning, Mr. Birch. We can't tell you how excited we are to have you here," Jason said.

"Thank you for hosting me. It is a real pleasure to meet you folks. I've been following your progress here, it's all very impressive," Edward said.

Jason introduced William.

"Very nice to meet you. I'm Edward Birch."

"Hello, sir, it's very nice to meet you, too."

"Sir, no, no, that won't do. I'm Edward, please; I should be calling you sir; your work here has been nothing short of miraculous."

Edward held William in his piercing blue eyes. The pull of Edward's charisma was unshakeable. In the brief exchange, William felt like he was the most important person in Edward Birch's life. Edward clasped William's shoulder and moved on to Tabitha.

"I'm a huge fan," Tabitha said, extending her hand stiffly.

"I'm not looking for fans, dear, just proponents," Edward said, taking Tabitha's hand.

Tabitha stumbled forward. Edward reached out with his left hand, grabbed Tabitha's shoulder, and steadied her. "Easy dear, are you okay?" Edward asked.

"Thank you. I'm fine."

"Have we met before?" Edward asked.

"Never in person. I've watched you speak several times."

"Well, then it's a pleasure to make your acquaintance."

The middle-aged woman stepped forward and spoke with brisk efficiency to Edward.

"We have to get moving," the woman said. "Several reporters are joining us for the tour. You have a sit-down interview with CBS in thirty minutes."

"Very good," Edward said to the woman. "I hope you folks will join me for the day, so long as I'm not imposing," Edward said to William, Tabitha, and Jason.

"Yes, of course," Tabitha said.

Tabitha stepped forward, laced her arm through the crook of Edward's arm, and led him towards the school. William trailed after Tabitha and Edward with the security detail and woman with the iPad. Half-dozen reporters with notepads and a camera crew met the entourage and followed along. Edward listened as Tabitha offered a history of the school during a tour of the facility. They paused at the entrance to the Beacon Café.

"This is the Beacon Café," Tabitha said. "I hope you'll have an opportunity to eat here, you won't be disappointed."

The woman with the iPad interjected, "This is where we're setting up for the CBS interview this morning?"

"Oh, perfect. Maybe you can have a snack after the interview. Everything here is made from scratch. It's gourmet quality. We haven't invited Zagat's in, but I'm sure we'd merit a five star rating," Tabitha said.

"I'm sure it would. As far as I can tell, everything here is five-star quality. Do faculty and students eat here every day?" Edward asked.

"Not exactly. We'll be passing the main cafeteria in a minute. That's where most of the students and teachers eat on a day-to-day basis. Students and faculty also prepare everything we serve there. You won't find a finer dining facility in any public school. The Beacon Café is reserved for students and faculty who excel. At the end of each month, performance reviews are given to each member of the faculty and student body. Individuals who rate the highest each month are placed on the VIP list for the Beacon Café," Jason said.

"Ah, yes, I've heard about this. Other Beacon Academies are doing the same thing. Tell me, what do you base your monthly performance reviews on?" Edward asked.

"A mixture of performance and effort. We use monthly benchmark assessment data to evaluate both the students and teachers. That's the main part of the rating. Students and teachers are also assigned various responsibilities in the building. William, for example, is assigned responsibility for facilities and school security." Jason said, turning to face William. "Each month, we assess the upkeep of the facilities and review any lapses in security."

"So, William, how'd you do this month? Did you make the VIP list?" Edward asked.

"No," William said. "It's a long story."

"I'm sorry to hear that," Edward said. "How about you, Tabitha; what are your added responsibilities?"

"Communications. I'm in charge of all PR for the school," Tabitha said.

"Well, if you're the face of Beacon Academy, somebody made a very wise decision."

Tabitha's face erupted in a crimson blush. "Thank you, that's sweet," she said.

A pang of jealously rippled through William.

After a tour of the Dojo and firing range, the woman with the iPad told Edward it was time to get ready for the CBS interview. The entourage walked to the Beacon Café.

Tabitha and William stood off to one side of the café and watched a woman on the CBS production staff cover Edward's face with make-up. Production assistants hustled around the room, adjusting lights, chairs, and the cameras on the makeshift set. The CBS reporter arrived on location. The production crew scurried around the set, applying make-up and reviewing last minute logistics.

"I recognize that guy, who is he?" Tabitha asked William quietly, pointing towards the reporter.

"Scott Pelley," William said. "He's the CBS Nightly News anchor."

"Quiet on set," a man wearing a photographer's vest hollered.

The restaurant lights dimmed. Four enormous set lights on tripods washed the room in bright light. A sound technician lowered a boom microphone over Edward and Scott's head.

"In three... two... one... action," the man in the photographer's vest hollered.

Scott Pelley opened the interview with a brief introduction. "I'm here with Edward Birch, candidate for Governor of the State of Virginia. Edward is the mastermind behind a growing conservative movement in America, known to supporters as The Movement. He is on a tour of America, visiting organizations and institutions started by The Movement. Mr. Birch believes these institutions epitomize his particular brand of libertarian conservative principles. Mr. Birch, good afternoon."

"Good afternoon, Scott," Edward said.

"We're visiting with you today at Beacon Academy in New Haven, Connecticut. Beacon Academy is a public school founded on the conservative libertarian principles of the movement you started," Scott said. "So, tell us, Mr. Birch, what makes this school so special?"

"I'm here to deliver the commencement address to two hundred and fifty remarkable young men and women. Beacon Academy is a charter school that educates public school students from districts throughout the region. Local school districts pay tuition for their students to come here. Tuition is determined based on how well students perform on standardized tests. The school is unique because all burdensome laws, regulations, and public policy governing traditional public schools have been eliminated; so long as students perform at the highest levels, the teachers here are free to focus on delivering educational services in any way they see fit - they are free from the abuse of state and federal legislation and regulation," Edward said.

"Teachers are paid according to student performance, is this correct?" Scott asked.

"That's correct. Unlike traditional public schools, teachers at Beacon Academy operate as a faculty, but are considered independent contractors. They negotiate individual contracts. These contracts reward them for student performance on measures like standardized tests, and other achievements and contributions to the school."

"This approach has irritated many teachers' unions, who claim that the approach pits teacher against teacher, and undermines the traditional student-teacher relationship by forcing teachers to view students as commodities to be tapped, rather than individuals to be developed. How do you respond to this criticism?"

"Teacher-against-teacher, huh, I haven't heard that one before. I imagine teachers here rely on one another; student performance and school success is a team effort. I encourage you to ask Beacon Academy teachers; we've opened the school up to the public, come on in and see for yourself. As for the student-teacher relationships, well, let's face the reality; traditional public schools are failing miserably, they have been for decades now. We flush billions of dollars into the sewer of public education every year. America's students dramatically underperform compared to students around the world. If this is a result of the student-teacher relationships the unions are trumpeting, well, then I argue it's time for us to ask some tough questions - our nation can't afford to waist the potential of America's youth - our kids deserve better."

"Your campaign is unique. You're running for a state office, but you're mounting a national campaign."

"That's right. The Movement is not limited to Virginia. We're reaching into communities across America."

"Do you have long-term plans to run for national office? Perhaps even President of the United State?"

"One step at a time. I want Virginia's voters to see what we have built, and examine how our philosophy matches our practice. If Virginians vote for me, we will replicate our values by creating a state system of government modelled on our values. In four years, Americans will have the opportunity to examine what we create in Virginia, and decide if this is what they want our national government to look like," Edward said.

"It's a unique approach," Scott said.

"I think so, too. Unlike most politicians, I will not be out there talking theoretically about what might be. Over the summer and fall, I will be travelling across America showing what The Movement has created in education, business, and every sector of our economic and civic life. I will explain how The Movement's practices can be replicated by getting government out of our lives, and allowing liberty to thrive."

"Edward Birch," Scott said. "Thank you very much for speaking with me. Best of luck with your campaign, we will be following you closely."

"Thank you, Scott. The pleasure has been all mine."

The set lights went out, and the flat, fluorescent light in the Beacon Café washed the room.

"Thank God he's on our side," William whispered to Tabitha.

THE graduation ceremony was rich with pomp and circumstance. A line of graduates snaked its way out of the school and across a long, lush field. Parents and well-wishers cheered the graduates. The sound of whistles, cowbells, and air horns filled the air. After the pledge of allegiance, national anthem, and a prayer, the graduates were asked to sit down. Jason greeted the graduates, offered some welcoming remarks, and then introduced Edward Birch. The crowd erupted with applause as Edward stepped to the podium clad in a black academic gown, a colorful hood, and a mortarboard.

"Good afternoon, graduates of the Class of 2021, how do you fare?" Edward asked the students.

"Hale and hearty, hearty and hale," the Class of 2021 boomed in unison.

"Hale and hearty indeed. I would rather be here delivering this commencement address to you Beacon Academy graduates than any other public, private, or parochial school graduating class. Beacon Academy students, you have earned the right to be called the Class of 2021. The values you have learned here at Beacon Academy have equipped you with everything you need as you head out into the world.'

'Let's take the lessons you have learned here at Beacon Academy, and compare them to those of your counterparts in traditional public schools across this state and nation. You have learned that simply showing up is not enough; you have learned that hard work alone is not enough; you have learned that not everyone gets a trophy, or earns a diploma; you have learned that performance and outcomes are all that truly matters. Life will not grade you based on effort. Life will reward your successes, and punish your failure - no matter how hard you try. You have learned this because you have learned from a faculty that is rewarded based on your success. Your failure was their failure. Over the past four years, those teachers who failed you are no longer here; only the strong have survived in the classroom. Now, let's compare these lessons with those lessons learned by students graduating from traditional public schools. They have learned that simply showing up is the better part of success. They have learned that effort alone will earn them a B-plus, and that half-an-effort will earn a B-minus. They have learned that fair does not mean the same, and therefore, everyone is entitled to differentiation based on perceived ability and disability. They have learned that failure simply means a second chance. They believe their diplomas are something they were entitled to, not something they were expected to earn. They have learned these lessons because their teachers did not truly care if students succeed; their students' failure had no negative impact on them. In such a system, mediocrity is considered excellence, and failure is explained away by apathy, demographics, poor parenting, and strokes of a pen across documents that ascribe special education disabilities and labels that have no place in the real world.'

'So, I ask you, which of these systems epitomize life's natural order? Which of these systems will produce individuals who possess the skills and habits of mind necessary to confront the realities of life? Will the greatness of this nation be maintained by individuals who believe that life owes them a living, or by those who believe that anything they are due will be reaped by talent, ability, and, at times, ruthless cunning?'

'Beacon students, I am counting on you. The trajectory of our nation is on a perilous path. Institutions have sprung up around you that will try to convince you that the expansive social contract offered by government can protect us from the realities of life. Too many Americans believe that the laws of men can insulate us from the laws of nature. Too many Americans are willing to turn over their liberty to the rule of tyrants, tyrants who supplicate us with the promise of cradle to grave care in exchange for indentured servitude. Too many Americans are willing to forego the blessing of liberty that is the birthright of this nation, and, instead, scurry around for the crumbs cast forth by a crumbling welfare state. Where will this inevitably lead us? Like lambs to the slaughter, this thinking will lead us to economic and social slavery, slavery not found in leg irons and chains, slavery found in the cycle of debt, deficit, and dependence that is the core of big government.'

'You Beacon students know better. You know the value of hard work. You understand the importance of self-reliance. When you leave here today, you will quickly discover something. People will be drawn to you in droves. Your strength and rugged individualism are powerful forces. Like steel to a magnet, the force of your character, your ability, your instinct, and your willingness to put trust in nothing but your own skill and ability, these traits will pull at the heart and inspire the minds of those who have been conditioned to place their faith in the progressive state. Let them come, Beacon students, let them come. Inspire them with the power of your sense of self. Lead them, and in the process, show them that faith in God, faith in family, and faith in self is the only true source of strength. Do not abide the false prophets who offer salvation in the laws of men. I call on you to lead, Beacon students; I call on you to lead us out of the wilderness."

The roar of the crowd echoed over the Long Wharf neighborhood, as though a legion of Spartans was preparing to lay siege to the city.

AFTER the graduates received their diplomas, a security detail escorted Edward back to the school. Several dozen dignitaries sipped champagne and talked politics with Edward at a VIP reception in the Beacon Cafe. Tabitha remained glued to Edward's side, mooning over him, and hanging on his every word. The woman with the iPad offered William a flute of champagne.

"Thank you," William said, taking the flute and downing the champagne in a quick gulp.

"He really is impressed with your work here," the woman said, nodding in the direction of Edward. "The Movement is grateful for everything you've accomplished."

"It has been a pleasure," William said.

"Edward would like a private meeting with you before he leaves."

"Really? With me? William asked.

"Yes."

"What does he want?"

"I'll let him tell you in person. Just hang around; I'll let you know when he's ready to speak with you."

William downed a few more flutes of champagne. Edward whispered something into Tabitha's ear. Tabitha nodded and followed Edward out of the café. William waited a moment, and then quietly slipped out of the café behind them. Tabitha took Edward by the hand and led him down a hallway towards her classroom. William tried to follow, but one of the men on the security detail stepped in front of him and put a hand in the center of his chest.

"Can't go down there," the man said.

William looked down at the man's hand. He considered grabbing the man's wrist and ripping his arm from its socket. He paused when he saw two more men from the security detail eye him suspiciously. "Where are they going?" William asked.

A smile curled at the corners of the man's lips. "Your guess is as good as mine."

William returned to the VIP reception. He gulped flute after flute of champagne. He wished for something stronger, but was grateful for the slow buzz that dulled his mind. William stepped back into the hall. Two men from the security detail stood at the entrance to the hallway leading to Tabitha's classroom. What the security detail didn't know was that there was another way to access the corridor. William swallowed two more flutes of champagne and made his way downstairs to the Dojo.

Alcohol surged through William, fueling a jealous anger that burned a white-hot pit in his chest. "Fucking slut," William hissed to the empty Dojo.

The armory was locked. Marc had the only key to access the guns, but William knew the combination to a stash of martial arts weapons locked in a faculty locker. He twisted the combination and opened the locker. He chose a small, six-inch scroll dagger from the gleaming array of weapons. William had been practicing with the scroll dagger for the past semester, honing his skills. He placed the sheath against the small of his back, held tightly by his belt. William walked to the center of the Dojo and began rehearsing the motions necessary to retrieve the dagger and slice a track neck-high through the air in front of him. The alcohol slowed his actions, but he still impressed himself with his speed and accuracy.

William quietly ascended the staircase, and slowly pressed the crash bar on the door at the top of the steps. He cracked the door open a few inches and peered down the corridor. Men from the security detail were visible at one end of the hallway. The other end of the corridor was empty. William pressed the door open just wide enough to slide through, and closed the door behind him. He walked on the sides of his feet across the hall, and pressed himself against the wall outside of Tabitha's classroom. He waited, keeping a close eye on the men at the end of the hallway.

"I'm gonna take a leak," one of the men said. "You got this?"

"Yeah, go ahead. I'm sure he'll finish with her soon enough," the other man said.

"I don't know. That one was pretty fuckin' hot. He might take his time with her."

The men laughed. One of the bodyguards walked away. The other guard leaned against the wall and began playing a game on his iPhone.

William stepped in front of the door and stared into the classroom through a long, narrow, rectangular window. Edward was leaning back against the teacher's desk, the palms of hands planted firmly on the desk, his head raised toward the ceiling. His pants were on the floor, bundled around his ankles. Tabitha was on her knees, her head bobbing up and down. Edward reached down with his right hand and grabbed a handful of Tabitha's hair. He steadied himself with his left hand planted on the desk, and stared at the top of Tabitha's head. His hips pounded violently, and then settled into a few rhythmic thrusts.

Tabitha's head stopped bobbing. She leaned back and wiped her lips with the back of her hand. She looked up and made eye contact with William. Red lipstick smeared across her chin, and her hair was a frenzied mess. Her blouse was open and bra unsnapped. William held Tabitha's gaze for a long second.

"William's outside," Tabitha said to Edward.

"Oh, good, I wanted to have a word with him. William, come on in," Edward said as he pulled his pants up over his hips and began tucking in his shirt.

William opened the door and stepped into the classroom. Edward reached out his hand to help Tabitha up. Tabitha accepted Edward's hand, and pulled herself up off her knees. She pulled the bra around her breasts, snapped the front clasp, and began buttoning the blouse.

"Well, aren't you quite the voyeur," Tabitha said.

"Now, now, Tabitha, it's all right. We're all adults here," Edward said. "Why don't you go to the bathroom and get yourself cleaned up. I have some things to talk to William about."

William stepped forward until he was six feet from Edward. His eyes never left Tabitha. The image of her on her knees seared into William's mind. He shook his head, trying desperately to displace the image of her bobbing head, and the euphoric expression on Edward's face. He reached his hand around the small of his back and gently caressed the handle of the scroll dagger. He turned his head and stared at Edward, estimating the distance between them. In two, quick, coordinated movements, he could draw the dagger and slice Edward's throat. Tabitha would undoubtedly try to stop him. If she knew the attack was coming, she could slow him down or possibly disarm him completely. Tabitha had sparred with William in the Dojo several times over the past semester; using Krav Maga under the close tutelage of Marc to practice repelling a knife-wielding assailant. But with surprise on his side, there was no chance for her to reach him before the blade sliced a course through Edward's jugular.

William's hand tightened around the handle of the dagger. In the moment before he unleashed the dagger from its sheath, Edward's eyes pierced William. William froze under the weight of Edward's glare. Invisible tentacles reached into his mind, leaving him physically paralyzed. In that brief, terrifying moment, William wondered if he was having a stroke. An electric current raced through his body, burning every nerve ending, and searing every muscle with a million pinpricks. William heard Edward's voice somewhere deep inside his mind - *Now, now, William, you don't want to do that. Let's save all that rage for a time when we really need it.*

Edward stepped forward and put his hands on William's shoulder. "Tabitha, dear. On your way back from the bathroom, please ask one of my men to bring me a bottle of water. Would you like anything, William?" Edward asked.

William couldn't find his voice or move his body. He was locked in Edward's hypnotic glare.

"Okay, then," Edward said. "Just the water. Run along, dear."

Tabitha obediently left the classroom. Edward reached around William's waist and pulled the scroll dagger from his belt. He held the dagger up to William's face. The tip of the blade hovered mere millimeters from William's right eye.

"She has quite a hold over you, huh?" Edward asked, twisting the blade in front of William's eye. "Shakespeare warned us about the Green-Eyed Monster."

Edward turned and walked to the teacher's desk. He dropped the scroll dagger on a pile of papers, and took a seat behind the desk. He leaned back in Tabitha's chair and lifted his feet onto the desk. "Grab a seat," Edward said.

The psychic vice grip released William. William exhaled a long gasp, and nearly collapsed to the floor. "You're okay now," Edward said. "Please sit down."

William fell back into one of the student desks. "What was that?" He asked.

"Just a little parlor trick. Let me ask you, would you really have slashed my throat for her?"

William looked down at the desk and shook his head.

"I didn't think so, but I have to say, I admire the gumption," Edward said. "So, let's just forget that little bit of unpleasantness."

"Thank you," William said.

"Good, good. I have a proposition for you."

"Proposition?"

"Beacon Academy has become a valuable proving ground," Edward said. "In addition to developing a legion of students who are bent on supporting The Movement, Beacon has also given us the opportunity to vet a cadre of teachers - individuals who we're looking to move up the ranks, so to speak. The Executive Committee has been monitoring your progress, William. We've kept tabs on the curriculum you write and the values you teach your students. Your instruction in social studies reflects the purest ideology of The Movement."

"Thank you."

"We also know that you practice what you preach. Your personal life has developed around some of the core conservative principles that we espouse. Your girlfriend, Mary, also has strong values. That's a positive. Who we choose to keep in our lives is an important reflection of our character."

William bristled when Edward mentioned Mary.

"Yes, yes, we know all about your relationship with Mary, and your infatuation with Tabitha. If it weren't for Tabitha, I imagine you would have already taken the next steps with Mary. That poor girl has been waiting a long time for your commitment. That biological clock of hers is ticking," Edward said.

"How do you know so much about me, and why do you care?"

"The Movement carefully vets people who we intend to move up."

"Move up?" William asked.

"Yes, move up. I have an offer for you," Edward said. Edward stood, walked around the teacher's desk, and took a seat in one of the student desks next to William. He reached out and placed a hand on William's shoulder. "I want you to come to Virginia. We're hoping you'll bring along that darling Mary of yours. I'm offering you a full scholarship to the University of Virginia Law School. The application paperwork has been taken care of; you don't have to take the LSAT's or apply. The school's administration is ready to welcome you with open arms. As you study for your law degree, which will take two years or so, I want you to work for The Movement. Then, once you complete the degree and pass the bar, I would like you to assume a senior position and commit yourself full-time to The Movement."

"What kind of work is it?" William asked.

"I expect to win my race for governor. In Virginia, the governor can only serve a single four-year term. I expect that you will finish your law degree in the middle of my term. So, you're going to sharpen your teeth by helping me reform Virginia State Law. You are going to help me create a blueprint in Virginia for a national model. After my term in Virginia, I have eyes on national office. Eventually, I'm taking The Movement to the highest office in the land. I need a team of lawyers with expertise in Constitutional Law to help The Movement shape and implement our vision. I want you on my team."

"You want me?"

"Yes. You and Mary. It's our time, William. It's your time."

William stared at Edward. Edward's strength and confidence was infectious. Even if he wanted to say 'no,' William knew he couldn't; he would follow Edward through the pits of hell. "Yes," William said.

"Excellent. Then you should be running home to tell Mary the good news," Edward said.

THE lump against William's thigh was heavy and warm. He dipped his hand into the side pocket of his cargo shorts and caressed the tiny, felt box. William and Mary parked in the student parking lot, and strolled casually across the Quinnipiac campus. A few students traversed the quad for summer classes, but the campus lacked the normal hubbub of the school year. They made their way to Mary's former dorm, where they found the front door locked with a sign that read - *closed for summer cleaning and repairs.*

"The campus sure has changed," Mary said.

"Yup. It's a lot bigger than when we were here. The law school, polling center, and addition of Division One sports changed everything."

"Too bad it's summer. I was looking forward to seeing the old floor."

"We'll come back for a hike this fall. So, are you ready to head up?"

"Let's do it," Mary said.

They walked back through the quad, across athletic fields, and crossed a street separating the school from Sleeping Giant State Park. William tightened the straps on his backpack as they stepped onto a trail leading up the side of Sleeping Giant.

"Look at that, what a shame," Mary said, pointing at two dilapidated huts covered in graffiti. A restroom sign hung sideways off one of the doors.

"Your tax dollars at work," William said.

"Quinnipiac should really buy this park. Nobody takes care of it."

"That's actually a good idea. But what would all those public employees in the Park's Department do without a park to pretend to take care of."

William and Mary walked slowly along a well-worn trail. The afternoon was cool and overcast; dark thunderheads rolled overhead, and leaves turned upwards, anxiously expecting a deluge. William was grateful for the dour forecast; it kept the onslaught of day hikers and joggers at bay, offering him and Mary a semblance of privacy.

"So, how was the graduation yesterday? Did everything go smoothly?" Mary asked.

"It was great."

"I watched the news coverage. It looked like quite the circus."

"It was intense."

"Did you get to meet Mr. Birch?"

"Yes. He and I had an interesting conversation. That's actually part of why I asked you to go on this hike with me. There are a few things I want to talk to you about."

"That sounds a little ominous."

"Mr. Birch made me an offer yesterday. The Movement wants to give me a full scholarship to attend the University of Virginia Law School."

"Law school? When?"

"Next fall."

"How? You haven't even applied, or taken the LSAT's."

"They have some pull. I don't need to do any of that, I just need to show up and register."

"I don't get it. Why do they want you to go to law school in Virginia?"

"According to Mr. Birch, I've managed to impress The Movement."

"Yeah, so?"

"He wants me to consult for his administration while I get the law degree. Then, assuming I complete the JD, they'll have a job for me in The Movement."

"What kind of consulting?"

"Education reform mostly, at least to start."

"Are you really ready to give up teaching? What about everything you've built at Beacon Academy? Are you going to just walk away?"

"I actually see it a little differently than that. I see this as an opportunity to build on everything we've done to help The Movement grow."

"Why a law degree? I mean, I thought The Movement was all about getting rid of laws, cutting back on government, not growing it. Lawyers are nothing more than the handmaidens of government."

"That's true. But it's going to take lawyers to unravel the glut of laws already on the books. They want me to get the degree, and then use that knowledge, in addition to what I already know about education, to help roll back all of the laws and regulations choking public education. It's my little niche; my contribution to The Movement."

They hiked in silence. A thunderhead crackled in the distance, and a cool wind rustled through the canopy of foliage above them.

"So, are you going to do it?" Mary asked.

"How can I say no?" The first pitter-pat of rain began landing on the leaves. "Come on," William said. "We'd better hurry up and get to the castle."

William grabbed Mary's hand and together they jogged up the trail. They reached the stone castle at the top of Sleeping Giant just as the clouds started to wail huge, cold, tear-shaped drops of rain. They sat on a picnic table in the castle and watched the skies unleash a sheet of rain.

"What about us?" Mary asked, staring into the deluge of water.

"I want you to come with me."

"You expect me to quit my job, pack everything in the trunk of my car, drive to Virginia, find a place to live, look for a new job, and basically start from scratch?"

"No, not exactly. We'll pack everything in the back of my truck and move into a place that we find together."

"Oh, this keeps getting better. Not only do you want me to start a new life, you want me to start a new life while living in sin. Great idea, William."

"You won't be living in sin. You'll be doing this as my wife." William slid off the picnic table, reached into the side pocket of his cargo shorts, and kneeled in front of Mary. "I want you to marry me, Mary. Will you be my wife?" William asked, opening the tiny, felt box.

"Yes," Mary said.

PART III

THE MOVEMENT

May, 2025

WILLIAM watched the numbers on the elevator panel illuminate. The elevator chimed and doors slid open when he reached the top floor of the downtown Richmond high-rise. He pushed his way through a small crowd, exchanging head nods and pleasantries with a few familiar faces. William walked down a hallway lined with doors to the private offices belonging to The Movement elite. He knocked softly and opened the door to the corner office suite.

"Good morning, Barbara," William said, stepping into the reception area.

Sage's administrative assistant looked up from her desk, and held out a finger. William cupped his mouth with the palm of his hand.

"Yes, sir, I understand, sir," Barbara said. "I will make sure Mr. Sage gets the message. Have a nice day." Barbara tapped the side of an earphone and ended the call, and then scribbled a quick note.

"Sorry about that, I couldn't tell you were on the phone," William said.

"Not a problem. How are you today?"

"Great. It's a beautiful spring day in Virginia. What could be better?" William asked.

Fine streaks of premature gray highlighted Barbara's dark, shoulder-length hair. A thick layer of concealer covered dark circles that rimmed the edges of her eye sockets. "How's Mary?" Barbara asked.

"She's doing great. Thanks for asking. You look tired today - is everything okay?" William asked.

"I haven't been sleeping too well these past few nights, that's all."

"What's keeping you up? Sage isn't working you too hard, is he?"

"No, no, it has nothing to do with work," Barbara said, staring down at her desk and rubbing her eyes. "It's my mother. We just moved her in. We're going through a bit of an adjustment."

"Did she move from out of state?"

"No. She has Parkinson's Disease. She was in an assisted living facility, but the disease progressed to the point where she needs round-the-clock care. The nursing home prices triple when you get to that level of care. She was a ward of the state up until a few months ago, so it would have been covered; but, well, you know how the laws are changing."

"Yeah, well, it must be nice to have your mother home with you. There's nothing more important than family," William said.

"I suppose so," Barbara said, looking down. Barbara pressed the earphone. "Mr. Blake is here to see you, sir," Barbara said "Yes, sir, I'll send him right in." Barbara tapped the earphone. "Mr. Sage is waiting for you, you can go right in. Would you like me to bring you a coffee or juice?"

"That would be nice, thank you. Can you make it half-decaf and half-regular?"

"Sure. Do you take cream and sugar?"

"Yes, please."

William walked into Sage's office. The corner office suite covered over eight hundred square feet of the top floor. Floor-to-ceiling windows along the two exterior walls offered a panoramic view of downtown Richmond.

"William my boy, how do you fare?" Sage asked.

"Hale and hearty, hearty and hale."

"Hale and hearty indeed," Sage said, standing up from his desk. "Did you get your results?"

"Not yet. They're going to be released sometime this weekend."

"I'm sure you passed with flying colors."

"I'm not worried about it, just a little anxious."

"Natural, completely natural. Make yourself comfortable," Sage said.

William sat on a leather sofa in the center of the office. There was a soft knock on the door and Barbara entered the office carrying a cup of coffee. Barbara placed the mug on a coffee table in front of William. Coffee sloshed over the side the mug.

"Oops," Barbara said, wiping the sides of the mug.

"Thank you," William said.

"Can I get either of you gentlemen anything else?" Barbara asked.

"No, that will be all. Please leave," Sage said, waving his hand at Barbara.

Barbara walked out of the office.

"She looks tired," William said. "She said something about her mother moving in with her."

"Do you need a secretary?" Sage asked.

"No, why? Are things not working out?"

"Let's just say that some of her work isn't up to par. I'm not sure how much longer I can string her along. I have to use the bathroom," Sage said, putting his hand over his stomach. "This morning's coffee has finally done its job."

"Do what you've got to do."

Sage walked into the office's private bathroom. William stood up from the sofa, walked to the windows, and stared down over Richmond. He walked along the windows, looking down on the hubbub of the city.

When William reached Sage's desk, he paused to look at a line of photographs. Most of the pictures were of Sage with his wife and children. A 16 x 20 inch photograph matted in a silver frame in the center of the desk captured an image from Edward Birch's inauguration ceremony. In the picture, Edward stood with one hand on the Bible while the Chief Justice of the Virginia State Supreme Court administered the oath of office. Next to the picture of the inauguration was a grainy, 1980s-era Polaroid that captured an image of Sage as a younger man. In the waxy image, Sage was bouncing a toddler on his knee. The toddler on Sage's knee stared out of the photograph with a deep, pensive expression, an expression that was equal parts intense and mesmerizing; the same expression Edward Birch wore as an adult.

William picked up the picture and stared at Sage. His real name was Travis Sage, but everyone called him Sage. Sage earned a bachelor degree from Princeton, an MBA from the London School of Economics, and a law degree from Harvard. As a graduate student in Europe, he wrote a thesis that updated the guiding principles of the Austrian School of Economics with twenty-first century economic, social, and political realities. The white papers Sage authored became the economic foundation that guided The Movement's macro and micro economic policy. With Sage in the background, Edward Birch and the Virginia State Legislature coupled libertarian ideology with economic legislation, policy, and regulation that was pragmatic and practical, and easy to explain to the bumper-sticker mentality of Virginia voters.

Sage was one of The Movement's founding fathers. He had been a close friend and business partner with Edward Birch's father, and part of a team that carefully groomed Edward, preparing him for his ascension through the spectrum of American political power. Under Sage's direction, The Movement operated as a parallel governing structure. On paper, The Movement was a registered consulting and lobbying firm. Elected and appointed officials from an alphabet soup of agencies and bureaus ran the official bureaucracy in Virginia. Behind the scenes, Sage chaired the Movement's Executive Committee, which was the true powerbroker in the state.

William returned to his seat on the leather sofa when he heard the toilet flush. He picked up his coffee and took a sip. The coffee was cold and bitter.

"Got to stay regular," Sage said, stepping out of the bathroom, drying his hands with a towel. "Once you get past fifty the wheels slowly start coming off the rails."

"Fifty? No way. I wouldn't peg you as a day over forty-five."

"You're a good boy, William. Flattery will get you everywhere," Sage said, throwing the towel on the vanity.

William smiled. Sage reminded him of Professor Wisan. His hair was thick and gray, and face long and covered with leathery skin that highlighted a pair of deep-set, dark eyes. He carried his large frame with a slight limp, an injury leftover from his days on the gridiron.

"I have some exciting news for you, assuming your exam results are what we hope they will be," Sage said. "I'm about to hand you your first official case."

"I'm ready for anything. What is it?"

"It's a big one. You pull this one off and it'll post a big 'W' for The Movement. This one cuts right to the heart of the battle for states' rights. I'm assigning you The Gellibrand Case."

"Holy shit," William said, sitting back heavily on the sofa.

"You think you're ready?"

"Absolutely," William said. "I know I am."

"What makes you so confident?"

"Lots of things," William said. "While you were in the bathroom, I was looking at those pictures on your desk. That one from Governor Birch's inauguration caught my eye."

"That was one of the greatest days in the history of Virginia."

"Absolutely. Three lines from the inauguration speech have framed my thinking about public education policy for the past three years. Every time The Movement Education Committee gets together, we begin each meeting by re-reading those three lines. We had them embroidered and framed; they hang on the wall of our committee workroom. We consider it a statement of our core values and beliefs; it frames every decision we make, every policy we recommend – everything."

"That speech was a masterpiece. Which lines are you talking about?"

William closed his eyes, leaned his head back and quoted verbatim from Governor Birch's inauguration speech, "Education is not a right; education is an opportunity. The government's need to compel children to pursue that opportunity is antithetical to the responsibilities that are God-given to the individual, and undermines the rights of the family. The state's use of taxation to redistribute provisions for education is an impediment to the concept of personal responsibility, and ultimately corrupts the strength that springs from the individual and the communities in which individuals choose to freely associate."

"It is brilliant."

"It's more than brilliant, it's perfect. That's how I know I'm ready to take on the Gellibrand Case. It's something I believe in with every fiber of my being. I can't lose."

"Excellent. I wouldn't give it to you if I wasn't completely confident in the outcome. Your work on The Movement Education Committee has been exemplary. Your committee's policy work has created the structures that match our vision."

William smiled when Sage called it *his* committee. "We've come a long way," William said, reflecting on the accomplishments of the committee since his arrival in Richmond three years earlier.

The Movement upended public education in Virginia after Governor Birch's election in 2022. In less than three years, William's committee wrote the policy positions that stripped public education from its traditional foundation, and reconstituted it on a foundation grounded in the principles of personal responsibility and free association.

The first education law that Governor Birch repealed was Virginia's truancy statute. With the stroke of a pen across an executive order, parents were no longer required to send their children to school. Within a matter of months, the Birch Administration abandoned Virginia's system of standardized testing, teacher certification, and all efforts to direct education policy. Governor Birch eliminated the Virginia State Department of Education. Only the constitutionally required Virginia State Board of Education remained as a centralized governing agency. Governor Birch neutered the authority of the Board by appointing members who failed to show up for meetings, denying the Board a quorum necessary to create policy. By the end of the Edward Birch's first year in office, the Virginia State Legislature repealed every state statute regulating education.

Towns and cities took over full responsibility for public education. Local boards of education were empowered to set graduation requirements, length of the school day, length of the school year, working conditions for teachers, and all matters of policy and regulation governing the operation of public schools. The Virginia State Legislature passed new laws that transformed public schools into schools of choice, and created a voucher system to subsidize public education. A five thousand dollar voucher per child was mailed to each family on August 1st. Families were allowed to use the money for any public, private, or parochial school they chose, or keep the money if they chose to homeschool.

By the end of Edward Birch's second year in office, the free market approach to public education was thriving. Marginal and failing schools closed. Charter and magnet schools cropped up in every corner of Virginia, online and distance learning programs thrived, and private and parochial school enrollment boomed. Students became clients - schools that served their clients well, survived; schools that failed to serve their clients well, closed. In less than two school years, districting based on residency collapsed as students began moving freely across town lines. The competition for the coveted five thousand dollar voucher was fierce. The elimination of the government's monopoly over public education drove innovation in the classroom as schools vigorously recruited and fought to retain students.

After eliminating Virginia's centralized role overseeing public education, The Movement Education Committee went after the unions. Governor Birch and his supermajorities in the Virginia State Legislature repealed all statutes prescribing collective bargaining rights, binding arbitration, and teacher tenure. When the dust settled, teachers found themselves serving at the will of local boards of education. Local boards of education were empowered to fire teachers without notification, just cause, or any right to due process.

The outcry from teacher unions was fierce in the first year of the Birch Administration. Equally powerful cheers from empowered students, parents, and taxpayers dampened the protest as quickly as it surfaced. Classroom teachers soon joined in and rejected the union outcry; despite the union's dire predictions, the best teachers saw their paychecks triple and gleefully watched as their lazy and mediocre colleagues were removed from the classroom. A new breed of high-quality teacher recruits entered the profession, lured by the prospect of a system that empowered them to market their skills to the highest bidder.

Without the financial burden of public education, the Virginia State Legislature repealed the income tax, and cut the state's sales tax in half. With the elimination of every regulatory burden, local boards of education slashed property taxes and cut education budgets in half during the first two years of the Birch Administration, and in half again in the third year. Of all the savings, the biggest cut to education budgets came with the complete elimination of all special education services.

Prior to the Birch Administration, multiple layers of federal and state legislation protected Virginia's neediest children. The federal Individuals with Disabilities in Education Act, Americans with Disabilities Act, Civil Rights Act of 1964, and a myriad of Virginia state civil rights and special education laws placed taxpayers on the hook for disabled students. Many of the most disabled students received services in highly specialized schools; the annual per student expense of these placements ran into the six figures. Local education budgets shouldered the expenses until the children reached the age of twenty-five, at which time the burden shifted to Medicaid, Social Security, and other disability entitlement programs. In addition to the most disabled students, students with learning disabilities consumed the costly services of special education teachers, paraprofessionals, school psychologists, speech and language pathologists, behavior intervention specialists, occupational therapists, specialized transportation, and other programming. In the third year of the Birch administration, the Virginia State Legislature repealed all special education laws. Governor Birch issued an executive order permitting schools to opt-out of federal education laws.

"So," Sage said. "Bring me up-to-speed. What you know about the Gellibrand Case."

"Heather Gellibrand is a ten-year-old student from Charlottesville. Late last year, she was forced out of a specialized residential placement for children with Cerebral Palsy. Without financial support from her local board of education, Heather returned home to her mother. Her mother is a real winner - Deborah Gellibrand. Deborah is a prostitute and meth-addict. She's been in and out of jail her whole life. Deborah squanders the five thousand dollar voucher she receives for Heather's education on drugs. For the past year, all of Heather's educational services and medical treatment stopped. Last summer, police responded to a trailer park during a domestic dispute between Deborah and one of her bereft boyfriends. The police found Heather on the floor in a small bedroom at the back of the trailer home. The police report is grim. Heather was dehydrated, malnourished, and covered in bodily filth. Deborah and her boyfriend were too busy cooking and shooting meth in the kitchen to bother with the girl."

"Damn it. I see where this is headed," Sage said. "We've still got work to do on those damned drug laws. They continue to jam us up with stuff like this."

"Yup," William said. "We knew these cases were going to crop up; it's part of the equation - personal responsibility meets human dysfunction."

"Tragic, indeed. Now that the government is no longer subsidizing this type of behavior, the laws of natural consequences are going to take a couple of years to root these things out. So, let me guess, because we still have those damned drug laws on the books, the police took the mother into custody, which of course left poor little Heather Gellibrand out there hanging."

"You got it."

"What happened next?" Sage asked.

"An ambulance transported Heather to an emergency room. Without medical insurance, the emergency room refused to admit her."

"Ah, I can hear the bleeding hearts already. Poor little Heather, kicked in the ass by the jackboot of education reform, health care reform, and welfare reform. We coldblooded conservatives are forcing poor little Heather and her mother to face the realities of personal responsibility."

"This narrative is playing out all over the state," William said. "The good news is that we're still winning the argument."

"For now. Go on with the story," Sage said.

"With her mother in custody, and a severely disabled, ten-year-old girl on their hands, the hospital had limited options. They would have had to literally drop a girl with Cerebral Palsy on the sidewalk in front of the hospital and leave her there."

"Yup, I see the dominoes falling. The private safety net hasn't caught up with us, yet. That will still take a few more years," Sage said.

"Actually, in this case, it did. The safety net is reforming exactly as we envisioned. For Heather, it worked the way it's designed to work. The hospital administration reached out to a local church. The church provided the funds to cover Heather's immediate health care expenses. After she was stabilized, the parish offered her shelter and care."

"Perfect. Like we've been saying right along; if it's in the best interests of society to care for the infirmed, it will be done. We don't need the overreach of government. So, then how did this end up in a federal court? I can't imagine Heather filed on her own behalf."

"One of the parishioners in the church is a local attorney. He offered pro bono legal services and filed suit on Heather's behalf. The attorney knows that the Virginia state courts are packed with Birch appointees. So, he brought suit in federal court, arguing that the State of Virginia is failing in its' responsibilities under the Individuals with Disabilities in Education Act."

"Still a few fucking liberal attorneys left out there," Sage said.

"Yup. The attorney's name is David Schekly."

"I'll pass the name along."

William felt a cold pang ripple up his spine. "I know him," William said.

"Who? Attorney Schekly?"

"Yes. He's an adjunct at UVA. I took a class with him," William said. A flash of two children materialized in William's mind. During lectures, Attorney Schekly hooked up his laptop to an LCD projector. The desktop image of two beautiful children greeted the class at the start of each lecture. William tried to shake the image of the toe-headed toddlers - a boy and girl smiling in front of a Christmas tree – from his mind. "Maybe I can talk to him."

"Don't bother. People like that can't be reasoned with; we'll just have to cauterize another wound. Active state progressives with law degrees will continue to be very dangerous until we can unwind all the laws that have empowered them for far too long."

"I understand," William said.

"Excellent. Keep me posted on your preparations."

"Yes, sir. The preliminary hearing is still a few weeks off."

"Okay. Will I see you at church Sunday?"

"Yes."

"Very good, hopefully you'll have the results by then."

"I'll let you know as soon as I do."

THE cursor hovered over the log in button on the screen. William's hand shook. He inhaled, held his breath, exhaled, closed his eyes, and appealed to God. The outcome was almost assured; he'd aced the practice tests, and even if he didn't pass, his connections in The Movement would pull a few strings to make sure he was admitted to the Virginia State Bar. But William wanted to do it on his own. The humiliation of telling Sage that he needed The Movement's connections to tweak his bar exam results would be unbearable. It would stain his reputation, and flatten the arc of his quickly rising star. He clicked the mouse. His results materialized on the screen; he scored well above the required mark. It was official; he could practice law in the State of Virginia.

"Yes," William said through gritted teeth.

"Sounds like good news," Mary said from the kitchen.

William walked into the kitchen and swooped Mary into his arms. "I did it," he said.

"Congratulations, Honey. I love you, Mr. Esquire."

William embraced Mary. He stood back and stared down at her belly, placing his hands gingerly over the bulge. "Is he sleeping?" William asked.

"Yes, he was kicking me a while ago, but he settled down."

"I'm going to take you out for dinner to celebrate. Anywhere you want to go," William said.

"Sounds good."

"All right, I've got a little work to do first, let's plan on getting out of here around five."

"Work? Oh, Honey, it's Saturday morning. You killed yourself prepping for that test. Take a break. Let's go to the park or something, it's a beautiful day."

"Sorry, Hon, can't. You know what they say about rest for the wicked. Go relax. I'm gonna take my laptop out on the deck."

"I'll bring you some lemonade in a little bit."

William kissed Mary softly on the cheek. He carried his laptop outside onto the back deck of the rented condominium in downtown Charlottesville. He logged on to a secure Internet connection. An email was waiting in his inbox. William opened the email and read a message from Sage - *Did you get them?*

William took his iPhone out of his pocket and found Sage's number in the contact list. The phone rang twice. An automated voice carried over the line, "Your party has been contacted, please state your name." William spoke his name into the iPhone. The automated voice immediately replied, "Identity confirmed, switching to secure cellular connection, please hold." There was a click on the line as the call routed through a private cellular network. A moment later, Sage's deep voice carried over the line.

"William, how do you fare?"

"Hale and hearty, hearty and hale."

"Hale and hearty indeed. Give me some good news," Sage said.

"I passed; ninety-eighth percentile."

"As if there was any doubt. Congratulations, welcome to the club, Attorney Blake."

"Thank you, Sage. I couldn't have done it without you."

"Nonsense. It was all you. The ink isn't even dry on your law license and already you've been handed one of the most important cases in Virginia. You'd better get ready; the progressives you're up against are pit bulls. They'll be backed by the full weight of the Office of Civil Rights. You win this one, and you're going to cut the heart out of the Individuals with Disabilities in Education Act."

"I'll be ready."

"I know you will," Sage said. "You earned this, William. Remember to consult with the media relations people on this. The plaintiffs are already out there pulling at the bleeding heartstrings. We want you to stay focused on the legal arguments, but make sure you let the PR folks know what you're up to so they can coordinate the message."

"Will do."

"Excellent. Congratulations, William. Get your team together for a strategy session bright and early Monday. I'd like a briefing in the afternoon. I'll see you at church tomorrow, right?"

"Yes."

"Good. I'm sending you an email. Look it over and email me any questions."

William hung up. An email from Sage landed in William's inbox. William opened the email - *Now that you're a full-fledged attorney, it's time to revisit your compensation package. Look over the attached contract. I'm sure you'll find it acceptable. Take that lovely wife and unborn child of yours out to celebrate. I'll see you at mass tomorrow. –Sage.*

William double-clicked a document attached to the email. A contract opened on the screen. William scanned the first few pages.

Thick legal language described a non-disclosure clause. The contract prohibited William from publicly discussing any of his deliberations or insights into The Movement. On the third page of the contract, he reviewed the benefit package. The package included a gold-plated health insurance plan, a ten million dollar life insurance policy for himself and Mary, a lease on a pair of BMW X-series vehicles with unlimited mileage and gas allowance, access to corporate jets and ground transportation, and a TPC golf membership that provided access to any TPC golf course nationwide. On the fourth page, William reviewed the salary schedule. The base annual salary was four hundred and fifty thousand dollars. The contract also included a performance bonus. The contract assigned William the Gellibrand Case as his primary responsibility for the 2025 calendar year. If he won the case, he would receive a lump bonus of five hundred thousand dollars.

"Hey there," Mary said, stepping outside onto the deck. "I brought you some lemonade."

"Thank you."

Mary placed the lemonade on the table. "What do you have there?"

"A new contract. Sage sent it over."

"Oh, that's exciting. What's the deal?"

"It's not bad. A little light on the bonus side of the offer. I'll get in there Monday and play hardball."

"Who are you kidding? You'd work for them for nothing."

"That's true, but don't let them know that," William said. William picked up the lemonade and took a long swig. He puckered his lips and wrinkled his nose as lemon pulp seared his taste buds. "So, you have a big decision to make this afternoon."

"What?"

"What color you want."

"Color for what?"

"Your BMW."

WILLIAM steered his BMW into the St. Stephen's Episcopal Church parking lot. Mass was still an hour off, but the lot was already three-quarters full.

"It's a good thing we got here early. Looks like it's gonna be standing room only," William said, pulling into an empty spot near the back of the lot.

William parked the car and retrieved a freshly-baked coffee cake that Mary made for the pre-mass reception. William walked around the car, opened the passenger door, and helped Mary out. They held hands as they walked across the parking lot.

"Beautiful morning," William said.

"Indeed," Mary said coldly.

William could feel Mary's consternation. He gave Mary's hand an extra squeeze. "I know what you're thinking, Hon. Don't forget, this is just for show, it's all part of the greater good."

"You've been saying that for three years. I'm telling you now; we will not raise our son in this Christian-light abomination," Mary said, caressing her stomach.

"I know, Hon. This is all business. We'll get back to our Evangelical roots soon, I promise. Besides, you have to admit that Reverend DeWitt has shown a little more spine recently. His last few sermons had some bite."

William and Mary entered the church through a massive set of double doors. The foyer was crowded. Mary leaned close to William as they walked through the crowd. A soft whisper ran through the room as William made his way towards the steps leading to the basement. Men and women tripped over themselves to shake William's hand, ask after Mary and the baby, and congratulate him on passing the bar. William and Mary moved quickly through the foyer; none of the parishioners congregating upstairs was worth William's time or attention. William and Mary made their way to a staircase leading to the basement. A hulking man in a business suit and sunglasses stood at the top of the steps, guarding access to the VIP reception in the basement.

"Good morning," William said.

"Good morning, Mister Blake, Misses Blake," the man said, stepping aside.

William led Mary down a flight of stairs to the basement. During the week, the basement housed a daycare center and preschool. Children's artwork adorned the walls. Classrooms with tiny desks and reading nooks flanked a large open area. William spotted Sage in the back of the room speaking with the Reverend. Sage waved William over.

"Here," William said, handing Mary the coffee cake. "I'm going over to see Sage for a minute. Bring this over to the baked goods table and mingle a little. I'll be right back." He felt Mary bristle and tighten her grip on his arm. "It'll only be a minute, I promise."

William gave Mary a quick kiss on the cheek and walked through the crowd. He did his best to nod and keep moving, lest he get pulled into any side conversations; holding his first Sunday-morning conversation with the two most important people in the room would signal his status to anyone observing the social dynamics.

"William, come on over here," Sage said, slipping his arm around William's shoulder and pulling him into the conversation.

William could feel many eyes on him. The physical embrace by the highest-ranking member in The Movement sent a subtle signal to everyone in the basement.

"Good morning, Sage, Reverend DeWitt," William said.

"Good morning," Reverend DeWitt said. "I understand that congratulations are in order."

"Thank you, sir."

"A law degree in hand and a first child on the way; this is shaping up to be quite a year for you," Reverend DeWitt said.

"The good Lord has been kind to me."

"He has indeed."

"So," Sage said. "I was just telling Reverend DeWitt that we've handed you the Gellibrand Case."

William wondered how Reverend DeWitt would react to the Gellibrand Case. Surely, he would want to see the poor and destitute cared for; that was one of the foundational tenants of Christianity. Religion and government often had a love-hate relationship, but in matters of caring for the needy and infirmed, William always saw church doctrine aligning with progressive demands that government assert its power to tax and spend in order to redistribute resources to the poor and destitute.

"We've been following your case closely," Reverend DeWitt said. "Our bishop sits on a statewide ecumenical council. The council is prepared to file an amicus curie brief with the Second Circuit supporting Virginia's position. We wish you the very best of luck. Feel free to call on us if we can offer any assistance. Now, if you'll excuse me, I have to prepare for mass."

Reverend DeWitt shook hands with Sage and William, and headed up to the main hall.

"Geez," William said. "You could knock me over with a feather right now."

"Why's that?" Sage asked.

"I figured the Church would line up against us on this one."

"Why would they do that?"

"Come on, Sage, you know what I mean; the desire to care for the needy is a basic principle of Christian ideology. Why would they support us? If we knock down the Individuals with Disabilities in Education Act, the federal government will be neutered; they won't have the ability to force states to spend one red nickel on education for the disabled. I can't see the Church supporting that."

"Oh, William, I'm disappointed. That's a very narrow way to look at it. Open your mind to the opportunity this hands the Church. They stand to gain in some very significant ways."

"How?"

"The greatest motivator of all - power."

"I'm not following you. How will the Church gain power if we prevail in the Gellibrand Case?"

"For over a generation, the clergy has watched Church membership drop. With that decline, the collection plates have been empty at the end of Sunday services. With a declining membership and coffers drying up, the power and influence of the Church has evaporated. There was a point not so long ago when there was a real possibility that churches would have to close their doors entirely. So, you tell me, why was this decline happening? Why were Americans turning away from institutions that built this nation into a shining city on a hill? Why did *In God We Trust* become a cliché, rather than an actual article of faith?"

"We've said it for years - the scourge of progressives and the liberal agenda."

"Yes, of course. Liberals convinced Americans to put their faith in government, not the Church. They've been out there since the 1960s preaching tolerance. In the name of respect for *individual difference,* we've had an agenda shoved down our throats that has caused a progressive cancer to spread unchecked. One of the first things that cancer destroyed was religion."

"I understand all that, but those are social issues, issues of morality. What does that have to do with government spending on special education? The Church has never abandoned the idea that we should pool our resources to care for the needy."

"It's all connected," Sage said. "Education has been one of the biggest drivers behind liberal social engineering. Progressives figured out a long time ago that if the poor and needy can rely on government, they won't need the Church. Progressives conditioned Americans to believe that if they pay high taxes, the government will take care of everything. With faith in government, why do we need faith in God? All we have to do is pay our taxes, and then run around without any meaningful accountability or personal responsibility to hold us back. Without the moral accountability of faith in God, Americans can do whatever they want – it's party time; homosexuality, adultery, pornography, go for it, if it feels good, why not? Gay marriage – sure. Unwanted pregnancies – ah, whatever, mistakes happen, go have an abortion. Liberals convinced us that every vice and immoral impulse is a function of individual choice; something our politically correct culture expects us to offer tolerance and acceptance. And when things start to go wrong, don't worry about it; government will pick up the pieces and the taxpayers will pick up the tab. Church officials see what The Movement has to offer. Our approach is going to bring an entire generation back into the fold of the Church. The Gellibrand Case is one more rung on the ladder. Reverend Dewitt and his ecumenical council is more-than-willing to see that resources are pooled and used to care for the needy; they just want the government to get out of the way so they can assume that responsibility."

"And at the same time enhance their own power," William said.

"Exactly."

"I get all that. But they must see how the case impacts the Gellibrand family. I thought for sure they'd come out in support of Heather and her mother."

"They are coming out in support of the Gellibrands. If Heather Gellibrand's morally decrepit mother can't rely on herself or Uncle Sam to take care of her and her daughter, then she'll have to turn to something."

"The Church."

"Yup. That's exactly what has happened. Since time immemorial, lost souls have found shelter and redemption in the Church. When Heather's mother returns to the Church, in exchange for the care they offer her infirmed child, she will be expected to live by the community's moral and ethical values. If she can't do that, they'll throw her out on her ass. In the end, Heather will be cared for, and her mother will be on a path to physical, mental, moral, and spiritual healing."

"It's brilliant," William said.

"Of course it's brilliant. It's what The Movement is all about – personal responsibility and free association."

"It's all coming together."

"Of course it is," Sage said, clasping William's shoulder. "Church membership in Virginia has doubled since Governor Birch took office. And without having to pay abusive taxes that sap wealth, people have money left over at the end of each week - collection plates are brimming. As government throws off the yoke of social programming, churches and communities of faith are stepping in to fill the void. Power is shifting from government to communities of faith - it's perfect synchronicity."

"So, people are finally coming around to see that all those bleeding heart liberals are actually the ones who lack humanity."

"It's funny you said that. Before you came over, that's exactly what Father DeWitt and I were talking about. The amicus curie brief the ecumenical council is filing focuses on that exact thing. They are going to appeal to the federal courts to return care for the sick and poor to where it rightfully belongs - in the family and communities of faith. Those communities bound together through faith and free association will determine the best outcomes for their parishioners. The government will have no further role in that formula."

"Exactly," William said. "And, as long as we prevail in the Gellibrand Case, no further ability to compel us. I get it; I completely get it. Sounds like low hanging fruit for our PR people."

"That's right. Speaking of PR people, have they been in touch with you, yet?"

"No."

"They will be. Have you ever watched a Sunday morning talk show called Face the State?"

"Sure, the NBC show, it's on right before Meet the Press. I usually DVR it and watch it over coffee after mass," William said.

"There's a segment next Sunday covering the Gellibrand Case. Attorney Schekly is going to be one of the guests. We've got one of our people going up against him. I think you might know her."

"Who?"

"Tabitha Couture."

William felt his knees go weak. "Tabitha?"

"Yup. She's going to be in touch with you this week to prep for the debate. Now, come on, let's get you back to that lovely wife or yours."

THE iPhone buzzed in William's pocket. He kept his eyes on the road, and gripped the wheel with white knuckles. William did his best to ignore the buzz, and hoped to God that Mary didn't hear it. He had remembered to turn off the hands-free technology in the car's navigation system, but forgot to set his phone to silent. William had been exchanging texts with Tabitha all morning, offering last minute advice as she prepared to step into the local NBC affiliate studio. The texting stopped when Face the State went live at roughly the same time William turned his phone off for the Sunday morning services at St. Stephen's. After the service, William checked his phone to see if Tabitha had texted him an update. There were no new messages. William knew it would only be a matter of time before she briefed him on her performance.

"Is that your phone?" Mary asked.

William closed his eyes and grimaced, the pending fight unfolding in his mind like a scene from a soap opera. "What?" William asked. The phone buzzed a second time. "Oh," William said, unable to deny the noise.

"How come you have the hands-free off?" Mary asked, reaching over and pressing a button on the dashboard.

The Blue Tooth turned on, and the system navigator spoke in a crystal clear voice through the BMW's high definition Dolby speakers, "You have one new text message, from... Tabitha."

William felt Mary's eyes burn a hole into the side of his face. "Play message," Mary said.

William immediately regretted setting the car's hands-free system to voice recognize both his and Mary's commands.

The navigator spoke, "Text message from, Tabitha, message begin, 'Did you see me, yet? How did I do?' end message."

William spoke to the system navigator, "Text message to, Tabitha."

"Begin message," the navigator said.

"Haven't seen it, yet. Heading back from church. Have it on DVR," William said.

The navigator repeated the message, and asked William if he wanted to, "Send now."

William replied, "Yes."

"Message delivered," the navigator said.

"Asshole," Mary said.

"It's work stuff, Mary. She went on a Sunday morning talk show to debate the merits of the case I'm arguing. I had to brief her."

"Brief her, huh. Is that what we're calling it now?"

"It's not like that. This is the first time I've seen her since we left New Haven."

"Oh, so you've been meeting with her, too. Nice. And I suppose it escaped your mind to tell me about it."

"Don't freak out, Mary. I'm not lying to you. This was all business; it had nothing to do with her and me on a personal level. If you don't believe me, then watch the talk show with me when we get home. You'll see what I'm talking about."

The iPhone buzzed with a new text message. The navigator spoke, "New message from… Tabitha."

There was a long pause in the car. "Well," Mary said. "If you have nothing to hide then let's hear her message."

William spoke, "Play message from Tabitha." He held his breath and waited for the navigator's voice to fill the car.

"Begin message… 'Call me later. Let's grab a glass of wine'… End message," the navigator said.

"I haven't laid a finger on her, Mary."

"Oh, I know that you've never laid a finger on her, but it's certainly not because of your chaste soul, not by a long shot. She wouldn't let you. She still has you right where she wants you - drooling over her like one of Pavlov's dogs, and then sending you home to me with an itch to scratch. You make me sick."

"You're wrong. Those days are over. This had nothing to do with her and me - this was all business. It's all for the good of The Movement. Why don't you watch the show with me when we get home? You'll see what I'm talking about; this is all about the case I'm arguing, nothing more," William said.

"Watch her, with you? Never. You've clearly lost your mind. If you think I'm going to sit there and watch you stare at that Jezebel, while your prick firms-up in your pants - forget it. You, and it, aren't coming anywhere near me."

A chill filled the car for the rest of the ride home. Mary bolted from the car the moment William pulled into the driveway. William parked the car and made his way into the condominium. He walked into the living room and turned on a flat screen television that hung on the wall above a gas insert fireplace. He scrolled through the recorded programs on the DVR until he found the Sunday morning show called Heart of Virginia. He sat back on the couch and fast-forwarded through the commercials and station identification, and hit play on the remote when the segment opened with a close-up shot of the anchor, a political pundit named James Saisa. The image widened to show Saisa seated at the vertex of a triangular table. Three coffee mugs emblazoned with the WSET-TV logo and *Heart of Virginia* rested on the table, and a green screen image of the Virginia State Capitol Building filled the space behind Saisa.

"Good Morning, welcome to the Heart of Virginia's Face the State, your source for Virginia politics," Saisa said. "Now heading into his fourth and final year as Governor, Edward Birch has been a transformational leader, galvanizing political forces across the state as Virginia strikes out on a bold new course. Over his term in office, Virginia has seen dramatic reductions in state and local taxes, and the near complete elimination of state regulation and oversight in virtually every corner of the private and public sector, all done in the name of full empowerment of individuals and communities at the local level. The result has been a booming economy, and a labor market at full employment. By every metric and indicator, the conservative approach to governance has taken a deep hold in Virginia. And while the benefits and blessings of the Birch administration's policies are apparent to most, there are still some naysayers who see a dark side to this renaissance; some refuse to believe that the call for personal responsibility is anything more than an effort to destroy the state's social safety net. Nowhere has the Birch administration's approach raised the hackles of progressive thinkers more acutely than the area of education reform. Since arriving in Richmond, Governor Birch has completely redesigned the state's system of public education. Governor Birch has transformed public education into a choice-based system by eliminating residency requirements and implementing a voucher system, through which education funding flows directly to students and to the schools that students choose to attend. Here to debate the merits of Virginia's education reform is Director of Communications for Governor Birch, Tabitha Couture. Good morning, Ms. Couture."

"Good morning, Jim. Thank you for having me," Tabitha said.

"Also joining us is prominent civil rights attorney, David Schekly. Attorney Schekly is representing a Virginia student named Heather Gellibrand. Heather Gellibrand is the plaintiff in a lawsuit filed by

Mr. Schekly in federal court. The suit alleges that Virginia's education reform initiative is denying Heather her right to a free and appropriate public education. Attorney Schekly, thank you for joining us today."

"Thank you for having me."

"Mr. Schekly, you have filed suit against Governor Birch and the State of Virginia. Your suit alleges that the Birch Administration's approach to education reform has undermined the funding formula for special education services. According to the merits of your suit, you believe that Governor Birch's approach has done great damage to educational services for students with learning disabilities," Saisa said.

"That's correct."

"Ms. Couture," Saisa said. "Let's start with you. Give us a little context. What are the Governor's goals for education reform?"

"Thank you for giving me the opportunity to speak to the citizens of Virginia. To start, I'd like to point out an error in your introduction," Tabitha said. "This is no longer the Gellibrand Case. Heather Gellibrand is no longer a plaintiff. Heather and her mother have asked to be removed from the case. They, like most citizens of Virginia, are directly benefitting from Governor Birch's vision for education. It's a deception to call this case the Gellibrand Case, when in fact Attorney Schekly isn't representing anyone or anything except his own narrow self-interests, and the interests of a discredited system of public education that for decades failed Virginia's students. He is representing an ideological viewpoint that in three short years Governor Birch has completely discredited."

"Is that true, Mr. Sheckly?"

"Of course that's not true. Heather and her mother have indeed opted-out of the case. The Gellibrands are living in a religious commune outside of Richmond. Like countless other Virginia families, they have been displaced by Governor Birch's draconian reform of the state's social safety net. I believe the Gellibrands were intimidated into opting-out of this lawsuit."

"That's a pretty serious charge. Intimidating a witness in a federal lawsuit is a felony."

"He has no proof to back up such a ridiculous assertion," Tabitha said. "Heather and her mother have found sanctuary in a community of faith. Mr. Schekly simply refuses to believe that there are communities and organizations outside of his beloved government bureaucracies that can do the job of caring for the needy."

"Heather Gellibrand has Cerebral Palsy. I find it disturbing that Ms. Couture and her Movement counterparts believe that the scope of Heather Gellibrand's many medical and educational needs can be properly managed in a religious commune, which is little more than a ramshackle compound in the woods, instead of a legally-required Planning and Placement Team comprised of medical professionals and educators."

William sipped his coffee, leaned back into the folds of his soft, Italian leather couch, and smiled at the optics captured in high-definition on the screen of his sixty-inch flat screen television. Schekly's brow furrowed, framing an angry burst of heat radiating under a thick layer of stage make-up that had been liberally plastered on his face in the studio's green room. The contrast with Tabitha was stark. Tabitha leaned forward in her chair, calm and collected, allowing her deep brown eyes to absorb the spectacle of her opponent, who appeared to be on the verge of a stroke. She projected youth and strength, and an intelligence that mixed with a sense of pity and compassion for the plight of the man who was the face of teetering opposition to The Movement in Virginia.

"What Mr. Sheckly finds disturbing is the fact that years of liberal social engineering has finally been revealed for what it is – a very expensive sham. Since the 1960s, the State of Virginia has been forced to comply with federal government overreach in the form of laws with well-meaning names like the Civil Rights Act, the Americans with Disabilities Act, No Child Left Behind, and the Individuals with Disabilities in Education Act. These laws were forced on Virginia by a succession of blowhard, know-it-alls like former Senator Ted Kennedy and other big government liberals. These are the laws that Mr. Schekly is fighting tooth and nail to defend. Governor Birch has turned back these laws in Virginia. He has returned natural rights to each individual by neutering government. As liberty begins to flow through the veins of every red-blooded Virginian, we have all begun to realize the evils that Mr. Schekly and his ilk have wrought for too long," Tabitha said.

"We've been listening to this poisonous propaganda for nearly four years now," Schekly interjected. "Let's take a minute to reflect on what Governor Birch has really brought to Virginia."

"Uh-oh," William said, sitting up a little on his couch. "Here come the stats."

"Under the Birch Administration, over two hundred and fifty million dollars has been cut each and every year for the past three years from the education budget. The sole source of assistance provided to students is a paltry five thousand dollar voucher. These vouchers barely scratch the surface of educational opportunities and resources that special education students need. And how have they gotten away with it? They eliminated the Virginia State Department of Education, so that now there is no one collecting data on any of our schools' progress. We have no way of knowing our graduation rates, dropout rates, percentage of students going on to college, or how well our students are doing on standardized tests. Governor Birch cut off that information because he knows that it would shed a light on the devastating impact of his administration's efforts to abandon responsibility for educating Virginia's children."

"There's the rub," Tabitha said calmly. "Mr. Schekly believes it is the government's responsibility to educate Virginia's children. Where in any of our state or nation's founding documents does it say that the government is responsible for education? That responsibility belongs to parents, to the family, and to communities of faith that parents choose for their family. We are simply restoring the natural order of things."

"That sounds all well and good, Ms. Couture. But we all know that some parents are simply unable to make those provisions. And while churches mean well, they do not possess the expertise necessary to provide educational services, particularly for students like Heather Gellibrand who have specialized learning needs."

William smiled. Schekly stepped into the bear trap; all Tabitha needed to do was slam the claws shut.

"I suppose your estimation of the ability to educate our children would come as a surprise to the millions of students who have been educated in this nation's system of parochial schools. But let's leave that assertion alone, I'll let Catholic and Christian schools defend themselves - after a comment like that, I'm sure there are hundreds, perhaps thousands of emails and letters to the editor that are about to be written in response. I would also remind you that communities of faith have filed an amicus curie brief supporting the state in this lawsuit. Virginia's religious communities are one hundred percent behind Governor Birch," Tabitha said. Tabitha paused for dramatic effect, took a sip of her coffee, and then turned to face the camera. "We've known for too long now that progressives like Mr. Schekly hold individuals in deep disdain, and believe that only government has the answers to our ails. Just like Governor Birch, I trust in the individual, and am far more comfortable placing my faith in the family, rather than government. It was not government that made Virginia great; it was the spirit of pioneering Virginians; the rugged individualism of one and all - that is the bedrock of Virginia's strength. Government has simply gotten in the way. I trust that parents, families, and communities of faith will do right by their children. Government has no role in that equation."

"Wake up, Virginia," Schekly hollered into the camera, his face exploding in a crimson blossom, veins throbbing in his temples. "See through this nonsense; think hard, before it's too late. You're being told that if you have a special needs child, too bad, you're on your own. Their logic has nothing to do with liberty; this is all a selfish ploy, they just don't want to pay their taxes, or assume responsibility for any of our citizens. This is nothing more than radical, right-wing social engineering at its most disturbing."

"Gotcha," William sneered at the television.

"And with that we have to take a break," Saisa said. "But stay tuned, we'll be back with more from the Heart of Virginia."

"Saved by the bell, you son-of-a-bitch," William said, lifting the remote and fast-forwarding through the commercials.

"Welcome back. We're here debating the merits and perceived dangers of the Birch Administration's education reform agenda. Before we left, Mr. Schekly argued that the rationale behind the state's education reform is a function of tax cutting," Saisa said, and turned to face Tabitha. "That's hard to dispute, Ms. Couture. Over the past three years, the state has eliminated the income tax, slashed the sales tax to two percent, and reduced or eliminated a laundry list of fees. Local property taxes have also been dramatically reduced across Virginia. Concurrent with all this tax cutting, social programming and education spending has been reduced to a small percentage of what it was four years ago. How do you respond to Mr. Schekly's charge that education reform is not truly about improving education, but rather an effort to slash the state budget and cut government services?"

"Education has benefitted tremendously from the free market forces Governor Birch unleashed. The state monopoly on education has been broken. Funds now follow the student. The result is that families have been empowered to choose public, private, or parochial school options best for their children. This reform has empowered individuals and local communities, and dramatically improved the quality of educational opportunities. Without the burden of abusive taxes, local communities have seen a boom in economic development. Corporations and small businesses are flocking to the state. Does anyone out there think that corporations would be pouring into Virginia by the hundreds if we didn't have an educated workforce? Local communities and corporations are supplementing state government spending, and are providing high quality educational opportunities for Virginia's students. This is another example of where the conservative approach is a proven a success, and the liberal agenda morally and financially bankrupt."

"Nonsense," Schekly barked. "You have abandoned the children of Virginia. You are putting the future well-being of this state at-risk."

"Mr. Schekly, may I ask you a question?" Tabitha asked coolly. Schekly glared at her. "You believe education is important, right?"

"Of course I do. That's why I'm fighting so hard. I believe firmly that there is nothing more important than the education of our children. High-quality education is the responsibility of each generation to the next; it is a key feature of our social contract."

"So do I; so do we all. If education is as important as we all agree it is, then why are you convinced that it will not be provided to our children?"

"Because you are attempting to starve public education of the funds it needs to flourish."

"Public education has never been more robust or effective in Virginia. Your problem is that you believe nothing as important as education can be accomplished without government. That is where we part ways, and where you are being proven wrong. Conservatives believe that nothing as important as education should be trusted to government. Fortunately, that is how the majority of Virginians see it, and with our continued success, that is how the majority of all Americans will soon see it, too."

"We're going to have to leave it with that. Thank you very much, Ms. Couture, Mr. Schekely. Tweet us your reactions and responses at…"

William picked up the remote and pressed the mute button. He stood up from the couch and walked to the doorway, searching the hallway for Mary. He heard her moving around upstairs. William took his iPhone out of his pocket and searched for Tabitha's contact information as he walked outside onto the back deck. The phone rang twice. Tabitha's voicemail message picked up, asking the caller to leave a message.

"Tabitha, it's William. I just watched it. Great job, you were pitch perfect…." The iPhone buzzed with an incoming call. William pressed the *end current call and accept incoming call* button on the iPhone, and said, "Hello."

"Hey, there you are," Tabitha said.

"I was just leaving you a message."

"I know. I didn't get to my phone quick enough. So, what did you think?"

"I think you kicked his ass."

"Thanks. It's pretty easy to kick someone's ass when you've got the facts on your side."

"Very true. In any event, you probably did him a service he'll never even realize. I can only imagine the tragic accident waiting for him if you hadn't beaten him up so badly."

"I don't think I'll get a thank you card anytime soon."

"I'm sure you guys in Movement PR would love to have him out there arguing the case for the opposition. You might want to send him a bottle of vitamins; the poor guy looked like a raving lunatic."

"That's how most liberals in Virginia look these days. And how did I look?"

"As good as ever."

"Just good, is that the best you can offer me?"

William turned and scanned the deck quickly. He looked up, saw both bedroom windows open, and instinctively knew that Mary would be eavesdropping on the call. It gave him an opportunity to win back some credibility "You did a great job, Tabitha," William said stoically, projecting his voice up to the bedroom window. "Look, I gotta run and check on Mary. Congratulations again, you scored a big win for The Movement today. I hope our paths will cross in the future."

William hung up the phone and walked into the house. He climbed the staircase to the second floor. As he suspected, he found Mary resting in the bedroom with an ice pack on her forehead.

"That was Tabitha," William said. "She did a nice job on the show today."

Mary sat bolt upright in the bed and screamed. William jumped. Mary groaned, wrapped her arms around her stomach, and rolled onto her side.

"Are you okay?" William asked.

"Quick, get the car. I think my water just broke."

* * *

July, 2027

WILLIAM walked into the conference room. Men and women in business suits mingled around the room. William recognized a few of the men and women; the rest were strangers who had flown in for the meeting. William made his way across the room and poured himself a cup of coffee from a barista station set up in the corner. A hand landed on William's shoulder as he stirred in cream and sugar.

"Good morning," Sage said, letting his hand linger on William's shoulder as William turned to face him.

"Good morning," William said.

"Exciting day."

"Is it? What's going on? Why are all the bigwigs in town?"

"I don't want to spoil the surprise."

A man in a dark suit walked towards Sage. The man held a pointer finger to his ear, and spoke into a microphone clipped to his lapel. The man sidled up to Sage and spoke softly into his ear, "Governor Birch has arrived, sir."

"Thank you," Sage said.

The agent returned to his post by the door. Two more agents stepped into the room and took positions around the conference table.

"Governor Birch has arrived," Sage said above the din of conversation in the room. "Please find your seats."

The sound of chairs scraping across a Persian carpet filled the room as everyone took a seat around a long, highly polished conference table. Within a matter of seconds, the only people left standing in the room were the agents on the governor's security detail. An agent opened the door and a tall, blonde woman dressed in high heels, a short skirt, and silky white blouse with two buttons undone at the top sauntered into the room. The woman paused at the entrance and dimmed the lights. The men and women seated at the table stood bolt upright as Governor Birch strolled into the room behind the woman.

Governor Birch walked casually to the head of the table and faced the group. "Good morning," he said. A collective "good morning" rose above the table. "How do you fare?" Governor Birch asked.

"Hale and hearty, hearty and hale," the men and women boomed in unison.

"Hale and hearty indeed. Please, let's all have a seat."

The men and women waited for Governor Birch to sit before sitting down and pulling their chairs up to the table.

"We've made great strides," Governor Birch said. "The Movement is breathing the sweet waft of liberty all across the great State of Virginia. The citizens of Virginia are reaping the bounty of liberty. They have turned their backs on the old, progressive models, and are embracing self-determination. We have accomplished this because of your hard work and dedication to the cause. Each of you around this table has been a pioneer in your own respective corner of The Movement; you have helped write and defend the policies that are the centerpiece of my administration; policies that have shredded the smothering social contracts of old, and replaced the power of government with the power of each rugged individual. I've asked you all here today because I want you to be the first to know. The time has come to take The Movement nationwide. Tonight, I will announce my intention to run for President of the United States in 2028."

An electric current filled the room on a rumble of applause. William clapped so hard that his hands began to sting under each snap. He stared around the table into the euphoric expressions plastered across the face of each of The Movement's architects. The men and women seated around the table had taken philosophy and turned it into policy. As he had done for education, so these men and women had done for energy, housing, labor, commerce, interior, transportation, and management and budget. This was the collective genius behind The Movement. William felt a ripple of pride as he realized that he held a seat at the table with those individuals whose names would echo through history – this was America's newest iteration of founding fathers.

"Thank you," Governor Birch said, holding up a hand to temper the applause. "There is much work to be done. We have laid the groundwork for a successful run. If the election was held today, I am confident we would win a strong majority of the popular vote. Nevertheless, we must not rest until we have captured the heart and mind of every American. Our victory must be absolute. If we do not cauterize every progressive impulse in America, the wound will continue to seep and fester on the body politic. In every corner of America, we have recruited and positioned a slate of charismatic individuals to run for all the down ticket offices that we need to capture in order to truly reform a nation. These individuals will be the face of The Movement, they will do our bidding, and it is you around this table who will operate the think tanks that they turn to for direction and guidance; you will help craft the policy that will propel our vision. You have proven yourselves to be The Movement's most valuable resource, my most valuable resource. There is a new calling for each of you as we take our beloved Movement and sweep across America."

Governor Birch motioned to his aide. The blonde woman began circulating the table, placing a folder in front of each of the men and women. William leaned to one side as the blonde woman placed a folder on the table in front of him. He felt her breasts brush against his shoulder.

"I'll see each of you shortly," Governor Birch said, standing up from the table. The security entourage escorted the governor out of the room.

Sage walked to the head of the table.

"Governor Birch and I have scheduled brief meetings with each of you individually. We will be meeting in my office. The time for your meeting is on the inside cover of your folder. In your folders, you will also find information about your new assignments. Review the information before you meet with Governor Birch and me."

Sage left the room. William picked up his folder, and carried it to his office on the first floor. He sat behind his desk and opened the folder. On the inside cover, William found a time for his appointment with Sage and Governor Birch – 4:30 pm. Inside the folder was a memo. The memo contained a username and password necessary to access to a secure website.

William logged on to his desktop computer and navigated to a secure website. He entered the username and password. Once through the security infrastructure, William accessed a series of files. The first file had his name on it. He double-clicked the file, and found a document inside. The document outlined a job description and new title – *William Blake, Director of Movement Operations for Southern New England.*

For the remainder of the morning and afternoon, William read about his new role. As the Director of Movement Operations for Southern New England, he would serve as the section chief for all Movement activity in Connecticut, Massachusetts, and Rhode Island. The job description outlined his role overseeing campaign activities, and coordinating policy in the region. The job came with enormous responsibilities, and an impressive package of compensation and benefits. He would receive a multi-million dollar base salary, and be authorized to bill corporations and private entities in Southern New

England thousands of dollars an hour for lobbying and consulting work. The compensation would catapult William and Mary from mere millionaire status, into the elite of America's nouveau riche.

At Four O'clock, William logged off his computer and took the elevator to Sage's office on the top floor. He waited patiently under the watchful eye of an agent posted in the reception area. Sage's receptionist told William he could go in.

William walked into Sage's dimly lit office. The only light in the room flooded in from the bathroom. The closed blinds robbed the room of any natural light. Sage and Governor Birch stood up from a couch when William entered. The blonde assistant who had distributed the binders in the conference room stood in the doorway to the bathroom, silhouetted in the room's only light source.

"Hello William," Governor Birch said, extending his hand. "It's nice to see you again. I hope you haven't got a scroll dagger tucked away somewhere."

William shook the governor's hand. A wave of warmth washed over him as he made physical contact. William swam in the soft, white energy that flowed from the governor.

"No, sir," William said. "That will never happen again."

"Well that's good. Even though, I must say, I admired your gumption the last time we met like this. I'm happy that we've been able to channel some of that passion in a direction that won't lead to my throat being slit."

"Never, sir. I still don't know what came over me that day."

"Oh, now, William," Governor Birch said with a patronizing tone. "We all know that's not true. Tabitha is a remarkable woman; she could drive any man insane with envy."

William stared down at his feet. "Things are different now."

"That's right. You're a father, congratulations. A boy, right?"

"Yes."

"And what's the lad's name?" Governor Birch asked.

"James."

"A son. You must be proud."

"The good Lord has been kind."

"No doubt. Please, have a seat," Governor Birch said, leading William to the couch. "I trust you've had a chance to review the information you were provided this morning."

"Yes, sir," William said, sitting down across from Sage and the governor.

"So, what do you think?" Sage asked.

"It's a very generous offer. I'm honored."

"Then you'll accept the appointment?" Governor Birch asked.

"Of course."

"Excellent," Sage said. "This is a remarkable opportunity, William."

"You've earned it," Governor Birch interjected. "We have a team already assembled for you in Connecticut, some of the best legal minds and policy wonks in The Movement. Southern New England will be a tough nut to crack. The region is moving in the right direction, but there's still some lingering vestige of progressive cancer. You're going to have be very surgical in your approaches."

"I know. New England is the land of stonewalls and steady habits. At least we've been able to get some Republican governors elected up there," William said.

"That's not going to be good enough," Sage said.

"The conservatives in New England are making some of the right policy changes, but their hearts aren't in the right place. With your leadership, we need the next wave of elections to usher in our breed of conservatives, those who'll truly move us in the direction of liberty," Edward said.

"I'm confident we'll be able to move the ball forward," William said.

"So are we. That's why we've tapped you. We have full confidence in your ability. And you're a Yankee at heart, that gives us a little of that insider knowledge that we're going to need," Sage said.

"When do we get started?" William asked.

"Right away. Time is of the essence," Governor Birch said. "We want you ramping things up within the week. Things are going to move fast. Once I announce my run, the momentum will be on our side. We will have to capitalize on that momentum. The Movement is only going to get one shot at this. Once we are in position, we are going to strip away the machinery of federal authority; dismantling the engine of oppression won't be pretty."

"It has gone pretty smoothly in Virginia. What makes you think it'll be any different when you roll things back at the federal level?" William asked.

"It's all degrees of scale," Governor Birch said. "The beast isn't going to go down without a fight. She's starving and backed into a corner right now, but she still has claws, and she'll lash out when we go in for the kill. The social and economic impact when we neuter the federal bureaucracy is going to shake the nation to its core. We can expect that historically liberal states like Connecticut, Massachusetts, and Rhode Island will try to absorb the vestiges of federal authority into their state bureaucracies. We cannot let that happen. We're going to have to be out ahead of it, and make sure that the redistribution of power flows from the neutering of Washington, DC, to the individual, not to Hartford, Boston, and Providence."

"I understand," William said.

"Then you understand the scope of your responsibility. Step one involves running the campaign and coordinating our message. Concurrently, you are going to lay the groundwork necessary to stifle any state-level effort to react by drafting regionalized social contracts. Our efforts must focus on returning power and liberty to the people – absolute freedom"

"I'm just concerned that I don't have a deep enough understanding of all the policies. I've been so focused on education reform; I'm not up-to-speed on all the other reforms that have been happening."

"You get the big picture, that's enough. You'll be surrounded by a team of policy experts who will help you work out the details," Sage said.

"Your team will guide you through the nitty gritty of the policy work," Governor Birch said. "Your role will be coordinating all the pieces, communicating, and staying out ahead of things."

"I understand," William said.

"Good," Governor Birch said, standing up and putting on his suit coat. "I'm proud of you, William."

William stood and shook hands with Sage and Governor Birch. Sage walked to his desk and used the intercom to let his receptionist know they were ready to leave.

"We have one more little gift for you," Governor Birch said.

"You've given me enough," William said.

"Oh no, not even close. All that Puritan missionary fumbling with Mary has turned you into a cold fish. When you tell me that you're hale and hearty, well, I just don't feel it radiating from your loins. It's time for you to have a good fuck for once in your life. It'll loosen you up a little."

The door to Sage's office opened and two agents stepped into the room. The agents led Governor Birch and Sage out of the office. The door closed. William heard the lock on the door click. He turned and saw the blonde aide silhouetted in the light of the bathroom door, slowly unbuttoning her blouse. She slid the blouse over her shoulder and let it drop to the floor.

"You can do anything you want to me, sweetie," the woman said, slowly crossing the room.

*   *   *

March, 2028

THE warmth of spring whistled through the driver-side window of the BMW as it climbed Cook Hill Road. The window was only open a few inches. William would have opened the window all the way, but Mary warned him that he'd be the one staying up all night if the baby got sick.

"Is he asleep?" William asked, looking in the rearview mirror at the infant dozing in the back seat.

"Out like a light," Mary said.

"We're almost there. Should we wake him?"

"Why, is he going to negotiate the deal for us?"

"Ha, yeah, we might need his help for that," William said. "I'm just thinking he might like to have his say before we seal the deal on the place he'll call home."

"I'm sure he'll wake up when we get there. Let him sleep a little longer."

Mud season still strangled the landscape, blanketing the world in a flat array of grays and browns. A few patchy clumps of dirty snow speckled lawns and clung to roofs, but the early spring tulips were beginning to creep into the world, offering the first color of the season, promising relief from winter's icy grip.

"Well, here we are," William said, nodding towards a sign shaped like an arrow with the words Blue Hills Orchard painted in blue next to a red apple.

William turned the BMW onto Blue Hills Road and drove towards the orchard. The overdeveloped, middle class suburbs of Wallingford, Connecticut gave way to a rural landscape. Rows of fallow fields used to grow pumpkins, gourds and squash spread out along the shoulder of Blue Hills Road. On the rolling hills above the estate, long, straight rows of barren peach, plum, nectarine, and apple trees stretched out to the horizon.

"How many acres are we talking about?" Mary asked.

"The entire farm is three hundred and fifty acres. Back in the day, it was over five hundred acres, but as you can see they sold off a lot of the land to developers," William said, head nodding towards a subdivision of raised ranch houses and a condominium complex that edged the border of the orchard. "There are about two hundred and fifty acres of apple orchards, thirty or so acres are used to grow nectarines, plums and peaches. The rest of the land is used for pumpkins, squash, gourds and other vegetables."

"Fruit," Mary said.

"What."

"Those are fruits, not vegetables."

"Oh, really, I've always thought they were vegetables."

"You're going to be one heck of a farmer," Mary teased.

"Yeah, well, you know what they say about hiring good people."

The BMW passed a country store next to a corrugated steel warehouse. William pointed at the warehouse. "That's the farm store and cider mill," he said.

"I know, I remember. Not much has changed," Mary said.

William and Mary had spent several late-October afternoons as undergrads visiting Blue Hills Orchard. The orchard opened to the public during the harvest season. Throngs of leaf peepers would descend on the farm to pick apples, buy fresh-pressed Blue Hills Cider, and nosh on cider donuts.

William turned the BMW onto a circular driveway in front of a whitewashed farmhouse. William's realtor was standing next to a silver Mercedes parked in the driveway. William and Mary climbed out of the car. William shook hands with the realtor while Mary retrieved James from a car seat and bounced him softly on her shoulder.

"Welcome home," the realtor said.

"That sounds promising. Did Mr. Bergeron accept the offer?"

"Not yet. But he will. He doesn't have much choice in the matter."

William and Mary followed the realtor up the porch steps. The realtor knocked on the door. A seventy-year-old man with grizzled features wearing a faded Carhartt jacket and overalls opened the front door. The man stood in the doorway and regarded William with a long, pensive stare through the eyes of a wizened New England farmer.

"Good morning," William said, stepping forward and shaking Mr. Bergeron's hand.

"Mornin'," Mr. Bergeron said.

"This is my wife, Mary, and our son, James. "

"Come on in," Mr. Bergeron said.

They followed Mr. Bergeron down a hallway to the kitchen. The 1860s farmhouse had undergone a few minor renovations and updates during its century-and-a-half on the same foundation, but the dwelling remained largely unchanged. The home radiated the strength that comes from six generations of farmers who tended to the home. Scuffs from countless work boots covered the floors, and hints of manure, dirt, and perspiration filled the air.

"Can I get you a cup of coffee?" Mr. Bergeron asked, motioning for everyone to have a seat at the kitchen table.

"No, thank you," William said.

William sat at the table. The realtor removed a manila folder from a briefcase and placed it on the table. Mr. Bergeron looked at the folder and sat down heavily in a chair at the head of the table.

"Your home is lovely. William and I met at Quinnipiac; just the other side of Sleeping Giant there," Mary said, head nodding out the window above the kitchen sink. "We used to come here to pick apples and pumpkins in the fall."

"You don't say," Mr. Bergeron said.

"I grew up on a farm," Mary said. "I know how important the land is. I can imagine how difficult this must be for you."

Mary's compassion took William by surprise. He'd never known his wife to show the slightest hint of empathy for anyone or anything. Perhaps a byproduct of her own experience losing a farm, the empathy Mary radiated filled the kitchen.

"You have a lot of memories here, don't you?" Mary asked.

"All of 'em. The good ones, anyway."

"Can I ask what happened?"

"Wife died. Kids're no damned good. I raised 'em up to know all about tendin' the land, now they're more interested in tendin' the devil's crop, rather than the fruit of Eden. Then the damned bank and government conspired against me. Can't keep up no more."

"Well," the realtor interjected. "With this offer you'll...."

William leaned forward in his chair, placed a hand on the realtor's arm, and gave him a look that could only be interpreted to mean *shut the fuck up.*

"I'm sorry about your wife," Mary said, adjusting James in her arms. "Not much we can do about the abuses of government. Seems to be an all-to-familiar story these days."

"Abuses of government, huh. I guess so," Mr. Bergeron said. He stood, walked to the sink, stared out a window, and let his gaze linger over the orchards and settle on an American flag that hung limp in the breathless air. "I've been flyin' the Stars and Stripes on that flagpole my entire life. I was drafted out of high school. The only time I ever spent away from this farm was when the government sent me off to fight in Vietnam. I earned the right to fly that flag. A few years back, my boys asked if they could fly the Gadsden Flag under it. I let 'em. I kinda liked the idea of remindin' anyone who cared to notice that we didn't appreciate the taxes and regulation. I was actually proud of my boys for it. I thought it was sign that I done a good job raisin' 'em up with a little steel in their spines, and a taste for independence – 'Don't Tread on Me' is as good a motto as any for a hardworkin' farmer."

"You were right to do it. Progressives have really done a number on Connecticut," Mary said.

"If you say so. Never paid much attention to politics. Always too busy tendin' to the farm to pay it no mind. I just paid my taxes and voted Republican, then went about my business. Didn't realize how much I counted on it 'till they started rollin' back the laws."

"What do you mean?" Mary asked.

"Lots a things. Open space conservation and farm bills always gave me a break on the property taxes and sales taxes on the produce, and the Connecticut Grown program gave us a boost with the marketing, and the subsidies was generous. When those programs went away, things got a little tougher. Then the banks seemed to start doin' whatever they darned well please – deregulation they call it. They tripled my interest rates, then they cut off my lines of credit altogether. Guess no one's left to tell 'em they can't pick on the little guy. But the nail in the coffin came when they repealed the marijuana laws."

"Marijuana laws?" Mary asked.

"Both my boys got pulled into tendin' the marijuana crops on those plantations in the northern part of the state where they used to grow tobacco wrappers. They done run off, lookin' for the easy money. That crop ain't nothing more than a weed; don't take half a mind a raise it up, not like the constant tendin' and hard work needed on an orchard. Can't eat it or drink it, no damned good for nothin' if you ask me. I wouldn't let 'em plant a single seed of that poison on this farm. So they turned their backs on me."

William's hands balled into fists, and his pulse quickened. "What'd you do with the flag?" William asked.

"Huh?" The farmer asked, turning from the sink to face his guests.

"What'd you do with the Gadsden Flag? I notice you're not flying it anymore."

"I didn't do nothin' with it. The boys must've taken it with 'em. I never paid no mind to what happened to it. Why?"

"Just curious, that's all. Do you think they still fly it?" William asked.

"Who?"

"Your boys, do you think they still fly the Gadsden Flag under the American flag?"

"Don't know. Maybe. Why're you so interested?"

"I just wonder if they're still drinking from the cup of liberty, that's all."

"Cup of liberty? Yeah, maybe, I suppose they're gettin' drunk as all hell off that cup, seems like a lotta folks are these days," Mr. Bergeron said, holding William disdainfully in his gaze.

"All right, so, let's get down to business," the realtor interjected, cutting through the quickly rising tension.

William and Mr. Bergeron held each other's gaze while the realtor prattled on about the terms of the deal. William felt the farmer's will break; Mr. Bergeron dropped his eyes and sat down heavily at the table. The only voice left in the kitchen was the realtor's. William and Mr. Bergeron took turns signing the documents. The realtor packed up the documents, and tucked them neatly into his briefcase. They all stood and left without a single goodbye.

"Congratulations," Mary said as William pulled the BMW back onto Blue Hills Road.

"Congratulations to you, too," William said bitterly.

"What's the matter?" Mary asked.

"Oh nothin'. I just wish I had lowballed him."

"I think we got a fair price. This is good land."

"It makes me sick to think that we let another taker get away with millions. I wonder how much he sapped from the public coffers over the years. It makes me want to throw up. Thank God Connecticut is finally heading in the right direction and starving leeches like Mr. Bergeron."

"Great things are happening, William. You should be proud."

William turned and looked at Mary. She reached across the armrest and gave his thigh a squeeze.

"Thanks," William said.

"You're welcome. Now, I can't wait to get started on Blue Hills Orchard. We're going to create something amazing, I promise."

* * *

August, 2028

William stood on the front porch and sipped coffee from a mug emblazoned with a giant red apple and the words *Blue Hills Orchard*. The sun crawled slowly over the top of Sleeping Giant and bore down on the orchard. William filled his lungs with a deep breath, the thick, wet air slipped down his throat in a soupy stream. He looked at his watch; it was only 6:30 a.m. William couldn't imagine where the temperature would settle when the sun reached its zenith. A black Town Car appeared on Blue Hills Road, rolling through a low haze of humid dew, and slowly rising screech of Cicada. William placed his coffee mug on the railing, picked up his suit coat, and walked down the porch steps. The Town Car pulled into the driveway. The passenger front door opened. An agent in a dark suit and mirrored sunglasses climbed out of the car and opened the back door.

"Good morning, Mr. Blake," the agent said.

"Morning," William said, climbing into the back seat.

William preferred to work from the comfort of Blue Hills, but he elected to head into the office that morning to close the deal for the telecom outfits, check-in with Nutmeg Gas and Electric, and work on campaign logistics. At the end of the day, he looked forward to running a personal errand, an errand that could only be accomplished in-person.

"The place looks beautiful, sir," one of the agents said. "I can't believe how fast you got it done."

"Thanks," William said. "The crew worked its' ass off."

William stared up at the farmhouse through tinted windows as the agent behind the wheel steered the Town Car onto Blue Hills Road. In less than five months, under Mary's watchful eye, an addition tripled the size of the home. The existing farmhouse was gutted and renovated to match the addition. The worn nineteenth century farmhouse was transformed into a stately home, towering over orchards and fields growing rich with the season's bounty.

The agent's comment reminded William that he needed to transfer the last installment to his general contractor. He used his iPhone to access one of his bank accounts and process the transfer of three million dollars. The debit put a dent in the remaining balance. William wasn't concerned, as long as things fell into place the way he expected, the account would bloom with a new deposit before the end of the day.

William's iPhone buzzed with a text message from Mary. *Didn't hear you leave. Quiet as a mouse.*

William typed a reply. *Glad I didn't wake you. James awake?*

Not yet. What time will you be home?

Late.

OK. New ovens r coming today.

Exciting. Text me a pic.

William placed the iPhone on the seat next to him and rubbed his eyes while reflecting on Mary's vision for Blue Hills Orchard. The addition of a commercial kitchen promised to open a new line of products. In addition to cider and apple juice, Mary planned a line fresh-from-the-farm baked goods. The front-end investment was huge, but William was happy to pay it; if for no other reason than it kept Mary busy and happy, which gave him the space he needed to focus on Movement business and campaign logistics.

The Town Car cruised along I-91 North. The sun bore down mercilessly on the steel snake of rush hour traffic that slithered along the banks of the Connecticut River. The car peeled off the highway and followed signs directing traffic to downtown Hartford. William stared out the window as the car cruised through a blighted neighborhood. Homeless men and women sleeping in makeshift dwellings of cardboard boxes and shipping pallets lined the streets. The car stopped at a red light.

A homeless man approached the car with a newspaper in one hand and spray bottle in the other. The agent cracked the window and hollered, "Stand back from the vehicle."

The homeless man ignored the order, aimed the spray bottle towards the Town Car, and rained brown water on the windshield. The agent driving the car stepped hard on the gas and turned slightly to the right, slamming the passenger side mirror into the homeless man's ribs as he leaned forward to wipe the windshield with the newspaper. A hollow thunk echoed through the car as the homeless man careened backwards onto the sidewalk, where he landed with a bone-crunching thwack. The agent sprayed the windshield with washer fluid and ran the wipers.

"Fucking animals," the agent hissed. "Someone should come down here with a Mac-10 and clean up this filth."

"Be patient," William said. "It'll just take a little more time to work the human excrement out of the system. The cycle of dependence that bred these vagrants is finally coming undone. It's not gonna be as quick and easy as the bark of a Mac-10, but the result will be the same."

"Thank God," the agent in the passenger seat said. "I just wish people'd get the message a little quicker."

"What people?" William asked.

"All the goddamned do-gooders who're sustaining this fucking menace."

"I'm not following you," William said.

"Well, the way I see it, now that government has wizened up and is no longer subsidizing this human filth with government handouts, you'd think the homeless would figure out that they have two choices - get a job, or starve to death. The problem is that there're still too many people giving handouts instead of a kick in the ass that those lazy fuckers need."

"That's an interesting observation," William said.

"It's true. Fucking charitable organizations and soup kitchens are doing more harm than good. They're getting in the way of natural consequences."

William stared pensively out the window. The agent was right. William made a mental note to reach out to the state-wide ecumenical council and advise against any further charitable work in the downtown area - at least no more handouts without strings attached.

The Town Car pulled up to the front entrance of a downtown office building. The agent in the passenger seat got out and opened the door for William. A brick oven wave of heat smacked William in the face. "Holy cow," William said, grimacing against the searing blast.

"Hotter than hell out here, sir," the agent said, surveying the urban landscape.

The agent followed William into the building. The conditioned air was a relief. William and the agent took the elevator to Movement offices on the top floor where William maintained a penthouse office suite.

"Good morning, Mr. Blake," his secretary said, standing up and snapping to attention when William entered the office.

"Good morning, Natalie, how do you fare?" William asked.

"Hale and hearty, hearty and hale."

"Hale and hearty indeed," William said.

"It's nice to see you, sir."

"It's nice to see you, too."

"Can I get you a coffee?"

"That would be nice, thank you."

"You have a busy morning," Natalie said.

"Very busy. I'd like to take care of the low hanging fruit first. Please get the communication's office in Richmond on the phone, and then we'll deal with the energy folks later this afternoon."

"Yes, sir. Mr. Sage's office called this morning to confirm that we're still scheduled for a call this afternoon."

"You can call them back and let them know I haven't forgotten," William said.

William spent the morning on a conference call with Movement communication consultants in Richmond. The consultants briefed him on policy positions for internet deregulation.

The Net Neutrality Acts passed at the end of the Obama administration tied the hands of internet service providers. Most states, including those in Southern New England, followed the federal government's lead and passed a series of regulations and statutes that required internet service providers to ensure equal access to all broadband. William confirmed that the deregulation underway at the federal level matched his efforts at the state level to roll back the laws and regulations in Hartford, Boston, and Providence.

After identifying the state statutes slated for repeal with a team of Movement lawyers, William arranged a conference call with the CEO's of the three largest internet service providers in the region. He reviewed the statutes and regulations, and explained how the repeal of state regulations would occur in tandem with federal deregulation after Governor Birch's election. The CEO's were delighted. The deregulation would allow them to tier internet access, providing fast-track bandwidth for anyone willing to pay a premium. At the end of the process, the service providers would have carte blanche authority to squeeze or eliminate internet service for anyone they wanted. The profits they would reap were potentially limitless; the economic equation was simple - pay up, or find your service nixed. And with the three major internet providers collaborating on the tiered pricing structure, there would be no way for disgruntled consumers to jump ship and move to a different provider. William was careful to remind the CEO's that in exchange for the promised deregulation, they would be beholden to the wishes of Movement leadership. The CEO's gladly agreed.

William leaned back in his chair and smiled, reflecting on the power that would flow from The Movement's ability to control access to information over the internet. With internet service providers in their hip pocket, The Movement's reach was limitless. William placed calls to his connections in Southern New England state houses and governors' mansions. The deal was sealed. It wasn't even Noon, and already he'd wrapped up the process of deregulating an enormous sector of the region's telecommunications economy. William documented his billable hours and consulting fees, and sent the internet service provider CEO's a bill for over two million dollars each - a fee they'd be all-too-happy to pay.

William buzzed Natalie and asked her to come into his office.

"Okay, chalk that one up. Now for the bigger fish, please get me Richard Clifford at Nutmeg Gas and Electric," William said.

"Yes, sir."

"Oh, and order me a turkey and Swiss on toasted rye with lettuce, tomato, mayonnaise and a thick layer of black pepper. I'm going to have a working lunch."

Natalie nodded and stepped out of the office. William walked to the office window and stared out over the city. Hartford shimmered in a layer of heat that radiated off baking steel, glass, and concrete. The phone on William's desk buzzed. William walked to his desk, sat back in his comfortable Italian leather chair, and pressed the speakerphone button.

"Dick, is that you?" William asked.

"Hello, William," Dick said.

Richard Clifford was the CEO of Nutmeg Gas and Electric. William had been consulting and providing lobbying services to Nutmeg, guiding the company through the intricate process of unwinding a labyrinth of state regulation. In less than three months, William navigated the process of deregulating decades' worth of state-monitored electricity pricing structures, and rolling back utility anti-trust statutes. Nutmeg Gas and Electric moved aggressively to consolidate control over electricity generation in the region. William advised the company not to move too quickly to raise prices. Nutmeg Gas and Electric complied, then went a step further and reduced the price for electricity in the region, cultivating good will while they consolidated their stranglehold over the region's energy production infrastructure.

"How do you fare?" William asked.

"Hale and hearty, hearty and hale."

"Hale and hearty indeed. It's nice to hear your voice," William said.

"I bet it is. Every time we speak, I can hear the clock ticking with billable hours. You're running up quite a tab at my expense," Dick said.

"Don't give me that crap you cheap bastard. You know damned well that for every penny I charge you, you're making ten times that amount off my efforts."

"Yeah, well, I'm just saying, your consulting fees have caught the attention of my Board of Directors."

"Then I guess you don't need my services. Have a nice day...."

"No, no. I'm just saying that the bill is getting a little steep."

"Bullshit. Now you listen to me, Dick. You'll pay what I tell you to pay and you'll do it with a fucking smile on your face – do you understand me? Otherwise, you're on your own, and good luck getting anything done in Hartford, Boston, or Providence, and never mind Washington, DC."

"Okay... okay... I'm sorry," Dick said, kowtowing audibly.

"Good, you were starting to piss me off. Just for that, you can expect the next round of billable hours I submit to reflect my ire."

"I humbly apologize."

"You've tested my patience. Now, before I get any more frustrated with you, tell me what's on your mind."

"I need to talk to you about some environmental regulations. They're still a pain in my ass."

"Which ones?"

"Clean Air Act. We're going to have to invest millions in the coal plants installing new scrubbers on the stacks to comply with the federal and state regulations. The cost for maintenance and replacement of those scrubbers is huge. We have two coal powered plants scheduled to come on line this winter; it'd save us a bundle if we can forego those scrubbers."

"You'll definitely have to wait until after the election on that one. I can lay the groundwork at the state level, but this all begins with federal law. We can't roll anything back locally until the feds make a move."

"Election is in November. How fast can we get things rolling in DC after the election?"

"I think you're assuming we're going to win."

"I've seen the polling data. There's no way for Birch to lose."

"Yeah, well, then we'd better hedge our bets, hadn't we? I'm sure Governor Birch's campaign would appreciate another donation."

"We just gave three million last quarter."

"That's all?"

"You guys are unbelievable."

"Excuse me," William said coldly.

"Nothing, nothing. Fine, you can expect another donation before the end of the week."

"Don't cheap out on us, Dick."

"I guess it's true what they say."

"What's that?"

"Freedom isn't free."

"It certainly isn't. But for the right price, I'm sure we'll be able to get things done for you before your plants go on line. Now, I have one more request."

"What?"

"It's for my orchard. I want a standalone micro-grid powered by a combination of propane, wind, and solar. It needs to be robust enough to generate power for the entire operation, and set up to give me the option of powering myself entirely, or supplementing what I draw from your grid."

"What do you want that for?"

"Hurricanes, tornados, blizzards… or just plain old self-reliance."

"Why? Don't you trust the good folks at Nutmeg Gas and Electric?"

"I don't trust anyone but myself."

"A top end unit like that runs a few hundred grand at least."

"I want more than just top end. I want the premium package, state-of-the-art. I'm sure you can have some of your guys out there to get me set up before the end of the month, right?"

"I'll have a crew out to survey and draw up some specs on the generators and infrastructure."

"It's always a pleasure working with you fine folks at Nutmeg. Have a good one, Dick. I'll be in touch," William said, ending the call and leaning back in his chair.

Natalie knocked once and walked into the office carrying William's turkey sandwich. "I got you a Coke and a bag of chips," she said, placing the lunch on his desk.

"Thanks."

"You look nice and relaxed today. Has it been a good morning?"

"Excellent morning," William said.

"Great. Can I get anything else for you?"

"No. I'm going to work through lunch. I have some hours to bill and policy positions to review. Please call Mr. Sage's office and let them know I'm ready when they are for the conference call."

"Yes, sir."

William spent the afternoon updating his billable hours, researching statutes and policy briefs, and reviewing requests from corporations clamoring to dip their beak in the tsunami of deregulation. Just as the sun was beginning to set, the intercom on William's phone buzzed.

William pressed the answer button. "Yes."

"I have Mr. Sage's office on the line," Natalie said.

"Excellent."

William waited while a secure line connected. "William. Are you there?" Sage asked.

"I'm here."

"How do you fare?"

"Hale and hearty, hearty and hale."

"Hale and hearty indeed. And how is Mary?"

"Good. We just started our second trimester. Everything is tiptop. We're having twins."

"Twins! Oh, how wonderful, I'm so happy for you."

"Thanks. Two baby girls."

"A son and two daughters, you are a blessed man."

"The Lord has been very kind."

"So, I hear things are going well up there."

"We're making progress. We still have a few obstructionists here and there, but the message has gone out loud and clear. Governor Birch's poll numbers have shocked any elected officials who remain on the fence. The writing is on the wall; get on board, or you're gonna be out of a job come November."

"Good," Sage said. "That matches up pretty well with what we're seeing across the country. We just need to make sure that our sweep in November is complete. We can't have any lingering doubts about our agenda, or anyone left standing in the way of our progress."

"Last check, Governor Birch was polling in the mid-seventies in Connecticut, pretty much the same in Rhode Island and Massachusetts. And all of the down ticket candidates who have The Movement's seal of approval are kicking ass in just about every poll. Heck, the Democrats aren't even running candidates in most of the races – they're essentially flat broke," William said.

"And believe it or not, the numbers in Southern New England are the softest in the nation. We're running in the eighties and nineties across the South and Central U.S. So, we're going to shore up the support with a stadium tour in early September right after the debate."

"We'll be ready." William said.

THE sun dipped into the horizon, submerging the office in a soft, grey hue. A knock at the door interrupted William's concentration. "Come in," William said, looking up from the glow of his desktop computer.

"I'm sorry to disturb you, sir. I'm going to head home now. Is there anything you need before I leave?" Natalie asked from the doorway.

"What time is it?"

"Past Nine O'clock."

"Boy, time flies when you're having fun."

"It's dark in here. Would you like me to turn on a light for you?" Natalia asked.

"Yes, please."

Natalie flipped a light switch. William rubbed the bridge of his nose and squinted against the flood of neon light.

"You haven't had anything to eat since lunch. Would you like me to order you something?"

"No, thank you. I'm about finished here. I'm just gonna wrap up a few things."

"Are you going to be in the office for the rest of the week, or will you be working from home?"

"I'm not sure, yet. I'll let you know."

"Have a nice night."

"You, too."

William saved a document and logged off his computer. He texted his security detail - *Transport in 10.* The iPhone chimed with an immediate response – *Transport standing by.*

William took the elevator to the first floor. One of the two agents on his security detail met him in the lobby.

"Good evening, sir. It's nice to see you again," the agent said.

William paused and looked at the agent. The agent towered over six feet tall, with a clean-shaven head, thick salt and pepper goatee, and build of an NFL linebacker. The agent had escorted William on a handful of other occasions, mostly to and from Blue Hills, and once to a state dinner at the governor's mansion, but he was not a member of William's regular security entourage.

"Oh, hey. Alan, right?" William asked, struggling to recall the agent's name.

"Yes, sir."

"I was expecting Nick and Mario."

"Mario's driving tonight. He's waiting in the car. Nick is home sick. I'm filling in. Where are we heading tonight, sir?"

William briefly considered altering his plans, wondering if the agent could be trusted. His errand demanded complete secrecy; like a junkie in search of a fix, William had a scratch that needed to be itched.

"Mario knows where we're going," William said.

"Yes, sir."

The agent followed William through the cavernous lobby towards the exit. William paused when he reached the sliding glass doors and turned to face the agent.

"How long have you been with Movement security?"

"This is my second year."

"Do you know how to keep your mouth shut?"

"Yes, sir, discretion is my middle name."

"It had better be," William said, turning and walking through the sliding glass doors.

The Town Car was idling curbside. The agent opened the back door and waited for William to settle in the backseat. He closed the door and sat in the passenger front seat.

"Good evening, Mr. Blake," Mario said, looking at William in the rearview mirror. "Where are we heading?"

"Hello, Mario. Usual spot - Asylum and Constitution."

The Town Car pulled away from the office building. William stared out the window at the urban landscape. The Town Car cruised through downtown Hartford, an area hopping with trendy nightclubs and restaurants. The urban landscape altered as the car ambled through the city's college district. The University of Hartford and Trinity College campuses were quiet - only a handful of summer school students co-mingled in coffee shops and open-air bistros, sipping iced lattes in the still-baking heat of the evening. A chill of excitement tickled the nape of William's neck when the car rolled into the city's red light district.

Two fluorescent green crosses glowed in the night, marking the border of Hartford's red light district. The green crosses hovered over a storefront where marijuana was sold in increments of two ounces or less. William stared through the window at customers sniffing various strains of marijuana in glass Mason jars. Next to the marijuana storefronts were coffee shops and lounges where customers could rent hookahs or puff on hashish cigarettes over a cappuccino or a glass of wine. The Town Car rolled past several men dressed in crisp, cotton summer suits. The men looked like brokers on Wall Street just getting off work. The men mingled with customers ambling to and from the coffee shops and lounges. William watched a customer stop and casually pull two, twenty-dollar bills from his wallet. The customer handed the cash to one of the men in a summer suit. The well-dressed man reached into the inside pocket of his suit jacket and handed over a small baggie filled with white powder.

"That still blows my mind," Alan said.

"What does?" William asked

"Drug dealing out in the open like that. I used to be a Hartford metro cop. I patrolled this neighborhood back in the day. I'll never get used to all this change."

"As long as they aren't hurting anyone, what's the problem?" William asked.

"No problem at all as far as I'm concerned. Don't get me wrong, this neighborhood used to be a complete shithole; now it's one of the safest and well-kept parts of the city. It's just that after all those years throwing drug dealers on the hood of my patrol car, well, it's strange to see them dealing in the wide open without a care in the world."

"Sort of makes you wonder about all those laws you used to enforce. Were you actually doing more harm than good?" William asked.

"Not sure I'm following you."

"Think about it. When America finally smartened up and surrendered the war on drugs, a completely new economy burst forth from the shadows. The economic impact has been unbelievable. Think about how many new millionaires have been created; think about how many people are finally earning an honest living doing what used to get them slammed on the hood of your cruiser; think about how much we're no longer spending on the entire law enforcement apparatus and justice system. Drug dealers have been transformed from underground scum into upstanding citizens."

"I don't know if I'd go that far. You don't know some of those maggots the way I do," the agent said.

"The way you *did*," William said. "They were only maggots because the laws you were enforcing turned them into maggots. Now, they're solid entrepreneurs and upstanding citizens out to do well and do good in their communities. You said it yourself - this is one of the safest neighborhoods in all of Hartford. Look around. Do you see any petty crime or vagrancy? Absolutely not. No one even dares drop litter in the streets. And do you see any overwhelming police force here to impose law and order? No, you don't. These people are tending their own neighborhoods - they're thriving."

"I know. It's just hard for me to let go. I spent twenty years on the force locking people up for selling that stuff. Then overnight they just threw open the prison doors and said, 'oops, hey, we're sorry, that shit you were selling actually isn't all that bad after all.'"

"You're missing the bigger point. Think about it this way: How many riots have occurred in inner city neighborhoods in the last five years? None. The domestic programs that spawned those riots started with President Roosevelt's New Deal in the 1930s, got exponentially worse with President Johnson's obnoxious Great Society programs in the 1960s, and were exacerbated by the war on drugs in the seventies, eighties, and nineties. Those riots were a direct result of government intervention and left wing social engineering. Now that we've finally cut all that nonsense, what do you see in inner cities? Sure, there is poverty, but people are no longer trapped in the cycle of poverty caused by dependence on government programming. The elimination of the welfare state and other social programming has ended the cycle of dependence. Inner city residents have to fight their way out of poverty, or end up starving to death. Hunger is powerful motivator. Today, if poor people turn to drug dealing, prostitution, gambling, it's completely legal; there's no longer a police force to harass their communities and throw people in jail for trying to make a good living. And if they do riot, well, the police aren't going to step in and prevent them from destroying their own neighborhoods. We've eliminated the police state and let the power of liberty and freedom take its natural course."

"I agree with all that," the agent said. "There's no question, these neighborhoods have changed for the better. It's just hard for me not to think of these people as criminals."

William sat back in his seat and wondered how closely The Movement had vetted the agent; he was talking and thinking like an old school conservative, rather than a libertarian.

"Ah, whatever," the agent said. "I guess it's just hard to get it through my thick skull that I've been proven wrong. All those drug dealers, pimps and prostitutes they let out of jail ain't hurtin' no one; at least no one who's not bringing it on himself, and I certainly don't begrudge a man or woman the right to make a living."

William breathed a sigh of relief. "That's right. Chalk it up to one of liberty's blessings."

The Town Car rolled past a strip of pawnshops, gun stores, and gold exchanges, and then rolled by a strip club with a neon sign boasting the letters V.I.P under a woman's face locked in an expression of orgasmic delight. A block-and-a-half past the strip club, the first in a series of storefronts offering gentlemen's services and full body massages came into view. William stared out the car window at half-naked women dancing in windows, enticing pedestrians who paused to consider the merchandise. The Town Car cruised by the largest of these establishments. A black awning stretched out over a red carpet. A man in a power blue zoot suit stood under the awning, soliciting passerby's with the promise of the 'time-of-your-life.' William's favorite parlor came into view, perched on the corner of Asylum and Constitution Avenue.

The Town Car pulled up to the parlor. "How do you want to do this?" Mario asked. "Same protocol as last time?"

"Yes. Alan, you stay with the car and keep an eye on the entrance. The parlor's closed to the public; I booked the whole place for myself. Mario, you're inside with me. I need you guys keepin' a close eye out while I'm here."

"Don't worry, sir. We'll keep the place on lockdown," Mario said.

"I do worry; last thing I need is someone trying to blackmail me, understand?"

"Yes, sir," Mario said.

William felt a pang of guilt as he stepped out of the car and followed Mario into the massage parlor. Bells above the door jangled as William stepped into the parlor's dimly lit waiting room. A wave of erotic excitement replaced the guilt when William caught his first whiff of sandalwood incense. A beaded curtain separating the back of the massage parlor from the waiting room jangled as the parlor madam pushed through the beads and stepped into the room.

"Missssster Blake. So good see you," the parlor madam said as she floated through the beads.

"Nice to see you, too," William said.

"You here for Ang Lei, no?" The madam asked through a thick Asian accent.

"Yes."

"You careful, Misssssster Blake. You fall in love."

William gave a low laugh and let the parlor madam take his hand and lead him through the beaded curtain. He followed her down a hallway lit with a soft, red light. Hand-drawn characters from the Kama Sutra covered the walls. The characters reached out to William as he past, calling to him, begging him to explore their pleasures. The one missionary position he and Mary posed in on those rare occasions when they explored the erotic side of their relationship was absent from the poses on the wall. William knew it would be absent from the repertoire he explored with Ang Lei that night.

"This way, Misssssster Blake," the parlor madam hissed. "You start shower, then see Ang Lei."

The madam led William to a small room where two Asian women in satin robes were waiting. The women peeled William out of his suit. They led him to a large shower stall with multiple showerheads. The water ran hot, filling the stall with steam. The women slipped out of their robes and led William into the shower. They lathered his body with soapy sponges. William leaned his head back and closed his eyes as the soft warmth of the sponges slipped across his flesh. The women slithered around William like a pair of serpents, sliding up and down, lathering his body with soap and oil. William's toned muscles flexed under the soapy caresses; his years of workouts in the Dojo impressed the women as they lathered and rubbed every inch of his body.

"Nice body," one of the Asian women whispered in William's ear.

"Poor Ang Lei, she in trouble tonight," the other woman teased, running a sponge up and down the shaft of William's fully enflamed phallus.

The women put their sponges aside and let the warm water strip their bodies of soap and oil. They turned off the water, slipped back into their robes and towel-dried William. The women rubbed a soft layer of talcum power over William's back, chest and stomach, then slipped a satin robe over his shoulders, cinched it shut with a satin belt, and led him out of the shower stall.

The women led William back into the hallway to a new room. They giggled as they opened the door for William. William stepped into a dark room. There was a massage table on one side of the room and a bed on the other. A petite, fifteen-year-old, Asian girl who was reserved for the parlor's highest paying customers stepped forward from the darkness. The girl untied the satin belt cinching the robe shut, and slipped her arms around William waist, pulling her lingerie-clad body into his embrace.

"So good see you," Ang Lei whispered.

William exhaled a deep sigh of relief and let his hands begin exploring Ang Lei's impossibly petite body.

"Good to see you, too," William said.

He knew he could do anything he wanted to her. It was time to feed the addiction that had started months ago in Sage's office; that night, William would feast.

*   *   *

October, 2028

THE popcorn in the microwave oven filled the kitchen with the sound of kernels exploding in a rapid succession. The oven beeped.

William removed the bag, tore open the top, and poured the buttery popcorn into a bowl. He carried the bowl into the living room and sat next to Mary on a leather sofa.

"Smells good," Mary said, helping herself to a handful.

"Remember when we were kids we used to make JiffyPop on the stovetop?"

"Oh, yeah, of course. You had to shake it like hell while the tinfoil expanded and that little hole in the top steamed."

"Yup. Those were the days. That popcorn always tasted better than this nuked stuff."

"The popcorn may have been tastier, but I'm inclined to believe that *these are the days*," Mary said, resting her hands on the twins sleeping in her belly.

"You won't get an argument from me. Okay, here we go," William said, turning up the volume on a flat screen television mounted on the wall.

"Good evening. Welcome to the fourth in our series of five presidential debates. I'm Peter Senge. I'm joining you live from Independence Hall in Philadelphia, Pennsylvania. I will be moderating tonight's debate featuring the three presidential candidates. Tonight's debate format provides each candidate ninety seconds for introductory remarks, and ninety seconds to make closing arguments. After the opening remarks, I will begin asking a series of questions. Each candidate will have ninety seconds to respond, and then another ninety seconds for rebuttal. Let's begin with an introduction to each of the candidates...."

James's cries reached into the living room.

"I'll get him," Mary said.

"No, it's all right, I'll go. Enjoy your popcorn," William said. "I'll get him.

"What, really? You don't want to watch the debate. I'm shocked."

"The DVR is recording it; I'll catch the highlights later," William said, standing up from the couch.

"You could knock me over with a feather right now."

"Why? I've read every word Edward Birch has written, and listened to every speech he has made for the past eight years. Do you think there's anything he's gonna say tonight that I haven't already heard?"

"If you say so."

"Besides, I'm going to be spending the entire day on the stump with him tomorrow. You sit back and enjoy the debate. I'll take care of James."

THE helicopter slowly descended and settled in a field near the farmhouse. "There's my ride," William said.

"Be safe," Mary said, adjusting James in her arms.

"Always," William said. William took James from Mary and gave him a kiss on the forehead. "All right, little man, you take care of your mommy and sisters," William said, rubbing Mary's belly. "I'll see you tomorrow."

William handed James back to Mary, gave Mary a kiss on the cheek, walked across the field, and climbed into the helicopter. He pulled on an aviation headset.

"Good morning, Mr. Blake," the pilot's voice carried over the headset.

"Good morning," William said.

"Exciting day," the copilot said. "That was one hell of a debate last night. Governor Birch kicked some serious ass."

"He sure did," William said.

"He's just about got this election all sewn up. He was already polling in the seventies. After last night's performance, he'll definitely get a bounce on top of that," the pilot said.

"I'm sure he will. But don't forget, it's not just him. We have a whole slate of other candidates we need to get elected, too. Some of them aren't polling as strongly. Let's hope that today's rallies get the ball rolling in the right direction."

The helicopter lifted off. William stared down at his orchard. September had slipped into October, and the crop was coming into full bloom. The harvest would begin within weeks. A few hints of red and yellow on some of the less hearty trees sprinkled Sleeping Giant. The helicopter flew towards a long, thin, blue strip that snaked through the green, early fall canopy. The pilot used the Connecticut River as a guide as they flew north towards the first of the stadium rallies.

The helicopter flew several hundred feet above the Connecticut River as it approached Hartford. A line of traffic stretched as far William could see in both directions approaching the city along Interstate 91 North and South, and Interstate 84 East and West. The helicopter slowed and took a position in a line of helicopters hovering over the Meadows Theatre. The pilots waited their turn to land on a small helipad at the back of the theater. William stared down at the parking lot where hordes of people tailgated. People were beginning to abandon their vehicles on the highway and side roads leading to the parking lot, and walk towards the Meadows Theatre. The Connecticut State Police had all but given up on trying to manage the surge of humanity.

"Holy shit," the pilot said. "There must be hundreds of thousands of people down there."

"Looks closer to a million," William said.

"That's unbelievable."

"And this is only the first of three of these that we have planned for today. We're flying from here to Gillette Stadium in Massachusetts this afternoon, and then to Met Life stadium in New Jersey for a rally tonight. Governor Birch is packing stadiums across the nation from now through election day."

"Are you going to all of them?"

"No. I'm just attending today's events, and then I'm off the hook."

The helicopter landed on a helipad at the back of the Meadows Theater. William climbed out of the helicopter. Movement security escorted him off the tarmac. The helicopter lifted off to make room for a succession of helicopters ferrying VIP's to the event. Security led William to a reception in an enormous frame tent set up in a fenced-in area behind the theatre. A hodgepodge of big-dollar donors, debutants, politicians and celebrities packed the tent; all of Hartford's beautiful people mingled over shrimp cocktail and champagne. In the distance, a country band played for the capacity crowd filing into the outdoor amphitheater.

From behind, someone grabbed William by the shoulder and spun him around. He stumbled sideways as an open-handed slap landed suddenly on his right ear. Instinct took over. William found his balance and settled on the balls of his feet in a guard stance, tactfully backing away from his attacker to buy himself time to process the onslaught and plan a defense and counterattack. His assailant closed the distance between them and threw two jabs in quick succession. William side-blocked the jabs, but couldn't defend himself against a lightening quick knee planted in his stomach, forcing the air violently from his lungs. He doubled-over and tried to step back. The assailant grabbed William's left wrist and spun him sideways, twisting his arm at an angle that would guarantee a compound fracture. William found himself locked in a Jiu-Jitsu chokehold, his assailant's arms wrapped skillfully around him like a boa constrictor, slowly squeezing the oxygen from his lungs, and denying lifeblood to his brain. He felt his spine bend to the breaking point, and neck strain against an impending snap. In the second before he was choked out, the man attacking him let go and pushed him forward. William doubled-over and coughed, then filled his lungs with a deep breath. He stood up and found himself encircled by a crowd watching the spectacle like a gaggle of high school students anxious to see a fight in the hallway after homeroom.

"What the fuck," William said, pulling himself into a guard stance and facing his attacker. He dropped his fists when he made eye contact with Marc.

"Come here you son-of-a-bitch," Marc said, stepping forward and pulling William into a bear hug.

"Marc! Holy shit. What the hell are you doing here?" William asked, pulling himself from the bear hug and staring into his old colleague's eyes.

"Working."

"Damn, it's good to see you," William said. "It has to be, what, seven years?"

"It's good to see you, too. Been a long time since our days at Beacon. I was psyched when I saw your name on the VIP list."

"Are you working security?"

"I don't just work it; I'm in charge of security for the whole damned thing. These are all my boys," Marc said, pointing out a perimeter of agents in dark suits.

"Wow. I'm impressed. It's nice to see Beacon folks doing well."

"Beacon folks are doing more than well. Half my agents are Beacon alum. Every time I review the dossiers of guests at the governor's highest-level meetings it's a freakin' honor roll of Beacon graduates and former teachers, lots of 'em from New Haven. We conquered the world."

"It's something to behold, that's for damned sure."

"And look at you," Marc said. "You've made quite a name for yourself."

"Have you been snooping on me, too?"

"Dude, I have access to information on everyone and everything. I told you, I'm in charge of the governor's security detail for this whole stadium tour. This shit's off-the-hook."

"Not bad for a sweaty old gym teacher," William said in his most condescending voice.

"Fuck you, dude. That's physical education, you pencil-pushing geek."

"Glad to see nothing's changed."

"Who are you kidding? Everything's changed." Marc held up his hand abruptly and stopped the conversation. He lifted his pointer finger and covered a small, flesh-colored earbud. "It's show time. Governor's bird is T minus ten. Go stand over there by that stage entrance," Marc said, pointing to the north side of the tent. "I'll get you right up on stage. This shit's going to blow your mind."

Marc walked briskly towards the helipad. William pushed his way through the crowd towards the stage entrance. An electric current ran through the crowded tent as everyone simultaneously registered Governor Birch's arrival. People pushed and strained to get a glimpse of the candidate. The governor's personal security detail and Marc's event agents pushed through the crowd, making a corridor for Governor Birch. Governor Birch waved and shook hands as he walked towards the stage. An agent at the front of the entourage reached the stage entrance and stood in front of William. The agent kept his hand inside his suit coat, fingers wrapped securely around the grip of a Sig Sauer 9 mm handgun. The agent scanned the crowd, searching for potential danger. The crowd surged as the governor approached the stage entrance. William pushed forward, throwing his shoulder into a man who tried to wedge himself between William and the agent. The man swore at William as the surge of the crowd swept him back and away from the stage entrance. Governor Birch continued waving as he made his way through the crowd. A hand reached through the crowd, grabbed William by the arm, and pulled him along.

"Come on, keep moving," Marc said, half-pulling, half-pushing William behind Governor Birch's entourage.

The press of the crowd subsided as the entourage entered a secure backstage area. Only the governor, his handlers, agents, and event staff were allowed in a greenroom next to the stage. William watched the governor's team prep him for the speech, adjusting his tie and wiping a few bits of lint from his shoulder. A man's voice carried over the speakers in the room. The voice thanked the warm up band and began introducing the governor.

"Let's go," Marc whispered, poking William in the shoulder and nodding towards the stage.

William followed Marc up a small flight of steps. Marc led him to an area on the side of the stage behind a curtain.

"Here, put these on," Marc said, handing William a pair of mirrored sunglasses. "Stand next to me and try to look tough. Let's go."

William followed Marc out from behind the curtain. They stood about fifteen feet from a podium at the center of the stage. Two American flags framed the podium. A man was standing at the podium addressing the crowd. William stared out at the packed amphitheater. The crowd stood shoulder-to-shoulder; there wasn't an inch of space anywhere in the sea of humanity. Above the crowd, dozens of American and Gadsden flags waved in the breeze.

"And now," the man at the podium bellowed. "The next President of the United States, Edward Birch!"

It's a Beautiful Day by U2 poured through the speakers. Edward Birch stepped on stage and waved. The crowd erupted. The governor walked up and down the stage waving to the crowd. After several minutes of waving, the governor walked to the podium. He stood and stared at the crowd. In a quick motion, he raised his hand and held out his palm. The riotous applause stopped immediately, as though someone pulled a cosmic plug on the entire crowd, rendering every voice mute. The collective silence was complete. Edward exercised total control over the crowd. He stared down at the sea of faces.

"How do you fare?" Edward asked.

"Hale and hearty, hearty and hale," the crowd boomed collectively. The stage rumbled under William feet.

The governor coolly asked a second time, "How do you fare?"

"Hale and hearty, hearty and hale," came the reply.

William shuffled on his feet as the stage shook against a sonic wave raised by the crowd. William looked into the transfixed faces. The scene reminded him of World War Two videos he played for his students at Beacon Academy; Adolf Hitler standing at a podium, crowds packed shoulder-to-shoulder, reacting to the Fuhrer's every word with arms outstretched in a show of complete devotion.

"Hale and hearty indeed," Governor Birch said. "A president of our nation once said, 'ask not what your country can do for you, ask what you can do for your country.' I come with no such request. I ask you to serve no master. I ask you only to serve as the master of your own house; to exercise control over your own dominion. Do not place your faith in me; do not place your faith in any government; place your faith in the power of self."

The crowd swooned under the Governor Birch's spell, hypnotized into complete submission. Instead of using his power to enslave his minions, Edward Birch used his influence to liberate. For the next hour-and-a-half, William watched the Movement's conquest. In contrast with the countless stump speeches of all previous politicians, Edward Birch's message was simple – power to the people.

Marc leaned over and whispered into William's ear, "Welcome to the revolution."

"Unbelievable," William whispered back. "I had no idea how far we'd come until right now."

Then, ominously, Marc whispered, "Maybe we should have been more careful about what we wished for."

PART 4

A SHINING CITY ON A HILL

October, 2030

WILLIAM stood at the crest of a valley and stared down over his orchard. The trees stretched out in both directions in long, perfectly straight rows. The sun cut a path through thin, wispy tendrils of fog, and shimmered off morning dew that clung to the leaves and grass; the entire orchard glimmered. The apple trees reminded William of his former students at Beacon Academy, attentively arrayed before him, hanging on his every word. A crisp, late-October breeze swept across the valley, offering a subtle hint at the approaching winter chill. The trees were bursting with red and green apples, the branches bowing under the weight of the bounty. Men and women moved methodically between the rows, using three point ladders to reach the upper branches. Baskets overloaded with apples were loaded in a trailer attached to a John Deere tractor bound for the cider mill.

"It's a bumper crop," Mary said.

"Not too shabby," William said. "That new Monsanto pesticide and fertilizer is amazing. Just look at the size of those Macintoshes, they're as large as softballs. Our presses are going to be working overtime."

"It is an amazing product."

"Now that the FDA and EPA is out of the way, the creative spark of corporate America has been unleashed. I'm telling you, Mary, we could end world hunger with crops this bountiful."

In 2028, during his first week in office, President Birch eliminated the Department of Education, Department of Commerce, Department of Energy, and the Environmental Protection Agency. With the stroke of a pen across a series of executive orders, President Birch placed a moratorium on the enforcement of all federal environmental legislation and regulation. The federal government returned power to the states while Congress weeded through volumes of legislation, draining the bureaucratic swamp of red tape. Without the burden of federal regulation and approval, corporations like Monsanto and DuPonte fast-tracked the release of a new generation of products that boosted the output of American farms. The corporations reaped huge profits, and American farms harvested record amounts of produce.

"What time are you meeting with the lawyers?" Mary asked.

"They should be here any minute now."

"Are we really getting the whole thing?"

"Every last acre."

William's radio chirped to life. "Gate one to Mr. Blake...."

William removed a radio clipped to his belt and responded, "This is Mr. Blake."

"Your guests have arrived, sir."

"Send them up to the house."

Mary hung on William's arm as they walked back towards the farmhouse. "I just can't believe it," she said. "Remember all those hikes we took when we were in college. To think then that someday we'd own the whole thing, it just blows my mind."

"This purchase should complete the estate. By the time I finish breakfast, we'll be the largest landholders in the State of Connecticut."

"Good luck," Mary said.

"It's not really a matter of luck anymore. The good Lord has blessed us with all the luck we could have hoped for, now it's a matter of negotiation."

William gave Mary a kiss on the cheek and watched her head off to tend to James and the twins. He walked into the kitchen and poured himself a cup of coffee, and then walked outside onto a veranda at the back of the farmhouse. William sipped the brew as he sat back in an Adirondack chair under a gazebo next to an in-ground pool.

"Mr. Blake," one of the house servants called sheepishly. "Your guests have arrived."

Three men stepped onto the veranda. Two of the men were dressed in crisp Brooks Brothers business suits, and one was dressed in the olive drab and green uniform of a Connecticut State Department of Environmental Protection officer.

"Gentlemen," William said, extending a hand to each of the men in business suits. The attorneys introduced themselves. William asked how they fared, and was comforted when they each replied, "Hale and hearty, hearty and hale." The attorneys fawned over William as he offered them a seat and directed the house servants to bring out refreshments. William turned to the DEP officer and extended his hand, "I'm William Blake, it's nice to meet you."

The man refused to shake William's hand. "Officer McFarlane," he said curtly.

"Won't you please have a seat?"

"I prefer to stand."

The two attorneys for the state shifted uncomfortably in their chairs. "Mr. McFarlane," one of the attorneys said. "There's no need to be discourteous. We are guests in Mr. Blake's home. Let's not make this an unpleasant experience for anyone involved in this transaction."

"Please, sit down. Let me offer you something to eat or drink," William said.

"I'd sooner take a meal with Satan himself. I have no interest in being here any longer than necessary. Let's just get it over with. Is there somewhere I can lay this out?" Officer McFarlane asked, holding up a long tube.

"The table here will be fine," William said.

Officer McFarlane opened the tube and removed a three-foot-by-three-foot topographical map. He unrolled the map on the table and placed silverware on the corners to hold the ends down. The topographical map detailed the elevation and GPS coordinates for Sleeping Giant State Park.

One of the attorneys removed a document from his briefcase. "This is the deed," he said. "All the GPS coordinates are documented according to this map. I just got off the phone with your attorney and the governor. The state has agreed to the terms of your last and final offer. I am authorized to sign the agreement."

William rubbed his chin. Even though the terms were agreed to, he didn't want to appear overly anxious. For twenty-five million dollars, he would take full possession of Sleeping Giant State Park. His estate holdings would span fifty square miles of Southern Connecticut.

"It's a real shame," Officer McFarlane said. "I hope you'll reconsider raping the public like this."

"Excuse me," one of the attorneys said, turning briskly to face Officer McFarlane.

William held out his hand. "No, it's okay. Officer McFarlane has something he wants to get off his chest. Let him say his peace."

"I see what you and your Movement has done; pillaging the state like this, it's a shame. You should all be thrown in prison."

"Prison, huh. That seems a bit extreme," William said. "I'm paying a fair market value for this property, what public trust have I violated?"

"I've spent twenty-five years as a DEP officer in this state. I've committed my adult life to protecting public land. To see it all slip away in four election cycles is an outrage. A few signatures across a piece of paper, money shifting from one account to another, and poof, all public resources are transferred to private ownership – it's beyond my ability to comprehend."

"You love this park, don't you?" William asked, tapping the map lightly.

"I love it dearly. It's one of Connecticut's treasures."

"If you love it so much, why would you leave it in the hands of a public agency like yours? You must see that you can't protect it and maximize its value. You should welcome this transfer."

"Welcome it? Bullshit. I see through all your self-sufficiency and rugged individualist bullshit. The government is collapsing from within. And what's going to replace it? Greedy oligarchs like you who are going to destroy the land."

"That's enough," one of the attorneys snapped. "You're here to help facilitate this sale, that's all. You're out of line."

"No, he's not. I welcome this conversation," William said. Both attorneys and Officer McFarlane stared at William. "It's refreshing to find a few holdouts who still believe that the public good is something that can be forced on free citizens. Officer McFarlane has clearly invested many years working for the state. I'm sure he enjoyed the artificial authority he was handed. He must be disappointed to see his agency dismantled."

"My agency along with just about every other state agency."

"That's right. So, let me ask you something, do you believe that preserving public space like Sleeping Giant is good for us?"

"Yes, of course."

"I agree with you. And, if it is good for us, then why do you believe that it won't be preserved? Why do you believe that only the government is capable of managing this land?"

"Because I know the history of Sleeping Giant. I know what happened when it was in private hands."

"Enlighten me."

"In 1924, the park was used as a quarry. If you look at the park from afar, you can see that half of the giant's head is gone, chipped away to harvest rock and stone by a private corporation. When the people of Hamden saw the giant's head slowly being chipped away, they formed an association to protect it. The association purchased the land from the corporation. It entered a trust and was eventually turned over to the state to manage and protect," Officer McFarlane said.

"Ah, see, you've just made my point. It wasn't government that stopped the destruction; it was a collection of individuals who banded together to protect their community. Sleeping Giant's preservation had nothing to do with government. If anything, government has only gotten in the way, which has led to more destruction of the land."

"What kind of twisted logic is that?" Officer McFarlane asked.

"It's not twisted at all. I've hiked Sleeping Giant countless times. I'm disgusted by what I see. The garbage, graffiti, and neglect that park is subject to is an outrage, and no one's doing a darn thing to stop it. The DEP's care for the park has been a disgrace."

"Yeah, well, after four election cycles of Republican governors, our budget has been slashed to the bone. What do you expect? We don't have the resources."

"Ah, there you go, the typical government argument, more, more, more; give us more, tax the people more, throw money at the problem. You're wrong. All the taxing and spending in the world isn't going to protect the land and maximize its value. You see, I know my history, too. If that park had stayed in the hands of the original citizens who banded together to purchase the quarry, instead of being turned over to the state, if it had been loved and tended to by a community of local citizens who recognize its value, then how well would it be preserved? Do you think people like that would have allowed the park to fall into the deplorable condition it's in now? Of course not. By turning it over to the state, you guaranteed is destruction."

"More twisted logic."

"Not at all. You assume that I'm going to turn that park back into a quarry and finish beheading Sleeping Giant. You're wrong. Look," William said, fanning an arm out over the view of his orchards. "I live here. Sleeping Giant is my home, my neighbor. I have every incentive to protect her. Her abuse is my abuse. Do you really think a bunch of bureaucrats in Hartford can do a better job preserving and maximizing the value of this land than me? You place your faith in government; my faith is in the people."

"You'll be stopped. I just hope it isn't too late to put an end to this insanity," Officer McFarlane said.

"The arc of history bends towards liberty. The people are getting a true taste of freedom. They're going to become addicted to it. I understand how hard that adjustment is going to be for state employees like you. But, in time, you too will come around, and when you do, you will see the error of your ways. Right now, you're just afraid."

"Afraid?"

"Yes, of course. You see your authority melting away, and with it, your livelihood. I'm sure that must be terrifying," William said with a calm, deliberative tone. In his voice, he felt himself channeling the magnetic charm of Edward Birch, as though the universe had loaned him the same hypnotic power of persuasion. "You have to trust me; more importantly, you have to trust yourself. When you are free from the bonds of government, you will reap the full bounty of liberty. As for your livelihood, you have a valuable skill set that will be in demand if you trust in yourself and your skills."

Officer McFarlane took a slight step backwards and dropped his chin. "I don't know what I'm going to do," he whimpered. "I have a family to support. The DEP is all I've ever known."

William stepped forward and placed an arm around his shoulder. "You're going to be fine. Instead of the state, you're going to come work for me, or someone like me. I need good men like you to help me manage and protect this land; people who know and love this park; people who can help me maximize its value. You are about to be handed true authority, and the unfettered ability to truly protect this land." William removed the radio from his belt and said, "Mr. Blake to Mr. Crocco."

The radio crackled. A voice carried onto the veranda. "Go ahead," Crocco said.

"Adrian, I have someone I want you to meet. His name is McFarlane. Please meet him at Gate One."

"Yes, sir."

William placed the radio on the table. "Adrian Crocco is a foreman on my estate, he's a good man. Meet with him. Tell him your background. There is a place for you and your family in my organization, if you're interested."

"I'd like that."

William raised his hand and signaled to one of the house servants. "Please show Mr. McFarlane to Gate One."

"Thank you, sir," McFarlane said.

William and the attorneys watched the officer leave. William sat at the table and removed a pen from his shirt pocket.

"All right, let's get this done," William said.

"That was a very kind gesture," one of the attorneys said.

"What was?" William asked.

"Offering that man a job."

"Kindness had nothing to do with it. I need the service of men like Officer McFarlane. He has nothing to worry about; his skill set will serve him well as we advance as a society of individuals who embrace and are embraced by communities formed around the concept of free association. In the right community, he will become a valuable asset. He just needs to get over his fear, and learn to trust in himself. Frankly, the only people on this veranda who have anything to worry about are you two gentlemen. Take my advice; if I were you, I'd start developing some new skills. Learn to use your hands for something. I don't see much use for pencil-pushing lawyers in the new world order."

William signed the documents, rolled up the map, slid the map into the canister, and said goodbye to the attorneys. He carried the canister with him to his office on the second floor of the farmhouse. He removed the map and unrolled it on his desk. He leaned forward with his elbows on the desk, and studied the topography. He picked up his radio and spoke, "Blake to Crocco."

"Go ahead Mr. Blake."

"I need a transport. Please have someone bring the Polaris up to the house. I need a lift to Butterworth."

"Yes, sir. Transport in fifteen."

"Let Butterworth know I'm on the way. I will be riding this afternoon," William said

"Yes, sir. Will you need a security detail?"

"Yes, two riders."

"Roger. Transport in fifteen and a security detail will meet you at Butterworth."

On his way out, William checked in on Mary. He found her playing with James on the floor in the living room. The twins were down for their afternoon nap.

"Hey, there you are. So, how'd it go?" Mary asked.

"Done deal. We are the proud owners of Sleeping Giant."

"How exciting," Mary said. She stood, lifted James off the ground, and carried him to William. James reached for his father when they were within an arm's length.

"Hey there," William said, gathering James into his arms. "Oh, my goodness you're getting so big." William gave James a kiss on the forehead and placed him on the floor. "I'm heading down to Butterworth. I'm gonna take a ride up Sleeping Giant this afternoon."

"Be careful," Mary said.

"Always. I'll be back before dark."

William gave Mary a soft kiss on the cheek, and walked outside. A farmhand drove a Polaris all-wheel-drive vehicle up to the porch. William sat in the passenger seat and directed the driver to take him to Butterworth. The driver put the vehicle in gear and drove down a gently sloping valley. Farmhands tending the orchards removed their hats and waved as Mr. Blake rode through the rows of apple trees. The Polaris climbed a rise. Lush fields spanned out towards the western boundary of the estate. Cornfields swayed in a soft breeze, the stalks bristling with fat, green husks. Combines would be rolling over the fields by the end of the week, reaping the year's bounty of feed corn and hay. The Polaris zipped down a narrow dirt road and bounded onto a paved secondary road leading to Butterworth Farm.

Two farmhands dressed in jeans, flannel shirts, and workbooks greeted the Polaris. The farmhands led William into the barn, where three horses were saddled and ready to ride.

"Where are we riding today, Mr. Blake?" One of the farmhands asked.

"Let's open them up across the polo fields and the old par five, and then we'll take the white trail up to the summit."

William climbed into the saddle. The farmhands double-checked the action on their rifles and snapped the safeties shut. They slid the rifles into leather saddle scabbards and climbed onto the horses. William led the men out of the barnyard to the edge of a long pasture used for Sunday afternoon polo matches. He kicked his heels into the side of his horse and screamed, "Ya ya, let's go, ya ya."

The horse reared back on its' hooves and leapt forward. The horse broke into a trot, then a cantor, and finally a full gallop across the field. William leaned slightly to the right and gently tugged the reins, directing the horse off the polo field and down the fifth-hole fairway of a former nine-hole golf course that he added to his estate shortly after acquiring Butterworth Farm. When he reached the end of the fairway, William pulled back on the reins and said, "Whoa, easy big fella... whoa." The horse slowed to a trot, then a walk, and finally stopped. William waited for the farmhands to catch up. The farmhands and a Springer Spaniel that belonged to one of the farmhands pulled up next to William. William led the men into a thicket trees, and down to a brook that ran along the edge of the golf course. The brook served as the eastern boundary of his estate. The horses and the dog stopped at the brook and took a long drink of water from the bubbling currents.

"You said the white trail, right?" One of the farmhands asked.

"Yes."

"Are you absolutely sure you want to go that way?"

"Yes. I want to see if the encampment is still there," William said.

"They're definitely still there," the farmhand said.

"I want to see it for myself. I have a message to deliver."

The farmhands loosened the tie downs on their rifle scabbards. They pulled the rifles upwards; making it easier to yank the guns free if needed in a hurry. The horses walked slowly along the bank of the brook, and then onto a trail marked with white dots. The trail snaked around the edge of Sleeping Giant into a picnic area at the entrance to the park. William smelled the smoldering fires of the encampment when they entered the picnic area. He pulled back on the reins and the horse stopped. William stared at the encampment. The residents arranged their tents and pop-up trailers in a haphazard semi-circle around the picnic area.

"Disgusting indigents," William said.

"What's that, sir?" A farmhand asked.

"Nothing, come on," William said, kicking his horse.

"I wouldn't head in there if I were you, sir. I recommend calling for some back-up first," a farmhand said.

William shot the farmhand a menacing glare. The farmhand lowered his eyes, kicked his horse, and followed William into the encampment. William rode through the center of the encampment, staring at the ragtag group of drug addicts, alcoholics, and vagrants.

Reforms to the nation's social safety net displaced a wave of leeches when the government eliminated Section Eight housing, food stamps, Medicaid, Social Security disability, and unemployment insurance. Those individuals who couldn't shake their dependence on government handouts formed ragtag communities of the disenfranchised and indigent. Encampments of the wretched were becoming a regular feature of life on what was left of America's public land. William and other Movement officials were enraged when the media began referring to the encampments as *Birchvilles*.

William rode to the end of the encampment, and then turned and kicked his horse. The horse trotted through the center of the camp, crashing through a spit grill hanging over an open fire. Pans of water and a cast iron coffee pot collapsed into the fire. The fire sizzled and barked a hail of sparks and embers. The horse leapt away from the fire. William yanked on the reins, regained control of the horse, and turned the animal around to face the encampment. Residents emerged from their tents and trailers, staring up at William with wide, bloodshot eyes.

"Listen up you huddled mass of human excrement. My name is William Blake. I am the owner of this land. As of right now, you are all trespassing. You will vacate this park within twenty-four hours, or you will be forcibly removed. Now start packing your shit up."

"What if we don't?" A man in a tattered and filthy Boston Red Sox sweatshirt shouted.

"This time tomorrow my men will be standing at this very site. Anyone still here will be severely beaten. Anything left in this camp will be burned."

"Where are we supposed to go?" A woman asked.

"Your problem. Try getting yourselves cleaned up and go find a job. You all disgust me."

The Springer Spaniel began barking wildly. William turned and saw two men creeping up behind his horse. One man was holding a baseball bat, and the other man held an ax handle. The dog barked and growled at the squatters. A shot rang out. The squatters reeled around and stared down the barrels of two .30-06 Springfield rifles.

"Degenerate trash," William hissed.

William kicked the side of his horse and pulled the reins upward and to the right. The horse jumped forward and spun one hundred and eighty degrees. William hollered, "Ya ya," and kicked the side of the horse. The horse responded by galloping toward the squatter holding an ax handle. William leaned back in his saddle, slid his right foot out of the stirrup, and kicked the man in the side of the head with his right heel. A wet crunch and the sound of hooves trampling the ground echoed through the camp. The man collapsed to the ground. William pulled back on the reins and turned to face the encampment.

"Twenty-four hours, you disease-ridden mob. Get off my land. If you've got nowhere to go, then here, take this." William reached into a saddlebag, removed a length of rope, and threw it to the ground. "My gift to you. Go fashion yourselves a noose and feel free to borrow one of my tree branches. You're useless, all of you, this nation has no further use for you; you've taken enough."

William dug his heels into the sides of the horse. The horse trotted a few hundred yards up the white trail. William pulled back on the reins and waited for the farmhands to catch up.

"Good job back there," William said.

"That was one ballsy move, Mr. Blake," a farmhand said. "Those people can be unpredictable; they'd slit your throat for a dime bag or handle of rotgut whiskey. They've been getting more and more desperate lately. We found a few of them casing the barnyard last week. Later, half dozen chickens were missing from the coop."

"I heard about that. We're not going to put up with that nonsense anymore. I just purchased Sleeping Giant. They're trespassing on private property, my property."

"You gonna clean 'em out?"

"Yup. Twenty-four hours, that's all they've got left. Come on, let's head up the Giant and see what else we have in store. I heard there's another encampment at the castle," William said.

William led the men up the white trail. Heat radiated from the horses' necks and hindquarters, steaming in the crisp afternoon chill. The fall foliage along the trail burst forth in a cascade of yellow, orange, and red. The season had already peaked; the gray and brown of the woods overpowered the colors of fall, threatening to cast Sleeping Giant into the dull, flat iron embrace of winter. The men rode in silence, lulled by the gentle sway and squeak of the leather tack, and clipity-clop of hooves. The white trail connected to the blue trail. The blue trail was the largest of the trails, snaking from the stone castle at the top of Sleeping Giant, down to a parking lot across from Quinnipiac University. William immediately recognized the well-worn trail. In normal times, the trail would be crawling with hikers and joggers, and Quinnipiac students clearing their minds with a crisp, late-autumn walk. Instead, the trail was eerily quiet. William pulled on the reins and stared up and down the trail.

"Everything all right?" A farmhand asked.

"Quiet," William said. "Follow me."

William led the men off the trail. The horses tromped a few hundred feet through the trees.

"We'll tie the horses here and walk the rest of the way," William said, throwing his leg over the saddle and lowering himself to the ground.

William and the farmhands tied the horses to low hanging tree branches. The farmhands removed their rifles from the saddle scabbards, and followed William through the forest up the side of Sleeping Giant.

"Why aren't we riding up?" A farmhand whispered.

"There's a perfect firing position from the top of the castle. We're going to scout it before we go tromping in there with a bull's eye painted on our foreheads," William said.

When they reached the top of the mountain, William paused, hunched over, and held his arm out to halt the farmhands. He crawled a few hundred feet into the brush on his belly, and pushed back branches to get a view of the castle. The castle was crawling with men and women. A handful of children played in the dirt and grass in front of a fire pit.

"Give me your rifle," William said to one of the farmhands.

William took the rifle and peered through the scope. He slowly moved the rifle back and forth, watching the crosshairs traverse the ragtag band of indigents.

"The infestation is worse than I thought," William said, holding the crosshairs on the forehead of a particularly decrepit looking squatter.

"I don't see any guns," a farmhand said.

"I'm sure they're armed. They must have a few handguns tucked away, at least."

"Are we going up there to talk to them?"

"No, we'll send a posse up here tomorrow to deliver their eviction notice. I don't want to lose the element of surprise."

THE windows on the farmhouse rattled violently as the blades of the helicopter cut the air. William, Mary, and James watched from the veranda behind the farmhouse as the chopper descended into an open field a few hundred yards away. James bounced up and down on the balls of his feet, pointing at the helicopter as it settled to the ground.

"We go in that, we go in that?" James asked excitedly.

"Sure, honey. I'll take you for a ride this afternoon," William said.

William had ordered the helicopter to support the raid. If needed, the air support would provide cover for the posse, and evacuate any wounded. William had been monitoring the sweep of the vagrant camps all morning.

The last time they spoke, Crocco reported no resistance at the camp at the base of the park. The vagrants had cleared out. Two of the vagrants took William's advice; the bodies were found hanging from a tree. William's men cut the bodies down and buried the vagrants in a shallow grave. Crocco was concerned that some of the vagrants at the base encampment had walked up to the castle to warn the residents at the top of Sleeping Giant that a posse was coming. If that was the case, Crocco was worried that the vagrants at the castle would have had twenty-four hours to prepare a defense.

William walked into the kitchen so Mary and James couldn't overhear his conversation. He removed a radio from his belt. "Blake to Crocco," William said into the radio. There was no response. There hadn't been a response for over an hour. William assumed that Crocco turned the radio off while he led the men up the blue trail. They still had the element of surprise, and didn't want the chirp of a radio giving away their advantage. "Blake to Crocco," William said a second time, anxiously waiting for a response.

Static filled the air when Crocco keyed his radio. William could hear voices of men screaming profanity, ordering the squatters to *move your ass, you fucking scumbags.* "Go ahead, Mr. Blake," Crocco said.

"What's the latest?"

"We just finished taking the encampment at the top of Sleeping Giant. They were waiting for us. A sniper picked off two of our men from the top of the castle. But he didn't have enough ammunition to hold us off for long."

In the background, William heard a woman screaming for help and begging someone to stop.

"What's that?" William asked.

"Nothing, sir. The boys are just having a little fun with one of the vagrant women."

William heard a ripping sound that he recognized as clothes being torn. A man's voice screamed in the background, "Leave my wife alone, she didn't do nothing." The radio cut-off Crocco's voice in mid-stream as he hollered at the men to, "Shut that bitch…" When Crocco's voice returned to the radio, there was no background noise. "We're all set, sir," Crocco said. "I can pretty much assure you that these squatters won't be back any time soon. We're definitely delivering our message loud and clear."

"Nice work," William said. "I have a helicopter standing by. Do you need air support?"

"No. We have things under control."

"Do you need a medical evacuation? You said the vagrants got two of our men."

"Yes. Two dead. Two more were wounded before the sniper ran out of ammunition."

William's mind flashed to the community of Blue Hills' employees who lived in a condominium complex called Heritage Woods. The Heritage Woods condominiums were constructed on farmland sold off by the Bergeron family during the recession in the 1980s. The condominiums were cheap and poorly built, but their proximity to the orchard made them prime real estate for Blue Hills' permanent and seasonal employees. William began purchasing the Heritage Woods condominiums one-by-one shortly after he closed the deal on Blue Hills. He offered a purchase price well above market value, which encouraged most of the residents to sell. There were still a few units with residents who didn't work for William, but the majority of the fifty units was rented to Blue Hills' farmhands, laborers, and staff who worked the farm and cider press. William wondered if news of the dead farmhands had reached Heritage Woods, yet.

"Who did we lose?" William asked.

"New guys. They weren't deep in the community," Crocco said. "Just a couple of drifters who were helping us with the harvest. They weren't planning to stay long. They won't be missed."

William breathed a sigh of relief. At least Heritage Woods wouldn't suffer the news that some of its residents had been left widows and orphans. A pair of migrant laborers was a loss, but William calculated the loss was negligible.

"Any idea where they were from? Did they have family in the area?"

"Don't think so?" Crocco said. "Jamaicans. No connections to anyone nearby."

"Okay, then I won't send the helicopter for them."

"What do you want us to do with them?" Crocco asked.

"If you're sure they won't be missed, bury them in the woods. There's no need to parade their bodies back here if no one's around to mourn them. Was anyone wounded?"

"Yes. They're just scratches. One guy had his ear nicked by a bullet - friendly fire. He's a little shook up, but no worse for the wear. One guy sprained an ankle; it might be slight fracture, nothing major. We can bring them back on horseback."

"How many vagrants are dead?"

"Most ran off into the woods. We're still mopping up. Body count is eight for the time being."

"Okay, bury them in the woods, too." William said.

"Got the guys already digging. What do you want us to do with the ones we catch alive?"

"Make sure they get a clear message," William said. "Beat 'em, brand 'em on the neck, and then escort them off Sleeping Giant. Tell them that if they're caught anywhere near Sleeping Giant or Blue Hills in the future, we'll recognize them by the burn. Tell them that next time they'll have a noose around their neck instead of a brand."

"Got it."

"Good. Have regular patrols visit the area for the next few weeks. Patrol size should be no fewer than five men until we're sure we've cleared out the infestation. After we know the camps are gone, we can drop to two-man patrols and cover more area. We're going to have to maintain an active presence in the park for the foreseeable future; at least until word gets out loud and clear that the park is closed to vagrants."

"Yes, sir. I've already assigned a rotation. I don't think we'll have any more trouble with Birchvilles sprouting up on Sleeping Giant."

"You call them Birchvilles one more time and you'll be out of a job. You got me?"

"Yes sir. I'm sorry."

"You should be. You sound like some fucking liberal activist."

"I understand; you're right. I'm sorry. Over and out."

William clipped the radio to his belt and walked outside onto the veranda. "You guys wanna go for a helicopter ride?" William asked. "It's a beautiful fall afternoon. The colors should be amazing."

"Yahoo," James squealed.

"What about the twins?" Mary asked. "Should I go get them?"

"Nah, leave them here, we'll just make it the three of us this afternoon. Tell one of the servants to keep an eye on them," William said.

Mary walked into the farmhouse to tell one of the house servants to keep an eye on Susan and Catherine. William took James by the hand and led him to the helicopter. William lifted James into the helicopter, and helped him put an aviation headset over his ears. William climbed in behind him and put on a headset. The pilot's voice carried through the noise-reducing earphones.

"Are you ready to go, Mr. Blake?" The pilot asked.

"Just a minute. My wife is coming with us."

Mary climbed into the cabin of the helicopter and put on a headset.

"All right," William said. "Ready to go?"

James squealed excitedly, "Ready, Daddy."

"Take us out low and slow over the top of Sleeping Giant, and then run us up and down the shoreline," William said to the pilot.

The helicopter growled to life. The blades cut a deep, concussive, thunk, thunk, thunk, through the air as it lifted off. William stared over Blue Hills Orchard as the helicopter rose. He watched farmhands moving through the orchards, tending to the apple, peach, and nectarine trees.

"Look," William said, pointing to a corn maze that his crews designed in a three-acre square plot. "Cool, huh?" William asked. Mary and James nodded in agreement.

"Smoke," James said, pointing to the top of Sleeping Giant.

The helicopter flew over the castle. Thick tendrils of black smoke floated in the clear blue sky above Sleeping Giant. William stared down at the scene. His men built several bonfires. The men moved in and out of the castle, carrying armloads of sleeping bags, clothes, and camping gear. The men threw the gear into the bonfires, and returned to the castle for additional loads. Several of the men looked up and waved as the helicopter flew over.

"What they doing?" James asked.

"Nothing, honey," William said. "Just a little spring cleaning. They're probably roasting marshmallows."

"Oh, yummy, I want marshmallow. Mom, can I have a marshmallow?" James whined.

The helicopter rose. Late-autumn colors streaked to the north and west as far as the eye could see; to the south and east, a long, blue strip of Long Island Sound cut off the color. Within minutes, the helicopter reached the coastline and flew north over Long Wharf. William stared down, searching for the former campus of Beacon Academy. The helicopter moved too quickly over the area for William to find his bearings in the labyrinth of city streets. The helicopter flew south over New Haven and along the Fairfield Country shoreline. They flew over New York City, circled the Statue of Liberty, and then flew north back towards Blue Hills. The sun was beginning to set as the chopper closed in on New Haven.

"What's that?" William asked, pointing to thick tendrils of smoke that floated high into the sky.

"Looks like a pretty serious fire," the pilot said.

"Let's go check it out," William said.

The helicopter flew towards the Westville section of New Haven, where thick tendrils of smoke billowed into the sky. William's eyes followed the smoke to flames licking the sides and roofs of a row of multifamily houses.

"Geez, look at that," the co-pilot said. "That's pretty messed up."

"What is?" William asked.

"Those firemen. They're just parked there in their trucks watching those houses burn. I don't see a single one of 'em trying to douse the flames."

"Well, that's what you get when you don't pay your association fees," William said.

"What's that?" The co-pilot asked.

"New Haven eliminated almost all city property taxes by privatizing city services like the fire department. Now, if you want fire protection you have to join an association and kick in your fair share. The FD comes out and sticks these little brass badges on all the houses that are current with their dues. No brass badge, no fire service."

"Wow, that's pretty hard core," the pilot said.

"It's not hard core at all; it's called personal responsibility. Why should I expect anyone else to take care my property? People need to learn to take care of themselves. Those flames are a function of natural consequences," William said.

"Yeah, but what about all the people who own houses around them? Even if they paid their association fees, those flames don't know the difference; brass badge or not, your house is a goner if your neighbor's goes up."

"I see the firefighters hosing down the surrounding houses. Look. They're gonna fight the fire when it reaches the responsible homeowners. Like I said, personal responsibility pays off."

"When the fire reaches the oil tank in the basement of that house the whole block is gonna explode," the pilot said. "Soaking those houses isn't gonna do one bit of good."

The helicopter circled the blaze and paused, hovering a few hundred yards over the home. Flames consumed the house. In the window of the third-floor apartment, a man stuck his head out from underneath a stream of black smoke that rolled like an inverted waterfall out the window. The man surveyed the surroundings, and then pulled his head back into the apartment. A moment later, the man leaned out the window holding something in his arms. The man leaned forward, reached down as far as his arms could stretch to minimize the distance separating the third floor from the ground, and opened his hands. A toddler dropped three stories to the sidewalk below. Mary's scream pierced the headset. Mary turned quickly and covered James's eyes. A mother, desperate to escape the blaze, followed the toddler out the window, cradling something in her arms. Then the father jumped, also cradling something tiny and fragile in his arms. A second later, as the pilot predicted, the flames devoured the home's oil tank in the basement and the entire structure was awash in a dazzling fireball. A thick, black tornado of smoke and debris swallowed the entire block.

"Get us out of here," William said.

THE last glimmer of sunlight dipped over Sleeping Giant as the helicopter settled to the ground. Mary carried James into the farmhouse. William followed them into the farmhouse, walked to the kitchen, poured himself a pint of beer, and retired to the den to watch the evening's local newscast. He was anxious to see how the local reporters would cover the blaze in Westville. He turned on the television just as the broadcast began.

"Reporting live from New Haven, Channel 8's Ryan Connors reports from the scene of a deadly fire that raged through a large portion of Westville, and took the lives of two children and their mother, and left a third child and a father in critical condition. Ryan," the newscaster said from the studio.

The newscast switched to an image of a reporter standing in front of the still-smoldering wreckage of several multi-family homes. In the background, firefighters were dousing steaming debris.

"Good evening. This is Ryan Connors reporting live from the Westville section of New Haven, where earlier today the scene behind me was an image of pure carnage."

The broadcast switched from the live shot to video recorded from earlier in the day. The image of four multi-family homes engulfed in flames materialized in high-definition on William's television. The reporter's voice narrated the scene.

"Sometime around One O'clock this afternoon, a blaze broke out in this quiet Westville neighborhood. The blaze quickly spread to surrounding homes. Local fire departments responded to the scene, and fought the blaze for several hours before finally gaining an upper hand on the inferno. The deadly fire claimed the lives of three, including a mother and two infants, and left one man and a toddler severely injured."

William took a long swig from his pint of beer, desperately trying to drown the image of the family leaping from the third-floor window. The live broadcast returned to the screen.

"The cause of this deadly fire is still being investigated. Here with me is Fire Chief Douglas of the Westville Ladder Station Two. Chief, do you have any idea what caused this afternoon's blaze?"

"We're still investigating, but have no definitive leads, yet. Many of these multifamily homes have ancient electrical systems, which have a hard time absorbing the power surges that we've been experiencing lately. If I had to guess, I'd say this was probably an electrical fire that started in the walls and spread through the structure," Fire Chief Douglas said.

"Chief, when our news crew arrived, your men were standing-by while the first home burned. I assume that's because the homes that burned are not members of your association. Is that accurate?"

"Yes. The blaze started in a home that was not part of our association, and then spread to a home that was also not part of our association. We began fighting the blaze when it reached the homes that are members in good standing."

"Chief, to what extent do you credit the privatization of fire services for the spread of this blaze?"

"Motherfucker," William said, draining his pint in one long swig. The political spin that the reporter was putting on the blaze was predictable.

The fire chief bristled for a minute, then turned and faced the camera. "This is a harsh reminder for all property owners in the city of the need to pay your association fees. Much of this could have been prevented if landlords took responsibility for protecting their property."

"Yes, but to what extent do you blame the city for this tragedy? Scenes like this are playing out all over the city ever since the New Haven Board of Aldermen and the Mayor decided to eliminate universal fire protection and replace it with private stations like yours."

William held his breath and waited for the fire chief's response. The man looked younger, so perhaps he wasn't acculturated when unionized fire departments held the city captive, and trapped property owners in a cycle of ever-increasing mill rates.

"As long as property owners are responsible for the safety of their properties, then tragedies like this won't happen. It's when homeowners fail to take personal responsibility that this occurs."

William breathed a sigh of relief. "Good boy," he said to the screen.

"Yes, but," the reporter said. "These are rental properties, the owners don't live here. The people who lost everything, the people who died in this blaze today, they're not the ones responsible for paying the association fees, and yet they're the ones who paid the steepest price. Don't you believe it would be better to go back to a property tax system that funds universal fire coverage?"

"No. I don't think socialism is the answer. The private system works fine," the Chief answered.

"Ata-boy," William said.

"If anything," the Chief continued. "I'd place the blame on deregulation of the power companies. The inconsistent flow of electricity in the city is killing my department. The blackouts and brownouts are bad enough, but the surges through the grid are causing electrical fires in record numbers."

"Oh, shit," William said.

"Thank you, Chief," the reporter said. "Reporting live from Westville, this is Ryan Connors. Back to…"

William turned off the television and walked to the kitchen. He poured himself another pint, and then walked to his office on the second floor. He logged on to his computer and accessed a secure web portal for Movement officials. He stared at a desktop image of Edward Birch standing in front of a crowd in a packed stadium while he waited for the portal to open. When the portal opened, William clicked a link labeled *Movement Communications*. The link directed him to a chat room moderated by a Movement communications facilitator.

The chatroom facilitator wrote, *Good evening, Mr. Blake. How do you fare?*

Hale and hearty, hearty and hale, William wrote.

What can I do for you, sir?

William typed, *Need to report left-wing bias in a local news report. I will take the report now.*

Reporter's name is Ryan Connors. Reporting for Channel 8 News in New Haven, Connecticut. Bias detected at 6:00 p.m. local broadcast time on Monday, November 5, 2030. Reporting on fire in New Haven. Bias related to city's recent moves to privatize fire protection services.

Report received. Investigation will begin. Thank you for your report. Have a nice evening.

William logged out of the chat room. He leaned back in his chair and finished his pint in one long swig. "There you go, Ryan Connors. Welcome to a world of pain," William said to the empty room. He slid open the bottom drawer of his desk, removed a half-pint of Jameson Irish Whiskey, and poured two fingers into his pint glass.

William clicked a link in the portal titled *News Feed*. The news feed linked him to a section of the portal that detailed national and international news, and explained how The Movement communications officials were managing the reporting of events. The news feed also outlined official talking points, and provided guidance on how to detect any left-wing spin that might be left in the few unbiased outlets that remained on the national media stage.

William scanned the international headlines on the site: *Chinese and Russian Troops Mass on Manchurian Border... Japanese Troops Evacuate Citizens from Sunkakhu Islands - Attack Imminent... Taiwanese, South Korean and Japanese Military Forces Begin Joint Military Drill - China Calls Drill Act of War... Saudi Troops Break Iranian Defense, Pour Into Baghdad... Israel Annexes Lebanon... European Leaders Sign Pact - Maastricht Treaty Declared Null and Void.*

William read the headlines, but didn't click on any of the reports. He knew the gist of the evolving stories, and understood the talking points. He sipped his whiskey, and reflected on the geopolitical realignment underway.

The United States no longer played the role of the world's police officer. The Birch Administration orchestrated America's withdrawal from the United Nations, NATO, and every other international entanglement. The Birch Administration's isolationist policies complemented the hollowing out of America's military, and drawdown of American troops in bases around the world.

International affairs did not concern William; domestic challenges consumed William's attention and the attention of most Americans, and if there was any domestic reality that threatened The Movement's agenda, it was unfolding events in the Mid-West. William clicked the link to *Domestic Affairs* and scanned the headlines: *Miami Struggles to Manage Key's Refugees in Wake of Hurricane Mitchell... Keystone Pipeline Spill Clean Up Continues in Nebraska... Tuberculosis Outbreak Contained... IRS Officially Closed - Federal Reserve Audit Continues... Texas Marshalls Skirmish with Mexican Special Ops... Reservation Natives and Colorado Minutemen Exchange Fire - 12 Killed... Work Continues on Colorado River Dam After Two Explosions at Constructions Site.*

"Fuck, fuck, fuck," William said as he continued reading the headlines. He drained his whiskey and poured two more fingers of Jameson.

There was a knock on the door. William looked up as Mary pushed the door open and stuck her head in the office. "You okay?" She asked.

"Oh, hey, yeah I'm fine. Come in." Mary stepped into the room. "Are the kids asleep?" William asked.

"Yes, out like a light. Why are you dropping the F-bomb in here?"

"Just reading the news."

"What's happening?"

"Stuff is still bad out West."

"The water wars?" Mary asked.

"Yes. Oklahoma's quiet, but Texas and Mexico are at each other's throat. Mexico sent Special Forces across the border; there have been some skirmishes along the Rio Grande."

"That's too bad. But, hey, look on the bright side. That's all a thousand miles away. Things are fine around here."

"I know, but still, we have to keep it together, at least until President Birch is re-elected. We need four more years to finish taking it all apart. Then we'll be able to rest easy."

"Well, try not to let it stress you out. The Lord will provide."

"I know."

"You're a good man, William Blake - a good man. Hurry up and come to bed. I'll help you forget about the news," Mary said.

"I'll be right in."

Mary stepped out of the office. William picked up the half-pint of Jameson and drained the bottle in one shot. He stood up and walked out of the office, lacking any vim or vigor in his step. The fifteen minutes of missionary position sex with Mary promised to be as enjoyable as a farmhouse chore. Before he left the office, William texted his security detail to plan on a trip to Hartford early next week. He hoped the prospect of a visit to the massage parlor would fill his imagination with enough prurient fuel to coax his loins into action when he slipped into his marital bed.

THE smell of bacon and coffee filled the kitchen. William poured cream into his mug and stirred in a spoonful of sugar. The twins played in a playpen in the corner of the room. James sat across the kitchen table from William playing with a Matchbox car instead of eating a mound of scrambled eggs that was quickly turning cold on the plate in front of him.

"Eat your eggs, Buddy. We've got to get going soon," William said.

James took a tiny bite of scrambled eggs and continued playing with the Matchbox car.

"Reverend Flowers shared his sermon with me last night, it's good. Is there anything you would like him to focus on?" Mary asked.

"Focus on? What do you mean?" William asked.

"Do you want him to weave any messages for the farmhands into his sermon? He's very clever at that."

"I don't know. Tell him to keep it light today. The boys did a nice job clearing the vagrants off Sleeping Giant. I want them to know how much I appreciate their work."

"Appreciate them? You put money in their pockets and food on their plates, how much more appreciation are they entitled to?"

"I know, but, come on Mary, the community lost two men in the raid on the vagrant camps, and two more were wounded. Tell Reverend Flowers to go easy today."

"You don't *go easy* when it comes to the Word of the Lord. And I don't think it's wise to spoil the workers, either. Shared values and a firm interpretation of the Word of God hold that community together. We need to make sure that those values are clearly communicated. Don't show them any weakness; if you do, trust me, you'll be sorry."

William finished his coffee and poured himself another cup from a plastic carafe on the table. Mary jumped up from her seat when a man in dark blue jeans and a black shirt with a clerical collar entered the kitchen.

"Reverend Flowers," Mary said. "Good morning, would you like something to eat?"

"No, thank you. A cup of coffee will be nice, but I'm going to wait until after services to fill my stomach," Reverend Flowers said.

"Good morning, Reverend," William said, getting up from the table and retrieving a coffee mug from the cabinet.

"Good morning, William. And how are you today, Sir James?" The Reverend asked, ruffling James's mop of hair.

William looked at Reverend Flowers from the corner of his eye as he placed the coffee mug on the table and filled it from the carafe. At 45-years-old, the Reverend looked younger, as though time had trapped him somewhere in his early thirties. He had stringy, shoulder-length, sandy brown hair that fell in curls around his shoulders. He stood a shade under six feet tall, with narrow shoulders and long, thin arms. When William first met Reverend Flowers, he reminded him of someone, but William couldn't connect the Reverend's face with a name that always seemed on the tip of his tongue. Months later, when William was watching a documentary on America in the 1990s, an image of David Koresh filled the television screen. It was then that William made the connection; Reverend Flowers was the spitting image of the Branch Davidian leader.

"Here you go," William said, sliding the coffee mug across the table. "Would you like cream and sugar?"

"Yes, please," Reverend Flowers said.

"Are you feeling a little more settled?" Mary asked.

"Yes. The accommodations are lovely. I'd be lying if I said I didn't miss Virginia, but Connecticut is starting to grow on me."

Mary met Revered Flowers at an Evangelical church she joined when she and William were living in Charlottesville. She abided the Sunday visits to St. Peter's, but the rest of the week, she attended the Evangelical church, where fire and brimstone sermons mixed with a heavy-handed, literal interpretation of the Old Testament. Reverend Flowers was one of several preachers at the church, and by far the most charismatic. When William and Mary moved back to Connecticut, Mary made William promise that their days as Episcopalians were over. She searched the area for a parish that could satisfy her Evangelical fervor, but the stoic Southern New England ecumenical landscape was too bland for her taste. With a little cajoling, Mary convinced William to bring Reverend Flowers to Blue Hills to start an in-house parish. William agreed. Reverend Flowers moved into the pool house adjacent the farmhouse, and began preaching every Sunday morning in the Blue Hills warehouse next to the cider press.

"We should start heading over," Mary said. "James, would you like to ring the bell."

"Yes," James said excitedly.

James jumped out of his seat and ran out of the kitchen. Mary and William each lifted one of the twins out of the playpen, and followed Reverend Flowers and James outside to the front porch. They found James jumping up and down under a triangular, cast iron dinner bell that hung from the eaves of the overhang at the top of the porch steps. William handed Susan to Reverend Flowers and lifted James. James reached up and grabbed a cast iron wand that hung from a leather strap. James used the wand to strike the triangular bell as hard as he could. The bell dinged softly under the toddler's blows.

"Good job, Buddy," William said, setting James down gently. "Should I give it a try now?"

"Yes, yes, Daddy," James bubbled, putting his hands over his ears.

William wrapped his fingers around the wand and began swinging the wand inside the triangle. The wand landed a powerful strike against each side of the triangle. The separate clang, clang, clang of the bell combined into a single sustained ring that echoed clear and loud over the orchard, reaching all the way down to the still-sleepy community at Heritage Woods. Minutes later, a line of men, women, and children appeared on Blue Hills Road walking towards the farmhouse. Some of the older children took a short cut through the orchard, running and skipping as a crow flies through the apple trees in the direction of the cider mill. The adults from the community trudged in their Sunday best up the paved road, carrying infants, herding toddlers, and pushing strollers. The line of farmhands and laborers wound past the farmhouse. The men removed their John Deere hats, and women nodded in a show of respect to Mary, William, and the Reverend. Mary stood at the top of the steps, arms folded in front of her like a schoolmarm taking attendance. When the last family in the procession walked past the porch, Mary carried the twins and led James off the porch steps towards the cider mill. William and Reverend Flowers followed.

"You have built something amazing here," Reverend Flowers said.

"Thank you."

"I appreciate being a part of it; part of what America really should be – a shining city on a hill."

"The Lord has been very kind to us," William said. William felt Reverend Flowers bristle, and heard him suck at his teeth. "What's wrong?" William asked.

"Calling the Lord *kind* always concerns me; the Lord may be *just,* but that is far different than kind. I've never found an ounce of kindness in the true Lord."

William contemplated Revered Flowers' words as they walked the rest of the way to the cider mill in silence. William always sought solace and comfort in the Lord; whereas, he knew Mary sought firm rebuke. It was clear that Reverend Flowers also chose to wield the Word of the Lord like an iron fist. In days past, when their faith was a matter of personal conviction, that difference could linger quietly in the background of their relationship. Now that he and Mary commanded the loyalty of an entire community, William wondered where that iron fist would lead.

*   *   *

November, 2035

William carried a birthday cake outside onto the veranda. The crowd around the table parted for William as a chorus of *Happy Birthday to You* began. William placed the cake in front of the twins. The twins stared at two flickering candles in the shape of the number five. The song ended with an out-of-tune *tooooo youuuuu....* The twins stared up at William.

"Go ahead, girls. Blow out the candles," William said.

The girls leaned forward and began blowing on the candles. After several huffs, the flames went out in a puff of black smoke. The guests offered a gentle round of applause. Mary leaned forward, cut two enormous slices from the sheet cake, and set the slices in front of Susan and Catherine. The girls looked up at Mary and waited patiently.

"Go ahead," Mary said.

The twins dug into the cake with both hands. Mary cut a third giant slice of cake and set it in front of James. James plunged a fork into the yellow cake, and shoved a gigantic forkful into his mouth. Mary began cutting smaller pieces and handing them out to the partygoers.

A hand landed on William's shoulder. William turned and faced Crocco.

"What?" William asked.

"I'm sorry to disturb you, sir. But I need a minute," Crocco said.

William followed Crocco out of the crowd to the edge of the pool. "What is it?"

"The shipment is here."

"It's here, right now? Geez, they're only three days late."

"I know. I had the truck pull up to the cider mill. I have several men keeping an eye on things. The driver won't let us unload anything until he talks to you."

"I have to deal with this shit on my daughters' birthday. What the fuck."

"I'm sorry, sir. It'll just take a minute, and then the men and I will unload everything."

William and Adrian walked around the farmhouse and headed towards the cider mill. William spotted a box truck parked in front of the main entrance to the cider mill. The men from Blue Hills stood off to the side, staring suspiciously at the truck driver and two deliverymen who accompanied the driver. All the men were armed. The Blue Hills men had shotguns and rifles slung haphazardly over their shoulders. The deliverymen wore compact Sig MPX submachine guns tight across their chests. If a firefight broke out, the Blue Hills men wouldn't stand a chance; they'd be mown down in a hail of 9 mm rounds before the single-shot .30-6 rifles and pump action shotguns could put up much of a defense. William approached the strangers. The driver stepped forward. The deliverymen separated a few feet and covered the driver. The Blue Hills men fanned out around the truck to cover William, each planning his next move if the shit hit the fan.

"Are you William Blake?" The driver asked.

"Yup. It took you guys long enough to get here. You were supposed to be here three days ago."

"Interstate travel sure ain't what it used to be," the driver said. "I need to confirm your identity before I turn this stuff over to you."

The driver removed a scanner from his pocket and held it up to William's face. The deliverymen shuffled uncomfortably on their feet, and flicked the safeties on the Sig MPXs' to the firing position. A retina scanner flashed a red light in William's eyes. The scanner beeped, confirming William's identity as the buyer. The deliverymen flipped the safeties back to the safe position.

"It's all yours, Mr. Blake," the driver said. He turned to face his men. "All right boys, let 'em get this stuff unloaded so we can get out of here."

The deliverymen opened the back of the box truck and pulled out a ramp extending from the bed of the truck to the ground. The Blue Hills men began unloading green, military-issue crates of various shapes and sizes. Stenciled on the side of the crates were the letters U S A. William, Crocco, and the driver walked to the side of the warehouse and opened a garage door leading to a shipping bay. They walked through the bay to a set of stairs leading to an underground bunker.

"You can go back to the birthday party, sir," Crocco said. "I'll oversee the unloading and inventorying of the shipment."

"This is a three million dollar investment. I think I'll stick around for a little while to make sure I'm getting my money's worth," William said, staring at the driver.

"I don't think you're gonna be disappointed," the driver said, fidgeting a cigarette out of a pack of Marlboro. "Don't mind if I smoke, do you?"

"That's fine," William said.

"You must have some friends in high places," the driver said, flicking a lighter and igniting the end of his cigarette. "This is top shelf stuff. We pulled it right out of Fort Bragg. A full bird colonel personally oversaw the manifest. No ifs, ands, or buts - we drove right out the front gate like we owned the place."

"If it was so easy, then why are you three days late?" William asked.

"Ride up from North Carolina was a bitch. Have you tried crossing state lines on the interstate highways these days? The tolls, weigh-ins, and other bullshit is getting out of control. We sure as shit didn't want any state troopers sniffing around the back of the truck. We stuck to the secondary and back roads, which, I'm here to tell you, ain't no picnic either. Every local-yokel from here to Fayetteville has some toll or inspection point set up; everyone's looking for a payoff."

The men walked down four flights of stairs, deep into the professionally constructed bunker complex. The construction of the bunker took nearly two years to complete, and cost upwards of six million dollars. The bunker was equipped with self-contained water, air, septic and electric, a mountain of freeze-dried food, and a hydroponic greenhouse. The specifications called for the structure to withstand an indirect nuclear strike, and sustain a party of twenty-five people for two full years. William led the men through a common area, sickbay, and bunkroom to a space near the back of the bunker lined with empty racks, gun safes, and cast iron cabinets.

"Holy shit," the driver said. "This is some hardcore doomsday prepping. You getting ready for the zombie apocalypse or what?"

"Something like that," William said.

Two men carried the first crate into the arsenal. "One at a time, boys," Crocco said. "This is gonna take a while to unload and inventory, but we're going to get it done right the first time. Tell the boys to stack the crates outside the room, we'll bring 'em in one at a time, and stow the weapons slowly and methodically."

One of the men stepped out of the arsenal to relay Crocco's orders. The other man kneeled, unlocked the crate, and threw back the lid on a neatly lined rack of six M4 carbine assault rifles.

"Isn't that pretty," William said. He reached down, took one of the rifles and lifted it out of the crate. "That's what I'm talking about," he said, pulling back the bolt and snapping it shut.

"It's all here," the driver said, handing William the manifest.

William reviewed the manifest: Fifty Beretta M9 pistols, twenty-five M4 carbines and twenty-five M16 assault rifles, twelve M40 sniper rifles, twenty-five Mossberg 590A1 semi-automatic shotguns, six M249 light machine guns, two M32 multiple shot grenade launchers, and a full assortment of accessories, including tripods, night vision, suppressors, laser sighting, and tactical lights. Each of the weapons came with thousands of rounds of ammunition. William special-ordered ammunition reloading equipment, including presses, case preparation, measures, scales, brass, casings, bullets, and hundreds of pounds of gunpowder.

"It looks good," William said to Crocco. "Get all this stuff inventoried and stowed away. I'm heading back to the party. I'll be back tonight to check on things. Make sure the arsenal is locked up tighter than a drum; from now on, no one's allowed down here without my permission, got it?"

"Yes, sir."

WILLIAM sat on the edge of Catherine's bed and finished reading the story. "Good night noises everywhere," William said, closing the book and placing it on the nightstand.

"Can we read another?" Susan asked.

"Not tonight, Honey. Now hop into bed."

Susan jumped down from her sister's bed and climbed into her matching twin bed a few feet away. William pulled the covers over Catherine's shoulders and gave her a kiss on the forehead. He paused and inhaled deeply, swimming in the sweet scent of his daughter's hair. He walked around the bed and tucked in Susan, also pausing for a kiss and a deep waft of her matching scent.

"Did you both have a nice birthday?"

"Yes, Daddy," the girls replied in unison.

"Good, five-years-old, you're big girls now. Sweet dreams. Don't let the bedbugs bite. I love you."

William flipped off the light and stepped out of the girls' bedroom. He walked down the hallway to James' bedroom. James was sitting at his desk building with Legos.

"All right little man, time for bed," William said.

James jumped into bed. William sat next to him and read a chapter from *The Lion the Witch and the Wardrobe*. William closed the book and ran his fingers through his son's hair, pushing it back and landing a soft kiss on James' forehead. "All right Buddy, time to get some shut-eye," William said.

"Okay, Daddy. Daddy?"

"Yes."

"Can we go horseback riding tomorrow?"

"Sure. Now, lights out."

William turned the light off and gave James another kiss on the forehead. He walked downstairs and found Mary in the kitchen putting dishes away.

"Nice job today, Hon," William said.

"Thanks. Even though you disappeared in the middle of the party. Where did you go anyway?"

"The weapons arrived today."

"Right in the middle of the party, that figures."

"Yeah, well, anyway, they're here. Crocco and some of the farmhands loaded them under the cider mill. I'll show you them tomorrow."

"Okay. I'm just about cleaned up here. I'm gonna turn in. Are you coming to bed?"

"In a bit. I need to do some work first," William said.

"No rest for the weary."

"Something like that."

"Don't stay up too late. We have a full day tomorrow."

"I won't be on the estate tomorrow. I have to head into Hartford to meet with Governor Sterling. We have a bit more convention prep to get through."

"Can't you do it by Skype?"

"I would, but I need to meet face-to-face. I don't have one hundred percent faith in the woman. I need to look her in the eye and remind her of the stakes."

"If you say so. Goodnight."

William poured himself two fingers of Johnny Walker Blue Label over ice and walked to his office. He sat behind a Mahogany desk facing an enormous pane glass window that in daylight offered a view of the Blue Hills orchards stretching up a gently sloping hill on the north side of the estate. Beyond the orchards, Sleeping Giant slept peacefully.

William turned on the desktop computer. He entered his username and password, and nursed his cocktail while he waited for the computer to boot up. Two high definition monitors on the desk flickered to life, offering a desktop image of William standing with Reverend Flowers, Mary, James, Susan and Catherine next to the family hearth on Christmas Eve. The twins were newborns in the picture, swaddled close in their mother's arms. William stared at the image, and took a swig of the Blue Label blended whiskey.

William swiped the screen with his finger and opened a public internet browser. He began surfing local and state news outlets, including the New Haven Register, Hartford Courant, Channels 3 and 8 broadcast news sites, and local online outlets covering towns in greater New Haven. The local and statewide news was loaded with upbeat reports of record high employment rates, a burgeoning local gross domestic product spurned by a revitalized manufacturing base, balanced budgets, and the elimination of the state debt. Human-interest reports featuring the surge of individual freedom and personal responsibility complemented the rosy economic news. The lead story in all of the local newscasts focused on the pending Constitutional Convention in Philadelphia, and featured the amendments and revisions the Connecticut delegation would support.

William turned his attention to national news, surfing CNN, FOX News, NPR, and NBC websites. The national news was equally as upbeat as the local news. The international news desks reported on

President Birch's successful negotiation of a Mid-East peace accord that expanded Israel's boundaries to include all of Gaza, the West Bank, the Sinai Peninsula, and large tracts of land in Syria, Jordan and Lebanon. Egypt agreed to absorb the Palestinian population, and redraw the map to create a Palestinian state along a slim strip of Egyptian territory that ran from the Mediterranean Sea to the Nile River.

William closed the public internet browser and double-clicked on an icon accessing a secure Movement browser. He leaned forward and waited while the camera in his monitor ran a facial recognition scan. He placed his thumb on the keyboard track pad and said his name. The computer ran a biometric scan and audio scan confirming his identity. A woman appeared on the monitor.

"Good evening, Mr. Blake. My name is Angela, concierge number 4527. How do you fare?"

"Hale and hearty, hearty and hale," William said.

"Hale and hearty indeed. Your biometric scan indicates a pulse of fifty-five beats per minute, blood pressure is one twenty-five over eighty-three, and all other markers are within the normal-to-superior range. You are the picture of health, Mr. Blake."

For the past year, access to the private Movement internet browser required a biometric scan, facial recognition scan, and audio scan. Once the security protocols identified the user, Movement agents called concierges facilitated and monitored all communications conducted over the secure ISP. The stringent security and monitoring of online activity followed in the wake of several leaks. A few Movement officials had gone rogue, and leaked Top Secret news and information to underground opposition groups. The opposition groups posted the information in chatrooms. The information spread like wild fire over social media. Movement IT officials identified the perpetrators and Movement security eliminated the leakers, but by that time, the damage was done.

"How may I help you this evening," Angela asked.

"Messages."

"You have two messages, sir."

"Play."

Sage appeared on the monitor. "Hello, William. I got your message. I'm sorry to hear you won't be joining us in Philadelphia next week. You're going to miss out on a seminal moment in American history.

Schedule a call for tomorrow; I want to go over some last minute updates for the New England delegates."

"Angela, schedule a call with Mr. Sage for tomorrow," William said.

"Accessing Mr. Sage's calendar. He is available at Two O'clock tomorrow afternoon."

"Schedule."

"Meeting scheduled."

"Play message two," William said.

An image of the Connecticut Governor appeared on the monitor. "Hello William," the governor said. "I just read your memo. Looks good. I'll see you tomorrow."

"Angela, inform a security detail that I'm planning to meet with the governor tomorrow at the Governor's Mansion in Hartford."

"Transport and security alerted, sir."

"Access Movement news feed."

"Domestic or international?"

"Let's start with domestic."

A newsfeed available to Movement personnel with top-secret clearance appeared on the screen. William began surfing the feed, catching up on the true status of America. He clicked a hyperlink titled *drought monitor*. The headlines reported what William was hoping to see - all was calm in the American heartland.

Southwestern Oklahoma and Northern Texas had been a flashpoint in the early days of the water wars. The Texas National Guard and Oklahoma National Guard openly battled for the few precious trickles of water that flowed across the bone-dry plains. The Texas National Guard and local militias mopped up any formal resistance from Oklahomans, and lay claim to the quickly evaporating water sources that rippled across state lines. In the wake of the defeat, Oklahomans began fleeing their homes; a wave of water refugees clogged state highways and surged across a wasteland of dusty, shriveled fields.

In the early years, neighboring states tried to offer some relief, but the flood of water refugees became too great. Eventually, local militias in Arkansas, Kansas, Missouri and Colorado closed the borders, completely isolating two-thirds of western Oklahoma. The region transitioned into an uninhabited wasteland, but fortunately for Movement officials, a quiet wasteland. Movement communications officials snuffed out any source of underground news that tried to supplant the iron fist of Movement-sanctioned reporting. Spotty ham radio broadcasts were the only remaining source of information from inside the dust bowl. Those reports were easily jammed or written off as the ravings of some lonely lunatic.

There was more good news on The Movement newsfeed. The desalinization plants in Southern California were successfully irrigating the parched state. The technical brilliance and collective genius of Silicon Valley turned its full attention to the drought. California threw everything left in its coffers into the construction and deployment of desalinization plants that speckled the coastline. The Californian economy would not have been able to absorb the massive expense if not for the resources thrown at the problem by every billionaire and millionaire in Southern California who still hoped to call the Golden State home. The massive desalinization plants wreaked havoc on the fragile Pacific coastal ecosystem, but produced enough fresh water to keep the population hydrated and irrigate the state's parched agricultural resources.

William sipped his Johnny Walker and breathed a sigh of relief. He knew there would be no way for The Movement propaganda machine to cover-up the ensuing unrest if California spiraled into environmental chaos caused by global warming. William sat back in his chair and threw the rest of his whiskey back in one shot. He sucked an ice cube out of the glass and spat it back, then opened the bottom drawer of his desk and pulled out a half-pint of Wild Turkey. He preferred the Blue Label, but was too lazy to make the trek back to the kitchen. William poured two fingers of Wild Turkey into the glass and turned his attention back to the news reports. All the other national reports were upbeat. The economy was humming along. The nation collectively held its breath in anticipation of the pending Constitutional Convention.

"International news, please," William said.

"Yes, sir," Angela answered.

William clicked the headline - *Tel Aviv Holocaust.* Images of the decimated city appeared on the screen.

"Poor bastards," William said under his breath.

The Palestinian Liberation Organization detonated a dirty bomb in downtown Tel Aviv on Easter Sunday. The blast ripped an enormous hole through the center of the city, and spewed a radioactive cloud over half of Israel. The initial blast killed thousands of Israelis, and the fallout killed tens of thousands.

Israel responded by unleashing all of her military might. The Israeli military pushed deep into Lebanon, Syria, and Jordan, and captured the entire Sinai Peninsula from Egypt, including the Suez Canal. Years of civil conflict between Sunni and Shiite militias had depleted Lebanon, Syria, Jordan and Egypt's military resources to the point where no meaningful resistance could stop the Israeli military push. In less than a month, Israel annexed enough land to triple her size and create an enormous security cordon around the Jewish homeland.

Israeli intelligence confirmed that Iran built the PLO's dirty bomb. Iran had developed an arsenal of nuclear weapons, but had not yet developed the missile technology necessary to deploy the weapons. With the political and military support of Saudi Arabia, a nation locked in a prolonged proxy war with Iran in Iraq and Yemen, Israel began bombing Iranian military and civilian targets. The Israeli strikes successfully destroyed all Iranian nuclear facilities and weakened Iranian industrial centers and military forces to the point where Saudi Arabia was able to push Iranian-backed forces out of Iraq and Yemen.

Along with the military push, Israel began the expulsions. Israeli Defense Forces herded all non-Jews into military trucks and trains, and expelled them from Israel, the West Bank, and Gaza Strip. Israeli death squads exterminated those Palestinians who refused to go peacefully. The streets of Gaza and the West Bank ran thick with Muslim blood. Israel deposited the refugees on the border with Egypt; dumping tens of thousands of desperate men, women and children on an unwilling Egyptian population. The Egyptians treated the Palestinians as poorly as the Israelis did. A Palestinian genocide ensued. The genocide lasted until the only remaining powerbrokers in the region – Iran and Saudi Arabia – put aside their differences long enough to force Egypt to cede a piece of its territory to create a Palestinian homeland.

William poured himself another two fingers of Wild Turkey and finished half the glass in a quick swig. He decided against checking in on the brewing tension between China and Russia - he'd had enough bad news for one night, and the whiskey buzz was making it difficult to read.

"I've had enough, Angela."

Angela's face appeared on the screen. "Is there anything else I can do for you, sir."

"No. Goodnight."

THE Town Car pulled up to the front gate of the governor's mansion. The driver rolled down the bulletproof glass. A Connecticut State Trooper stepped out of a small guardhouse, and peered into the driver-side window.

"William Blake to see Governor Sterling," the driver in mirrored sunglasses said.

The state trooper checked a clipboard. He said something garbled into a radio, and the double gates swung open. The trooper waved the car through. William stared out the dark, tinted windows as the Town Car drove along a circular driveway to the front door of the stately, brick mansion. A Movement security guard in the front passenger seat stepped out, scanned the area, and opened the back door for William. William stepped out of the car. Two plain-clothed Connecticut State Troopers walked out of the mansion, and waved to William's security detail. William followed the troopers inside. The troopers led William down a hallway to the governor's office at the back of the mansion. William checked his watch; it was still early, plenty of time to finish his business with Governor Sterling and the Speaker of the Connecticut State House before his afternoon phone call with Sage. William stepped into the dark, wood-paneled governor's office. Governor Sterling rose from an armchair, and Speaker Russo stood up from a matching red leather sofa in front of an Oak desk.

"William," Governor Sterling said. "How do you fare?"

"Hale and hearty, hearty and hale," William answered as he walked into the office and shook Governor Sterling's hand. "Speaker Russo, it's nice to see you."

"It's nice to see you, too, William," Speaker Russo said.

"Would you like something to drink, it's a little early for a cocktail, but a cup of coffee or juice?" Governor Sterling asked.

"No, I had a coffee on the way. I think it's best that we get down to business; I have a call scheduled with Sage this afternoon, and I'd like to be back at the orchard before dark."

"I agree. Let's get to work. We're on the brink of history. This is a great day for America," Speaker Russo said.

Governor Sterling wrinkled her nose and recoiled slightly at the speaker's comment.

"Everything all right Governor?" William asked.

"Everything's fine," Governor Sterling said, dropping her eyes and crossing her arms.

"Before we review the content of each of the amendments, let's talk about how things will unfold over the next six-to-eight weeks. Is everything in order?" William asked.

"Yes. We're in excellent shape. All the pieces are in place," Speaker Russo said.

"Good. Let's review what's going to happen here in Hartford once the convention closes in Philadelphia. Concurrent with the approval of the amendments to the Constitution of the United States of America at the end of the convention, the Connecticut State Legislature will move immediately to adopt the amendments, and then call for a Connecticut state constitutional convention. Are all the towns ready?"

"Yes," Speaker Russo said. "We have all one hundred and sixty-nine cities and towns lined up and ready to go."

"It's gotta be quick, like pulling off a Band-Aide," William said.

"It will be. The Connecticut State House and Senate will vote concurrently to ratify the federal amendments to the constitution. The ratification will be on Governor Sterling's desk within forty-eight hours of the close of the convention in Philadelphia. Governor Sterling will join the House and Senate and call for a state constitutional convention once she signs the federal amendments. City and town councils across the state have already selected their delegates. The convention will be held in the Connecticut State Armory here in Hartford," Speaker Russo said.

Governor Sterling walked across the room and stared out the window. "These gardens are so beautiful in the fall, but nothing is as beautiful as when they're in bloom in the spring. It's sad to watch it all wilt away like this." The Governor turned and placed the palm of her hand on her desk. "This desk is White Oak; crafted from the original Charter Oak Tree that concealed Connecticut's Royal Charter from the British so many decades ago, back when America was in her own spring. It seems ironic that in a few weeks I'll be signing a document on this very desk that will reverse so many years of constitutional democracy in this state."

"You're not getting cold feet, are you?" William asked.

"No," Governor Sterling said, walking around the side of the desk and sitting in an armchair. "Let's get down to business. I'd like to review the amendments one more time."

William eyed the governor suspiciously. For months, President Birch and The Movement had been establishing the framework for a constitutional convention. In the last year of the Birch Administration, a plan was hatched that would use a constitutional convention to neuter any remaining federal authority left in the United States. The amendments would strictly limit the authority of the executive and legislative branches. Only the judicial branch would have any real scope of power. A system that term-limited all federal judges, including Supreme Court justices, to four-year terms would check the power of the judicial branch. The term-limits would guarantee that any meaningful precedents or lasting judicial actions would be vacated with a new bench every four years.

Concurrent with the ratification of the new amendments at the federal constitutional convention, Movement officials in all fifty states planned state constitutional conventions. In Connecticut, William worked hand-in-glove with the Speaker of the State House, President of the State Senate, and Governor Sterling to prepare the state amendments. The Connecticut state constitutional convention would do to Hartford what the federal constitutional convention did to Washington; the new amendments would annihilate state power and return full authority to govern to local town and city councils. By the time President Birch left office, Americans would be free from the bonds of federal and state government. The only thing standing in the way of the revolution was any potential last-minute sabotage by delegates at the convention, or elected officials in the states.

William, Speaker Russo, and Governor Sterling spent the next three hours reviewing the logistics of the convention, and discussing the content of the amendments dubbed The Liberty Amendments by President Birch. By Noon, they had reviewed all but one of the Liberty Amendments. When they reached the last amendment, Governor Sterling stood up from a leather armchair, walked across the office, and stared out the window.

"I don't know about this last one," Governor Sterling said. "I've been losing sleep over it. All the others are fine, but if I rise in support of the *Supremacy Amendment*, well, the word treason comes to mind."

"Treason?" William asked. "How do you see this as treason?"

"America has stood the test of time since 1776. I feel like we're on the cusp of committing national suicide."

"Governor," Speaker Russo said. "Let's just go over it one more time; I think you're making too much of it. I don't see the *Supremacy Amendment* as anything but a victory for liberty."

"Liberty, huh, it's a thin line between liberty and anarchy. The *Supremacy Amendment* gives states the right to annul any federal laws they object to. Now, let's follow the bouncing ball on this: Once the Connecticut State Legislature ratifies the federal constitution as amended, the plan is to call for a state constitutional convention. At that convention, you want me to support a state *Supremacy Amendment* that will allow towns and cities in Connecticut to annul any state laws that they object to. And, William, I know your Movement think tank has already drafted town and city resolutions that will amend town and city charters to allow individuals to ignore any local regulations and statutes that they object to. Once all the Dominoes fall, the entire system of government will be hollowed out - the social contract will be null and void; government will be a paper tiger. I can't support an amendment that essentially tears government from its foundation. I'm all for limited government, but to completely destroy our system of governance - to take away all authority - that's treason."

"Governor," Speaker Russo said. "I think you're missing the point. The *Supremacy Amendment* returns authority to the only place where God intended - the individual. That amendment revives natural rights; this will begin a return to God's natural order."

"I'm not missing anything. My eyes are wide open. I know exactly what the *Supremacy Amendment* is going to do. You see God's natural order as freedom and liberty; I see it as a place of desperation. The Liberty Amendments will destroy government. By the time this is over, we're going to have a loose confederation bound by the whims of a federal judiciary that won't have any ability to implement its' rulings. If I rise in support of the *Supremacy Amendment*, I am rising in support of complete dissolution of the union - America as we know her will cease to exist."

"All empires fall," William said. "America grew into a bloated mass of laws that crushed individual freedom. Our choices were simple: Either watch America collapse into rubble when we rose up and threw off the yoke of oppression in a violent fit of revolution, or use the constitutional and democratic process to bring her down in a non-violent revolution that ensures she falls in the direction of liberty. You are part of a revolution, Governor; what you are about to do will ensure that liberty thrives."

"I'm not buying it," Governor Sterling said. "Revolutions are designed to replace one system of governance with another, not leave the government vacant. Power despises a vacuum. It scares the hell out of me to think what's going to rise up and replace our democracy. What kind of country will we leave to our children?"

William stood up from the red leather sofa and crossed the room. He placed a hand on Governor Sterling's shoulder. "I know you're scared. But you have to take a longer view of things," William said. "Look beyond this office of yours. Look at what liberty has already brought to Connecticut. People are thriving like never before now that we've unleashed a true spirit of freedom. What's going to replace the power of the state is the power of the individual; hundreds of millions of Americans will rise up on a tide of self-reliance and self-governance."

"And what about our fellow Americans in Oklahoma? Has that spirit of self-reliance lifted them?"

"Okies should have learned their lesson from the Great Depression. It's not our responsibility to prop up the lives of those who chose to inhabit a land that never should have been inhabited. They're experiencing the laws of natural consequences. Natural consequences are part of the natural order. Life is not easy, and government should not try to inoculate individuals against the harsh realities of life. Government would have only made the problems in Oklahoma worse. Instead, natural consequences are working out the details, not government. Life is short and brutish only for those who make bad decisions and refuse to accept personal responsibility."

"I've always believed in strictly limited government. But there has to be some common good in our system of governance; there must be something that binds us together to stave off anarchy. We cannot completely abandon the social contract."

"We don't need government to compel us to care for one another. If there is such a thing as the common good, then the common good will arise naturally from liberty. Think about it governor; don't you remember when we started down this road? They said that the cities would burn when we eliminated the welfare state. Did that happen? No. It took a while to wash the streets clean, but look at the cities now - they are thriving; there's no more police state, we're at full employment, and the people place their faith in themselves now that we've torn away the faith people used to place in government. And what about those progressive dimwits who told us we were throwing grandma off a cliff when we eliminated Social Security and Medicare. Did waves of the elderly end up dying in the streets? No, of course not. Families and communities pulled together to care for their own. No one said it would be easy, but think how much we've strengthened families and local communities. We're riding a wave of progress spurned by liberty and personal responsibility."

"Limiting government is different than abolishing it."

"No, it's not. This is part of the natural progression from conservatism to libertarianism; you're riding an unstoppable tide of momentum. Think about what we accomplished when we eliminated the Federal Reserve and liberated our nation's currency from the illusion of full faith and credit of the United States. When we linked the value of the dollar to gold, how many progressives promised us an economic catastrophe? Did it happen? Of course not. The nation's economy is booming. We've wiped out debt and deficit spending, and created a wave of unprecedented prosperity."

"Some see it that way," Governor Sterling said.

"This is the last step in the revolution," William said. "You can't turn back now."

"No. This is the last step before the fall." A stream of tears rolled down Governor Sterling's cheeks. Governor Sterling stared at William. "This is what it's like to see an empire collapse. This will be the birth of a failed state."

William removed his hand from Governor Sterling's shoulder. "This is what it's like to see liberty rise," William said. William turned and walked out of the office.

"William," Speaker Russo called. "William, where are you going?" Speaker Russo followed William into the hallway. "William, wait, please." William paused and waited for Speaker Russo to catch up. "William, please, don't leave like this. Governor Sterling is just nervous; we're all a little anxious."

"No, it's more than fear. She can't be trusted."

"Don't be hasty. I've known Governor Sterling for many years. She'll come around. She'll do the right thing."

"This is too important to leave to chance. Are you planning on travelling with her to Philadelphia?" William asked.

"Yes. We're flying out in the morning."

"I'd make other plans if I were you. Make up some excuse. You'll be better off finding your own way to Constitution Hall."

THE Town Car cruised through downtown Hartford. William's iPhone buzzed. He pressed the *accept call* button and a woman's face appeared on the six-inch screen.

"Good afternoon, Mr. Blake. My name is Samantha, concierge number 6421. I have Mr. Sage on the line for you."

"I'll take the call," William said.

"Please remain on the line…"

Sage's face appeared on the screen. "Hello William. How do you fare?" Sage asked.

"Hale and hearty, hearty and hale."

"Hale and hearty indeed. It's nice to see you."

"It's nice to see you, too," William said.

"Uh-oh, I can tell by the sound of your voice, something's wrong."

"Big time," William said.

"What happened?"

"It's Governor Sterling. I just had a very disappointing meeting with her. We can trust her to support all the amendments except the *Supremacy Amendment.* I think she's going to turn her back on us. "

"Are you absolutely sure?"

"Speaker Russo thinks she'll come around. But I don't."

"That's disappointing."

"I agree."

"You know the stakes on this, William. So I'll ask you one time, are you absolutely sure that Governor Sterling is compromised?"

"Yes, one hundred percent confident."

"You understand what this means."

"Yes. I've already begun making alternative arrangements."

"Okay, keep working on those arrangements. This will happen quickly, the convention begins in two days."

"I'm on it, Sage. You can trust me."

"Is there anyone else besides Governor Sterling in the Connecticut, Massachusetts, or Rhode Island delegations that you have doubts about?"

"No, the rest of the delegation is rock solid. The only wild card is Sterling."

"Good."

"How about the other state delegations? What are you hearing from the rest of the country?" William asked.

"We'll have a sizable majority, but pulling together unanimous consent may prove difficult. We're doing our best to clean up a few votes, so knowing about Governor Sterling is important – nice work."

"Thank you."

"Where does Connecticut stand with respect to the state convention? President Birch expects the state conventions to proceed immediately after the federal convention. Have you got everything lined up?"

"I have a conference call tonight with the state house and senate whips. They've turned their attention to the local delegates who will represent Connecticut's towns and cities. I'll have the list ready to go before The Cleanse," William said.

"Good. We'll need the names in the next forty-eight hours. Once President Birch gives the order for The Cleanse to begin, we won't be able to add any more names to the list, or remove any names."

"I understand. It's going to be a busy month," William said.

"More likely a matter of weeks."

"You have my full commitment."

"Good, we're going to need it. This will be The Movement's crowning accomplishment," Sage said. "Goodbye, William."

William said goodbye to Sage and ended the call. He dialed a secure number for Movement communications. A woman's face appeared on the screen. "Good evening, Mr. Blake. My name is Robin, concierge number 6139. How do you fare?"

"Hale and hearty, hearty and hale," William said

"How can I help you?" Robin asked.

"I need to get a message to the President of the Connecticut State Senate, Alfred Graves. Inform Senator Graves that I need to meet with him in-person first thing tomorrow morning at my estate. Please alert transportation, and have him picked up at his home by Six O'clock."

"Accessing Senator Grave's schedule. He has a Senate hearing in the morning."

"Cancel the meeting and clear his schedule."

"Yes, sir."

WILLIAM stood on the front porch holding a cup of coffee in both hands, milking the warmth that radiated through the porcelain to stave off the blanketing wet chill that clung to the orchard. Tendrils from the piping hot brew caught in a soft morning breeze and drifted above the mug. The entire orchard shimmered in the quickly rising sun that arched over Sleeping Giant. William watched workers move methodically between the trees, gently shaking the branches to cast off morning dew that clung in thick droplets to the leaves and obscenely large fruit. The weight of the unnaturally large, fully ripened apples, peaches, and nectarines combined with the heavy morning dew, bowing the branches to the breaking point. It was another bumper crop; within a matter of weeks, the cider press would be working overtime to juice the fruit. Mary's commercial kitchen would soon cast off the sweet scent of baking pies, cider donuts, apple fritters, and an assortment of fresh-from-the-farm treats.

Leaf peepers would soon descend on the orchard for hayrides, apple picking, and to challenge the Blue Hills corn maze. They'd fill their bags with produce, and stop off for autumn delicacies at the Blue Hills Farm Stand. The entire enterprise wasn't turning a huge profit, but it was enough to break even, and leave a little left over for the family at the end of each harvest. Money wasn't the goal; self-sufficiency was the objective. And if self-sufficiency wasn't enough, William could always count on the hundreds of millions of dollars he had stashed in his portfolio. His insider knowledge and investments in gold in the months before President Birch orchestrated the elimination of the Federal Reserve and returned the dollar to the gold standard reaped him a fortune that no man could spend in a single lifetime.

A Town Car rolled up Blue Hills Road towards the farmhouse. William took a sip of coffee, and stepped off the porch. He walked towards the Town Car as it drove up the driveway. The Town Car stopped, and a Movement agent climbed out of the front seat. The agent waved to William, and opened the back door. A portly man with a ruddy complexion and thick salt and pepper sideburns climbed awkwardly out of the backseat. William immediately recognized the President of the Connecticut State Senate.

"Senator Graves," William said, stepping forward and extending his hand. "How do you fare?"

"Hale and hearty, hearty and hale. It's nice to see you, William."

"It's nice to see you, too. Thank you for coming on such short notice."

"Didn't sound like I had much of a choice. I'm not used to being summoned in this manner. Is everything all right?" Senator Graves asked.

"Everything is fine. Let's just say that your visit represents the better part of prudence."

"Well, if prudence dictates, then I'm happy to oblige."

"Come on inside and let's get you settled. I figure we can talk business over a tour of the orchard. We'll take a ride up to the top of Sleeping Giant. After lunch, we'll do some trap shooting off the veranda, I hear you know your way around a shotgun."

William led Senator Graves into the farmhouse. They shared a cup of coffee in the kitchen while waiting for Crocco to bring a vehicle up to the farmhouse.

"Why don't you lose that suit coat and tie? I'm sorry I didn't tell you to dress for the occasion. You're on a farm now, not in some senate hearing room. There's a little nip in the air today, put this on," William said, handing Senator Graves an XXXL sweatshirt emblazoned with the Blue Hills logo.

Senator Graves took off his suit coat and tie, and unbuttoned the collar of his shirt. He slipped the sweatshirt over his head. William led him back outside to the front porch. Crocco was waiting with a John Deere Gator 850i, and two horses saddled and ready to mount.

"We aren't riding on those, are we?" Senator Graves asked, nodding towards the horses.

"No, we'll take the Gator. A couple of my men will ride along with us."

"Are there security concerns on your estate?" Senator Graves asked, nodding towards the rifle scabbards.

"No, no, of course not. I just like to have a couple of the men with me when I'm entertaining guests as important as you, Senator."

Crocco and one of the Blue Hills' farmhands climbed into the saddles. William helped Senator Graves into the passenger seat of the Gator. William sat in the driver seat and turned the ignition. He put the Gator in drive, and drove down a trail through the apple trees.

"This is a beautiful piece of property. My wife and I always purchase Blue Hills' products. She's particularly taken with your Apple Crisp," Senator Graves said.

"Thank you," William said. "I give all the credit to Mary. She's the mastermind behind the success of Blue Hills. I'm more of a gentleman farmer. I really just try to stay out of her way."

"Did she grow up on a farm?"

"Yes, her parents were dairy farmers in upstate New York."

William drove the Gator up a small rise. "You get a bird's eye view of the corn maze from here," William said, pointing towards the maze.

"Very nice," Senator Graves said.

"Over there is our sunflower maze. It's not as spectacular as it was a few weeks ago; the sunflowers are just about dried out by now."

"What are those men doing?" Senator Graves asked, pointing to men moving between the flowers, tying cheesecloth over the quickly drying sunflower heads.

"That's how we harvest the sunflowers. As the flowers dry, we tie cheesecloth over the flower heads. The men will cut the flowers and hang them upside-down. The sunflower seeds collect in the cheesecloth. We've had Blue Hills Sunflower Seeds on the market for a couple of years now. This year, Mary's got it in her mind to start a new line of Blue Hills Sunflower Peanut Butter."

"Very interesting," Senator Graves said. "But I'm sure you didn't bring me here for a lovely tour and to enlighten me about harvesting sunflowers. Let's talk a little shop."

William stepped on the gas. The Gator bounced along a dirt logging road winding up the side of Sleeping Giant. The men on horseback followed behind the Gator.

"You know the convention opens tomorrow in Philadelphia," William said.

"Yes, of course. It's a very exciting moment in America's history."

"I figure you and I should spend some time together going over the amendments just in case you have to make an appearance."

"Make an appearance? I'm not following you."

"You're Connecticut's understudy. If something were to happen to Governor Sterling or Speaker Russo, you'd be the man stepping in."

"Oh, don't be silly. Nothing is going to happen to them. What's the worry?"

"Like I said earlier, prudence dictates that we prepare for all contingencies. Tell me, how familiar are you with the Liberty Amendments that are going to be proposed."

"I know all the Liberty Amendments quite well," Senator Graves said. "The limits to the powers of the federal executive, legislative, and judicial branches are long overdue. It's time to clip their wings; especially the executive branch. I also like the idea of a part-time legislative branch. As for the judicial branch, the term limits on judges makes sense."

"I assume you fully support all of the Liberty Amendments."

"Yes."

"What about the *Supremacy Amendment*? What are your thoughts on that?"

Wrinkles formed across Senator Graves' forehead. He turned away from William. The Gator turned a corner and the castle came into view.

"Wow, what's this?" Senator Graves asked.

"My castle," William said, pulling the Gator up to the base of the castle at the top of Sleeping Giant.

"You built a castle?" Senator Graves asked.

"No. The Works Progress Administration built it in the 1930s during the Great Depression. It was here when I bought the park. Come on, let's take a walk up to the top, there's an amazing view. On a clear morning like this we'll be able to see all the way across Long Island Sound."

William led Senator Graves up a narrow, dank walkway that led to the top of the castle. "Here we are," William said when they reached the top.

"It's spectacular," Senator Graves said, scanning the panoramic, three hundred and sixty degree view of Greater New Haven. "You can see all of New Haven from up here. What is that, Long Island way out there?"

"Yup. And there's my alma mater, Quinnipiac University, right down there."

"Very impressive. I understand you've made quite an investment in Quinnipiac."

"Quinnipiac did a lot for me. An old Quinnipiac professor of mine introduced me to The Movement. I wouldn't be here if not for him. I figure I owe everything I have to that university. Do you know what the word Quinnipiac means?"

"No."

"It's a Native American word meaning 'bend in the river.' I always thought that name was appropriate; I certainly found a bend in the river when I was a Quinnipiac undergraduate."

"You've built something amazing, William. It's quite the shining city on a hill - Jefferson would be proud."

"Now we need to make sure that Jefferson would be proud of you, too. That is, of course, if you're called upon to serve."

"William, I appreciate the concern, but nothing is going to happen to the governor or speaker. I'm sure they've safely arrived by now and are getting on with all the pomp and circumstance to start the convention."

"I'm sure you're right," William said. "Come on, let's head back to the house. We have a delicious lunch waiting for us."

William and Senator Graves spoke idly as the Gator descended Sleeping Giant and returned to the farmhouse. After lunch, they sipped brandy and smoked cigars on the veranda.

"Would you like to do some trap shooting?" William asked.

"Sounds like fun."

William asked Crocco to bring up two shotguns from the armory, and set up a clay pigeon thrower on the veranda. William and Senator Graves finished their brandy and cigars while a farmhand set up the clay pigeon thrower. Crocco handed two gun cases to William.

William placed the gun cases on the table and opened the clasps. He pulled out a 1906 Boss over-and-under twelve-gauge shotgun. He inspected the handmade weapon and handed it to Senator Graves.

"It's beautiful," Senator Graves said, inspecting the intricate detailing on the metalwork, and rich texture of the wood stock. "I have a 1946 Browning at home, but nothing this exceptional. This must have set you back quite a bit, what thirty, forty thousand?"

"You know your shotguns," William said.

"Oh yes, family tradition. I've been shooting since I was a boy. I've fired my fair share of outstanding shotguns, but I've never seen anything this remarkable in real life."

William opened the second case and pulled out a matching shotgun.

"Holy cow," Senator Graves said. "Not one, but two. Where did you get them?"

"I have my sources. Please, be my guest," William said, handing the senator a pair of tinted shooting glasses and earmuffs.

Senator Graves put on the glasses and earmuffs, cracked open the over-under barrel, and dropped two shells into the barrel. He clapped the barrel shut and stepped forward. "Pull," he yelled. A farmhand pulled a string connected to the spring-fed arm on the clay pigeon thrower. A clay pigeon spiraled off the arm and flew high into the sky. Senator Graves took aim and pulled the front trigger. A wave of pellets launched from the barrel and nicked the side of the clay pigeon. The senator re-aligned his site and pulled the back trigger. The Boss twelve-gauge barked and the clay pigeon vanished in a puff of black dust.

"Excellent shot," William said."

"It's hard to miss when you have a weapon this smooth in your hands. Let's see what you've got."

"Load two for me," William said to the farmhand. The farmhand placed two clay pigeons on the thrower. "Pull," William yelled.

Two clay pigeons rocketed over the yard. William pulled the front trigger in the nanosecond after the first pigeon took flight. The pigeon disappeared in a puff of black debris. William paused for dramatic effect; letting the second clay pigeon sail far out over the yard separating the veranda from the orchard. Just as the clay pigeon was about to lose velocity and drop to the ground, William adjusted his aim and pulled the back trigger. The clay pigeon vaporized.

"That's impressive," Senator Graves said.

"Your turn," William said.

Senator Graves and William took turns shooting. After a few rounds, William paused before his turn.

"We never finished our discussion about the *Supremacy Amendment*," William said.

"It's certainly a clear win for states' rights. The ability for the states to annul federal legislation will be a transformational moment," Senator Graves said.

"And what about the proposed amendments here at the state level?"

"I see how the Dominoes will fall; I think we all see the progression. The state will amend the Connecticut State Constitution to allow the towns and cities to reject state legislation, and the towns and cities will soon amend their charters to allow individuals to reject local statutes."

"A clear victory for individual rights?" William said.

"Many people see it that way."

"And what about you, Senator? It that how you see it?"

"I suppose."

"That's not the most convincing stance. I need to hear a little vim and vigor."

"Come on, William. It's no big deal; my feelings are irrelevant. Speaker Russo and Governor Sterling are already in Philadelphia awaiting the opening gavel. My opinion doesn't matter for squat - they're the ones who are going to be casting Connecticut's votes."

Senator Graves and Williams' cell phones began buzzing. William stood still, holding the shotgun in the crook of his arm with the barrel cracked open. Senator Graves reached into his pocket and removed his iPhone. The breaking news reports and text messages from senate colleagues filled the screen.

"Holy shit," Senator Graves said.

"What happened?" William asked.

"There's been an accident. Governor Sterling's helicopter went down shortly after takeoff. She's dead."

"What about Speaker Russo?"

"They weren't travelling together."

"I guess we need to get you down to Philadelphia," William said.

Senator Graves looked confused. He began mumbling and playing aimlessly with his iPhone.

"Senator," William said, stepping forward and taking Senator Graves' phone away. William dropped the phone in his pocket and stepped back a few feet from Senator Graves. "I need you to answer me; will you support all of the Liberty Amendments, including the *Supremacy Amendment?*"

"Oh, um, yes, I think I can support it," Senator Graves said.

"Look at me, Senator," William said.

Senator Graves stared William in the eyes. William dropped two shotgun shells in the barrel of the over-under Boss. He clapped the barrel shut, and pointed the shotgun at Senator Graves' face. Senator Graves stared into two dark holes at the end of the shotgun. William pushed the safety off, and pressed his pointer finger lightly against the front trigger.

"I need to be absolutely sure, so I will ask you one more time, will you support the *Supremacy Amendment?*"

Senator Graves' voice shook, "Yes."

"Pull!" William hollered.

Two clay pigeons released from the thrower. William raised the shotgun a few inches above Senator Graves' head and fired both barrels in quick succession. The clay pigeons disappeared in a puff of black debris. William lowered the shotgun and stepped forward.

"For you," William said, handing Senator Graves the Boss shotgun. "Both of them; my gift for your loyalty to The Movement."

"I can't," Senator Graves said.

"Sure you can. Please. I insist."

"That's very generous. Thank you," Senator Graves said.

The roar of a helicopter filled the air. William and Senator Graves watched the helicopter land.

"There's your ride," William said. "You might want to change back into your suit and tie; I'm not sure how it would look to have you on the convention floor in a Blue Hills sweatshirt."

Senator Graves pulled the sweatshirt over his head, handed it to William, and walked into the farmhouse to change. After changing, William walked Senator Graves to the helicopter.

"You have nothing to worry about with this machine," William said. "My helicopters are tip top."

"That's reassuring," Senator Graves said.

"I had my men load your shotguns. They'll be waiting for you on your flight home."

"Thank you," Senator Graves said.

"No, thank you. Now get down there and do the right thing."

WILLIAM turned on the television in his office, sat behind his desk, and flicked on his computer. He turned up the television volume on a live FOX News broadcast from Philadelphia while he waited for the computer to boot up. The newscaster covering the convention reported on the crash of Governor Sterling's helicopter, and the last-minute arrival of the governor's replacement. Footage of the crash scene filled the television screen. A FOX News' chopper captured a bird's eye view of helicopter wreckage strewn across a field in Windsor, Connecticut, a short distance from where Governor Sterling took off from in Hartford. The helicopter crash-landed next to a long, red tobacco shed used to cure tobacco leaves for Connecticut-grown cigar wrappers. An image of a chair reserved for the Connecticut delegation in Independence Hall flashed on the screen. Convention organizers tied a black ribbon around one of the two chairs reserved for the Connecticut delegation.

"Nice touch," William said to the empty office.

William pressed the mute button on the television remote and logged-in to the Movement's secure internet browser. He placed his thumb on the biometric scanner, and leaned forward, allowing the built-in camera to run a facial recognition and retinal scan. The face of a pretty, blond woman in her early twenties appeared on William's monitor.

"Good afternoon, Mr. Blake. I'm Amanda, concierge 4015. How do you fare?"

"Hale and hearty, hearty and hale," William said.

"Your blood pressure is one-ten over sixty, and pulse is fifty-six beats per minute. All vitals and biometric indicators are in the superior range. You are hale and hearty indeed, Mr. Blake. How may I assist you?"

"Messages?"

"You have three email messages. The messages are from Mr. Whitkin, Mr. Francois, and Ms. Amato."

Whitkin, Francois, and Amato were Movement whips from Rhode Island, Massachusetts and Connecticut. As whips, they were responsible for reviewing vote counts. Normally, they would count the votes of elected representatives in the Connecticut, Massachusetts, and Rhode Island statehouses. With state constitutional conventions on the horizon, William directed the whips to count the votes of the delegates who town and city councils across the region had nominated for the state conventions.

"Let's start with Connecticut. Let me see Amato's email," William said.

An email appeared on William's screen:

William,

My team and I finished the preliminary count for each of the 169 towns and cities. The attached list contains the names of the delegates. I've placed a star next to the names of the people who we should be concerned about. There's an asterisk next to the individuals who we suspect will be on the fence. Those without anything next to their names are solid. We have a strong majority; I'm projecting about 60%. However, to get to the three-quarter supermajority, we'll have to neutralize the names with a star next to them, and hope that at least half of the asterisk names vote 'Yea' when the amendments are proposed for ratification.

William double-clicked the document attached to the email. A long list of names and addresses appeared on this screen. William recognized a few of the names on the list, but most were strangers. There were stars next to fifty names, and an asterisk next to forty-five names; the Connecticut whip identified over forty percent of the delegation as individuals who would not, or might not support the state constitutional amendments, particularly the state version of the *Supremacy Amendment*. William was disappointed that the number was so high; he thought for sure The Movement had made deeper inroads into the conscience of Connecticut's citizenry.

William saved the document with the Connecticut delegates to his desktop, and reviewed the counts from the Massachusetts and Rhode Island whips. Things were not as bad in Massachusetts and Rhode Island, but the numbers were still substantial. In total, one hundred and seventy-eight state convention delegates in Connecticut, Massachusetts, and Rhode Island would need to be cleansed to ensure that the state constitutions were amended to include language that freed cities and towns from the dictates of the state legislative and executive branches in Hartford, Boston, and Providence. Once the towns and cities ratified the Connecticut, Massachusetts, and Rhode Island State Constitutions, William and his Movement affiliates would spread language that amended town and city charters to allow individual citizens to opt-out of local statutes. Once complete, federal, state, and local authority would be neutralized - individual freedom would be unfettered.

"Time to water the tree of liberty," William said to himself.

"Excuse me, sir. Did you say something?" Amanda asked. "I couldn't hear you."

"Nothing. Please combine the Connecticut, Rhode Island, and Massachusetts' names and addresses into one list. Remove the names and addresses that do not have a star or asterisk next to them. Bold the names with stars, and italic the names with asterisks. Once you've combined the lists, attach the list to a single email from me with the subject line *The Cleanse.* Send the email and attachment to Sage."

"Yes, sir. Is there anything else I can do for you this evening?"

"No, that will be all."

William stood up from his desk, walked to the window, and stared over his orchards. Sleeping Giant rested under a slowly arching sun that descended from its zenith, and settled into the horizon. The forecast called for stormy weather in the wee hours of the morning, but for the moment, the orchard was placid as the sky transitioned from brilliant blue into a soft pink hue.

"Pink at night, sailor's delight," William said to himself.

William's mind wandered. He wondered how Sage would orchestrate The Cleanse. The Movement had a chokehold around the throat of the national and state media. There was little chance that The Cleanse would stir a public backlash amid news reports of state delegates disappearing, winding up dead in tangled masses of car wrecks, falling prey to unexpected heart attacks and strokes, or simply ending up in a pool of blood that flowed liberally from slit throats or bullets to the back of the head. The Movement mastered a thousand ways to kill; unleashing The Movement's killing machine on public officials would certainly draw attention.

William shrugged. "Oh well, not my problem," he said to himself.

William walked downstairs and outside onto the veranda. A table was set with a white tablecloth and fine China. Propane heaters around the table chased away the chill. Mary, Catherine, Susan, and James were waiting for William. The girls squealed, ran to their father, and jumped into his arms. William lifted the girls off the ground and gave each daughter a bear hug and kiss on the forehead.

"How did your meeting with Senator Graves go?" Mary asked.

"Very productive. Things are coming along. I'm looking forward to the convocation tonight. We'll have to keep an eye on the time. The President is speaking at Eight O'clock."

"Can I stay up and watch?" James asked.

"Sure." William said.

James fist-pumped under the table.

"Can we stay up, too? Please, please, please," the twins pleaded.

"I suppose so," William said.

The girls squealed with delight. Mary shot William a glare across the table. "Come on, Mary," William said. "If there was ever a time to let them stay up after bedtime it would be on a night like this, this is history in the making; they'll be telling their grandchildren about this someday. But only if they promise to sit quietly and listen to what President Birch has to say, and then straight to bed."

"We promise," the twins replied in unison.

Housekeepers brought out the dinner. The children were served chicken strips, fresh fruit and mac-n-cheese. Mary and James were served New York strip steak with scalloped potatoes and steamed broccoli.

"Who would like to say grace," William asked. No one volunteered. "Well, then I guess it's up to me. Let's hold hands and bow our heads. Lord, thank you for the bounty we are about to receive. Thank you for the blessings you have bestowed upon this family, the Blue Hills community, and our nation. Please look after us and guide us as we seek to walk in your footsteps. In the name of the Father, Son, and Holy Ghost. Amen." The family followed William's 'amen,' and dug into their meals.

"How's the steak?" William asked.

"A little well-done for my taste, but okay," Mary said. "I need to talk to you about something."

"Uh-oh, that sounds ominous," William said. "What's up?"

"I know what's going on out at the winery, and I'm not happy about it. I never gave my blessing for a distillery. I looked the other way when they started making hard cider in the cider mill, and I agreed to let them plant the vineyard and open a winery, it's a money-maker for sure, but I'm not at all comfortable with them producing vodka. I never consented to hard alcohol. I understand you gave permission."

"We grow the potatoes, it's farm-produced. I thought our rule was that anything homegrown was permissible. This is just another Blue Hills product. I figured you wouldn't mind. Besides, it's a small still, nothing substantial. I don't see us moving into a commercial line anytime soon."

"That's even worse. If it's only for community consumption, we're going to end up with a farm full of drunkards."

"What's a drunkard?" Susan asked.

"Nothing, honey," William said. "Let's talk about this later."

"We will," Mary said.

The family finished their dinners and hot fudge sundaes for dessert. The sun dropped over Sleeping Giant, and a chill kicked up across the orchards. The family moved indoors to the living room. William played Chess with James, while Mary helped the girls with their spelling homework.

"Check," William said, sliding his bishop across the board.

"I resign," James said, turning his king onto its side.

"Nice game," William said, shaking hands with James. "All right everyone, it's Eight O'clock, let's see what's happening in Philadelphia."

William turned on the television and chose Fox News. The camera panned over Independence Hall. The delegates sat in pairs at small wooden desks. President Birch sat alone at a table at the front of the room. A Sergeant at Arms stood at a lectern placed at the front of the hall. He banged a gavel on a wooden lectern.

"The delegates will come to order," the Sergeant at Arms said in a deep baritone voice. The dull murmur in the hall quieted. "We will begin these proceedings with an opening prayer. The delegates will please rise and bow your heads."

A priest stepped to the lectern and delivered an opening prayer.

"Beautiful," Mary whispered.

The Sergeant at Arms stepped to the lectern. "The President has asked you to join him in a moment of silence in memory of Governor Edith Sterling from the great State of Connecticut." The delegates bowed their heads for the moment of silence. "Thank you. Ladies and gentlemen of the convention, the President of the United States of America."

The delegates began applauding wildly as President Birch stood up from his desk at the center of the hall and stepped behind the lectern.

"Very interesting," William said.

"What?" Mary asked.

"No pledge of allegiance or singing of the national anthem. Just the prayer."

"What does it mean?"

"Nothing. It's just interesting. It's also interesting that a Sergeant at Arms is opening the convocation. They usually ask an assembly speaker to open legislative sessions."

"I'm not following you," Mary said.

"It's nothing, just a little unique. It's certainly setting a different tone."

President Birch raised his hand to temper the exuberant applause. The delegates quieted down. "How do you fare?" President Birch asked.

The delegates boomed in unison, "Hale and hearty, hearty and hale."

"Hale and hearty indeed," President Birch said. "It is my pleasure to stand before you today. You have an important task ahead of you; a task that if effectively accomplished will inscribe your names in the annals of the American experience alongside the names of the great men who were our nation's founders. We assemble here today to reconstitute the seminal document that frames the powers of the Federal Government – the Constitution of the United States of America. In so doing, we aim to ensure that no future tyranny arises from a president, senators, representatives, or judges who comprise the three bodies of our national system of governance.'

'America is and always has been a philosophical entity. Unlike much of the world, whose evolution arose from the history of men who engaged in repeated civil war and tribal conflict, America's evolution is a journey of ideas, founded on the principles and belief in natural order and natural rights. This is the basis for American exceptionalism. Today, we strive to enshrine those God-given rights into the document that forever frames the destiny of our nation. As a philosophical development, America is framed by the belief that our Constitution is a reflection of human nature. Within this framework, the individual must be placed at the center of all power; personal autonomy, equality, the belief that the governed must give their consent to be governed, and the need for governance to be limited in scope; these are the core values that are the basis of American exceptionalism.'

'We have made great strides rolling back the tide and abuses of a progressive government; a government that wantonly taxed and regulated every action of the individual. For the past eight years, we passed no laws designed to constrain individual liberty. Instead, we used the power of the legislative and executive branches to drain the bureaucratic swamp of law, policy, and regulation. The result of this effort speaks for itself. Americans are once again reaping the full bounty of liberty, liberty steeped in the belief that we are nothing if not for the full measure of our rugged individualism and personal responsibility. You great men and women assembled here today are responsible for reconstituting the powers granted to government. In so doing, you will ensure that Americans are forever blessed with the full measure of liberty and independence. Ladies and gentlemen, I declare this convention open."

The delegates filled Independence Hall with raucous applause. The voice-over of a Fox News pundit began narrating the scene.

"All right," William said, hitting the mute button on the remote. "Time for bed."

James, Catherine, and Susan walked to their bedrooms. William tucked-in the children, and walked back downstairs.

"Are you going to stay up and watch the convention?" Mary asked.

"No. They won't start any official business until tomorrow morning. The only thing that will be on tonight are the talking heads and analysts opining about the Liberty Amendments. I don't need to watch them; their opinions are meaningless."

"What are you going to do?"

"I'm going to have a cocktail on the veranda, take in some fresh air, and then go to bed."

"Do you want some company?"

"No, you go to bed. I want to be alone. I have a few things to mull over."

"What kind of things?"

"Oh, nothing too crazy; just trying to figure out what the new world order is going to look like."

PART 5

A MORE PERFECT UNION

April, 2046

WILLIAM stood at the back of the cider mill and stared at the makeshift classroom. Twenty-five students ranging from five-years-old to eighteen-years-old sat at tables arranged by grade level. Mary taught a lesson on long division to a group of eight-year-olds while Reverend Flowers monitored the rest of the students as they worked independently at their desks. Reverend Flowers walked to an eleven-year-old boy in the second row who was doodling in the margins of a notebook. Reverend Flowers grabbed the boy by his ear and yanked him out of his seat.

"This is the second time I've had to speak with you," Reverend Flowers said. "There will not be a third time."

Reverend Flowers dragged the boy by his ear to the front of the classroom. Mary stopped her lesson and directed the class to put down their work and pay attention to the discipline meted out by Reverend Flowers. The students put down their pencils and looked up from their assignments.

"Hands out," Reverend Flowers said.

The boy raised his hands in front of him with the palms down, closed his eyes, and gritted his teeth. Reverend Flowers lifted a yardstick and slapped the boy's knuckles three times. The boy began to cry.

"Return to your seat and focus on your work," Reverend Flowers said. "If there is a third time, it will mean a visit to the woodshed."

Mary and Reverend Flowers oversaw the education of Blue Hills' children. Dozens of children, pre-teens, and teenagers lived on the estate. Mary and Reverend Flowers handpicked a small number of children for academic classes that met in the cider mill. Mary vetted the cider mill children with academic aptitude tests. Students with top scores received instruction in core academic areas during the late-fall, winter, and early-spring months. Students who did not measure up academically participated in a vocational and agricultural training program also designed by Mary.

Students in the vocational and agricultural program received only basic literacy and mathematics instruction. The lack of education kept the farmhands in a state of ignorance, and helped solidify the social structures at Blue Hills, further indenturing the farmhands to a system that dictated every aspect of the living and working conditions. The vocational and agricultural program provided Blue Hills' children a broad insight into how all activities on the estate contributed to the community. The training created a flexible workforce with the skills necessary to work in any area of production.

"All right, children. Put your pencils down," Mary said. The children stopped working and looked up. "As you know, tomorrow will be the last day of regular classes. The sowing season is here. We will only meet as a class on Wednesday and Thursday mornings until the harvest next fall. You are expected to keep up with your assignments during the spring and summer months. The evening tutorials will continue as normal. Your work and apprenticeship schedule is posted in Heritage Woods and here outside the cider mill. Class dismissed."

William stood in the doorway and watched the children filter out of the cider mill. The boys were dressed in work boots, overalls or jeans with suspenders, and button-down hemp or cotton shirts. The boys retrieved worn, hand-me-down Carhartt jackets hung on hooks near the entrance and scampered outside. The girls were dressed in homespun cotton prairie dresses with wool shawls thrown over their shoulders. William stepped to one side as the children filtered out of the classroom. The children nodded respectfully to William as they passed him. Two girls paused at the door.

"Good morning, girls," William said.

"Hi Dad," Susan said.

"Hello, Daddy," Catherine said.

"I can't believe how big you two are," William said. William gave each of the twins a kiss on the forehead. "I remember bouncing you both on my knee, and now here you are on the doorstep of your seventeenth birthday. Where did the years go? What do you have planned for the rest of the day?"

"Let's find out," Susan said.

The girls led William out the front door. The children gathered around papers posted on corkboard outside the cider mill, searching for their names in the handwritten columns. Catherine and Susan waited for the crowd to thin, and then stepped forward and scanned the lists headed carpentry, sewing, canning, plumbing, security, mechanical, farrier training, and electrical training.

"There you are," Susan said to Catherine, pointing at the carpentry list.

"Ugh," Catherine said.

"What's wrong?" William asked.

"Oh nothing, another week in the lumber mill isn't all that exciting."

"Yeah, but it's important. That mill provides the roof over our heads," William said.

"I know, I know. It's just all that sawdust and noise. It's not exactly the most enjoyable way to spend the day. I'd rather be sewing or canning."

"There I am," Susan said, pointing to her name on a list under the heading *mechanical*.

Susan ran her pointer finger down the list of names. Her finger paused briefly under the name of a boy in her class. Susan turned and shared a quick smile with Catherine.

"What's up?" William asked, noticing the exchange between his daughters.

"Nothing," Susan said. "What are you doing for the rest of the day?"

"Lots to be done," William said. "It should be an exciting day. The first plows will be in the fields."

"Okay, well, have fun, Daddy. We'd better get going," Susan said. "Don't want to be late for our apprenticeships."

"See you later, Daddy," Catherine said.

The girls giggled and skipped off together. William stepped forward and strained his neck to see the names on the *mechanical* list. He read the name that had filled Susan with joy – Eric.

"Good morning, William," Reverend Flowers said as he stepped out of the cider mill.

"Good morning, Reverend."

"Beautiful day here in God's kingdom."

"It is now that we survived February and March," William said. "That was one bear of a winter."

Climate change at Blue Hills was dramatic. Summers were long and hot, with at least thirty days each year topping one hundred and ten degrees. The fall was long and warm; the growing season extended into late-October, and a few crops continued to grow into mid-November. For the first time that previous season, Blue Hills' harvested cotton, a crop that previously only grew south of the Mason Dixon Line. Decembers on the estate ushered in a bizarre mixture of seventy-degree days and thirty-degree days. The temperature rarely dropped into the mid-twenties until late-January. After each New Year, the community braced for the dreaded month of February. In February, the temperatures dipped below freezing, just cold enough to turn rain into heavy, wet snow.

That February, the temperature at Blue Hills dipped into the teens, and three blizzards struck the estate in quick succession, each blizzard socking the community with three feet of snow. An impossibly heavy blanket of snow and ice buried the estate for weeks. Not even the strong backs and hungry stomachs of the farmhands could dig out from under twelve feet of snow and drifts that topped twenty feet.

"Fortunately for us all, spring has arrived early. You certainly aren't going to have any drought conditions this spring," Reverend Flowers said.

"Yeah, but now we have the opposite problem - the flooding is pretty bad. Please ask the Lord to spare us any rain until the Housatonic and Quinnipiac Rivers get back inside their banks."

"Good morning," Mary said, stepping out of the cider mill.

"Good morning," William said. "How were the lessons today?"

"They're coming along," Mary said.

The whine of an internal combustion engine filled the air. William turned and saw Crocco driving a John Deere Gator up to the cider mill.

"What in the Sam hell are you doing?" William asked.

Gas was a precious commodity on the estate. Mary and William strictly limited the use of vehicles with internal combustion engines. Transportation around the estate was limited to foot traffic, bicycles, and horseback.

"There's something you need to see right away," Crocco said, pulling the Gator up to the cider mill and putting it in park.

"It'd better be important if you're burning gas," William said.

"It is. Hop in, please. There's something I have to show you. I ain't never seen nothin' like it."

"What is it?" Mary asked.

"I don't know," Crocco said. "Something's killing off the wildlife down by the river. There're dead birds and fish everywhere."

"You're using the Gator because you found a few dead birds?" William asked.

"It's not just a few birds, sir. Trust me; you need to see this right away."

William said goodbye to Mary and Reverend Flowers and sat in the passenger seat. Crocco put the Gator in drive and drove down Blue Hills Road. He steered the Gator through the orchards, and up the side of a sloping hill. From the top of the hill, William and Crocco had a clear view of fallow fields that snaked along the Housatonic River. Crocco stepped on the brake and paused at the top of the rise.

"Geez, the flooding is worse today than it was last week. It's gonna be weeks before we can till those fields," William said.

"I don't know that we're going to be able to use these fields at all," Crocco said.

"What's got you all upset? I don't see anything except acres of flooded farmland."

"You'll see," Crocco said.

Crocco put the Gator in drive and drove down the hill towards the river. He parked the Gator a few hundred yards from the river on the edge of one of the fields.

"We'll have to walk from here. The Gator will get stuck in the mud," Crocco said.

William climbed out of the Gator and followed Crocco across a fallow cornfield. When they were within a few hundred feet of the river, William saw the first goose carcass. "Holy shit," William said. Hundreds of geese lay dead and dying on the flooded plain. William hunched down next to half-dozen dead geese and inspected the carcasses. "What the fuck happened to them?" William asked.

"I don't know. I saw them all flying in this past week. A couple of the boys came down here yesterday with their fishing rods and found 'em like this. Whatever killed 'em, killed 'em quick," Crocco said.

"Yeah. And all at once. Geez, I never thought a bunch of dead geese'd upset me; I always hated these filthy animals, they shit everywhere. But this is too much."

"Come on, there's more," Crocco said.

Crocco led William to the edge of the river, and pointed at dead fish floating in the currents and washed up along the banks. The smell of dead fish filled the air.

"Wow," William said.

"What do you think did it?"

"Must be something in the water."

"I was thinking the same thing," Crocco said. "That can't be good; we irrigate our crops with this water."

"Get a bucketful and let's head over to Butterworth," William said. "I have an idea."

CROCCO drove the Gator into the barnyard at Butterworth Farm, parked, and unloaded a five-gallon bucket full of water from the Housatonic River.

"Go park the Gator. There's no need to burn any more gas," William said.

Crocco parked the Gator in a shed behind the barn and returned to the barnyard.

"So, what's the plan?" Crocco asked.

"Where's that mangy old dog I always see laying around here?"

"You mean Flash?"

"Yeah. It's time for Flash to take one for the team," William said.

Crocco walked into the barn. A moment later, he returned with one of the farmhands. An old Springer Spaniel walked slowly behind the farmhand.

"This is Jack," Crocco said, introducing William to the farmhand. "Flash is his dog."

"It's nice to see you again," Jack said, stepping forward and extending his hand.

"Have we met before?" William asked, shaking Jack's hand.

"It's been over a decade. I'm not surprised you don't remember me. I was with you the day you purchased Sleeping Giant. You rode into that vagrant camp and kicked some ass," Jack said.

"Oh, yeah, I remember you now."

"We still talk about that around here. You had balls of steel doing that. You must remember Flash, he rode out with us that day," Jack said, reaching down and scratching Flash between the ears.

"Oh, sure. Flash, huh, it looks like it's been a long time since he lived up to his name."

"He definitely has a little gray on his snout, but don't we all. He's still a good boy. A little slow these days, that's all."

"He looks thirsty," William said. "Where's his water bowl?"

"Over there in the shade."

William walked across the barnyard and picked up a red water bowl placed under a Weeping Willow tree. William emptied the bowl, carried it to the five-gallon bucket, and filled it with water from the Housatonic River. William carried the bowl to Flash."

"Here you go, boy," William said, placing the water bowl in front of Flash.

Flash walked slowly to the water bowl. He sniffed the water and looked up at William. He sniffed again and looked at Jack.

"It's okay, boy. Go ahead," Jack said.

Flash lowered his nose to the bowl and began lapping the water. After a good long drink, Flash lifted his head, licked his lips, and walked to his favorite spot in the shade under the Weeping Willow. He stretched once and lay down under the tree.

"What do you need with him?" Jack asked.

"Hopefully nothing," William said.

"You ain't gonna hurt him, are you?"

William ignored the question. William pulled three cigars from his shirt pocket and handed one to Jack and one to Crocco. "Come on, boys. Let's enjoy a cigar."

William handed Jack a lighter. Jack lit the cigar, puffed deeply to get the ember burning, and gave the lighter to Crocco.

"So, what do you need Flash for?" Jack asked.

"Tell him," William said.

"There's been a fish and fowl kill on the estate down by the Housatonic River," Crocco said.

"Fish and fowl kill? What's that?"

"Just what it sounds like," Crocco said. "We've got a hundred or so dead geese sprawled across fields flooded with water from the Housatonic, and all up and down the river there are dozens of fish floating belly-up. We think something in the water might be poisoning the animals."

"And I suppose that bucket there is filled with water from the Housatonic," Jack said.

"That's right," Crocco said.

"Son-of-a-bitch."

Jack walked to the five-gallon bucket and dropped his cigar into the water. He walked over and sat down next to Flash under the Weeping Willow. Flash rested his head in Jack's lap, and rolled over on his back to let Jack rub his belly.

"He seems okay," Jack said.

"Give it a few minutes and we'll know for sure," William said, puffing on his cigar.

Nothing happened for the first half-hour. Forty-five minutes after drinking, Flash began to foam at the mouth and retch. An hour into

Charles Britton

the experiment, Flash twisted in a series of violent seizures and began vomiting blood.

"I guess we have our answer," Crocco said.

"Yup, that's enough. No need to make him suffer; better to put him down," William said.

Crocco and William reached for the Glock 9 mm handguns strapped to their thighs. Crocco pulled the gun from his holster and racked a round.

"I'll do it," Crocco said.

"Stay the fuck away from him," Jack said. "He's my dog, I'll do it."

Jack leaned over and gave Flash a kiss on the snout. He ran his hand up and down Flash's back, and then stood up. He removed a Smith and Wesson .38 Special Police Revolver from his holster and stepped back. He aimed the revolver at Flash's mid-section, raised his left hand to steady the weapon, and pulled the trigger twice.

Crocco held his Glock at his side, and William kept his hand on the butt of his handgun. Both men stood ready to cut Jack down if he turned away from Flash and drew down on them. They relaxed when Jack returned his revolver to the holster on his hip. Jack walked into the barn, and returned with a wheelbarrow and a shovel. He lifted Flash and gently placed him in the wheelbarrow next to the shovel.

"Need any help burying him?" Crocco asked.

"No. I'll do it myself."

"It would be crass for us to say 'thank you,'" William said. "Flash didn't die in vain. We needed to know if it was the water. You have a credit with me, Jack. Feel free to cash it in whenever you need something."

William and Crocco puffed their cigars and watched Jack wheel Flash towards the woods.

"Well, we know it was the water that killed those fish and geese. We've got to assume that if it's polluted enough to kill animals, it's gonna kill the crops, too," William said.

"Yup. It actually squares with some of what I've been hearing at Heritage Woods."

"What's that?" William asked.

"Folks have been complaining about the smell of chlorine. It's bad depending which way the wind is blowing, and on humid days when the air is thick."

"Ammonia."

"What?" Crocco asked.

"It's not chlorine, it's ammonia. It's one of dozens of chemicals used in steel production. Back in the day, I did some consulting work for the steel industry. Ammonia was one of the chemicals they were anxious to get out from under EPA regulation. The EPA fought like hell to keep the mills from dumping ammonia into the water supply. The EPA lawyers and agents got their panties in a bunch when we won."

"That makes sense. There are at least half-dozen steel mills upstream."

"Yup, steel mills and dozens of other manufacturers line the Housatonic as far north as Massachusetts. It was only a matter of time before the chemical concentrations reached toxic levels."

"What're we going to do?"

"I'm not sure we can do anything," William said.

IT was near dark when William walked into the farmhouse. He found Mary in the kitchen. William said hello, filled a rocks glass with ice and Wild Turkey, walked to his office on the second floor, and booted up his desktop computer. There hadn't been cellular service or Wi-Fi hotspots on the estate for many years. The only connection William had to the outside world came through a spotty satellite uplink reserved for high-level Movement officials. William expected the connection to fail, and was pleasantly surprised when his computer connected to the satellite. He clicked a link to a secure Movement ISP and waited for access.

In the decade after President Birch left office, cyberwars erupted across the internet. Anonymous hackers and foreign governments attacked America's internet infrastructure. Movement agents in the NSA allowed the attacks to go unchecked, and in some cases facilitated deeper access to American servers and ISP hosts. The internet was the last remaining threat to The Movement; Movement officials viewed the ease of access to information and news, and the ability to use the internet to organize progressive and federalist counter-movements as the sole remaining threat to individual liberty. The cyberwars obliterated America's internet, and left a pernicious collection of spyware and malware that could seek and destroy any effort to reconstitute internet service. The attacks also destroyed America's system of cellular and satellite communications. Cell phones, GPS, satellite television, and all satellite-based communication systems were permanently disabled. When the dust settled, America was dark; the crippled infrastructure and decimated electrical grid beyond repair. Spotty AM radio broadcasts dominated by right-wing pundits, printing presses, and aging landlines that were easily cut and abused by Mother Nature were the only remaining sources of information.

A female face appeared on William's monitor. "Good evening, Mr. Blake. My name is Jennifer, concierge 7477. How do you fare?" The woman asked.

"Hale and hearty, hearty and hale."

"Hale and hearty indeed. How may I help you this evening?"

"International news," William said.

William sipped his whiskey and surfed Movement-sanctioned international news headlines: *Saudi and Israeli Forces Break Republican Guard Lines, Pour into Tehran.... Brutal Urban Combat in Tehran, Kuds Force Vows No Surrender.... China Annexes Taiwan... Chinese and North Korean Forces Shell Seoul.... Pakistan and India on Brink of Nuclear Exchange... Russian Forces Push East Across Aleutian Islands... Ebola Spreads Through Central Africa.*

"That's enough," William said. "I'd like to see domestic news, please."

"Yes, sir," Jennifer said.

The first three headlines caught William's attention: *Canada Closes Border... Riots Reported at Dozens of Border Crossing... Canadian Border Patrol Opens Fire, Hundreds of Refugees Killed.* Waves of American refugees began surging north to the Canadian border in the years after President Birch left office. In the early years, Canada provided humanitarian help and visas to many in the legions of America's economic refugees. The Canadian public backlash had been predictable; Canadian voters swept waves of nationalist, right-wing politicians into office. The politicians invested billions of Canadian dollars in new fences, closed the border, and ordered the military to begin deporting the estimated eleven million Americans in Canada illegally. Canadian Mounties set up concentration camps along the border to warehouse American wetbacks.

"Fuckin' assholes," William said, tipping back his whiskey.

There was a soft knock and the door opened. Mary stuck her head into the office. "You okay in here?"

"Yeah, I'm fine, come on in."

"Let me guess, you're reading the news," Mary said.

"Yup."

"Why do you do that to yourself? You know how angry the news makes you. What's got you all riled up this time?"

"Fucking stupid Americans trying to get into Canada. I'll never understand why anyone would choose to give up the blessings of liberty for the socialist confines of Canada."

"Some people are unwilling to accept the responsibility that comes with freedom."

"Well, they'd better start figuring it out. The Canadian government is fed up; they're deporting Americans by the millions, and they just gave Canadian Border Patrol agents the green light to start shooting border jumpers."

"Try not to let it get to you. It's just part of the evolution"

"I guess you're right."

"There's something I need to talk to you about," Mary said.

"What's up?"

"I need to give you a heads up on Reverend Flowers' sermon this Sunday, and the community notes I'm going to make after the service."

"Okay. What's the plan?"

Mary required everyone on the estate to attend Sunday services in the cider mill. She assigned Catherine and Susan the responsibility for taking attendance. Absent farmhands were summoned to appear before Mary and Reverend Flowers to explain the absence. Any farmhands who claimed to be too ill to attend services could expect a bedside visit from Mary. Firm rebukes and public shaming during community notes followed unexcused absences. Repeated unexcused absences resulted in docked wages, provision reductions, and the promise of expulsion from Blue Hills.

Mary took full advantage of the community notes at the end of each service to share her observations of sloth, sin, and other malfeasance at Blue Hills. She regularly matched her observations with Reverend Flowers' firebrand sermons and promises of eternal damnation

"I am deeply concerned about some of the couples in the community using birth control," Mary said.

"Birth control?" William asked.

"Yes. With so many women of childbearing age, we should have more pregnancies on the estate. I know for sure that none of the women has access to birth control pills. I suspect that someone is smuggling condoms into Heritage Woods. I think they're getting them at the

Redwood Market. It might be time for us to begin limiting access to Redwood, and monitoring what's being brought onto the estate."

William stared at Mary. The last thing he wanted to do was monitor the family planning practices of couples at Heritage Woods. William didn't want to come right out and say it, but he hoped to God that the farmhands were using condoms. More mouths to feed on the estate promised to strain the finite resources the community produced. The community stemmed the influx of new farmhands, which meant the only new mouths to feed were newborn infants.

"I don't see how limiting access to Redwood is going to stop condom use in Heritage Woods. They're nearly impossible to detect. Besides, you don't even know for sure that they're being used," William said.

"Oh, I know they're being used. We need to root out every evil on this estate."

"All right, look, I have no objection to some firm rebukes during your community notes, but I'm not going to limit access to Redwood. The farmhands look forward to those visits; it's the only place they have to barter or buy new provisions."

"Fine, but I will be monitoring this carefully. Our women need to be fruitful and multiply – praise be to God," Mary said, looking up at the ceiling. "There's something else I have in mind."

"What?"

"It's time for us to build a stockade."

"A new fence?"

"No, not a fence; a stockade, like the kind you used to pose in for pictures at Sturbridge Village. But we need a real one, one that locks around peoples' wrists and neck."

"You're kidding, right?" William asked. "What the hell do you need that for?"

"Discipline. Right now, the only recourse we have with the community aside from firm rebukes is withholding provisions and wages. We need something with a little more bite."

"Jesus, Mary, you've got to be kidding. What's next, whipping posts and an iron maiden? Sounds pretty medieval to me."

"A firm hand, William. The Word of God and discipline from a firm hand is the only thing that will bind this community."

"Let me think about it. I haven't seen any behavior around here that warrants public shaming in a stockade," William said.

"Then you're not looking hard enough."

"All right, let's say there is something, what do you have in mind? Do you really want to shackle men and women in a stockade while the rest of us throw rotten tomatoes at them?"

"If that's what it takes to root out immorality, so be it."

"All right, all right, like I said, I'll think about it. What are the plans for the Sunday afternoon activities?" William asked.

Every Sunday after church services, the men and women separated by sexes and engaged in community activities. The men combined labor for barn raisings, fence construction, and sprucing up around the orchard. If there were no community projects, or they finished early, the men would spend the afternoon throwing horseshoes, racing horses, or holding shooting contests. The women would convene for sewing bees, canning sessions, or knitting circles. On Sunday evenings, the community would share dinner, then meet in a large, empty barn for square dances and hoe downs.

"I was going to ask the menfolk to build the stockade," Mary said.

"No, Mary, please…. Not this Sunday. I need to think about it."

"Fine, then I'll ask them to ride out to the eastern edge of Sleeping Giant and run some barbed wire. We chased off a few poachers last week."

"That sounds better. They just finished building a couple new wagons at the lumber mill. They can pack the boys and barbed wire in the back, and break 'em in on the ride over Sleeping Giant. What are the women doing?"

"We're going to spin the last bit of cotton from last year's harvest."

"Good. And what's the plan for the Sunday dinner?"

"Pig roast."

"Perfect."

"Is there anything I can do to get you to reconsider the stockade?" Mary asked.

"No."

Mary offered William a 'harrumph,' and stormed out of the office.

WILLIAM and Mary stood next to a fire pit watching three, ninety-pound pigs rotate on spits over coals. Grease from the pigs sprayed and sputtered over the fire. The pigs had been methodically spinning over the coals for twelve hours, slowly roasting into a culinary masterpiece.

"They look like they're almost done," William said.

"Yes, sir," a farmhand wearing an apron said. The farmhand had tended the pigs all night, carefully basting the pigs with beer brewed in the Blue Hills Brewery.

"Should I call everyone to dinner?" William asked.

"So long as the ladies have everything ready, the pigs are good to go," the farmhand said.

A group of women roasted potatoes and tossed salad with lettuce, tomatoes, onions and cucumbers grown in a greenhouse over the winter. Mary walked over to check the progress of the side dishes.

"Go ahead and call everyone," Mary said. "Everything'll be ready by the time everyone gets up here."

William followed Mary up the porch steps. They stood next to the dinner bell hanging from the eaves. William lifted the wand and began ringing the iron triangle. A sustained clang, clang, clang rang out over the estate, calling the community to dinner.

"How was the knitting circle?" William asked.

"It went well. We spun the last bushel of cotton and made onesies and blankets for the newborns at Heritage Woods," Mary said.

"That sounds like an appropriate thing to do following your community notes and Reverend Flowers' sermon."

"I thought so, too," Mary said. "The older women and I had a nice talk with some of the younger women. One young woman admitted to using birth control. She told us that her husband was pulling out, but I suspect something a bit more. She didn't come right out and admit to using condoms, but it was on the tip her tongue."

"Can you blame her? Would you have admitted to using condoms after Reverend Flowers' sermon and your community notes? She was probably scared to death."

"I suppose you're right; we got the message across."

"Good, firm rebukes is all you need. We don't need a stockade," William said.

"We'll see about that," Mary said. "And how did the men do? Did you get the barbed wire strung?"

"We fixed a portion of the fence that the poachers cut. The barbed wire should slow them down a little. We posted signs warning that trespassers will be shot on sight."

"What were they poaching?" Mary asked.

"Turkey and white tail deer most likely."

"Is there anything else you can do to stop them? I hate the idea of strangers stealing from us."

"We're gonna run some more regular patrols out there. Next time we catch a poacher, we'll string 'em up on the border of the estate. A few stretched necks should get the message out there."

"Good idea."

"What are the party favors tonight?" William asked.

At the end of the Sunday evening cookout and barn dance, Mary sent each family home with a treat as a way of saying thank you for their hard work.

"Honey and maple syrup," Mary said. "We're still pretty well stocked from last year, but it'll be nice to get production ramped back up now that spring has sprung, especially if we need to do some bartering at Redwood."

"I know. We need some replacement parts, and our propane is running dangerously low," William said. "Make a big deal out of the syrup and honey; the community pulled together this week to get the fields cleaned-up and tilled. We took a big step forward into the planting season."

"Here they come," Mary said.

William and Mary stood on the front porch watching the men, women and children from Heritage Woods walk towards the farmhouse. The dinner bell and the aroma of roasting pork had stomachs grumbling up and down Blue Hills Road. The men were dressed in white cotton or beige hemp button down shirts with suspenders and wool pants. The women wore colorful, full-length, cotton prairie dresses with lace bodices covering their necks. Mary would spend the better part of the night inspecting the dresses to make sure the hemlines rose no higher than the ankle. Mary reprimanded and sent any woman found with a high hemline back to Heritage Woods.

"All right, come on," William said. "Let's eat."

A line of farmhands stretched out around several tables loaded with roast pork, potatoes, and salad. The community loaded their plates, filled glasses with apple cider, and took seats at picnic tables and on blankets set up in front of the farmhouse.

William moved between the tables and blankets, asking how everyone fared, and spending a few minutes with each family to extend his appreciation for the backbreaking work it took to run the horse and bull drawn plows across the fields. When William visited each family, all conversation immediately stopped, and the men removed their hats in a show of respect for their benefactor. Blue Hills employed over three hundred farmhands. All the farmhands regarded William with a mixture of respect and fear. Despite the hardships and unending physical labor, each of the farmhands knew that things would be much worse if William or Mary expelled them from the estate. At Blue Hills, they could count on three meals a day, a roof over their heads, and a semblance of security.

The community's collective appetite picked the pigs clean. The farmhands enjoyed shortbread and strawberry preserve for dessert as darkness slowly settled over the orchard. The women led their children into a barn lit by kerosene lanterns while the men slipped into the darkened orchards around the barn to share mason jars filled with hard apple cider. A guitarist, fiddle player, standup bass player, drummer, and accordionist tuned their instruments, and a caller reviewed the set list and mentally rehearsed the steps for each dance. William stood off to one side of the barn watching the men and women line up for the first dance. The band began playing, and the caller hollered the first step.

William spotted Catherine standing off to one side of the barn with half-dozen teenage girls. The girls were giggling and staring at the dancers. William spotted the subject of the girls' gossip. Susan was dancing with a blonde-haired boy with high cheekbones, thin lips, and broad shoulders. William could tell by the way Susan stared at the boy that she was smitten. From across the barn, William saw Mary observing her daughter's flirtation with the young farmhand.

Mary stormed across the barn onto the sawdust covered dance floor. Susan and the blonde-haired boy turned a gate hollered by the caller to the 6/8 time of *Country Sunshine*. Mary grabbed Susan by the arm and pulled her off the dance floor. On her way out of the barn, Mary shot a nasty glare at Catherine and the gossipy teenagers. The girls quickly separated. William walked across the barn and stood next to Catherine.

"Hi, Dad," Catherine said.

"What was that all about?" William asked.

"What?"

"Don't play coy with me, Catherine. You know exactly what I'm talking about."

"His name's Eric Richard. He's a nice boy; you'd like him, Daddy. He's really smart and a hard worker. Susan likes him, and he adores her."

"How long has this been going on?"

"Since last fall. They didn't see much of each other in February, but they exchanged a few letters when the couriers shuffled from Heritage Woods to the farmhouse and cider mill for supplies."

"Letters, huh…I'm only going to ask this once," William said. "How far has it gone?"

"How far has what gone?" Catherine asked.

"Has their relationship turned physical?"

"No, Daddy, I promise. Susan's a good girl. She would never do anything like that. Eric's a good boy, too. He has been trying to work up the courage to come speak with you. He wants to court her."

WILLIAM and Mary sat at the kitchen table reading dozens of love letters written by Eric. William found the letters where Susan hid them under a loose board in her closet. The tender letters painted a picture of a boy in love for all the right reasons. William was impressed with the quality of Eric's writing, and the depth of his sentiments. William finished reading the last letter and looked across the table at Mary.

"Do you still think a stockade is a bad idea?" Mary asked.

"You're not serious, are you? You would put Eric in a stockade for falling in love with our daughter?"

"Absolutely. I have it in mind to walk down to Heritage Woods and send the Richardson family packing right this very instant."

"Come on, Mary. Let's not get carried away."

"He's too old for her."

"Nonsense, he's twenty-year-old. Susan and Catherine are almost seventeen; they're young and beautiful. This was bound to happen."

"What are you telling me? Do you want that boy having sex with your daughter while the whole community laughs and calls her a slut?"

"Of course not. You read these letters. The relationship is laid out in the boy's words right there in front of you. He's clearly taken with Susan for all the right reasons. Catherine told me Eric has been working up the courage to come speak with us and ask permission to court Susan."

"Never! You disgust me. You'd allow some filthy farmhand to slobber all over your daughter."

"You can't lock your daughters away forever."

"The hell I can't."

"And what, have them grow up to be lonely spinsters? Didn't you just reprimand the community for not being fruitful and multiplying? Don't you want grandchildren some day?"

Mary stood up from the table, turned her back to William, and walked across the kitchen. She crossed her arms and stared silently out the window.

"They're going to want their own lives, Mary. They want their freedom. You can't hold that against them; it's the natural course of things," William said.

"James and Annaliese will be married this summer. We're bundling them the month of July before the wedding in August. After that, I will consider allowing the girls to begin courting. When we allow them to see young men, it will only be with our blessing. Until then, that boy is no longer allowed to be with Susan."

"Okay, now you're sounding a bit more reasonable," William said.

"One more thing," Mary said, turning from the window and leveling a gaze at William. "I want the stockades built next Sunday."

"All right, you win; I'll have the men build a stockade after services next Sunday. You and Reverend Flowers can start planning the service and community notes."

"Two."

"What?"

"I want two stockades built in front of the cider mill."

"Fine, then in exchange, I want you to leave Susan and Eric alone for the time being. I'm going to Redwood tomorrow. I will take Susan with me and talk to her. Let me handle this situation with Eric. I don't want you going off the rails and doing anything crazy. If you push too hard, you will push her away," William said.

"Agreed. This situation is yours to handle, but I will be keeping a close eye on that boy. If he crosses the line, he and his family will rue the day."

CROCCO lifted the trailer and dropped the hitch onto a two-inch trailer ball on the back of a Ford F150. Farmhands loaded the trailer and bed of the truck with crates of fresh vegetables, five-gallon milk cans loaded with cream and whole milk, coolers filled with bacon, eggs, cheese, and butter, and boxes loaded with clothes and blankets sewn in the cider mill. Each of the fresh-from-the-farm staples would sell quickly, or be bartered away at the Redwood Market. The quickest selling items were loaded into the trailer last – mason jars of hard apple cider, sixty-four ounce growlers of beer, and bottles of moonshine and vodka. In the glovebox of the F150, William stashed bags of marijuana grown in the Blue Hills' greenhouses. The alcohol and marijuana were the most prized possessions at the market. Men would clamor around the Blue Hills Farm Stand as soon as the tables were set, and vigorously barter for the alcohol and pot.

William climbed into the cab of the Ford, and Susan pulled herself up into the truck and sat in the passenger seat. A dozen farmhands with assault rifles slung over their backs surrounded the truck on horseback. Another half-a-dozen farmhands would be waiting at the Redwood Market. The advance team would set up the tables, and prepare the farm stand for the arrival of Blue Hills' produce. William turned the key, put the truck in drive, and drove slowly down Blue Hills Road. The men on horses flanked the truck, keeping a close eye on the road as the truck drove off the Blue Hills estate and rolled onto Route 5.

"So, tell me about Eric," William said.

Susan rolled down her window and stared outside. "What do you want to know?" She asked.

"I read the letters, and I saw how you looked at him at the barn dance last Sunday. It's pretty clear to all of us that something's going on."

Tears filled Susan's eyes and began rolling down her cheeks. William reached across the seat and put his hand on Susan's shoulder.

"Come on, Honey. What's wrong?" William asked.

"I love him, Daddy. He's all I can think about. And he loves me. I want to be with him. I know mom will never let us be together."

"Your mom and I talked. She thinks you're too young."

"That's not it. She'll never allow me to be with a farmhand, no matter how many years separate us."

"Look, you're our daughter. That comes with certain responsibilities on the estate. People look to our family; they count on us to be an example of how to live a moral life."

"I am living a moral life. Eric and I aren't doing anything wrong. We're in love, and we're going to be together."

"Here's how it's going to go down: Your brother is marrying Annaliese in August. He and Annaliese will be bundled the month of July. After James's wedding in August, we will consider allowing you and your sister to court. But until then, you have to promise me you will stay away from Eric. Your mom will be watching you closely; she will find out if you see him. I'll look the other way if you two continue exchanging letters. But don't let your mother catch you, or see you with him."

"I wish I could believe you, Dad. You know she'll never let me or Catherine be with anyone on the estate. She looks down on everyone. No one will ever be good enough. And even if there was someone she thought was good enough, I'm not going to be married off in some arranged marriage. I love Eric; I'm going to be with him."

William stared out the window and kept his hand on his daughter's shoulder. He knew she was right. Mary viewed the farmhands the same way she viewed livestock on the estate. Eric or any of the men at Heritage Woods would never be good enough.

"Then you're going to have to trust me. I will work on your mother, I promise. You just have to promise me that you'll play along for a little while. Just wait until your brother is married."

"You promise?"

"Yes, Honey. I promise."

"I love you, Daddy."

"I love you, too, Sweetheart. Now, grab that clipboard on the seat next to you and let's go over what we need to find at the market."

One of the men on horseback rode up to the driver-side window and motioned for William to stop. William stepped on the brake and leaned out the window. "What's up?" William asked.

"There are some men on the shoulder of the road up ahead. I can't see how many, but it's more than a handful."

"Thieves?"

"Maybe."

"Take a couple men and ride up there to take a look," William said.

Three farmhands slung their assault rifles across their laps. They checked the action on the rifles, flipped the safeties to the fire position, and rode ahead. The remaining farmhands took defensive positions surrounding the truck. William pulled a Glock 9mm out of his holster and held it on his lap. He reached over and opened the glovebox. He removed a .38 Smith and Wesson revolver and handed it to Susan. William watched the farmhands ride up to the men on the side of the road. After a few minutes of conversation, the farmhands waved the truck forward. William drove towards the farmhands. One of the farmhands rode back towards the truck and spoke to William through the window.

"They're sketchy motherfuckers for sure. Oops, I'm sorry, I didn't realize there was a young lady in the truck," the farmhand said.

"It's okay," William said. "What did you tell them?"

"I told them we were from Blue Hills, and they saw our firepower. We've got 'em outmanned and outgunned," the farmhand said. "We're definitely not a soft target; we should cruise through without a problem."

"All right, but keep an eye on them."

"Absolutely."

The farmhands kept their rifles pointed at the highway robbers as they passed. The bandits were sitting on the shoulder of the road at a curve that was perfect for an ambush. William glared at the men as they passed. One of the thieves had the gall to wink at William. William considered ordering the farmhands to open fire and cut the men down, but Susan's presence in the cab of the truck made him think twice. He decided to wait until Susan was out of earshot before ordering his men to ride back to the curve in the road and kill the thieves.

William drove the truck into a long, narrow parking lot that spread out along Route 5 in the shadow of Sleeping Giant. A sign at the entrance to the market announced their arrival at the *Redwood Country Flea Market*. The market was once a smalltime operation only open on Saturday and Sunday afternoons. It was a place for people to empty out their garages and sheds, and sell off junk and extra stuff without having to organize garage or tag sales. With the collapse of interstate commerce, and closure of the big box stores and supermarkets, Redwood transformed into a bustling farmer's market, and eventually grew into an indispensable feature of commerce in the greater New Haven area.

William parked the truck and helped the farmhands unload the trailer. The men placed Blue Hills produce on tables under a *Blue Hills Farm Stand* banner. Men and women in the market immediately flocked to the tables. Blue Hills' farmhands only accepted Canadian dollars for their goods and produce. William kept a reserve of produce, alcohol, and marijuana in the bed of the truck while his men spread out across the market searching for gasoline, propane, spare parts for the community's generators and vehicles, penicillin, and medical supplies to barter for. When his men found the supplies on the list prepared by Crocco and Mary, they returned to the truck to review the negotiations with William and finalize the details of the trade. By Noon, the Blue

Hills Farm Stand was bare, and the trailer and bed of the truck loaded with fresh supplies.

"Take the truck and my daughter back to Blue Hills," William told one of the farmhands. "Bring a dozen men with you to make sure you get back without incident. I'll ride back with the rest of the men in a few hours."

"How come you're not coming back to the estate?" Susan asked William when he told her she was riding back without him.

"There're a few things I need to check on. I'll meet you home in a few hours."

"What do you need to check?" Susan asked.

"The men and I are going to ride around the perimeter of Sleeping Giant over by Quinnipiac University. I want to check on the condition of the fences."

"Be careful."

"Always. Tell your mother I'll be back before dark," William said.

William watched the Ford and mounted escort pull out of the market and turn north on Route 5. William waited for the truck to roll out of sight before walking towards the back of the market. Two farmhands stayed with the horses, and four men followed William to an RV parked in a corner of the lot. The farmhands stood guard while William walked up to the RV and knocked on the door.

"Yeah, what do you want?" A man's voice hollered from inside the RV.

William knocked a second time. The door opened and a man with a beer belly, wearing a stained t-shirt, and filthy boxer shorts opened the door.

"Mr. Blake," the man said.

The man stepped aside and William climbed a set of steps into the RV. A 15-year-old girl in a short, paisley sundress sat on a sweat-stained couch, and an older woman missing several teeth stood at the sink smoking a cigarette.

"Same price as last time?" William asked.

"She's the same," The man said, nodding towards his decrepit wife. "It's an extra ounce and growler for the girl."

"Is she clean?" William asked. "Last time she smelled like shit."

The man nodded to his daughter. The girl stood up from the couch and lifted her sundress to show William that she was wearing a pair of clean, white panties. William walked over to inspect the teenager. A sweet waft of vanilla filled his nose as he ran his fingers across the girl's tight stomach.

"You smell good. Were you expecting me today?" William asked. The girl smiled at him. "All right, an extra ounce and growler."

William walked outside and spoke to his men. One of the farmhands accompanied William into the RV. They placed three, sixty-four ounce growlers of homebrewed beer, four mason jars of hard cider, and a milk jug of vodka on the table. William threw two ounces of marijuana at the man in the stained t-shirt and told him to get the fuck out of the RV. The man pulled on a pair of pants and told William and the farmhand to have fun. The farmhand moved towards the man's wife. William led the girl into a small bedroom at the back of the RV.

July, 2046

WILLIAM stood in the doorway watching Catherine, Susan, Mary, and Annaliese's mother bundle James and Annaliese by the light of candles and a kerosene lamp. The women slowly and methodically sewed the couple into separate bundles. In the morning, Mary and Annaliese's mother would inspect the bundles to make sure that the soon-to-be husband and wife hadn't torn open the seams. If they did, they would put their relationship at risk; Mary would call off the wedding if she determined that her prospective daughter-in-law was a harlot willing to succumb to lust outside of wedlock.

The month of July had been blisteringly hot. William felt sorry for James and Annaliese. Even though they were sewn into light cotton sheets instead of the normal wool blankets, they would spend the night sweltering in the dead, humid, ninety-five degree air of James's bedroom. The solar generators outside the farmhouse only provided enough power to run the well pump and hot water heater. The excess wattage was used to power a few lights in the kitchen and run the ice chest. Air conditioners and fans were a luxury of a long-gone decade. Even so, William suspected that James and Annaliese would not object; they were in love, and anxious to be married. The month spent bundled in bed together was enough of a tease to get their juices flowing in preparation for their wedding night in August. William smiled each morning when he saw suspiciously stained sheets hanging on a clothesline outside the farmhouse. Even through the bundles, it was clear that James and Annaliese had found a way to share intimacy, which was to be expected as they explored one another's naked, young bodies through the light cotton sheets.

Mary led the family in prayer after the last stitch sealed the bundles. At the end of the prayer, everyone said goodnight and left James and Annaliese alone. Susan grabbed William's arm as they stepped into the hallway outside of James's bedroom.

"Dad," Susan said. "Can I talk to you for a minute?"

"Sure." William led Susan into his office and closed the door behind him. "What's up, Hon?"

"It's been three months since Eric and I spoke. I've seen him around the estate plenty of times, but I haven't said a word to him. Are you still working on mom? You promised that after James's wedding you'd allow me to see him."

"I haven't forgotten, Sweetheart. We made a deal. You're keeping up your end, and I will keep up my end of the bargain. I assume you two are still exchanging letters."

Susan smiled at her father.

"Well," William said. "Make sure you keep them in a good hiding place, or burn them after you read 'em. We don't want your mother finding out."

"Thank you. I love you, Daddy."

"I love you, too."

William kissed Susan on the forehead and walked downstairs to the kitchen. He poured whiskey over ice in a rocks glass and prepared to adjourn to the family room to read when there was a knock on the farmhouse door. William opened the door and found Crocco standing on the front porch.

"I'm sorry to bother you at this time of night," Crocco said. "There's a lady asking for you at the front gate. She's says she knows you."

"I'm not expecting anyone. It's probably just a vagrant or beggar dropping my name. Send her packing," William said.

"We tried. But she seems to know an awful lot about you. Says her name is Tabitha Couture."

The rocks glass slipped from William's hand and shattered on the front porch.

"You all right, sir?" Crocco asked.

"Where is she?"

"Front gate."

"Let's go," William said.

William arrived at the front gate and found two men and a woman standing outside the fence. The men wore black Kevlar vests and carried assault rifles. Three farmhands stood inside the gate watching the strangers carefully. William suspected that if a firefight broke out the men outside the fence would easily gun down the farmhands. All the men held assault rifles, but the strangers held their weapons differently. The men outside the gate wore their gun straps tight across their shoulders and chest, which would make it easier to shoot and move at the same time if a fight broke out. This contrasted with the farmhands, who held their rifles haphazardly across their stomachs. The strange men were clearly seasoned ex-special forces soldiers; William suspected they were Army Rangers or Delta Force.

William opened the front gate and stepped outside the fence. A woman in a hooded sweatshirt carrying something in her arms stepped forward from between the soldiers. The soldiers watched closely as she approached William.

"Hello, William," Tabitha said, pulling back the hood. Tabitha adjusted the bundle in her arms, and William saw she was holding an infant.

"Tabitha, is it really you?"

"It's me," Tabitha said. She stepped forward and gave William a kiss on the cheek.

"And what's this?" William asked, looking down at the infant.

"His name is Edward. He's named after his grandfather."

William stared at Tabitha and the infant for a long moment. "His grandfather?" William asked.

"Yes. We have a lot of catching up to do," Tabitha said.

"Please, please, come in," William said, motioning for his men to open the gate.

William and Crocco escorted Tabitha and the soldiers to an empty condominium in Heritage Woods. William stepped into the vacant condominium and flipped on a single light.

"You still have electricity. That's amazing," Tabitha said.

"Yes," William said proudly. "We get electricity from our solar and wind generators. Each family in Heritage Woods gets about one hundred watts of electricity. We use the rest of the power to keep the water pumps running. Every condo has running water in the kitchen and bathroom, and all the toilets flush. The condos also have solar hot water heaters, so you're welcome to take a warm bath or shower."

"Electricity, toilets, and hot water; you're doing well for yourself," Tabitha said. "I don't suppose you have air conditioning."

"That's a luxury we do without. You're welcome to stay here. The condo next door is also vacant if your men want a place of their own to crash."

The soldiers looked at Tabitha, expecting her to say no.

"Are we safe here?" Tabitha asked.

"Safe? From what?"

"Things that go bump in the night," Tabitha said.

"Blue Hills is as safe as it gets. The estate is fenced-in and we have sentries patrolling the grounds twenty-four seven."

"Well, I suppose that's as safe as it gets in this brave new world of ours. It's okay, boys," Tabitha said to the soldiers. "Go on next door, I need some time alone with Mr. Blake."

"Take them next door," William said to Crocco. "Oh, and tell the men at the fence to keep their mouths shut. No one is to know we have guests on the estate."

"They'll have to stay indoors," Crocco said. "Heritage Woods will be bustling with farmhands when the sun comes up."

"Right," William said. "You guys have to promise to stay indoors until we can find more private housing."

The men nodded and left with Crocco.

"Let me get him fed and into bed," Tabitha said, nuzzling the infant. "Then we can talk."

Tabitha followed William to the second floor of the condominium. William drew the shades and lit a kerosene lantern in the bedroom, and another lantern in the bathroom. Tabitha changed the baby's diaper, and fed him a bottle of formula. Tabitha rocked the infant to sleep and put him down on a mattress in the bedroom. She used the warm water in the bathroom to clean herself up, and changed into clean shorts and a tank top. When she was sure the baby was asleep, she walked downstairs, where William was waiting under the sharp glow of a single, naked lightbulb hanging from the ceiling.

William stared at Tabitha as she descended the staircase. Even in the unflattering glare of the single, eighty-watt bulb, and past middle age, Tabitha was as beautiful as ever. There was a slight osteoporotic bend to her back, but she still carried herself with the sleek, avian movements that William remembered from their days at Beacon Academy. Her hair was thinner and shorter with a few streaks of gray, and crow's feet clawed at the corners of her eyes, but her face still held the glow of youth, and her eyes were as deep, intense, and mesmerizing as ever.

William was at a loss for words as Tabitha crossed the room and sat down next to him on a dusty couch. "How do you fare?" William stammered.

"Oh, William," Tabitha said, reaching over and putting her hand on his thigh. "There's no more hale and hearty in my life."

"Is that your baby?" William asked.

"He's my grandson."

"Where's his mother?"

"Dead. Baby Edward is all I have left in the world that means anything to me."

"I'm sorry," William said.

"So am I. I suppose we both have a lot to be sorry for."

"Where have you been for the last eighteen years?" William asked.

"Rosewood."

"With President Birch?"

"Yes. Rosewood has become a fortified commune, a little like what you have here. I was kept there by Edward for many years."

"You had children with him. Were you married?"

"We had one child together, but were never married."

"Where is he now?"

"I'm not sure. I imagine he's searching every corner of Earth for me and his grandson."

"You left him?"

"I more than just left him. Can I trust you, William?"

"Yes, of course. What's going on?"

There was a knock on the condominium door. William stood up from the couch, crossed the living room, and cracked open the door. He opened the door when he saw Crocco standing on the doorstep. Crocco stepped into the condominium and William shut the door behind him.

"Your wife has people looking everywhere for you," Crocco said.

"Shit. Already. All right look, I've got to get back to the farmhouse," William said to Tabitha. "Crocco will get you and your men anything you want to eat or drink, and anything else you need. Does the baby cry a lot?"

"No, he's a very easy baby."

"Good. The walls between the condos are paper-thin. Things haven't changed with Mary, even after all these years, she's still as jealous and controlling as ever. You have to promise me you'll lay low."

"My men and I have many reasons to keep our presence here a secret," Tabitha said. "And for reasons far more compelling than a jealous wife."

"Okay, good. Spend the night here and stay out of sight tomorrow morning. I'll send someone for you tomorrow afternoon. We'll move you somewhere else tomorrow night," William said. William turned and spoke to Crocco, "Come see me first thing in the morning and we'll figure this out."

William walked back to the farmhouse. Mary was waiting for him on the front porch.

"Where the hell did you run off to?" Mary asked.

"They needed me at the front gate. There were some vagrants trying to get on the estate."

"You dropped your glass on the porch and ran off like a bat out of hell because of a few vagrants? That seems a little excessive. You had me worried."

"Oh, yeah, I'm sorry. I'll clean it up," William said.

"Already done," Mary said.

"Thanks. Everything is fine. Come on, let's go to bed."

William followed Mary up a staircase to the second floor of the farmhouse. They paused in the hallway and listened to James and Annaliese giggling through James's bedroom door. William brushed his teeth, changed into pajamas, and climbed into bed next to Mary. He knew it would be a long, sleepless night.

WILLIAM stood in the doorway to James's bedroom drinking a cup of coffee and watching Mary and Annaliese's mother inspect the stitching on the bundles. Once they determined that James and Annaliese hadn't freed themselves from the bundles during the night, they used scissors to cut the stitches and release the young lovers from the cotton cocoons. William saw Crocco riding a horse towards the farmhouse through James's bedroom window. He walked downstairs and stepped onto the front porch. It was only Seven O'clock in the morning and already the temperatures topped eighty degrees, and promised to spike in the one hundreds by mid-day. Crocco rode up to the farmhouse. He held the reins to a second horse, and led the animal behind his horse to the front porch.

"Mr. Blake," Crocco said. "I need you to see something at Butterworth. A few of the livestock have come down with something. The vet's there now."

Crocco projected his voice loud enough for anyone inside the farmhouse to hear the ruse. William told Crocco to hold on. He stuck his head inside the farmhouse and yelled to everyone that he was riding to Butterworth Farm. James called down the steps from the second floor and asked William if he wanted company. William told his son to enjoy a quiet breakfast with Annaliese. William stepped off the porch and mounted the horse. He and Crocco turned and directed the animals towards Butterworth.

"Good job," William said when they were far enough from the farmhouse that he was sure no one would hear.

"No problem. So, what's the game plan?"

"Send a group of men on horseback out into the suburbs around the estate and find a house in relatively good shape where we can put them up," William said.

"You mean outside the fence?"

The suburbs surrounding Blue Hills had fallen apart. The collapse of Connecticut's infrastructure and shortage of gasoline crippled private ownership of cars that were the lifeline to suburban existence. When public services fell apart, the middle class houses and McMansions were left without electricity, city sewer, or city water. Suburbanites abandoned their neatly manicured lawns and began renting or buying houses and apartments in cities and town centers where they could rely on walking or biking for transportation, and where there remained some semblance of city services. The middle class homes and McMansions on cul-de-sacs and leafy suburban roads were pillaged and looted for copper, scrap metal, and spare parts, most of which was sold at Redwood. Without upkeep, many of the homes had partially collapsed or burned to the ground.

"There must be a house or two in relatively good shape. Take a generator and hook it up for them. Make sure it's close to the estate, but far enough away where they won't raise any suspicions," William said.

"Okay, I'll have some men ride out this morning and see what they can find. Are you worried about security? There're still some sketchy people trolling the suburbs."

"I'm not worried. I'm sure those men with Tabitha know how to handle themselves, and trust me, Tabitha is no slouch when it comes to self-defense."

'Okay, I'm on top of it," Crocco said.

"Good. I have one more thing I want you to do. Find a female farmhand who is good with babies and you trust will keep her mouth shut. I want her to babysit Tabitha's grandson for the day. Ride into Heritage Woods this afternoon, give Tabitha clothes that will help her blend in on the estate, and bring her to me. She and I are going to ride up Sleeping Giant and talk. I need to figure out what the hell is going on."

William spent the morning at Butterworth Farm anxiously waiting for Tabitha and Crocco to arrive. Shortly before Noon, William spotted Crocco and Tabitha riding towards the farm. Tabitha was dressed in a light blue prairie dress. William walked up to her horse and grabbed hold of the bridle.

"Hey," William said. "You look nice. Sorry we couldn't let you wear your normal clothes; you'd stick out like a sore thumb."

"No problem. I actually like the dress. It's very retro," Tabitha said.

"How did you and the baby sleep?"

"Very well."

"Are you comfortable with the babysitter?"

"Yeah. Edward's an easy baby; he won't give her any problems."

"Good. Did Crocco tell you about our plans to move you off the estate tonight?"

"No."

"We have men searching the suburbs for a nice place. I'll have a generator hooked up for you. Hopefully, we can find a house that still has wiring intact and a well so we can hook a generator directly into the electrical box and get the water pump, hot water heater, and lights working."

"That's very kind of you," Tabitha said. "I can't thank you enough. But it's not necessary, we won't be staying long."

"We'll see about that; I'm going to do my best to talk you into staying for a little while, at least. I was thinking we could take a ride up to the top of Sleeping Giant. I have a lunch packed for us," William said.

"Sleeping Giant?"

"Yeah, he's right there behind you - Sleeping Giant Park," William said, nodding towards the mountain range. "It's very peaceful up there, we can talk privately."

"Sounds good to me."

"All right, let's gear up."

William retrieved two M4A1 assault rifles with leather straps from a gun safe in the Butterworth barn. He handed one to Tabitha and slung one over his shoulder. Tabitha slung the rifle across her back and waited for William to mount up.

"Want me to ride with you guys?" Crocco asked.

"No," William said.

"How about a security detail?"

"We'll be fine," William said. "We need to talk in private."

THE horses walked single file up a narrow trail. Halfway up Sleeping Giant, the trail widened enough for the horses to walk side-by-side. William pulled on the reins and waited for Tabitha to ride next to him.

"It's the surprise of a lifetime to have you here," William said. "Fill me in on what's been going on."

"Geez, I don't even know where to start."

"Start with your family. You said the baby is your grandchild."

"Yes. After Edward left office, we all retired to Rosewood. He took me, and I had his child – Isabella. She was a beautiful girl. Even with his dark presence in my life, I had one beam of light to keep me going – Isabella. When she turned sixteen, Isabella fell in love with one of the men on Edward's security detail. She got pregnant. She died giving birth, the doctors just couldn't stop the bleeding," Tabitha said.

"That's awful. I'm so sorry. Why did you leave Rosewood?"

"I had to. I couldn't take it any longer. The lies, the deceit; Edward is an evil force."

"Evil? That sounds a little extreme. What did he do to you?"

"He has done things to me that would break most women. But this isn't about me, I'm not here to ask for your help protecting me, I'm here to ask for your help with the counter-movement."

"Counter-movement? What's that?"

"A counter-movement is growing state-by-state, city-by-city, town-by-town across this nation. People are starting to come together to throw off the damage done to our communities by reconstituting social order. It's a counter-revolution, William; a chance to pull this nation back together before it spirals completely out of control."

"Why?"

"Oh, William. How can you even ask why? Look at what we've become. Look at the suffering across the land. We were wrong. We were so blind, and so wrong. The Movement destroyed this nation. I was the face of that destruction while you helped pave the path to anarchy through your policy work. We owe it to the throngs of people suffering out there to make every effort to roll back the forces we unleashed."

"Even if you could convince me of the *why*, *how* do you propose to begin this counter-movement?"

The horses reached the castle at the top of Sleeping Giant. Tabitha and William dismounted. William tied the reins around low hanging branches, lifted a picnic lunch out of a saddlebag, and led Tabitha to the top of the castle. William spread out a blanket and set up a lunch of fried chicken, cornbread, hardboiled eggs, and canned peaches. Tabitha stared down from the top of Sleeping Giant while William set up the picnic lunch. William joined her and stared out over the crumbling remains of Quinnipiac University. They watched smoke and smog choke New Haven and blanket Long Island Sound.

"There's your why," Tabitha said, waving her hand out over the wasteland.

"What?" William asked.

"You asked me why we need a revolution - there's your answer. Everything has gone to shit. We tore away all the structures that used to bind and protect people in this country. We declawed the institutions that constrained the excesses of men and women fueled by greed and want. We created this cesspool."

"It's not that bad," William said. "People who embrace personal responsibility are thriving. Just look at my estate."

"How long do you think your farm can last? Do you have any idea what's happening around you?"

"What do you mean?"

"Do you know what's happening across this nation? Do you know what's clawing its way towards your farm?"

"Sure. I still have access to the Movement newsfeed over a satellite connection. I know that there are some tough situations out there. But there have always been tough situations."

"Tough situations, is that what you call it? William, you're blind; don't believe a goddamned thing that you read on that Movement newsfeed. It's all sanitized propaganda. Here's the truth: Edward Birch has unleashed chaos and anarchy on this nation. I believe that was his goal from the very beginning, to use The Movement to unleash war, pestilence, famine, and death on the United States. He used the promise of liberty and freedom to soften us up, and push aside all the structures that stood in the way of anarchy. He conned Americans into believing that the natural state of man is liberty and free will; it is not, the natural state of man is war and death in all its' miserable forms. All those social contracts and government structures we fought so hard to destroy were actually a thin bulwark against chaos. Edward Birch is no hero; he is a demon. Trust me, I know. I've stared deeply into his beady, black eyes; I've been held in his cloven hands; I've smelt the sulfur and brimstone on my body when he's finished raping my flesh. He is a dark force that is reveling in the wrath and ruin that has befallen this nation."

"That all sounds a little extreme."

"It's the furthest thing from extreme. You may have carved out a sweet little community for yourself, but you are an island in a sea of misery - the tide is rising quickly. It's only a matter of time before you and your estate are consumed by famine, pestilence, and death. We have a small window; I'm thinking maybe three to five years to try and put the genie back in the bottle."

"How?"

"We have men and women in place in state capitols across the region who are working to reconstitute local and state governments. Many of these people are the same men and women who you worked with during the movement. If we can get some structures re-established, the goal is to hold a second round of constitutional conventions and repeal all the Liberty Amendments and the Supremacy Amendment at the state level. Once the Liberty Amendments and Supremacy Amendment are gone, we can begin making and enforcing laws once again. As soon as we can enforce law, we can begin to rebuild society based on those laws."

"So, let me see if I've got this straight," William said. "You took your grandson and fled Rosewood, leaving Edward Birch in the dust, and now you're bent on starting a counter-movement, and you want me to help you foment this revolution."

"That's exactly right."

"You're doing this because you believe that Edward Birch is some demon, perhaps even the anti-Christ himself, whose goal all along has been to unleash an apocalypse on America. You believe Edward Birch did this by duping Americans into believing that pure freedom and liberty is a good thing, when in reality it has been a pathway to anarchy. By throwing off the yoke of centralized government, you believe Edward Birch has doomed us to an existence of war, famine, pestilence, and death. Now you believe that if we don't start a counter-movement immediately, the four horsemen of the apocalypse will ride, and the end of days will befall us. Have I got all that right?"

"You're the one coloring this situation with all types of Christian imagery," Tabitha said. "I'm not some crazy Evangelical out there hollering for people to repent because the end of days has arrived. Those Biblical allusions you just threw around don't resonate with me; perhaps they will with whatever Evangelical fervor your wife has stoked down there at Blue Hills. My view of what's happening is far more secular. It goes like this: The Movement and Edward Birch effectively fucked America up. We're on the brink of complete chaos. Even now, it may be too late to save America from spiraling into anarchy. As far as Edward Birch himself, it's not for me to say if he is an actual demon or the anti-Christ. What I can tell you is that he is a man possessed of a powerful charisma and an ability to control people that goes far beyond any normal sphere of influence. I can tell you firsthand that I have been possessed and used by the man; he has done some terrible things to me; things I would never allow any other man to do. If there is evil in the world, I believe Edward is possessed of that evil. So, to sum it up, whether you choose to describe what is happening to America in Biblical or secular terms, the current state of the nation is not some utopic natural order in which every man is free and the master of his own domain. America is decaying into a wasteland in which people are suffering very badly. It's a wasteland that you and I helped create, William. I think of it like the old Pottery Barn rule; we broke it, now we own it. I'm here because I need your help putting the pieces back together."

William stared over the expanse of greater New Haven from the top of the castle. Black tendrils of smoke curled into the air from homes burning in the blighted suburban neighborhoods of North Haven and Hamden. In New Haven proper, tendrils of smoke from burning tires marking gangland territory twisted over the city and floated over Long Island Sound. William took a deep breath. The oppressively humid, hot, and stagnant air did little to refresh the capillaries in his lungs.

"You're asking me to reject everything I've believed in and fought for my entire adult life," William said. "And here's the irony of it, you were the one who recruited me at the very beginning. I'm only here because of you."

"I bear the full weight of knowing that you are part of this because of me. It's not just you, William; I was the face of The Movement for many years, I helped con an entire nation. I convinced hundreds of millions of people to swallow Edward Birch's poisoned Kool-Aide. I now intend to spend the rest of my life trying to put Humpty Dumpty back together again."

"Let's pretend for a minute that I'm willing to go along. What do you want from me? What exactly are you asking me to do?"

"I'm gathering the support of as many former top-ranking Movement officials as I can. Many have joined me. I'm not prepared to share their names with you, but trust me when I tell you that people are turning on The Movement. You and the others know exactly how America was dismantled, and I believe you and the others are the only people with the knowledge and skills necessary to put her back together."

"What are the first steps?"

"We're starting at the state level. I want you to reach out to the delegates who you groomed and assembled for the state constitutional convention in Connecticut. Reassemble them and repeal all of the Liberty Amendments and the Supremacy Amendment. Then have them reconstitute a Connecticut State Legislature and appoint a new governor. There won't be time to elect a governor, so have them pass emergency legislation that allows for the appointment of a governor until such time that an election can be organized. The same process will play out concurrently in other states. Once the states have regained centralized control, we'll go after Washington D.C."

"That's not going to be easy. The internet is long-gone, phone lines are barely functional, cellular service is dead, and there is no working postal service," William said.

"You have men, women, and a barn full of horses. Start a new Pony Express. Get the word out quickly and quietly to every corner of Connecticut. I recommend convening the convention on your estate. You have the facilities and the security. You might even want to consider making Blue Hills the seat of state government until you can gain control over the cities once you create a new state police force," Tabitha said.

"And you think Edward is going to allow us to pull government back together without a fight."

"Definitely not. We can expect a fight. I guarantee bloodshed. We're going to have to be cunning and move quickly. When we're ready, we will also need muscle."

"I have about two hundred men on my estate. I have one small group of men who have some paramilitary training, but the vast majority are plain old farmhands; we wouldn't stand a chance against a professional military."

"That's when you can count on me. Several former high-ranking military officers have joined the revolution. As we speak, they're pulling together their units and reorganizing a standing militia. We'll be ready to protect your convention and stand up to whatever The Movement has left to throw at us. You'll also be able to count on them to enforce Connecticut state law until you can assemble a state police force."

"When do you want me to hold this convention? It will take me time to get the word out to the delegates, and that's assuming I can even locate them."

"We're moving quickly. Time is not on our side. We're hopeful that we can hold the conventions before Thanksgiving this year."

"November, huh, three months from now; it's ambitious, but I guess it's doable."

William contemplated the logistics. He could send Blue Hills' farmhands all across Connecticut. If they rode like Paul Revere, there was a chance they could spread the word across the state and meet the November deadline.

"All right," William said. "I could probably organize Connecticut. But I couldn't get Massachusetts and Rhode Island together, too."

"You worry about Connecticut. We've got people organizing the other states."

"It's doable," William said.

"Good. Are you in?" Tabitha asked.

"I need some time to think."

"We don't have the luxury of time, and I don't know what there is to think about. Face reality, William; the island of tranquility you've built at Blue Hills is a mirage. It's only a matter of time before you're swallowed in the sea of misery swirling around you."

William stared pensively off the top of Sleeping Giant. Tabitha walked behind him and wrapped her arms around his back and across his stomach. She leaned her head against his back.

"I need you, William."

William turned and hugged Tabitha. Tabitha buried her face in William's chest while William rested his chin on her head. Tabitha leaned back, tilted her head, and lifted upward on the balls of her feet. Their lips met. For the first time in his life, William felt himself slip into a swirl of passion that wasn't paid for. Tabitha leaned back, stared William in the eyes, and began slowly unbuttoning his shirt.

"I've wanted this for so long," William whispered.

"I know. I was so bad to you when we were kids. I'm so sorry. I'm going to make it up to you," Tabitha said, sliding down to her knees and unbuttoning William's pants.

William pulled his shirt off and let his pants and underwear bundle around his ankles. He grabbed two handfuls of Tabitha's hair and leaned back against the castle wall. After several minutes, Tabitha stood and kissed William. William unbuttoned the buttons on the back of the prairie dress. Tabitha let the dress fall off her body when William released the final button. Tabitha took William's hand and led him to the picnic blanket. They made love for hours. When they were finished, Tabitha rested her head on William's chest. William felt Tabitha's breath against his neck and chest as he swam in the post-coital glow.

"Will you stay for a while?" William asked. "We'll find a nice place for you and baby Edward."

"No. There's much to be done, and I have to keep moving. The Movement is hunting me; I'm usually only one or two steps ahead of them."

"Where are you going next?"

"It's better that you don't know."

"How are you getting there? You and your men don't have horses or a vehicle. Are you walking?"

"The counter-movement has set up an underground railroad."

"When will I see you again?"

"I don't know."

"How can I reach you?"

"Get the convention organized as quickly as you can. Once Connecticut and the other state governments get organized, we'll open interstate communications by establishing a new Post Office. Until then, I'll send word to you by courier."

"So, what you're telling me is that the only way I'll ever see or hear from you again is if I join your counter-movement?"

"Yes," Tabitha said. "I have one more favor to ask."

"What?"

"I need you to keep baby Edward. He's not safe with me."

"I can't," William said.

"Please, William. I know you can't keep him yourself, Mary would never allow that, but you must have families on the estate who can take him in. There must be someone you trust to look after him and keep him safe."

William leaned his head back on the blanket and stared up at the hazy sky. The weight of Tabitha's naked body against his, and caress of her fingers as she played with the hair on his chest left him lightheaded. He knew that taking-in baby Edward would offer the best chance of ever seeing Tabitha again.

"Okay," William said.

"Thank you. I love you, William."

"I love you, too."

Tabitha and William dressed, packed the picnic lunch, and rode back to Butterworth. Tabitha's men were waiting for them in the shade of the Willow Tree in the barnyard. Tabitha nodded towards the men as she dismounted. One of the men removed a satellite radio from his pack and established an uplink. Moments later, the unfamiliar sound of a helicopter filled the air. It had been years since anyone on the estate had seen a plane or helicopter. The helicopter flew low over the tree line, hovered for a minute over the barn, and set down in a field next to the barn.

"There's my ride," Tabitha said.

"Stay, Tabitha. I'll keep you safe. We can launch the counter-movement from Blue Hills," William pleaded.

"I have to keep moving," Tabitha said.

"We need to go, now," one of Tabitha's men yelled. "We have a report of two gunships en route."

"Don't you want to see baby Edward before you go?" William asked, desperately searching for a way to keep Tabitha on the estate.

"I can't," Tabitha said. "Take care of him, William. Someday I will come for him, and you."

Tabitha kissed William on the lips and ran off towards the helicopter. She and her men climbed into the helicopter. The helicopter lifted off the field and rocketed over the top of Sleeping Giant. When the helicopter was out of sight, William turned and looked around the barnyard. Dozens of farmhands had watched him kiss Tabitha. News of a helicopter swooping in and gathering three strangers, and William's public display of affection would surely reach Mary's ears on a buzz of farmhand gossip.

THE sun was setting over Sleeping Giant when William reached the farmhouse. He walked slowly up Blue Hills Road, rehearsing how he would tell Mary that Tabitha had paid a visit to the estate. He felt like a condemned man walking towards the gallows. Before he spoke with Mary, William hoped he could find time to shower. The smell of Tabitha lingered on his fingers. He was sure Mary would be able to smell and sense her presence. His hopes were dashed when he looked up at the farmhouse and saw Mary standing on the front porch staring down at him. She stood prim and proper in her prairie dress with her hands folded in front of her waist, the stern expression of an angry schoolmarm plastered across her face.

"Hello, Mary," William said.

Mary glared at William, burning a hole into him with the fury in her gaze.

"I suppose I have some explaining to do," William said. The script William rehearsed on the walk from Butterworth to the farmhouse unfurled in his mind; honesty was the best approach, but he didn't want to overplay his hand and reveal everything, especially the fact that Tabitha's grandson was still on the estate. "She showed up uninvited," William said, holding out his hands as if he could stem Mary's consternation. "It was a complete surprise."

"I suppose it conveniently slipped your mind to let me know that she was here. How long did you hide her in Heritage Woods?" Mary asked.

"It was only one night. I was going to tell you tonight."

"You're a liar and a son-of-a-bitch."

The sound of helicopters interrupted the inquisition. The farmhouse began to shake. Two Apache attack helicopters swooped over the orchard and hovered a few hundred feet above the farmhouse.

The Apaches' boasted Hellfire missiles mounted on the sides, and 30 mm chain guns on the nose of each helicopter. The chain guns swept back and forth across the farmhouse and orchard as the gunners in each Apache searched for a target. The helicopter gunships covered the descent of a CH-47 Chinook. The double blades of the Chinook rattled the ground beneath the farmhouse with the intensity of a minor earthquake. The Chinook landed in an attack position with its nose up. The back gate of the Chinook opened and dozens of soldiers in black tactical outfits carrying assault rifles poured out. The men ran across the field separating the Chinook from the farmhouse in a tactical attack pattern. The soldiers began throwing farmhands to the ground and binding their hands with zip ties. The men reached the front porch, pointed their assault rifles at William and Mary, and hollered at them to "get the fuck down." Two soldiers grabbed William, pulled his Glock from the holster on his thigh, and forced him to his knees.

"What the hell's going on?" William hollered.

"Shut the fuck up," a soldier said. The soldier used the butt of his rifle to crack William on his back.

The men entered the farmhouse and began moving room-to-room yelling "clear" when the room was empty, and hollering at people to "get the fuck down" when they found a room occupied. Soldiers led Susan, Catherine and two farmhands to the front porch. The soldiers tied their hands with zip ties, and forced them to kneel next to William and Mary.

"Daddy, what's happening?" Catherine asked.

"Shut the fuck up," one of the soldiers screamed in Catherine's ear.

Catherine began to cry. William glared at the soldier. The soldier raised the butt of his rifle and prepared to smash William in the mouth.

"That's enough," a man's voice hollered.

William recognized the voice. He turned and looked at the man giving orders as he walked up the porch steps. It took William a minute to recognize the man; the years had grizzled his face, covered his hair and short beard with a sprinkle of salt and pepper, and left his face worn under a leathery layer of skin ravaged by too much sun.

"Hello, William," the man said.

"Marc?" William asked.

"How you doin, man?" Marc said. Marc reached down, grabbed William under his arm, and helped him to his feet. "Stand down, boys," Marc said to the men on the porch. The men lowered their assault rifles and relaxed. "First things first," Marc said to William. "I know you've got an arsenal here on your farm and a boatload of men who know how to use it. Tell your men to put down their weapons. My boys have itchy trigger fingers; I'd hate to see this get ugly if someone out there tries to be a hero."

In the fading light of dusk, William saw armed farmhands moving between the rows of apple trees. A dozen men in black uniforms kneeled in the field separating the orchard from the farmhouse, taking dead aim at the farmhands. The Apache gunners aimed the chain guns towards the orchard. If a fight broke out, a maelstrom of 30 mm rounds from the Apache chain guns would shred the orchard and anyone hiding among the trees.

"This is William Blake. Lower your weapons and come out," William hollered towards the orchard. "That's an order."

Farmhands began wandering out from between the rows of apple trees. The men on Marc's assault team disarmed the farmhands and corralled them in an area next to the farmhouse. Marc used a radio clipped to his Kevlar vest and told the Apache pilots that everything was under control. The Apaches flew off over the top of Sleeping Giant.

"There," Marc said. "Now everyone is going to play nice."

William watched more men walk out of the orchard towards the farmhouse. All except one man kept his rifle pointed at the ground. William recognized the man who pointed his assault rifle at the men on Marc's assault team.

"That's my son, Marc. Please. Tell your men to hold their fire."

"Stand down, stand down," Marc hollered in the direction of the men on his assault team who were pointing their rifles at James. The men lowered their guns. "You better go get him," Marc said. "My boys won't appreciate a rifle pointed at them like that."

William stepped off the porch and ran towards James with his hands raised. "James. It's okay, Son. Take it easy. Lower your rifle."

"What the fuck is going on Dad?" James asked.

"It's okay. It's under control."

"Bullshit. They're not going to treat you, mom, and the girls like that. Who the fuck are they?"

William reached out and took the rifle from James. "Trust me, Son. You wouldn't stand a chance against them. Just relax. I've got things under control. This is all a big misunderstanding. I know their commander. Tell everyone to chill out while I talk to him and figure this whole mess out."

"Are they here because of those people who were on the estate last night and today?" James asked.

"Yes. I'm sure it has something to do with them. I'll explain everything later."

William clasped James on the shoulder and led him to the farmhouse. William handed Marc James's rifle when they stepped onto the front porch.

"All right," Marc said. "Now that we're all playing nice, let's cut to the chase. Where is she?"

"I suppose you're talking about Tabitha," William said.

"Don't play dumb."

"She left a few hours ago. You just missed her. What the hell is going on, Marc? Is this freakin' invasion really about Tabitha?"

"Yeah, that fuckin' crazy bitch is stirring up some serious shit."

"Sounds like we need to talk. Let's go inside to my office. But you gotta promise me your men are gonna chill out. We're peaceful folks here; we don't want any trouble. It'd really be better if they get back in that helicopter and get outta here. We're not gonna cause you any trouble. I'll tell you everything Tabitha told me."

"Don't worry about them," Marc said. "They're pro's. I trained 'em myself. As long as your people are cool, they won't have a problem."

The sound of a helicopter filled the air. Marc and William looked up and watched a Blackhawk slowly settle in the field next to the Chinook.

"What's this, more soldiers?" William asked.

"No. Special guest," Marc said.

The Blackhawk landed in the field. The side door slid open and a soldier jumped out. The soldier extended a hand and helped an elderly man out of the helicopter.

"Is that Sage?" William asked.

"Yup," Marc said. "In the flesh."

Sage walked slowly across the yard. Two soldiers walked on each side of him, ready to extend a hand if he stumbled.

"William, my boy," Sage said, walking slowly up the front porch steps. "How do you fare?"

"Hale and hearty, hearty and hale," William said.

"Hale and hearty indeed," Sage said, pulling William into a hug. "Let me get a look at you. Ah, the years are treating you well"

Sage's hair had turned stark white and his face was covered with age spots and wrinkles, but his blue eyes were as bright and piercing as ever.

"I can't believe you're here." William said.

"Good evening, Mr. Sage," Mary said, stepping forward and taking Sage's hand.

"Ah, Mary, you look wonderful. It has been too long. Don't tell me these are your children. Last time I saw James he was still a toddler, and I don't think I've met the twins."

William introduced James, Susan and Catherine. Sage shook hands with everyone and apologized for the dramatic entrance.

"You have a beautiful family, William. Now, I don't mean to be rude, but is there somewhere we can talk in private?" Sage asked.

"Yes, I was just about to invite Marc up to my office for a cocktail and some conversation."

"Lead the way," Sage said.

William led Marc and Sage into the farmhouse to his office on the second floor. The evening was cooling off. A cross breeze in the office chased the day's humidity out of the room.

"Can I get you guys a drink?" William asked.

"That would be great," Marc said. "What do you have that's cold?"

"Everything we have is homemade. I can offer you a homebrewed beer, vodka, hard cider, wine, or straight up moonshine. I wouldn't recommend the moonshine unless you're ready to tie one on. I have an ice chest in the kitchen, so everything is cold."

"A beer sounds good," Marc said.

"I'll have a glass of wine," Sage said.

William walked to the kitchen and poured two beers and a glass of wine. He carried the drinks to his office.

"Here you go," William said.

"Ah, nice and cold," Marc said. "I admire a man who can still serve an ice cold beer on demand. You're living in the lap of luxury."

"We're doing okay," William said.

"Now, now, William. There's no need for modesty. You've created something beautiful here at Blue Hills. You should be proud. This is exactly what we had in mind when we started The Movement," Sage said.

"Thank you. We work hard around here. So, tell me, what the hell is going on? I don't hear from anyone in over a decade and then all of a sudden Tabitha shows up talking about some counter-revolution, and you guys show up ready for World War Three."

"Ah, yes, Tabitha," Sage said, sitting back on a leather sofa, crossing his legs, and sipping his glass of wine. "That's good Chardonnay. You say you make it here on the estate?"

"From grapes to glass. You'll excuse me if I'm not really interested in talking wine right now."

"Yes. Where were we? Oh, right, Tabitha. So you say she was here."

"Yeah, she was here. I assume you know that already."

"Did she have an infant with her?" Sage asked.

"Yes. She told me he was her and Edward's grandson."

"Where is the baby now?"

"I don't know. Tabitha took off with him a few hours before you guys showed up."

"Did she say where she was going?"

"No. She talked about some underground railroad, but didn't tell me where she was headed."

"It's important for you to tell me if you know where she or the infant is, or if you know where they are going. Edward is prepared to lay waste to anything and anyone standing between him and his grandchild."

"I swear, I don't know. I'll tell you everything she told me, but she didn't tell me where she was going."

For the next hour, William told Sage and Marc about Tabitha's plan to reconstitute state governments by reconvening state constitutional conventions and repealing the Liberty Amendments and the Supremacy Amendment. Sage nodded along as William detailed all of the plans Tabitha shared about the counter-movement. Marc looked on and half-listened, throwing back beer after beer.

"I appreciate the honesty. Nothing you've told me is a surprise. Tabitha Couture is a traitor. When we catch her, she will be hung as a traitor." Sage paused and stared at William. "Does that upset you?"

"No. A traitor is a traitor. She's obviously made her bed."

"Then can I assume you are not drawn to her cause? I'm sure you must at least be considering it. I know how, shall we say, *committed* you've been to her in the past."

"I'm not interested in her plans. I remain committed to what we started."

"Good," Sage said. Sage stood up from the couch and clasped William on the shoulder. "I can tell you that anyone who falls in behind her and her liberal revolutionaries is going to face a holocaust of repercussions. An officer in the Vietnam War once made history by saying that he had to destroy a village in order to save it. I believe that is exactly how Edward Birch views this little revolution Tabitha is stirring up. I would hate to see anything like that befall you or your beautiful family."

"Never. You can assure President Birch that I remain loyal to The Movement."

"Good. Then I suppose it is time for us to go."

"Sage, before you go, tell me, how much support has Tabitha generated? She talked about some former high-ranking military officers who are pulling their troops back together. Where is this whole thing heading?"

"Tabitha has created some waves, no doubt. But we believe the situation is under control. Do you still have access to Movement communications?" Sage asked, nodding towards William's computer.

"The satellite uplink is spotty. Once in a while I can get online."

"Okay. I'm going to talk to the communications people; they'll make sure your connection problems are ironed out. If you see or hear from Tabitha again, contact me immediately. Otherwise, continue to monitor the newsfeed; you'll know if things start to get bad."

William walked Sage and Marc out of the farmhouse. Darkness had settled over the estate. Marc spoke into his radio, and his men ran off towards the Chinook. The Chinook rumbled to life and took off.

"Goodbye, William. I wish you continued success. I will be sure to extend your regards to Edward, and let him know that you remain committed to The Movement. I know he will appreciate your loyalty."

Sage stepped off the porch. Two soldiers escorted him across the lawn towards the Blackhawk.

"Hey," Marc said. "Before I get out of here, I've got to ask you."

"What?"

"Did you finally get to fuck her?"

"Huh?"

"Don't give me that, I'm not your wife. I'm just askin'. After all these years, did you finally get to fuck that little slut? Hell, before Edward Birch started knocking the bottom out of her, I used to bang her a few times a month. Back at Beacon Academy she was the school slut, all the guys used to pass her around."

"No," William said. "I did not fuck her."

"That's too bad, dude. I always felt bad for you. The way she used to tease you all those years when she was out there spreading her legs for anything with a cock, and at the same time acting like a prude for the one dude who actually gave a damn about her."

William considered calling Sage back to the farmhouse and leading him to baby Edward. Instead, he bit his tongue, turned his back to Marc, and walked into the farmhouse.

*　　*　　*

August, 2046

WILLIAM and Mary sat in the front row. The chairs were arranged in long, straight rows under a tent set up in the field next to the farmhouse. The farmhands and family stood as a fiddler played *Here Comes the Bride*. Annaliese's father led Annaliese down an aisle between the rows of chairs. James and Reverend Flowers stood at the end of the aisle, waiting for the bride and her father to arrive. Annaliese was dressed in a long, white gown sewn by Mary and Annaliese's mother in the weeks before the wedding. William looked up and smiled at Susan, Catherine, and two other bridesmaids standing off to the side. Mary sniffled and dotted her eyes with a handkerchief as Annaliese's father gave his daughter a kiss on the cheek and shook James's hand. A soft, late-afternoon breeze swept through the tent, offering slight relief from the blistering heat and oppressive humidity.

Reverend Flowers addressed the community and led the couple in the exchange of vows. James and Annaliese kissed, and Reverend Flowers declared them husband and wife. The community applauded as James and Annaliese left the tent and walked towards the farmhouse. The guests left the tent and followed the newlyweds across the field to a reception set up on the veranda. The sun blessedly dipped behind Sleeping Giant. The evening promised to be hot and humid, but less oppressive without the inferno generated by the direct, brick oven blast of the sun. A diesel generator grumbled and lights strung up around the veranda flickered to life. The farmhands mingled and filled their plates from a buffet of chicken, beef, and vegetables. Hungry stomachs greedily devoured the feast.

Crocco walked up to William and shook his hand. "Congratulations," Crocco said.

"Thank you," William said.

"It's a nice spread. I know that everyone appreciates it. It should lighten the mood a little," Crocco said.

"Are things looking any better?" William asked.

"Unfortunately, no. I was at the vineyard today. Enjoy the wine tonight, because the grapes are gone."

"Grapes are the most fragile crop."

"Yeah, but they're also the canary in the coal mine. The orchards are struggling, and the rest of the crops ain't doing good either."

"It's a good thing we have the greenhouses."

"That'll sustain us. But we're going to have to cut back on rations if the fields don't start producing."

William closed his eyes and rubbed his forehead with the palm of his hand.

"Look, let's not worry about it now. Tonight is a night to celebrate," Crocco said.

William couldn't shake the image of trees shriveling in the orchard, and corn and wheat that should be tall and strong by late-summer, but instead barely poked its heads from the soil. All the crops on the estate were suffering. The fields contaminated by the Quinnipiac and Housatonic Rivers were bare. The orchards and crops grown across the estate were showing signs of disease and infestation. Decades of over fertilizing burned the soil. William suspected that the DuPonte fertilizer and pesticide that for years yielded an overabundance of produce had ended up scorching the earth. He also suspected that the chemicals were responsible for an uptick in cases of cancer that plagued Heritage Woods. There wasn't a family left in Heritage Woods that hadn't been touched by cancer; it seemed that barely a week went by without a funeral on the estate.

After the reception and buffet, the farmhands moved to the barn for dancing and celebration. There was still enough hard cider and moonshine on the estate to fuel the party. The farmhands knew not to imbibe the libations too deeply. Displays of drunk and disorderly conduct on the estate met with Mary's ire, and earned farmhands a few days in the stockades. Mary and Reverend Flowers regularly filled the stockades in front of the cider mill with farmhands they accused of malfeasance. Behavior on the estate had deteriorated once the stockades were constructed. Fighting over provisions, theft, and drunkenness was the new norm. These behaviors combined with the moral indecencies that Mary and Reverend Flowers persecuted without any evidence beyond their own perception earned dozens of farmhands days on end in the stockade. As opposed to serving as a deterrent, the stockades had become a catalyst for a decline in kindness and compassion across Blue Hills. It didn't surprise William when several weeks after construction of the stockades, Mary and Reverend Flowers came to him and asked him to build a gallows next to the stockades. William denied the request, but he knew it would only be a matter of time before Mary pushed him.

William carried the growing problems on the estate with him as he entered the barn. He stood on the side of the dance floor and watched James and Annaliese dance. Halfway through the dance, the farmhands began to join the newlyweds on the dance floor. William felt a hand slip into his hand. He looked over and made eye contact with Susan.

"Want to dance?" Susan asked.

"Sure, Honey."

Susan led William onto the dance floor. She slipped her arms around his waist, and he laced his arms around her shoulders. They moved slowly to the beat of the waltz.

"So, are you excited to have a new sister?" William asked.

"Yeah. We all love Annaliese. She's sweet," Susan said.

"Good. I'm happy for them. They're a great couple."

"Daddy…"

"Yeah."

"You said I had to wait until James was married before you'd talk to Mom about Eric. Well, James is married. I haven't said a word to Eric in months."

"I know, Sweetie. You've been very patient."

"And?"

"I'll talk to your mother tonight."

"Thank you, thank you, thank you," Susan said. She pushed up on the balls of her feet, gave William a quick kiss on the cheek, and hugged him.

"Do you want to dance with him?"

"What?"

"Eric. Would you like to dance with him?" William asked.

"Yes, more than anything."

"Well, go ahead."

"What about Mom?"

"You have my permission. I'll deal with your mother."

'Oh, Daddy. Thank you. I love you."

William watched Susan skip off across the dance floor to find Eric. He scanned the crowd looking for Mary. William knew that if Mary saw Susan dancing with Eric before he caught up with her there would be hell to pay. He spotted Mary standing to one side of the barn with Reverend Flowers. Mary and Reverend Flowers lorded over the farmhands, searching for any hint of drunkenness, and measuring the appropriateness of the slow dancing between unmarried couples. William could feel the tension in the barn; the unmarried couples knew that Mary and Reverend Flowers were judging their every move. None of the farmhands wanted to spend a blisteringly hot day in the embrace of the stockade, so they robotically danced with their hips far apart. William walked across the barn and asked Mary if she'd speak with him outside. He knew the farmhands would enjoy a moment out from under Mary's reproachful gaze. Mary followed William outside.

"Exciting day," William said.

"Yes indeed. What do you need?"

"I want to talk to you about Susan."

"Okay. What?"

"Susan would like to begin courting Eric. I told her that she had to wait until her brother was married. She obeyed. As far as I know, she hasn't spoken with Eric since the night you pulled her out of the barn dance. I would like to give her our blessing to begin courting Eric."

"Absolutely not."

"Mary, let's try to be reasonable."

"Susan is spoken for," Mary said.

"What? Who?"

"Reverend Flowers."

"Have you lost your mind? He's more than twice her age."

"No matter. The Reverend and I have been talking this over for several weeks now. Reverend Flowers has been considering his options, and has made up his mind."

"What options?" William asked.

"Susan or Catherine. He has chosen Susan."

"Jesus, Mary. He's not picking out a pair of socks. These are our children. What gives him the right to choose between our daughters?"

"Do not use the Lord's name like that. I have given him my blessing."

"Neither of the girls want him."

"No matter. They will do what they're told."

"No," William barked. "I won't support this decision."

A commotion from inside the barn interrupted the conversation. The band stopped playing and the sound of a woman screaming filtered out of the barn.

"That sounds like Susan," William said.

William and Mary walked crisply into the barn. The farmhands had formed a circle around an altercation on the dance floor. William and Mary pushed their way through the crowd. In the center of the circle, they saw two farmhands restraining Eric. Susan was screaming at the men to let Eric go. Reverend Flowers was doubled-over at the edge of the circle, holding his hand against his mouth. He pulled his hand back and looked at the blood on his fingers.

"Take him to the stockades," Reverend Flowers hollered.

The farmhands stalled and waited for confirmation of the directive from William or Mary. The crowd quieted when William stepped forward into the center of the circle.

"What in God's name is going on?" William bellowed.

"Daddy," Susan cried. "He's crazy. Eric and I weren't doing anything wrong. Tell them to let him go."

Eric's body went limp in the farmhands' grasp. He lowered his eyes.

"Reverend," Mary said, inserting herself into the fray. "What happened?"

"I observed Susan being mauled by that young man on the dance floor. I interceded in order to end the immodest display, and the boy struck me," Reverend Flowers said, tilting his head to show William and Mary blood flowing from a split lip.

William looked at the wound. William suspected that Eric had pulled his punch; if Eric had thrown his broad shoulders and strong arms into the punch, William suspected he would have knocked out a few teeth, and likely broken Reverend Flowers' jaw. The small cut and slightly swollen lip was an indication that Eric had controlled the punch to lessen the impact and ensure that Reverend Flowers sustained no permanent damage.

"Take him to the stockade," Mary ordered the farmhands.

"Hold on a second," William said. "We haven't heard from the boy or Susan."

Mary stepped close to William and hissed in his ear, "Don't you dare contradict me in front of the community." William lowered his eyes and stepped back. "I said, take him to the stockades," Mary hollered.

The farmhands restraining Eric looked at William. William waved his hand. The farmhands led Eric out of the barn, and walked him towards the stockades in front of the cider mill.

"No, Daddy, please," Susan pleaded.

"You shut your mouth and go to your room. We'll deal with you later," Mary said.

Susan burst into tears and ran out of the barn.

"Show's over," William said. "Go back to the celebration."

William, Mary, and Reverend Flowers walked out of the barn.

"We need to talk," William said.

"Let's get some ice on that lip," Mary said. "Then we'll talk."

William followed Mary and Reverend Flowers to the farmhouse. Reverend Flowers made a great show of groaning and moaning over the relatively minor wound. William rolled his eyes and shook his head as Mary tenderly dabbed the split lip with a wet cloth, and gingerly placed some ice in a hand towel against Reverend Flowers' mouth.

"I'll be in my office when you're ready to talk," William said.

William walked to his office. He poured himself two fingers of straight vodka in a rocks glass and sat back on the couch. Reverend Flowers and Mary entered the office. Reverend Flowers continued holding the ice against his lip.

"That boy is an animal. Do you see what he has done to me?" Reverend Flowers asked, removing the hand towel and showing William the slightly swollen lip.

"I think you'll live," William said.

"That's not the point," Mary hissed. "That boy had no right to lay a finger on the good reverend."

"What happened?" William asked.

"I was watching the community dance. I observed Susan and Eric walk onto the dance floor together and begin dancing. I am well aware of your expectation that Susan not speak with Eric. I can tell you that the way they moved together was far from platonic; the devil was clearly stimulating the fire in their loins. I walked onto the dance floor and asked them to stop. Susan looked me straight in the eye and told me that she had your permission, William. Of course, I knew right away that she was lying. I asked them to stop a second time. When they ignored me, I grabbed Susan by the arm with the intention of removing her from the dance floor. That's when that animal attacked me."

"She wasn't lying," William said.

"What?" Mary asked.

"I gave her my permission to dance with Eric. She wasn't lying."

"How dare you," Mary hissed. "How could you?"

"I had no idea that you two were scheming and plotting her future. What makes you think I would ever embrace an arranged marriage? You're more than twice her age, Reverend."

"It's only logical," Mary said. "Their marriage will help solidify the power structures on the estate."

"Power structure? What in the hell are you talking about? Have you lost your mind? Let me ask you something, Reverend. Why Susan? It's clear to me that my wife is comfortable giving you the pick of our daughters. Why did you choose Susan over Catherine?"

"I'm drawn to Susan more intensely than I am to Catherine. I feel the blessing of the Lord at work in our relationship," Reverend Flowers said.

"Blessing of the Lord?"

"Yes, I've served as Susan's tutor and teacher for many years now. I feel God's will at work in my relationship with Susan."

"God's will? Sounds more like a scene out of Lolita if you ask me. Reverend, I'll ask you this only once - have you ever laid a finger on Susan or Catherine?"

"How dare you?" Mary hissed.

William was shocked that in all their years together, Mary never once suspected nor heard the whispers around the estate concerning Reverend Flowers' appetite for little girls and boys. While never confirmed, William suspected that more than a handful of Blue Hills' children had felt the molesting paws of Reverend Flowers. He further suspected that the children and their parents never came forward for fear of Mary's wrath.

"I asked you a question, Reverend," William said, levelling a cold gaze at Reverend Flowers.

Mary stepped between William and Reverend Flowers. "For you to even suggest such a thing makes my blood boil."

"Reverend?" William asked.

"No. Of course not," Reverend Flowers said.

"Reverend Flowers is a man of God. We have been planning this marriage in consultation with the Bible and in deep prayer. God has spoken to us; it is his will. I will not have it torn apart by some filthy farmhand."

"Now both of you listen to me carefully," William said. "I will not support an arranged marriage. Susan does not love Reverend Flowers, and I will not force my daughter into a marriage that promises to bring her nothing but misery. I know Susan well enough to know that she would never abide such an arrangement. She is in love with Eric. I have no interest in seeing this devolve into some Shakespearean tragedy. Susan deserves a chance to be happy, and I'm quite sure that you, Reverend, are not the man who will bring her that happiness. The answer is 'no.'"

"You think so?" Mary asked. "Now you listen to me, William. You will support this arrangement. Do you think I'm stupid? I know all about that infant you have tucked away down there in Heritage Woods. I'm willing to bet there are plenty of your old associates in The Movement who would love to know where to find that baby."

William stared at Mary. Her eyes were cold, calculating, and angry. In that moment, William felt nothing but hatred for her. "You have no idea how dangerous those words are," William said.

"I am well aware of what I'm saying," Mary said.

"Are you looking for some type of Pyrrhic victory?" William asked. "Cause that's what you'll get."

"I'll give you a few days to think about it," Mary said. "Reverend Flowers and I will not be denied."

William watched Reverend Flowers and Mary storm out of his office. His hands shook with anger as he poured himself another glass of vodka. He sat back on the couch and stared up at the ceiling.

That night, the alternating sounds of James and Annaliese consummating their wedding vows in James's bedroom, and Susan sobbing in her and Catherine's bedroom filled the farmhouse. The contrast between happiness and despair under the same roof resonated with William. Sometime around Four O'clock in the morning, William heard Mary return to the farmhouse from the pool house where Reverend Flowers resided. He wondered what plans Mary and Reverend Flowers had concocted, just as he wondered what plans Susan and Eric would hatch; a Machiavellian intrigue was sure to befall the estate, and William didn't like it one bit.

*   *   *

September, 2046

WILLIAM and Crocco sat on horseback at the top of a hill watching the sunset over withering cornfields on the north end of the estate. The cornstalks struggled to crawl from the grasp of the dusty soil. A patchwork of mold and disease covered the produce. The apple, pear, nectarine, tangerine, and peach orchards were rotting just as badly as the corn, wheat, hops, hay, sunflowers, cotton, and soy. Gypsy moths filled the branches, and Asian Longhorned Beedles bored into the trunks. The pumpkin, blueberry, strawberry, and raspberry patches also rotted in the oppressive heat.

"It's a damned shame," William said.

"Nothing we do does a bit of good," Crocco said. "We're gonna have to write off this year's harvest and make do with what we have canned from last year."

"Yup."

"Good news is that the greenhouses are still producing, we've managed to keep the disease out, and the livestock is in good shape. We'll have plenty of protein from the cattle, pigs, and chicken, and enough milk, cheese, and eggs for everyone on the estate."

"Sure, but what the hell are we going to do this winter? All the feedstock is dead or dying in the fields. The animals are going to starve come winter," William said.

"We have men scouring Redwood, and riding out across the land looking for feed corn and hay to buy or barter for. We'll find something," Crocco said.

"I doubt it. I'm sure every field across the state looks like that," William said, waving his hand over the decaying fields.

William looked towards the cider mill and saw a dust cloud rise high into the air. Two dozen men on horseback raced across the field. James rode at the front of the posse.

"Dad," James called, pulling back on his horse's reins and stopping next to William.

"What's going on?" William asked.

"It's Catherine and Susan. Last night, Annaliese heard them scheming through the bedroom walls. At first she didn't believe what the girls were saying, but this morning she found this in their bedroom."

James handed William a letter. William unfolded the letter and immediately recognized Susan's long, flowing script. He read the letter, and quickly folded the paper and placed it in the pocket of his t-shirt.

"When did she find this?" William asked.

"About an hour ago. The girls have been gone since early this morning. I figure they have at least a day's head start," James said. James tossed William and Crocco M4A1 assault rifles. "We've got your gear packed up. We'd better get going right away; you can change when we get to Redwood."

William stared at the men on horseback behind James. Gone were the overalls and homemade cotton or hemp shirts. All the men wore black Kevlar vests and tactical gear that William had purchased and stashed in the cider mill armory.

"Let's go," William said.

William led the men off the estate and down Route 5. They stopped a mile from Redwood. William and Crocco changed into black shirts, elbow pads, Kevlar vests, and black cargo pants with kneepads. They put on SWAT helmets equipped with night vision goggles and an embedded communication system. William tested the com system; all the farmhands reported that they received William's command signal in clear, high-definition. William double-checked the action on his assault rifle, and adjusted the flashlight and laser sights on the end of the rifle. William took a knee on the ground. James, Crocco, and a farmhand who was a former soldier and had trained the Blue Hills tactical team took a knee next to him.

"What's the plan?" James asked.

"James, you take eight men and ride around the market. You're going to lead the assault south down Route 5. I will lead eight men into the market northward from this position. Crocco, I want you to take four men into the woods on the east side of the market. Your job is to stop anyone fleeing to the east. If you catch anyone in the woods, check 'em over. If you suspect they're a coyote, tie 'em up. And you, what's your name again?" William asked.

"Reid, sir."

"Time to see if the training you provided these guys will pay off."

"It will, sir. I promise"

"You take four men and go down by the Quinnipiac River on the western side of the market. If you catch anyone wading through the river, stop 'em and check for coyotes," William said.

"What are the rules of engagement?" Reid asked.

"Use all necessary force. If anyone fucks with you or resists, put three rounds in their chest and one in their head."

"Yes, sir," Reid said.

"James, when I say go you move into the market hard and fast from the north. Kick in every door, check every truck, throw back the tarp on every table, search every square inch."

"What if the coyotes left and are already heading north towards Canada?" James asked.

"Then we're screwed. If girls have already been trafficked, then our only hope will be to catch some coyotes still in the market, beat the shit out of 'em, and hope the intel we get will point us in the right direction if we have to go after the girls. Now, let's get to it."

Crocco, James, and Reid led their teams out of the staging area. William waited for several hours while his men got into position. It was past Midnight when Reid, Crocco, and James reported that they were ready for the assault. William checked the com system. The men reported that they were receiving his transmission. William flicked on his night vision goggles, and turned on the laser sight on his rifle.

"Okay," William said into the headset. "If anyone finds the girls, call out and give us your location, the rest of the team will converge on your position." The men responded with a *Roger* over the headset, and William ordered the assault to begin.

William moved into the market from the south, moving northward along Route 5. His men pulled back tarps over tables, stuck assault rifles into tents, pulled open car and truck doors, searched trunks, and kicked in the doors on RV's parked throughout the lot. They moved quickly and methodically through the market, hollering *clear* as they searched the parking lot and vendor vehicles. From the north, William heard James's team moving south towards his position. A profanity-laced scream rang out through the night, and the pop of a handgun filled the air. A burst of semi-automatic rifle fire responded to the pistol shot and the screaming ended. There were a few more screams, and a few more bursts of semi-automatic fire as the teams converged. William spoke into the headset and warned the teams to be aware that they were in close proximity, and to hold fire unless sure of a target. The assault teams were within a few hundred feet, and still no one called out that they found the twins. Semi-automatic fire erupted from the Quinnipiac River. William asked Reid to report. Reid reported that he made contact with some resistance, but had everything under control to the east. William and James's teams met in the center of the market and converged on a single white van.

"Let's hope that's it," William said.

James and William walked towards the van. William tried to open the passenger side door. The door was locked. William reared the butt of his rifle back and prepared to smash the window. Three pops from a .38 Revolver exploded from inside the van. The bullets flew through the passenger side window and missed William's head by millionths of an inch. One of the rounds nicked his helmet. Through the night vision goggles, William saw a man jump from the back of the van into the driver's seat and try to start the ignition. William quickly flicked the switch from full-auto to semi-auto on his rifle. He fired one round clean through the driver's head. The man's head recoiled sideways against the driver side window and then slumped forward against the steering wheel.

"Hold your fire," William hollered as he made his way toward the back of the van.

The men took up positions around the van. James stepped forward and tried the back door. A semi-automatic pistol barked from inside the van. William and James dropped to the ground and watched thirteen rounds from the pistol punch holes in the back door of the van.

"Hold your fire," William yelled. "You, in the van. You're surrounded. Come out with your hands up."

They heard a click on the lock of the back door. The door opened and a man stuck his head out. Two farmhands grabbed the man, pulled him from the van, and slammed him face-first to the ground. James, William and several farmhands pulled off their night vision goggles, turned on the tactical flashlights on the end of their rifles, and shined the beams into the dark reservoir inside the van. They saw Eric and Susan sitting with their hands behind their backs. Their feet were bound and mouths gagged with duct tape. Towards the front of the van, they spotted a single coyote holding a knife to Catherine's throat. Catherine was unconscious, completely naked, and covered with a patchwork of blood and filth.

"Get them out," William ordered the farmhands.

The farmhands reached into the van and pulled Eric and Susan out the back door. William stepped forward and pointed his rifle at the man holding the knife to his daughter's throat.

"You listen to me you piece of shit," William said. "There are two ways out of this for you: One, you slice her throat. You do that, and I promise I will strip you naked, cut off your dick, and make you watch me shove it down your throat. Then I will surgically remove every extremity on your body, and pluck out your eyes with a fucking spoon. You will spend the last hours of your useless life in a world of pain while you beg for death. Or, you let the girl go, and I promise I will treat you humanely for whatever remains of your time on Earth, which either way isn't going to amount to much. You understand me, you fucking scumbag. Now let her go, asshole," William screamed.

The man dropped the knife, raised his hands, and began sobbing. Catherine flopped lifelessly onto the floor of the van. James grabbed the coyote and threw him to the ground next to his partner. William climbed into the van and cradled Catherine in his arms. William looked up and down the length of his daughter's ravaged body. She had been gang raped repeatedly in front of Susan and Eric, but she was still alive. William thanked God that she was unconscious, and hoped she had remained unconscious for the bulk of the brutality. A medic climbed into the back of the van and began looking over Catherine's wounds. William climbed out of the van and ordered two of his men to ride back to the estate and return with the truck and community doctor.

William walked over to Susan and kneeled down next to her. Susan was sitting with her knees against her chest and arms wrapped around her shins. William looked into her eyes. She stared blankly at him from a state of profound shock. Eric was standing behind her. William stood and took a step towards Eric.

"I'm sorry, I'm sorry," Eric whimpered.

William placed his rifle on the ground, angled his waist, steadied himself and bounced slowly on the balls of his feet, and then reared back and punched Eric in the eye with all of his God-given strength. William felt Eric's eye socket shatter under the force of the blow. He heard a wet thwack and felt the small bones in Eric's cheek crumble. Eric stumbled backwards and crashed to the ground. He instinctively covered his right eye. The socket would eventually heal, but for the rest of his life, Eric would view the world through a lazy eye.

*   *   *

November, 2046

WILLIAM stood in the doorway to Catherine and Susan's bedroom watching the doctor measure Catherine's blood pressure and pulse. The doctor sat on the bed and whispered encouragement to Catherine, trying to call her back from a dark corner of her mind where she hid. He held his hand to her forehead, pushed the hair back from her face, and shined a light into her eyes. Catherine stared up blankly at the ceiling. Susan lay in the bed next to Catherine's bed. The doctor stood up from Catherine's bed and moved to Susan. He removed a pair of white gauze bandages from Susan's wrists and inspected the wounds. Swelling formed around the deep slices in Susan's wrists, and a red outline of infection surrounded the cuts. The doctor cleaned the wounds and replaced the bandages. When the doctor finished changing the bandages, he stepped into the hallway to speak with William. A farmhand in a white prairie dress stepped into the room, sat in a rocking chair, and began knitting. The farmhand had orders to hold vigil for Catherine, and immediately report if the catatonia broke. The farmhand also maintained a suicide watch for Susan.

"How are they?" William asked.

"Catherine's condition is unchanged. Physically, she is fine, but the psychological impact of her experience continues to have a profound impact," the doctor said.

"It has been over three months; when will she snap out of it?"

"I'm not a psychologist. I imagine it could be any day now, but I don't have the expertise to hasten her recovery."

"And the baby?" William asked.

"The pregnancy is progressing normally."

William lowered his voice and whispered to the doctor, "Could you perform an abortion?"

"Yes, I possess the technical skills necessary to perform an abortion," the doctor whispered.

William quickly scanned the hallway to make sure no one heard the next question. "Could you make it look like a miscarriage?" William asked.

"Do you know what you're asking me?"

"I do."

"Then you know I can't do it without your wife's consent. Even if the pregnancy is a result of rape, I would surely swing from the cider mill gallows if Mary found out I performed an abortion. In addition, from a medical perspective, I advise against any major surgery with Catherine in her current state. The physical trauma combined with the ongoing psychological shock could kill her."

"And what kind of trauma do you expect when she gives birth?"

"I'm sorry. I can't do it."

"How's Susan?"

"The attempt was nearly successful. She lost a lot of blood. Thank God you found her as quickly as you did. Another few minutes in the bathtub and she would have bled out. Right now, my biggest concern is the infection. The wounds are not getting better by themselves. We need antibiotics."

"I have men scouring the countryside."

"Good. Assuming we can keep the infection away, she will be okay physically. But there's no telling what will keep her from another attempt."

"Yes, there is. We know exactly what she wants - Eric."

"That's an issue for you and your wife to discuss. It's clear to me that she'd rather be dead than live without him. The choice seems pretty simple to me."

"It does to me, too."

"I wish I could do more. I'll be back tomorrow."

William escorted the doctor out of the farmhouse. He stood on the porch and watched the doctor walk down Blue Hills Road towards Heritage Woods. William stared at the orchards. White netting from Gypsy Moths hung like gossamer from all of the branches. The tree trunks and branches were black and barren, denuded of apples, peaches, pears and nectarines. The crops on the estate failed to produce a single morsel for the autumn harvest.

A rider on horseback raced up Blue Hills Road. William recognized Crocco riding tall in the saddle as the horse closed the distance to the farmhouse. Crocco pulled back on the reins when the horse reached the porch.

"Where are you off to in such a hurry?" William asked.

"Coming for you. There's a man at the front gate. He says he's ridden from Boston. He claims to be a mail carrier for the postal service."

"Postal service?"

"Yes. He's handing out newspapers filled with articles about new state governments taking root. Here, take my horse and ride down there," Crocco said, climbing down from his mount and handing William the reins.

William climbed into the saddle and rode to the bottom of Blue Hills Road. He saw a man in a tricorn colonial hat standing next to his horse at the front gate talking to several farmhands. The man wore a satchel with the letters USPS branded in the brown leather slung across his shoulders. William pulled back on the reins, climbed out of the saddle, and handed the reins to one of the farmhands.

"Are you William Blake?" The man asked.

"Yes. Who are you?"

"Name's Jim. I'm a rider for the US Postal Service."

"How do you fare?" William asked.

"A little worn out from the road, but otherwise fine," the rider said.

William glared at the man. "Postal service?" William asked. "There hasn't been a postal service for over twenty years."

"There is now. We started up out of Boston. New state congresses are forming in Boston, Providence, Montpelier, and Augusta. Conventions will be held on Thanksgiving. The states are reforming central governments, and are gonna start the process of electing governors soon. Here, look," the rider said. The rider handed William a newspaper called the *New Republic*.

William took the newspaper and read the headline: *Hail Connecticut and New Hampshire! Where Do You Stand?* William skimmed the article. The article detailed efforts underway in Boston, Providence, Montpelier, and Augusta to reconstitute the Massachusetts, Rhode Island, Vermont, and Maine state governments. Massachusetts, Rhode Island, Vermont, and Maine had scheduled state constitutional conventions to meet on Thanksgiving Day to repeal and replace the changes made to their state constitutions, and reconstitute centralized authority. The article noted that Connecticut and New Hampshire were the only New England states that had not yet taken steps to reconstitute state government. The article appealed to the citizens of Connecticut and New Hampshire, urging them to come together and organize state government in Hartford and Concord. Once state governments were reconstituted, the *New Republic* called for the creation of a New England Confederation of States.

William unfolded the newspaper and scanned the articles. The articles detailed the collapse of a nation, and unabashedly documented how The Movement purposefully dismantled local, state, and federal governments, which led America to become a failed state. The *New Republic* editors and authors implored Americans to restore systems of centralized authority. The paper claimed that America was at its lowest point, but by reforming a new social contract, America could begin to pull herself back together as one nation, under God.

"How many of these do you have left in your satchel?" William asked.

"Few dozen," the rider said.

"And you say you've been delivering those newspapers across the state, right?" William asked.

"Yup. Been on the road for about two weeks now. Still have a ways to go before heading back to Boston."

William dropped his right hand to his side, and in a fluid motion, pulled the Glock 9 mm from the holster on his thigh. He raised the weapon and aligned the front and rear sites over the rider's chest. He fired two rounds at the rider. The rider took both rounds in the center of his chest. The impact knocked him backwards into the dirt.

"So much for not shooting the messenger," William said, stepping forward, aiming the Glock at the man's face, and firing an additional round into the rider's forehead.

William kneeled down next to the rider and removed the satchel from his shoulder. He threw the satchel over his shoulder, and climbed into the saddle of Crocco's horse.

"Bury the body and bring his horse to Butterworth," William directed the farmhands. William kicked the sides of the horse and rode back to the farmhouse.

As the horse trotted up Blue Hills Road, William spotted Crocco and James standing together on the front porch. James and Crocco walked off the porch as William approached. Crocco held the bridle while William climbed down from the saddle.

"What's that?" James asked, pointing at the leather satchel slung over William's shoulder.

"A satchel filled with propaganda."

"Did you take it from the rider?" Crocco asked.

"Yup. He won't need it anymore."

"What's going on, Dad?" James asked.

"It's not good news. According to this newspaper, state governments are reconstituting in Maine, Rhode Island, Massachusetts, and Vermont. They're calling on Connecticut to do the same, and join a new confederation of New England states."

"Why is that such a bad thing?" James asked.

"I can't believe you'd even ask a question like that. What the fuck have I been teaching you all these years? Have you learned nothing? We're talking about the rise of tyranny; a return to the bad-old-days of regulation and taxation."

"How close are they?" Crocco asked.

"According to this liberal rag of a newspaper, the conventions are convening on Thanksgiving."

"Thanksgiving? That's tomorrow," James said.

"Yup. Trust me when I tell you, this isn't going to end well. I don't know how or when, but there is no way The Movement is going to take this lying down."

"What's going to happen? Is there going to be some kind of war?" James asked.

"I don't know. When Tabitha was here, she mentioned that the counter revolutionaries had some former high-ranking officers on their side. I have no way of knowing what kind of army they've assembled, or what The Movement has left to throw at them."

William froze. He stared at the ground blankly as the darkest of all thoughts crossed his mind.

"What's wrong, Dad?"

"All right, now you two need to listen to me carefully and do exactly what I say. Starting right now, you need to begin prepping the bunker as quickly and quietly as possible. Stow as many provisions as you can fit in there. Think in terms of what we will need to survive for years, not months. That bunker needs to be fully prepped and ready for residents immediately."

"Why? What's happening, Dad? You're scaring the shit out of me."

"I don't have time to explain," William said.

William walked inside the farmhouse and retrieved a pen and a piece of paper. On the paper, he wrote fifteen names. He handed the paper to James.

"What's this?" James asked.

"I want everyone on that list to meet tonight in the cider mill. Tell them to pack clothes and keepsakes, not too much, just the essentials. And tell them to do it quietly; we don't need a riot in Heritage Woods."

James looked at the list, and then looked at his father. "Everyone?" James asked incredulously.

"Yes, everyone. Now get working."

James and Crocco walked off the front porch and jogged towards the cider mill. William walked to his office on the second floor. He turned on his computer and prayed for the satellite uplink to connect him to the internet. William fist-pumped under his desk when the connection opened and a young woman's face appeared on the screen.

"Good evening, Mr. Blake. I'm Charlotte, concierge 4576, how do you fare?"

"Hale and hearty, hearty and hale," William said.

"Hale and hearty indeed. How may I help you this evening?"

"I'd like to speak with Travis Sage."

"Mr. Sage has been expecting your call. I will patch you through."

The screen went blank. William panicked, convinced that the connection had failed. After a few minutes staring at a black screen, the monitor flickered back to life and Sage appeared on the screen.

"William, my boy. So good to see you. I was expecting this call."

"I knew you would be," William said. "A rider was here this morning handing out newspapers. The newspaper reported on constitutional conventions meeting tomorrow in Massachusetts, Rhode Island, Maine, and Vermont. They're reforming state governments and calling for the creation of a New England Confederation of States."

"We are aware," Sage said. "Tabitha has been more successful than we anticipated. She has re-infected New England with a progressive virus."

"What's going to happen?" William asked.

"Remember I told you about the officer in Vietnam who said he had to destroy a village in order to save it?"

"Yes."

"Well, we will have to destroy some states in order to save them. We're going to treat the liberal infection."

"How?" William asked.

"We have two treatments planned. A nuclear submarine in the Atlantic is targeting Boston, Providence, Augusta, and Montpelier. We will cauterize the progressive infection before it festers and spreads," Sage said.

"Liberty or death," William said.

"What?" Sage asked.

"Nothing. I was just thinking; this gives a whole new meaning to the motto *liberty or death*," William said.

"I suppose you're right."

"Isn't there another way?" William begged.

"I'm afraid not. William, you have always been loyal to The Movement. I know you have the ability to ride this out. I also know you have Edward's grandchild."

"What are you talking about?" William asked.

"It's too late to play dumb, William. Keep the child safe. The Movement will be sustained through the child; the boy is special, through him, the great works started by his grandfather will continue. He is destined to lead the world in the coming age."

"I understand," William said.

"Good."

"What's the second one?"

"Second what?" Sage asked.

"You said you're going to treat the liberal infection two ways. The first is the nuclear option, what's the second."

"I'll leave you with one final image," Sage said. "Goodbye William. Godspeed."

Sage signed off. On the screen, a satellite weather map of the entire Atlantic Ocean appeared. William had seen the map dozens of times back in the days when forecasters from the National Weather Service reported on the path of hurricanes that formed off the coast of Africa and churned northeast towards the Caribbean, Gulf of Mexico, or East Coast. William's mouth dropped open. He instinctively covered his mouth with the palm of his hand and sucked air through the back of his throat. On the screen, six fully formed, category five hurricanes swirled in the Atlantic Ocean. They looked like giant snowballs, each one bigger than the last, on a collision course with New England. The lead bands of the closest hurricane tickled Long Island Sound and promised to make landfall in Connecticut and begin cutting a path of devastation across New England within hours.

William pushed the *print screen* button. A color printer next to the monitor whined and churned out the image. William picked up the paper, flipped it over, wrote twenty names on the back of paper, and ran out of the office to find Mary.

THE John Deere Gator rumbled up a logging trail that snaked along the spine of Sleeping Giant. Mary sat in the passenger seat next to William with her arms folded across her chest and jaw set. She was angry that William interrupted her afternoon chores, and even more angry that he was burning gas in the Gator. She had demanded to know why he wanted to bring her to the castle, and was frustrated by his lack of a response. Mary initially refused William's request, and returned to her chores. William had grabbed the fat around Mary's triceps, squeezed, and pulled her close.

"Shut up and get in the vehicle, or I'll start slapping the shit out of you,'" William had hissed into Mary's ear.

William meditated on how he was going to tell Mary that it was time to move into the bunker under the cider mill. He knew that simply explaining the situation would not be enough. He would have to color the reality in Biblical terms if he hoped to inspire Mary to seek shelter; William knew that a secular explanation of the threat the estate faced would not move Mary to action.

William parked the Gator in front of the castle.

"All right, we're here. What do you want?" Mary asked.

"Come on. Let's walk up to the top of the castle," William said. "I need to show you something."

"I really don't have time for this. I have a million chores to get done this afternoon."

"Get your ass up to the top of that castle, now," William barked.

Mary climbed out of the Gator and walked up a dank hallway that led to the top of the castle.

"Oh my God," Mary said when she reached the top.

William and Mary stared out over Long Island Sound. A wall of black thunderheads formed as far as they could see up and down the shoreline. The clouds had slowly swallowed Long Island, and would soon descend on Connecticut.

"That's one hell of a storm," Mary said.

"It's not a storm," William said.

"What are you talking about?"

"It's one of the Four Horsemen," William said.

"What?"

"The first four seals have been broken, Mary. Behold the Pale Horseman, Death," William said, fanning his arm out over the black horizon. "He's not alone," William said. William removed the paper in his pocket, unfolded the weather map, and handed it to Mary. "I printed this half an hour ago."

"Oh dear Lord," Mary said, staring at the image. "Are these all going to make landfall here?"

"Yes," William said. "It is the Pale Horseman, Death, churning over the ocean, about to breathe ruin upon us all. But that is not the only demon."

"What are you talking about?" Mary asked.

"You can see the Black Horseman for yourself – Famine. Look at the trees here on Sleeping Giant, netted in the choking grasp of Gypsy Moths and slowing dying in the grip of insects and disease. I know you've seen the orchard and crops on the estate. We are staring into the dark eyes of the Black Horseman. He has already ridden across the land, trampled the fruit of Eden, and bestowed famine upon us all."

"My God," Mary said, folding her hands under her chin.

"Take a walk through Heritage Woods to observe the White Horseman – Pestilence. Tuberculosis, Small Pox, Influenza, Whooping Cough, cancer; not a day goes by that the doctor doesn't treat a new disease. It's only a matter of time before it reaches the farmhouse."

"Oh dear Lord. Two of the farmhands I labored with this morning took ill with fever. I sent them back to Heritage Woods with orders to rest."

"Hopefully it's not too late."

"Is there more?" Mary asked.

"Yes, the Red Horseman – War. He will begin his ride across the land on Thanksgiving Day."

"Tomorrow?" Mary asked. "How do you know?"

"Massachusetts, Maine, Rhode Island, and Vermont are holding conventions tomorrow with the aims of restoring state government. They're trying to return us to the bad-old-days; they aim to begin robbing us of our liberty. Edward Birch is going to annihilate the conventions, burn the traitors in an inferno. The Red Horsemen will ride on the tip of nuclear missiles. The time has come – Judgement Day."

"Praise be to God," Mary said, staring into the sky. "The end of the millennium. A thousand year reign of the Messiah; Christ will descend from the right hand of God."

"Yes, Mary, yes," William said excitedly. "And we must be here when he arrives. But first we have to survive the end of days; we have to bear witness for the Lord."

"Do you suppose that is why the Lord hasn't called us home?"

"What?" William asked.

"The Rapture. Is that why the Lord hasn't raised us up in Rapture."

"Yes, I'm sure of it. Instead of ascending to heaven, he wants us to take shelter underground, and survive the end of days. He wants us to bear witness to his power, and prepare the world for the return of Christ when we rise up from the cider mill bunker and reclaim God's kingdom."

Tears began to stream down Mary's cheeks. She raised her hands to the heavens and began turning in circles. The first drops of rain from the leading bands of the hurricane lashed the castle. The wind picked up and rumbles of thunder echoed over Sleeping Giant.

"There's one more thing, Mary," William said, grabbing Mary by the shoulders to stop her from spinning. "The Lord has spoken to me. He has told me to save the following people. James and Crocco are assembling them in the cider mill as we speak."

William turned over the printout of the weather map and showed Mary the list of twenty names he had written on the back of the page. The names included James, Susan and Catherine, Reverend Flowers, the doctor, Crocco and his wife, Eric and his parents, Annaliese and her parents, baby Edward, the couple caring for baby Edward, and two children belonging to the couple who cared for baby Edward.

Mary stared at the list. William braced himself for Mary's anger. On a normal day, the prospect of saving Tabitha's grandchild and the boy who Susan loved would stoke Mary's ire.

"Do you think he's the one?" Mary asked.

"Who?"

"The grandchild of Edward Birch? Do you think he is the Messiah?"

"I don't know. We will have two infants to care for," William said. "Edward Birch's grandchild and Catherine's ill-conceived child."

"Praise be to God," Mary said.

Mary walked down the dank hallway back towards the Gator parked at the bottom of the castle. William paused for a minute before following Mary. Mary's Evangelical fervor had rubbed off on him; he stared at the menacing clouds preparing to lay siege to Sleeping Giant, and wondered if they would bring forth the Messiah, the anti-Christ, or both when they rose up from the embrace of the earth.

"Welcome to liberty's wrath," William said to himself. He turned his back to the storm, and followed Mary out of the castle.

Printed in the United States
By Bookmasters